CROOKED
V.2

EDITED BY
JESSIE KWAK

CONTENTS

Introduction   v

NARROW ESCAPE   1
by Maddi Davidson

RENEGADE HAVOC   15
by C.E. Clayton

SPARROW   43
by G.J. Ogden

A CRUEL CYBER SUMMER NIGHT   61
by Austin Dragon

RISK MANAGEMENT   95
by Caitlin Demaris McKenna

SOLARMUTE   117
by Jim Keen

ION HUNTER   149
by E.L. Strife

ACE IN THE HOLE   179
by Kate Sheeran Swed

THE SILENT PASSAGE   211
by Patrick Swenson

CASE CITY COWBOY   241
by Greg Dragon

THE CRIMSON VIAL   267
by William Burton McCormick

TERMINAL SUNSET   297
by Erik Grove

DO-YEoN PERFORMS A COST-BENEFIT
ANALYSIS ON A CAREER BASED ON
QUESTIONABLE ACTIVITIES   319
by Mark Niemann-Ross

THE WESTERN OBLIQUE JOB   347
by Mark Teppo

LAST CHANCE   379
by Jessie Kwak

MARTIAN SCUTTLE   399
by Andrew Sweet

GOOD AS GOLD   423
by Frasier Armitage

LOVE & PICKPOCKETS   451
by R J Theodore

Contributor Bios   481
More Sci-Fi Crime   491

INTRODUCTION

Welcome to CROOKED V.2, the second installment in the *Crooked* anthology series. We had so much fun with volume one that I couldn't help but do it again.

In this volume you'll find eighteen more stories of mayhem, tangled loyalties, and space crime.

Easy jobs go wrong. Hunted bounties get wily. Mysteries are solved, only to lead to more horrifying mysteries.

Sometimes the bad guys win, sometimes the good guys do. And, hey. It's a crime anthology. Most of the time it'll be pretty damn hard to tell the two apart.

The folks in these stories are just trying to do their best—or not—in a morally gray world.

The goal of the *Crooked* anthology series is to introduce you, the reader, to authors who are currently writing sci-fi crime stories. Many of the stories in this collection are set in larger universes, which means that if you read something you like, you'll find plenty more in that author's catalogue to keep you busy.

To help you discover work you'll love, I'm trying something a little different than most anthologies. While you can certainly read the stories in order from beginning to end, I've also included "Pick Your Poison" prompts at the end of each story. Whether you finish a story and think, "Hell yeah, I want more of this!" or "Let's try a different flavor of sci-fi crime," use the prompts to find your next story.

Or, just turn the page.

(You can also head to jessiekwak.com/bad-intentions to take a story recommendation quiz based on your favorite sci fi and crime shows.)

Whether you're picking up this anthology because you like the premise or to read a story by an author you already love, you're sure to discover a new author or two you'll dig. Don't forget to follow the links at the end of each story for goodies, giveaways, and even more stories from the seedy underbelly of the Science Fiction shelf.

And if you want even more sci-fi crime in your life, head to jessiekwak.com/bad-intentions to pick up your copy of *CROOKED V.1*.

Have fun out there,

Jessie Kwak
September 27, 2022

NARROW ESCAPE

A TASTEE BRIOCHE TWISTLETOE STORY

BY MADDI DAVIDSON

MINING ORSOTHIUM ON GALINA 552 MEANT crawling along dark tunnels, breathing foul air, and using antiquated laser drills to extract the ore from surrounding rocks, all of which played hell on my manicure. When the whistle sounded, I took the tram to the mine's entrance and trudged the quarter-mile to the main building, my excitement growing with each step.

After stumbling into the women's locker room, I sat on a bench next to a large metal laundry bin and heaved a deep sigh as if I were exhausted. Verna Smootz, the gods bless her little heart, sat next to me.

"You okay, Smelda?"

"I'm fine, Verna. Need to rest a moment. Please don't let me keep you from getting cleaned up."

"I'm okay. I'll keep you company."

Damn.

Verna prattled on about her dinner plans for her boyfriend as coworkers ripped off their overalls, shoved them in laundry bins, and sauntered into the shower area.

About half the shift had departed when I reached into my pocket and pressed a button on a remote control.

"And of course I'll serve organic slugs for an appetizer," Verna said.

The sound of a distant rumble from an explosion deep in the mine penetrated the walls of the locker room.

"What's tha—" Verna started to say when blasts two and three near the mine's entrance rocked the building.

Amidst the cacophony of screams, shrieks, and wails, I added my voice. "Run for your lives!" I yelled.

Verna took off toward the showers as the smoke bomb I'd placed earlier under a locker room bench detonated. I dove into the laundry bin, whacking my left knee, but thrilled at the near perfection of the blasts—music to my ears. Or it would be once they stopped ringing.

Tossing out the dirty overalls, I made quick work of the false bottom, which hid the stash of orsothium nuggets I'd pinched over the past month. Moments later, I extricated myself from the bin and hobbled toward the showers, babying my sore, bruised knee.

Security protocol required miners to remove their boots and strip off the company-provided clothing before using the communal showers. Since orsothium was one of the rarest and priciest metals in the galaxy at 500č per gram, fine filters were used to capture the ortho-dust from the clothing and shower waste water. Exiting the shower room, miners encountered security guards and a top-of-the-line body scanning machine, lest anyone try to smuggle nuggets out in their orifices or hair. During my first week on the job, a woman stuffed a miniscule nugget into a tooth which had a hole but no filling. The body scan picked up the metal. A diligent guard pried her jaw open and extracted both tooth and nugget, not for the first time. As a consequence, Gummy Glenda lost her last molar.

The female guards had fled so I bypassed the scanner and entered the dressing room. I expected the area to be empty, but a dozen women who were unwilling to run naked through the building were putting on clothes. A handful, placing beauty before imminent death, were applying makeup.

I grabbed my small, hardside suitcase out of a locker, dumped the nuggets inside, and pressed the fire alarm button, just to add to the confusion.

Stepping into the building's lobby, I encountered a scene of pure bedlam. Dozens of guards, responding from across the compound, were pouring into the building. Suspecting the blasts had been a diversionary tactic to cover up a theft—even a trained ape could figure that out—security personnel were tackling anyone who moved. I limped toward an emergency exit but one of those apes intercepted me. Literally. A 300-lb trained gorilla held me in a bear hug—I know, I'm mixing metaphors.

I slipped a hand into my pocket and pressed the second button on the remote.

I submit to you that a mix of decomposing body, rotten eggs, the spray from a skunk's anal gland, and *odeur de* men's locker room can be considered no more than an unpleasant odor as compared to the gag-inducing stench of cirax feces. And why, you might ask, am I mentioning the cirax, the elephant-sized carrion eater from the Epsilon Eridani system? Because I'd arranged for cirax poop extract in sealed canisters to be hidden in the air ducts of the building. Pressing the remote control opened the containers.

Knowing a gods-awful smell would fill the building and lacking a severe head cold to block my sinuses, I closed my eyes and held my breath. I heard rather than saw the convulsing and retching around me. Note to self: carry a small spray can of *odeur de* cirax in case of unpleasant dating encounters.

When the gorilla's grasp loosened, I wiggled away, reached into my case, and pulled out a full-face gas mask. Everyone in the lobby was incapacitated, most still heaving. They'd be out of action for days. I tossed few smoke bombs to cloud the picture for anyone looking in from outside, made my way to a fire exit, and edged out.

I love when my scathingly brilliant plans work.

MY BIRTH NAME is Tastee Brioche Twistletoe and no, I don't know what my parents were thinking, though it may have been a reflection on their extreme dedication to carbohydrates of the French persuasion. In the Dark Space metaverse I'm known by many monikers, but I would have changed my name even if I weren't a thief.

I was six years old when my father left my mother for another woman: one who would not be as wedded—so to speak—to a lavish lifestyle. Mother says we were left destitute, her opinion of possessing merely two homes, a half-dozen large diamonds, 40,000 shares of Interspace Ships Ltd., and three bank accounts. Mother believed she had little choice but to turn to crime to augment our meager assets.

She specialized in fleecing older men. In possession of elfin features, a helpless mien, artificial lashes she batted often and coquettishly, and no mercy, she siphoned off millions of caloos from a series of rich men. Even when they realized she'd left them with depleted bank accounts, few of her victims were angry with her, believing the "poor, sweet little thing" too innocent to rob them blind by design. As one might expect, Mother's success required her socially backward and awkward child—me—be stowed out of the way, say, in a boarding school on an isolated planet near the edge of the galaxy with no regular spaceship service.

When cosmetic surgery and the application of makeup with a trowel became insufficient to mask her advancing age, my mother retired from her lucrative career. She brought me home and began teaching me the principles of the con. Mother expected that I, her sole offspring, would devote my life to keeping her in the lifestyle she deserved. To her great disappointment my gawkiness and clumsiness had increased rather than abated as I grew: regularly spilling food and drink, tripping on level ground, and careening into priceless and breakable antiques. Nevertheless she persevered, instructing me on how to assume a persona and use appropriate makeup, mannerisms, and clothing to support the mirage. She guided me in the ways of a femme fatale; how to make men drool at my beck and call. I tried, but despite my best efforts, only dogs drooled—Bassett Hounds loved me. After a while, Mother gave up, acknowledging that her flat-chested daughter with fly-away hair, a pot belly, and the legs of an anorectic stork would never be irresistible to men.

I MADE my way to the Hauler Maintenance Building and slipped inside to change. I shed my boots and the foul-smelling mining suit, and—bare for all the world to see—stooped to retrieve my clothes from the bag.

From behind me came an appreciative sigh. "A little skinny, but I don't mind."

I pulled my clenched hands out of the bag, stood, and turned to find a grease monkey leering at me. No, not a simian. This one was human and wearing oil-stained overalls labeled "Mechanic."

He licked his lips and took a step toward me.

I smiled, licked my lips, took a step toward him.

A flicker of uncertainty passed over his face a moment before I raised my right arm and electroshocked his jewels. His family jewels.

Five hours later I sat in a booth in a shadowy corner of a hoity-toity bar. To be clear, hoity-toity on this planet meant the operators guaranteed no vermin of the non-human kind would be found on the premises, alive. I'd assumed the disguise of a young male: bulky jacket and black pants, five o'clock shadow (paste on), bushy mustache (also paste on), and wet, foul-smelling boots. (I'd been leaning against a tree across the street waiting for my contact to enter the bar when a stray ghink—think porcupine-wolf hybrid—relieved itself against the aforementioned tree, and me.) I sipped eighteen-year-old fermented floraldehyde. My companion, who called himself Red Eye—don't ask me why, his eyes were dark brown like mine—discretely assayed the nuggets I'd stashed in a rubber-lined satchel. (I'd had to ditch the suitcase because of the lingering cirax odor. Fortunately, the nuggets and my clothes smelled no worse than sweat. My boots, though, were another matter.)

With a small dropper, Red Eye extracted hydrochloric acid from a bottle and dispensed the solution onto the nuggets to ascertain their purity. Satisfied with the results, he closed the satchel and passed a small navy string bag to me under the table.

Red Eye drank his expensive bourbon, imported from Earth, and I examined the contents of the money bag.

"You're short," I said after rummaging inside to ensure the bag contained nothing but currency. "This can't be more than 50,000 caloos. The deal was for 75,000č."

"You promised the goods would be delivered last month," he retorted.

"You promised me an accurate report on the security systems, but the scanners I found were several generations newer than what you'd stated."

"We warned you the information was six months old and we were not responsible for any subsequent changes to the situation. However, since the scanner upgrade caused you additional trouble, you may have another 8,000č, which I'll send to you after I'm off this planet."

Like I'd ever see the money. "10,000č," I countered. "You'll pay me now and I'll show you the fake nugget in which I've hidden a tracking device. The police would just love to know the frequency."

Red Eye sneered as he reached in to his jacket and pulled out five bank-issued packets, which he placed on the table. "10,000č."

I flipped through a packet before gathering the remainder and shoving them inside my jacket.

"There is no tracker; I lied about the nugget," I said.

Red Eye rose. His face flushed crimson and bright red flecks appeared in his irises. Fearing he would kill me then and there, I reached for a girl's best friend, my electroshocker.

"Our business is done," he said, although his tone suggested otherwise. He stalked out.

Hoisting my glass with a cheerful, "Here's to another successful theft" seemed inappropriate, so I finished off the fermented floraldehyde. I planned to skedaddle out by the back door to avoid Red Eye, expecting he or a compatriot would be lying in wait to hasten my demise and recover the money.

As I stood, the left side of my mustache came loose. Damn. I hadn't used enough spirit gum. Raising my hand to press the mustache back in place, I knocked my drink off the table. The shattering glass caused twenty heads to swivel in my direction. So much for a discreet departure.

I limped my way out the door, caught the first public skimmer I could, disembarked two stops later, and boarded another one traveling in a different direction. One hundred meters down the road, the vehicle broke down. I hopped on yet another skimmer, sat in the back, and kept an eye on the traffic behind the vehicle for signs I was being followed.

Red Eye worked for a criminal organization known as *Nemo Loquitur* or No One Speaks. Its operations never left witnesses. No doubt Red Eye had plans to eliminate Armani Q. O'Really—my current alias. Since no one appeared to be on my tail, I had to consider Red Eye had inserted a tracker in the bag or packets. I examined each credit chip and soon found the small device. The slimeball had counted on me demanding more money and had slipped the tracker into one of the bank packets, to which I'd given only a cursory inspection.

I pulled out a black shopping tote into which I transferred most of the money. I left the tracer stuffed under a seat, gave 500č to a young woman for her coat, and another 500č to an older woman for her hat. Leaving the astonished passengers behind, I disembarked.

······✳······

LACKING ANY CURVES, the femme fatale role was not the best use of my skills. However, because of my figure, or lack thereof, I had the advantage of being able to pass as a man—up to a point. Mother focused her lessons on how I could alter my appearance, mannerisms, and speech to appear male. She called in favors and hired experts from whom I learned how to hack security systems, create and handle explosives, and master other basics of thievery. However, Mother's greatest contribution to my professional career was her insistence on meticulous planning for every contingency.

"What happens if your explosives don't work, or someone recognizes you, or you are caught in the act? Any moment you might have to flee. How are you going to ditch whomever you might be with, leave the area, and make your way off the planet? How will you cover your tracks? Where will you go and for how long? What new persona will you assume? You must not enter any room, travel on any conveyance, or walk down any street unless you know how you will escape."

My first job, overseen by Mother, took me to Zebed-sneezer, a planet in the backwaters of the Gliese 357 system. Like many rural planets, Zeb did not trade in credit: all transactions were done in caloo chips. With Mother's help in planning, I knocked over the spaceport, earning 220,000č for Mother's upkeep—with one minor complication. Engaging in a bit of misdirection, I sent my suitcase on a ship I had no plans on taking. However, I forgot to remove my Interstellar Passport. In order to leave the planet, I had to stow away on an industrial transport, enduring a seventy-five day journey, which takes three days on a passenger ship. On the bright side, I did lose a pesky ten pounds.

On the next operation, I snared 25,000č from a casino on Pantpansynog before entering the wrong hotel room: 635 instead of 536. It's a mistake anyone could make. The occupants, a half-dozen male soldiers on shore leave, weren't too drunk or drugged to recognize an opportunity when she stepped across the threshold. I tossed money into the air to buy time to retreat, returning home with a mere 8,000 caloo.

My next job in Hendrerwydd netted me 12,000č and a month in the hospital for an intestinal worm my physician said was a record-breaking length—eww.

Mother declared me free to rob the galaxy without her help and asked I spare her the details of my jobs . . . and constant muck-ups. Since then I've worked alone, including my current caper. I was not in league with Red Eye.

Quite the opposite, in fact.

A tenet of my profession is don't operate in your backyard and don't let others, either. However, a number of major thefts on planets where Mother owned property drew the attention of the Stellar Police. When the police started turning over rocks, one never knew what they might find and I feared their efforts might uncover sensitive information about Mother's past, or mine.

Reports and rumors floating in Dark Space pointed to *Nemo Loquitur* being the force behind the thefts.

Working through back channels under the name Armani Q. O'Really, I secured a contract with *Nemo Loquitur* to steal two kilos of orsothium. I intended to bring *Nemo Loquitur* to the attention of the police, and perhaps earn a bit of money while doing so.

ESCAPING a planet after a major heist is often the trickiest part of a job. Searching for the reputed orsothium thief, spaceport security would be eyeing every passenger on public or private spaceship. I suspected Red Eye had his own ship and had bribed several officials to ensure smooth passage through security. I planned to disrupt his arrangements.

One of the first orders of business when arriving on a new planet is to hire help: those who have been on the wrong side of the law and don't fear it. My teenage associates—two boys and a girl—had placed the *eau de* cirax in the airducts of the Locker Room Building. Now, as I used a high powered scope from afar to keep watch on the private spacecraft terminal, they were parked by the edge of the terminal, pretending to work on a vehicle that had stalled.

When Red Eye stepped out of large skimmer with his entourage, I sent a signal to my team. The boys tossed cirax extract cannisters at Red Eye's feet and dove into the getaway skimmer, which, under the direction of the girl, had miraculously started. I triggered the opening of the containers. The effect was instantaneous. People collapsed like axed trees. Panic ensued in those who witnessed the effect, but were far enough away to not be affected, yet. Airport personnel ran toward the victims and joined the fallen.

I hoped the incident would draw the scrutiny of security personal who hadn't been bribed by Red Eye. Perhaps his capture would lead them to his employers.

I didn't wait to observe the outcome, but headed for my own ride out of town. I'd plopped down money to ensure passage in a cargo ship ferrying, among other items, a half dozen trained gorillas. It was the perfect cover; I'd arranged for a private cage and procured a gorilla costume. We were ready to go when, at the last minute, calamity struck.

I should have known the caper had gone too smoothly.

Three extra gorillas boarded and the loadmaster placed another female in my cage. Worse: she was in estrus, the males knew it, and the cages were flimsy.

Thank the gods I'd packed my gas mask and the last canister of cirax poop.

"Narrow EscApe" is the first story in a planned series of Tastee Brioche Twistletoe adventures.

Read more free short stories at maddidavidson.com/bitch-and-chips

PICK YOUR POISON

1. *I love me a good heist—but can you somehow dial* up *the weird?* Head to "Terminal Sunset" by Erik Grove

2. *I'm ready to join the crew.* Head to "The Western Oblique Job" by Mark Teppo

3. *Jobs gone wrong is so my jam.* Turn the page to read "Renegade Havoc" by C.E. Clayton

RENEGADE HAVOC

A EERDEN STORY

BY C.E. CLAYTON

JUST THINK ABOUT IT, YEAH?

For the past few weeks, that was exactly what Pema Tran tried *not* to do. Ellinor's voice was like a fucking earworm that no cigarette or case of beer could drown.

She refused to believe Ellinor's words of caution about her boss. Pema had worked for Cosmin von Brandt most of her adult life after he paid her bail following another fight at a synth-club—one she hadn't even started. Cosmin never explained why he paid her bail. Only that he recognized talent when he saw it and wanted to offer her a job in his organization: smuggling illegal, weaponized magitech throughout the city-state of Euria.

Pema didn't have anyone else at that point; her family was either dead or had cut her off. She was far too broke to say no to a job, even one that could get her more jail time than any of her brawls ever could. Cosmin had found Pema when she was two steps away from making a living on the toxic ground level of Euria without an air filtration unit. He had saved her, and had given her more than a job. He'd given her a purpose again, and, through working with him, Pema met the love of her life: Talin Roxas.

Pema owed Cosmin more than just her life.

She made a discontented growl deep in her throat and glanced around her cubicle apartment. It was the same small space she and Talin had shared when they first moved in together, back when they were still part of Ellinor's crew, before she'd left Cosmin's organization.

They had no windows in their two-room unit. This low in the sky-tower apartments, they wouldn't have had a view of anything anyway. Instead, there were two holo-windows on opposite walls in the main room that served as everything except their bedroom. Each holo-window showed a soundless scene of the city from higher up, above the pollution where the grimy air didn't hide the glitter of neon. Pema could have set it to anything: forests, beaches . . . But those vistas weren't as real or comforting to her as a bustling city. The mauve walls hadn't changed since they moved in, either. Pema never did get around to patching the dent that Ellinor had made when she tripped over the second-hand sofa, drunk and laughing.

Pema sighed, and dropped her gaze to the concrete flooring.

Ellinor popping back up had complicated things, leaving their crew fractured all over again in ways that could never be repaired. And Pema hated complicated.

Now Talin was starting to question things she never had before. Like if Cosmin saving Pema had really been as fortuitous, as *coincidental* as she had originally thought. Pema didn't agree with that. Cosmin got nothing from pulling Pema out of jail when he did. He had given *her* a chance to be more, be better than just some angry drunk prowling the synth-clubs for the rest of her life. But Talin kept wondering if Ellinor had been right to get out of Cosmin's organization.

That didn't go so hot for her, remember?

Pema lit a cigarette and put it to her lips, inhaling deeply. She shut her eyes, trying to escape the images that burned behind her eyelids of what happened when you "quit" on Cosmin, or, worse, betrayed him.

Pema was still furious at Ellinor. If she had never left Cosmin in the first place, Talin never would have gotten nearly killed on a botched delivery run. Her crew, her *friends*, would all still be working with Cosmin and things would still be good. But no. Ellinor had to go and *complicate* things . . .

Pema had leaned more into her vices—smoking and drinking—to help dull the edge of her anger, much to Talin's chagrin. Who, instead, lost herself in her work in order to avoid reality. But Pema didn't have her girlfriend's acumen for explosive work.

Talin could lose days in her workshop, forgetting to eat or drink entirely if Pema didn't go in and check on her. Talin had a real talent for taking pieces of junk, malfunctioning pieces of smart tech, and making them go *BOOM* in ways Pema would never have thought possible. Give Talin an hour, a seatbelt, a handful of broken cybernetic enhancers, and an empty beer can, and she could bring down a hypersonic plane like it was easy. Talin was one of Cosmin's most valued explosives experts, but despite that, Cosmin did not excuse Talin from witnessing the punishment that awaited traitors. Talin preferred to work long hours in her workshop after rather than risk the image of such torture plaguing her in her sleep.

Pema slapped the side of her head with the palm of her hand a few times to put an end to her spiraling thoughts. She took another long drag on her cigarette and held the smoke in her lungs until they started to burn, before slowly exhaling and getting to her feet.

Stretching, she moved to the cloudy mirror on the far wall of the bedroom and gave herself a long, hard stare in the mirror.

"Traitors deserve what they get, you follow me, Pema? Cosmin takes care of those who take care of him. And you, Pema, you take care of the boss. Got it?" Her voice was deep and gravelly, a bit more hoarse than normal with the recent nights of shitty sleep, but she liked to believe the pep talks were working.

Those purple bags under her narrow, rich brown eyes were *definitely* not because of the image of Talin nearly getting killed haunting her dreams. Those extra streaks of grey in her long black hair *definitely* did not have anything to do with the torment she witnessed Cosmin doling out. That ashen twinge to her bronze-hued olive skin was *definitely* not because she had replaced most meals with bottles of beer. And those extra lines around her thin lips and brows were *definitely* not from scowling all the time.

No, the pep talks were *definitely* working.

"You," she said, jabbing a finger into her reflection on each word as if that would help solidify the words. "Do not. Fuck. With. Cosmin. You *owe* him."

Then, as if her words manifested the man himself, her communicator chimed: *I have a job for you and your charming girlfriend, my dear.*

Despite her churning stomach, a spark of hope and relief clawed up from her gut to warm her chest. She was quick to respond in the affirmative, then stubbed out her cigarette on the way out of her apartment. Pema practically ran down the hallway, its moldy stains blurring into one greenish yellow streak, toward the rusty service elevator that would take her to Talin's workshop.

The elevator doors opened, and she darted down a new hall identical to the one on her floor. Pema stopped outside a narrow door and checked the hallway to make sure no one was snooping before slipping inside. Forced to walk sideways down the musty, steel hallway, she had to squeeze behind the building's air purifier before getting to Talin's "office".

It would have been safer for Talin to have a workshop in Cosmin's mansion, but he didn't want to have Talin's activities so obviously linked to him and his work. Which, sure, made sense. But it still seemed dangerous for Talin to do her work next to such a vital piece of technology for the whole of their complex. Cosmin wouldn't even let Talin operate from one of the money laundering businesses he had spread throughout Euria.

Plausible deniability. You know better than to question that shit, she scolded herself as she stepped up to the reinforced, metal door.

Pema punched in her private code to enter Talin's workshop without thinking about it, realizing too late that she should have absolutely let her girlfriend know ahead of time that she was on her way. The automatic door hissed up, and the smell of burning rubber slammed its acrid fist into Pema's nose, squeezing the air from her lungs.

Sputtering, she flung an arm over her face and gasped, "Babe, air filters!" before a fit of coughing overtook her completely.

Talin poked her head up, but all Pema could see through her blurring vision was the black, helmeted mask

Talin wore. There was a muffled curse, the clanky, industrial fans and purifiers kicked in, and the smell of burning rubber was replaced with a cool ozone scent so full of static energy that the hair on Pema's arms stood on end. She stumbled inside, coughing a few more times for good measure, then the automatic doors closed behind her. Ripping off her breathing apparatus, Talin caught Pema before she could knock anything explosive off the cluttered tables.

"Love, we talked about this," Talin chastised, but it was more out of habit, and there was no real heat in her smoky voice.

Pema blinked the tears from her eyes and looked up at her athletically tall girlfriend. Talin's jade green eyes were as bright as neon, shining as always with delight whenever Pema was around even if she pretended to be annoyed. Her smooth, deep ebony skin was dewy with sweat that glistened most noticeably on her skull, shining through the barely-there black fuzz. But her dark lips were turned up in a soft smile, her round cheeks making her eyes crinkle with the grin.

Pema couldn't help herself; she stood on her toes and gave Talin a gentle kiss on those incredibly soft, full lips.

Talin's eyes fluttered, half closing as she pulled back slightly. "What're you doing here? Not that I'm not happy to see you, but, you know," Talin said, waving vaguely to the random pieces of tech strewn about the steel tables.

Pema took a deep breath, committing Talin's soft smile to memory before she took it away with her news. "Cosmin's got a job for us."

⋯⋯✳⋯⋯

THEY WAITED until the service bot had left them in the vehicle depot. Only when they were alone, piling into the sleek, black transport, did either relax enough to fully exhale. The first step to the operation completed without being picked up on a government spy drone. So far, so good.

"Something feels off to me," Talin whispered.

Pema shrugged, waving her fob over the ignition and initiating the virtual intelligence auto-driver. "Seems standard to me. A simple drop and exchange. How's this any different than the stuff Cosmin's had us do a million times before?"

Talin rolled her big green eyes, picking at her lower lip. "Right, sure, that was the stuff we did when we were grunts, new little babies. We haven't done runs like this for decades, love. Haven't needed to since you ranked up, since Cosmin regulated me to arms and explosions. You're a *sergeant*, Pema. You don't send people like us do these drops. But hey, for argument's sake, let's pretend this still fits our job description."

Talin's voice rose an octave as she spoke, her words coming out in a rush to where Pema couldn't get a word in even if she did know what to say. "Cosmin's sending one o' his generals on this run with us. To man the op *from the ground*. Why? It's dumb as shit. Too risky for someone who's spent centuries as the undisputed king of magitech smuggling. Something about all this is different, and Cosmin doesn't do different when it comes to his shit. Not without reason."

Silence as thick as oil slithered between them, only broken when Talin added, "Is he cutting us loose? Because of Ell?"

Pema kept her eyes on the road, even though she

didn't need to. The auto-driver was handling everything, programmed ahead of time by Cosmin himself to take them where they needed to be so no one could leak the location. But there was a feeling in Pema's gut of perpetually falling, and she worried that if she looked at her girlfriend, even for a second, Talin would see her concern.

So she forced a chuckle and hoped it didn't sound like a cough. "You know the boss wouldn't do that, babe, and you know why? Because Ellinor lost her damn mind, accusing Cosmin of setting her and her man up. Her grief, I don't know, it fucked with her head or something. Sure, it was shitty how Cosmin made her come back, but if he was really worried about *us*, Cosmin wouldn't have had his medical team patch us up good as new *after* she ran off. Again. He'd have—well. You know what he'd have done instead. You feel me?" Pema took a deep breath, unclenching her fingers from around the steering console, and made an effort to relax. "We're loyal as fuck. This run? It's because he trusts us to kick ass. Maybe it's a test, you follow?" she added quickly, wiggling her eyebrows suggestively, trying to get Talin to smile. "Like he wants to see how we do before promoting us?"

"I don't know about all that, but . . ." Talin crossed her arms over her chest and snorted. "Shit, I don't know. I just think Ell may o' been on to something."

Just think about it, yeah?

Pema fished a cigarette out of the command console, masking her sigh of frustration by placing the cig to her lips and lighting it. "Come off it, Talin. We owe Cosmin. *I* owe him. Without Cosmin getting me when he did . . ." She shook her head, expression hardening. "No. Cosmin knows we're not like Ellinor. Fuck her."

Pema exhaled a cloud of smoke, and her shoulders

sagged under her girlfriend's disapproving glare. "Look, babe, no way Cosmin would cut us loose. Not *us*. Not now. If he thought, even for a minute that we were anything like Ellinor, he'd have gladly let us both die when we got back to the city. But he healed me, he had his docs heal *you* and then immediately put us back to work! Nah, no way is he demoting us or whatever, not when he's given us so much." She bit off her words before she could add: "Not when working for him brought me to you."

She squeezed Talin's knee. "No way would he partner us with the top echelon in the organization, and send us to the same distribution team he's used for decades, if he had any doubts about what side we play for. You know that."

"*You* know that's not what I meant," Talin grumbled in response. She rubbed a hand back and forth over her closely shorn hair, then sighed, shrugging her thin shoulders noncommittally, and said no more. Pema couldn't spend more time trying to convince her girlfriend that everything was fine, that Cosmin had only survived this long because he planned eight steps ahead and all their trepidation could be explained simply by them not seeing the bigger picture. It was a conversation she would need to have with Talin—again—just not now. Not when they were halfway to the rendezvous point where they'd be meeting up with the rest of the crew.

In silence, both women checked their loadouts one final time as the transport circled toward a discreet vehicle depot. While Pema busied herself with her pulse scattergun, Talin prepped the spy drones she had modified to scramble the government surveillance systems so it would look like none of their people were ever there.

As the transport slid into a vacant spot, they slipped disguise film over their faces, hiding their identities from the distribution team—as well as the rest of their own crew. Checking the perimeter one last time to make sure they hadn't been tailed, the women cautiously made their way toward the sub-levels where the convoy was waiting.

The delivery plan was simple enough; they would be riding in an armored convoy to a private launch pad where their distribution partners had a sub-hypersonic shuttle waiting. Where the shuttle went after that wasn't their concern. It was safer if they didn't know. Their job was to ensure the combat magitech—guns, ammunition, weaponry, and cybernetics that used too much magic for the Governor's liking—was safely handed over to Cosmin's partners. Once Cosmin's general confirmed the shipment was en route, then, and only then, would credits be exchanged.

Four unmarked black semi-vans, engines humming, waited for them in the first sub-level. Already crowded around the vehicles was a team of ten. At least two of the people waiting were Cosmin's general and their second; Pema just didn't know which ones they were. There were five generals in Cosmin's organization, only one of which Pema had ever worked directly with previously. Pema wasn't positive, but she was pretty sure that general wasn't with them. Which was for the best. That guy was an asshole. With the disguise films on, everyone had the same standard, expressionless face. Like mannequins with varying skin tones. They all knew better than to greet each other, to shoot the shit in such an exposed place. As soon as Talin and Pema arrived, on silent command, they all dispersed into the semi-vans.

Except there wasn't room for them in the same transport. Pema was directed to the lead van, and Talin two vans behind.

Talin hesitated, not leaving Pema's side, and all ten heads of the crew whipped around to stare at them. Pema didn't need to see their faces to know their muscles had tensed, that hands would soon be lowering to weapon belts if they didn't keep moving.

She gently ran her fingers down Talin's spine, her hand coming to rest on the small of her girlfriend's back, before giving her a gentle push in the right direction. Pema wouldn't dare utter words of encouragement, not here, not when they needed to stay off all comm channels.

Pema could feel Talin take a deep, shuddering breath that rattled all the way through her core, but she jutted her chin up all the same, heading for the second to last semi-van.

Like the transport Pema and Talin arrived in, the auto-driver virtual intelligence had been pre-programmed by Cosmin ahead of the delivery. One person remained in the driver's seat, for pretenses; the others sat in the back with the cargo. That was where Pema situated herself, tucked into a cramped space with barely any room to move. Just as the doors were closing, she saw Talin being put in the driver's seat of her semi-van.

Pema had only enough time for her eyes to widen in surprise before the door closed and she was cast in darkness. The driver's seat was the most exposed, the most vulnerable, the absolute last place you wanted to put someone who didn't have tactical training—like Talin. Pema would have been a better choice, but not by much. It was the first time since Cosmin gave them their orders that Pema started to doubt the plan.

The vehicle bumped along the poorly-maintained

aerial bridges, and Pema could only hope Talin was doing all right. Her girlfriend hated flying, and even though they weren't technically flying, these roads and bridges were high above the true ground of Euria . . .

Then the van began to decelerate, coming to a gentle stop.

Pema wiggled, attempting to stretch her cramped legs, when there was muffled shouting from outside. Their driver pounded four times in quick succession on the partition separating them from the front—the signal that things had gone tits up.

Flipping on her combat-tech armor and disengaging the safety on her scattergun, she kicked open the back door. She jumped out and rolled into cover before assessing the situation.

Pema always enjoyed a good fight. She liked taking center stage, lowering her pulse scattergun, and daring anyone to meet her head on. She crouched, poking her head around the side of the van, and—

"Oh, fuck me."

It wasn't a rival group of magitech engineers, or power-hungry casters looking to get their hands on a piece of Cosmin's magic. The district police of Euria had blockaded the road. Judging by the rose-gold and chrome badges on their heavily modified uniforms, these weren't *just* district cops, the ones Cosmin had a long-standing agreement with, but the elite district cops tasked with protecting the Governor and the other elected officials.

She whipped her head back into cover, but she had seen enough. The road was completely blocked by armored vehicles, and a pair of Ash Hawk helicopters circled above, tracking their every move. How had the district police caught up with them? Was there a mole in Cosmin's organization?

Impossible. We know better.

"Put the weapons down, disengage your armor, and come out with your hands up," one of the elite district cops barked, their voice tinny through the amplifier. "You know the drill. This doesn't have to get ugly."

But that was the problem. It did, it always did. Cosmin would accept no less.

Pema took a deep breath, scanning the rest of the convoy behind her, looking for Talin. But she couldn't see the lithe form of the woman she loved. All Pema could do was hope that Talin was being smart, that she was preparing something special to use in this shitty situation. She took another deep breath, the lingering taste of cigarette smoke in her mouth and lungs soothing her as she waited for the signal from Cosmin's general to engage.

And waited.

And waited.

Sweat was starting to trickle down her spine as milliseconds that felt like minutes passed, when finally, mercifully, a double buzz like a heartbeat issued from her wrist communicator. Without hesitation, a silver, cylindrical object—Talin's special brand—flew through the air with impeccable accuracy. It bounced, rolling to the feet of the first line of district police.

With an earsplitting *POP!*, a plume of electrified gas burst from the canister, disabling the mechanized armor of the first row of cops, locking them in their suits and preventing them from moving. Then, chaos erupted.

Pema poked her head out from cover, firing at the vehicles the district police were taking cover behind, disabling them as her driver dove for the semi-van to get it ready to haul ass once the way was clear.

The driver didn't make it.

The district police were using armor piercing rounds mixed with water magitech bullets. The shriveled husk of her driver crumpled to the ground; all fluid in their body stripped away.

The cops hadn't hesitated; they knew who they faced, and who they worked for. This was the most prepared—and lethal—Pema had ever seen the district police be when attempting to raid Cosmin's supply lines.

That's when the chain of command began crumbling. One of Cosmin's team was trying to surrender, another was still firing at the district police—their rounds ineffective. Another one of Talin's canisters soared through the air, but was shot down over the vehicle Pema was crouched behind.

Pema lurched to her feet, diving for the semi-van behind her. Its engine was vibrating, and she rolled away just in time to avoid getting crushed as the driver slammed on the accelerator, trying to ram the barricade. Pema remained prone, shooting at the district police as they dove out of the way—but not of the van careening toward them, or even Pema, whose aim was just as good as Talin's.

They dove away from the war automaton that lumbered from the back of their ranks.

The giant, square-shaped android with its cylindrical arms that nearly reached the ground stopped the van cold; the driver flew through the window and landed in the hands of the district police. They instantly wrestled Cosmin's man to the ground, cuffing them before all the plex-glass from the van landed.

"Oh, fuck no!"

Pema liked a good fight, relished a challenge. But dealing with a war bot? That was suicide. Pure and simple. Scrambling to her feet, Pema ran. But not away, not yet. She needed to get Talin.

Talin and the remaining four members of Cosmin's crew were taking cover behind the last semi-van. Pema slid into cover beside them, only recognizing Talin because she had spent so much time worshiping her in the dark. Pema had no clue if the four people the district police had arrested—or the two they had killed—included Cosmin's general or second. Either way, the odds weren't good.

Pema gave Talin a quick once over, didn't notice any blooming dark spots of blood, and went back to firing, hoping to find a weak spot in the bot's armor plating. That was all they could do. They could only buy Talin time to come up with a miracle, some device from the loadout she brought that could disable the bot, keep the district police back, and give them a chance to pile into the last van and get out of there.

Talin kept her head down, her nimble fingers digging through wires, rearranging outputs, adding the magitech stored in her bullets into one of her devices so fast Pema couldn't track everything she did. She could only pray Talin's fingers were fast enough.

The district police were hanging back, content to let the giant robot do the fighting for them. So far, the bot was merely disabling the vans, ensuring that they couldn't drive off with the magitech contraband they had been attempting to deliver. The bot didn't react to their shooting, their bullets leaving little more than scorch marks and dents on its body, and the ground vibrated as it rolled forward, moving to the next vehicle. The last one before it reached them.

"Babe," Pema pleaded, her voice breathy and raspy as panic began to settle in. Pema couldn't go to prison, couldn't risk Talin getting hurt . . . *Not again!*

Talin snorted. Leaning over Pema's lap, she gently let a wheeled canister go. The device took a millisecond to orient itself, just as the war automata started heading for them. The canister rolled toward the massive, chrome robot and *thunked* against its wheel. The bot didn't notice Talin's device, or, if it had, it hadn't been programmed to address whatever threat such a small thing may pose. It kept moving.

Nothing happened.

"Babe!" Pema yelled, her gravelly voice nearly shrill.

"Wait for it to engage," Talin barked back. But the four other crew members weren't content to wait, doubting perhaps that whatever Talin did would activate in time.

They split into two groups, flanking the vehicle and unloading everything they had on the war bot in one final grandstand. They might as well have been throwing pebbles at a sky-tower. Then Talin's canister finally began to hiss at the base of the bot, a gentle curl of steam twisting into the air . . .

Pema tried to provide cover as best as she could, but there were too many people to protect. Almost leisurely, a shoulder-mounted turret emerged from the bot's back. With a soft *poof* of air, almost like a gasp, industrial sized tranquilizers fired from the turret, each finding their home in the weak points between the crew's masks and the rest of their combat-tech armor.

All four of them fell in unison. Under different

circumstances, Pema would have found it comical. But, currently, when she was now the last person with any kind of firepower standing between a war bot and her girlfriend? She damn near pissed herself at the sight of all of Cosmin's people crumpling to the ground.

TWANG!

The canister at the bot's feet imploded at last.

The war android stopped dead as it was deploying the metal nets to secure Cosmin's incapacitated team. It teetered for a second, the district police shouting orders that sounded like garbled noise to Pema. Then the bot fell back, painfully slowly, giving all the cops behind it plenty of time to scatter.

Grabbing Talin's hand, Pema pulled her up. "Time to go!"

Talin tried to pull her hand away. "But what about —*oomf!*"

Pema's heart dropped, a fist squeezing her chest so tightly she thought her ribs would shatter. A crimson stain bloomed on Talin's arm. Talin's face twisted in pain, and she fell heavily to one knee, her hand clutching at her wounded arm.

Fire consumed Pema, racing from her core to engulf her lungs, sharpening her nerve endings as Talin's hand slipped from hers. And yet, Pema was able to draw in slow, steady breaths. Talin's eyes were scrunched closed in pain, teeth clamped on her lips to keep her scream of agony locked away.

Pure wrath enveloped Pema, and her logical brain shut down. A cold, efficient killer emerged in its place. She would make every last bastard out there pay for hurting her girlfriend. Her nostrils flared, and Pema pushed Talin into the back of the semi-van.

She slammed the door closed and marched to the driver's console almost calmly, ducking and swerving as needed, but firing relentlessly into the ranks of the district police. Who were, mostly, still scrambling to get back into position after their bot fell.

Pema saw only red as she fired over and over again, the same red as Talin's blood leaking down her arm. She was methodical in her shots, making sure the police couldn't poke their heads out of cover long enough to get a fix on their position beyond what the hovering Ash Hawks could provide.

Using the door as cover, Pema initiated the auto-driver virtual intelligence, overriding the commands Cosmin had given it to remain where it was, or proceed to the drop off point. The semi-van engaged, and as soon as the tires began spinning backward, Pema dove in, closing the door, and keeping her head down as the van turned sharply, nearly flipping itself over as it raced back the way they had come.

Pema flinched constantly under the endless barrage of bullets. She couldn't get the van to swerve properly, and large splintering cracks were starting to appear in the windows, the armor failing . . . When the back door of the van flew open.

"Talin!" Pema screamed, and could only watch through the rearview mirror as the love of her life stood, exposed, facing down the pissed-off district cops.

Talin shoved out a stack of magitech weapons and armaments into the scrambling ranks of the Governor's team. Then she shoved another, the stacks mercifully providing cover, even if only momentarily. As the plastic crates spilled onto the ground, slowing the cops, Talin tossed out one more grenade.

This one didn't have a delayed detonation. The grenade's explosion wasn't anything impressive, just thick smoke and sparkling electricity. But it was more than enough to ignite the fire magitech within the crates they were smuggling.

The following explosion nearly collapsed the entire sky-bridge. The toxic, billowing black smoke that rose from the wreckage blocked them from sight of the circling Ash Hawk helicopters. Pema wouldn't waste even a millisecond of cover in getting them out of there.

It took her a moment to figure out where in Euria they were, what route the auto-driver had taken them on, and how to avoid that direction like a venereal disease. Disengaging the auto-driver, Pema took direct control of the semi-van and raced down the sky-bridge. She turned sharply onto another platform, then down a hairpin turn roadway that was mainly used for service droids, before gunning the semi-van underneath another major thoroughfare, using the shadow of the street as cover from the Ash Hawks.

Only then did Pema risk slowing down, only then did she notice how loud her breathing was, and how rapidly her pulse pounded throughout her body. Maneuvering them into the normal ebb and flow of traffic, Pema cocked her head, straining to hear any sounds: horns, the wail of sirens, the *whomp-whomp-whomp* of propellers . . . but all she heard was the growl of ground bound traffic.

Taking a shaky breath, Pema turned the semi-van into the nearest mega-mall and parked it in the bottommost level. As soon as she cut the engine, she dove out of the van, finally able to assess the injuries Talin had sustained.

Talin was already stumbling out of the back of the van by the time Pema reached her. She grabbed the back of Talin's head, brought her face down so she could peer into those stunning jade green eyes she adored so much, and inhaled the scent of burning wood and cinnamon that was so uniquely the woman she loved.

"I'm okay, love," Talin said, her smoky voice wavering. She took a deep breath, wrapped a hand around the back of Pema's neck, and said again, "I'm okay. It was just a graze. I promise."

It wasn't until Talin brushed her soft lips over Pema's forehead that she finally released her. Pema gently took Talin's hand and examined her arm. She had somehow bandaged her wound as Pema drove like a mad woman, and the blood hadn't managed to seep through yet. Only then did Pema believe Talin when she said it was merely a graze.

That was too close.

Gripping Talin's hand as if she would slip away the moment Pema turned her back on her, she gently tugged her away from the black semi-van. "Come on," she said, her voice breaking with emotion. Clearing her throat, she said more firmly. "We've got to ditch it and find a new ride. No way am I taking our transport back. I'd bet my left tit they have a tracer on it by now."

"Aw, but that's my favorite one," Talin joked, but Pema couldn't even muster a chuckle in response.

IT TOOK them five hours to get back to their cramped apartment. Talin jokingly called Pema paranoid after the first hour and a half of her girlfriend, following Cosmin's protocol when assignments didn't go according to plan, took meandering paths, backtracking via public transportation, only to repeat the process. By hour three, Talin was no longer joking, and by the time they actually stumbled into their home, having long lost any tail that may have been on them, Talin had stopped speaking entirely. Pema took the protocol to obsessive levels that set Talin on edge, but she didn't care as long as she had Talin by her side, alive and whole.

Once safe in their unit, Pema helped Talin rebandage her wound by covering it with a skin-like wrapping that would help the tissue heal rapidly. Thankfully the bullet that grazed her had been simple armor piercing rounds and not anything full of caster magic. A graze from a bullet with magitech could be just as deadly as if Talin had been hit full force—Pema knew from experience. If Cosmin's doctors hadn't seen to her after Ellinor ruined everything, Pema would be half cyborg by now, at best. Instead, Cosmin had poured so many resources into her recovery that Pema was convinced that he wanted her to stay a part of his organization for a very long time, no matter what Ellinor said, or Talin's own trepidation.

Only once Talin was seen to, and both women had kicked off their boots and had cold bottles of beer in hand, did they ping Cosmin on a secure holo-channel. Pema sat on their bed, holding the device, and Talin sat next to her, folding her long legs under her, resting her head on Pema's shoulder.

Cosmin didn't answer.

Talin sat upright, her shoulders tense and spine straight. Pema took a long swig from her beer, and wiped her mouth with the back of her hand, grinning tiredly at Talin. "He's a busy man, babe. I'm sure he's already heard of the clusterfuck that went down and is securing what he can, getting our people out of custody, the works. You follow?"

Talin frowned, getting up and moving to the main room. "Oh, I follow, but this don't feel right. Ping him again."

Pema shrugged, complying if it meant putting Talin at ease. But when Cosmin didn't answer by the third ping, Pema became concerned. Was this a bigger raid? Had the Governor found a way to link Cosmin to all the money laundering businesses and shell corporations he used to shield his true business? Did his immunity from a deal he made centuries ago expire at long last?

"Pema, my dear, I didn't expect to hear from you," Cosmin said, finally answering.

Why not?

The holo-tablet picked up his image a moment later, displaying it over the device in three-dimensional, life-like perfection. Cosmin was lounging at his desk, his matte black hair pulled up into a tight, stylish braid. He leaned a bit forward, as if he needed a better view, looking for something. His pumpkin orange eyes flicked over Pema, and she tried not to wince. Like most people, Pema found Cosmin's eyes unsettling, too similar to the overabundance of fire magic he wielded. His orange eyes seemed to burn her skin if he looked at her too long.

"Lovely," Cosmin said, leaning back, his voice oddly expressionless. "It appears our darling Talin is with you as well."

Pema's heart beat erratically in her chest, and she hoped the nervous sweat collecting at her temples wasn't noticeable. "Cosmin, there was a raid," she said in a rush, worried that if she stopped to be more tactful, she'd never get everything out, or wouldn't be able to tell her boss that they fucked up somewhere along the way. "The Governor had his district rats all over us. They took, or killed, everyone else. We saved one of the vans, but lost some of the merchandise along the way." There was a phantom twinge in her side from where she had once been so grievously injured. She took a deep breath, putting her hand over the wound that Cosmin's people had so expertly patched up. "Orders, sir?"

Cosmin didn't react as she spoke. He tugged the cuffs of his black and gold brocade suit jacket down over the sleeves of his tailored silk shirt, but otherwise didn't move as she told him that the *Governor* now had possession of Cosmin's magitech. Magitech Cosmin himself supplied the fire magic for.

He waved his hand dismissively once she was done, clicking his tongue. "My dear, calm down before you give yourself an ulcer. Nothing happened that I didn't allow to occur."

Pema nearly dropped the holo-tablet at his confession. "What?" Her words were barely more than a raspy squeak. "I don't get it. Allow to happen?"

Cosmin sighed, leaning back in his throne-like seat, crossing his leg at the knee. "My dear, it's not so hard to understand if you don't spend all day overthinking it. Certain . . . concessions needed to be made after Ellinor ran off and made such a spectacular mess of the simple errand I had wanted her to complete. Really, the imposition she put me in was rather bothersome."

Pema glanced up as he spoke, spying Talin standing painfully still in their narrow hallway, gripping her bottle of beer so tightly that Pema was sure it would shatter. But, even as Cosmin spoke, Pema's mind rebelled against what he was saying. Cosmin wouldn't do that, not to her, not when she always, *always* did what he asked without question or hesitation.

"But," Pema said, holding on to the holo-tablet tighter so it wouldn't slip through her slick grasp. "You sent one of your generals and their second with the shipment. What about them? They could rat to the Governor!"

Cosmin chuckled, the sound like dead, rustling leaves and a blush of amusement entered his slightly yellowed pallor. "I suspect it's far too late for that."

When Pema merely blinked back at him uncomprehendingly, he shrugged, sighing again. "My dear, I really shouldn't have to spell this out to you, of all people, but very well. After the debacle that *is* Ellinor, I suspected there were others in my ranks who felt similarly. There were just so many annoying little messes to clean up that this seemed the easiest way. Give the Governor a little something of mine in order to return the status quo, and get rid of a few peons I felt were already feeding intel to those they had no business speaking to. Which reminds me, you'll have to tell me where you left that last van. I'll need to tip off the district police to ensure my arrangement is upheld."

"Then why send us?" Pema said, doing her best to keep the tremor of fear and rage from showing in her voice.

Cosmin shrugged, his black brows pinching together in annoyance. "To sell the ruse, obviously."

"But we could have been taken, or killed!"

Cosmin smirked at her for a moment, steepling his fingers in front of his dimpled chin. "Pema, darling, you know the job. Now, be a dear and send me the coordinates of the remainder of my shipment."

He disconnected the call, never once asking if she or

Talin were all right, never once showing any remorse for the people that died. Cosmin hadn't even bothered to tell them of the plan so they could have better prepared and gotten out clean, while still making sure that whatever deal Cosmin enacted stayed intact.

He doesn't trust us—me—anymore.

She tossed the holo-projection device aside, and jammed her palms into her eyes, rubbing until she saw spots. Pema had never felt so small, so *expendable* in her life.

She always thought—since Cosmin first busted her out of prison, paying her bail and giving her a job, giving her *life* back—that he valued her, that he wanted her. That he would always protect her and Talin like he had in the past. But now? Now she was beginning to realize that she was as disposable as toilet tissue. Talin and Ellinor had been right all along. Cosmin was more than able, and willing, to throw the life of the woman she loved away if it satisfied a *hunch* he had about *possible* rats in his organization. Pema didn't remove her palms until she felt Talin place her hand on her shoulder and squeeze gently.

"See, love?" Talin said, her words kind even if her tone said: I told you so. "Ellinor was right. We're nothing to Cosmin. Never have been. Just tools to be used when the mood strikes. Took a while but, yeah, I can see what Ell did. She was right this whole damn time about Cosmin. We just didn't want to listen."

Pema looked up into Talin's dazzling green eyes, the resigned frown on her perfect lips, before trailing down to her freshly bandaged arm. She placed her hand over Talin's long, elegant fingers, and held on tightly.

Pema Tran knew from a young age that she would never be the "good guy" in anyone's story. But then she met Talin and she figured that, if nothing else, she could be this woman's hero, that she would gladly spend her days protecting that brilliant mind that delighted in watching things explode. They were perfect together, and, when she really thought about it, Talin was the only good thing Cosmin von Brandt had ever truly brought into her life.

And he had been willing to destroy that on a *feeling*.

Just think about it, yeah?

Pema was more than just thinking about Ellinor's warning now as she stared up at Talin. Her chest ached realizing how close she had been to losing Talin, again, and her pulse quickened through her body, filling her blood with pure fury.

"I follow you," she said, voice weak but gaining strength. "We need to find a way out of Cosmin's organization. Before he gets us fucking killed."

Get a standalone Eerden novella and meet the notorious Cosmin von Brandt before he becomes a household name in Paradigm Flux! dl.bookfunnel.com/1uxhxjygo5

Pick Your Poison

1. *Let's stick with organized crime, but make it cyberpunk.*
Head to "Case City Cowboy" by Greg Dragon

2. *Let's stick with organized crime, but make it aliens.*
Head to "Risk Management" by Caitlin Demaris
McKenna

3. *Actually, do you have any stories about bounty hunters?*
Turn the page to read "Sparrow" by G.J. Ogden

SPARROW

BY G.J. OGDEN

RAMSEY LORCAN THREW OPEN THE DOOR AND FOUND himself charging down the barrel of a pulse pistol. The weapon discharged, but Lorcan's momentum had propelled him out of the line of fire and into the body of the gunman, Hector Malloy. The collision sent the two men barreling along the corridor, as if an airlock had ruptured and was blowing them into space.

Lorcan clawed at the deck plates of the transport and arrested his fall before Malloy had a chance to shoot again. He used his advantage to land a crushing elbow strike that smashed Malloy's nose, splattering blood over the man's face like an abstract artist tossing paint at a canvas. Malloy fell, clutching his broken nose, and allowing Lorcan to gather up his own weapon, which had cartwheeled down the corridor along with him after the two men had collided.

"Where is it, Malloy?" Lorcan yelled, aiming his pulse pistol at the man who was the only known lead to a Malfunct he'd been hunting for the last ten years. "I know it's on this transport with you, so give it up and you might still live."

"Eat shit, asshole!" Malloy said, spitting blood onto the deck. "I'm no synth, so you can't do a damned thing to me. Besides, if I tell you anything, then that freak of nature will just come after me next."

"Not if you tell me where it is!" Lorcan snarled.

Lorcan hauled Malloy up by his shirt collar and shoved him against the wall, before pressing the barrel of the pistol into the man's broad chest.

"I swear to God, if that Malfunct gets away because of you, I'll make you pay!"

Malloy sprayed a haze of blood-stained spittle into Lorcan's face then smiled, saliva dribbling over his nose and lips.

"Like I said, eat shit," Malloy said. "Unless you're going to pay double what that synth freak gave me—and I know you can't—you can kiss my sweaty asshole."

Lorcan gritted his teeth and added pressure to the trigger. The only thing he hated more than malfunctioning synths were the human bloodsuckers that helped them to avoid Menders like him.

"That thing has killed over a hundred people," Lorcan said, digging the barrel of his pistol deeper in Malloy's flesh. "Don't you care?"

"No, I don't care," Malloy hit back. "And I'll happily take two years in lock for helping that malfunct, because when they let me out, I'll still be rich."

Lorcan fought the urge to blow the man's heart out of his chest, but while he had a license to kill malfunctioning synths, he had no jurisdiction when it came to natural-born humans, even the degenerate ones. If Malloy didn't cooperate, he was back to square one.

"Are we done, or are we going to make a deal?" Malloy said, dabbing more blood and snot from his nose.

"Here's my offer, dickhead," Lorcan snarled, before whipping the frame of his pulse pistol across the side of Malloy's face.

The man's body went limp and landed in a crumpled heap at his feet. Lorcan slid his pistol back into its holster then stared at Malloy for a few seconds, lamenting the fact that his only solid lead was now drooling on his boots.

"God damn it!" Lorcan cursed, shaking his head at the obstinate man. "I was so close."

The satisfaction he'd got from decking Malloy had been fleeting, and now he was left with a sense of crushing disappointment. Malloy had been his only link to Malfunct SPR-0, a malfunctioning synthetic human that was better known by its ID code: Sparrow.

Sparrow had been responsible for more than one hundred brutal murders spanning a period of ten years. A freak mutation had screwed up the synth's artificial DNA, giving it the ability to metamorphose into a new body after each murder, like a snake shedding its skin. As a Mender, it was Lorcan's job to track down and eradicate these deviants. Yet, for ten long years, this was the closest he—or any other bounty-hunter from the Mender's Guild —had ever gotten to catching the galaxy's most notorious Malfunct.

"Sir, I am detecting elevated levels of adrenaline and stress hormones in your system," said Leah, Lorcan's personal synth, speaking through a bone-conducting transducer engineered into his skull. "Are you in danger?"

"No, Leah, I'm fine," Lorcan sighed. "At least, I am now."

Technically, the synth's official designation was Law

Enforcement Assistant, High-Functioning, but Lorcan preferred Leah for short.

"I also detect that Hector Malloy is in your vicinity. Are you in need of assistance?" Leah added.

"Unless you can tell me if Sparrow is actually on this ship, I don't think there's a damned thing you can do to help me," Lorcan hit back, tetchily.

"I regret that I cannot find any evidence that Malfunct SPR-o is aboard this vessel," Leah replied mournfully. "I presume that Hector Malloy is proving uncooperative in this matter?"

"You could say that," replied Lorcan, staring at the unconscious man at his feet.

"I am in the transport's data center, searching for clues," Leah continued, answering the question she had successfully predicted Lorcan would ask next. "The transport's complement is one hundred and twelve passengers and crew, including you and me. Seventeen crew are synthetics. All have been successfully verified."

"Shit, so it's not here then?"

"It would appear not, sir."

"Damn it!" Lorcan thumped his fist into the wall of the corridor. "I was sure we had that bastard this time."

"It would appear that Hector Malloy was merely a decoy," Leah said. "Our best course of action now is to return to Titan and inspect the security recordings and cargo manifests of all the other vessels that departed Huygens Station after this vessel."

"That could put Sparrow on any one of two dozen other ships, assuming it even left Huygens Station at all," Lorcan said, rubbing the bridge of his nose with his thumb and forefinger.

Lorcan sighed and shook his head again, wondering

why he kept putting himself through the stress and frustration of hunting an unfindable prey. The fact that this time he had felt sure he was going to get his man only made his failure to do so more depressing and humiliating.

"Screw it, Leah, I'm done with chasing this asshole all over the solar system," Lorcan said, making the decision to abandon his pursuit of Malfunct SPR-o; this time for good. "Get to the shuttle and file a request to depart with the bridge. We'll head back to Earth and run down some easier contracts. At least then we'll get paid."

"Yes, sir," Leah replied brightly.

There was a soft chirrup as the comm link between himself and his personal synth was closed. Suddenly, Hector Malloy groaned and began crawling around on the deck, like a drunk who'd dropped his house keys and was desperately searching the ground trying to find them.

"Come on, get up, I didn't hit you that hard," Lorcan said, jabbing Malloy in the ribs with the tip of his boot.

"I don't feel so good . . ." Malloy peered up at Lorcan through pained-looking, squinty eyes.

"That's because I broke your nose then cracked open your skull, shithead," Lorcan replied, still jabbing Malloy in the ribs with his foot. He then sighed and took pity on the wretched man. "Come on, I'll take you to the med bay. The last thing I need is you dying on me. The paperwork would be a bitch."

Lorcan hauled up the robust frame of Hector Malloy and guided the dazed man through the halls and corridors of the transport until they reached the medical bay. He dragged the man inside then threw Malloy down on a spare bed, startling the two on-duty medics in the process.

One of them, a woman aged about twenty, came over to inspect the patient.

"He fell and hit his head," Lorcan explained. Since it was a half-truth, he didn't feel bad for lying to the doctor.

The medic examined the cut to Malloy's skull then scowled at the man's badly broken nose.

"He walked into the door first," Lorcan added, embellishing his story. "What can I say, he's a clumsy son-of-a-bitch."

"I see," said the doctor, while shining a light into Malloy's eyes. "Well, we will take good care of him. Thank you for bringing this man to our attention. You may go."

Lorcan frowned at the medic. The nature of his job meant that he'd had plenty of experience with hospitals, but he'd never met a doctor with such a coldly clinical bedside manner before. Or such an odd way of talking.

"Don't mention it, doc," Lorcan replied, casually checking the name tag on the medic's scrubs. It read *Jane Baker*. He nodded to the medic then turned on his heels and headed for the door, feeling a sudden urge to lose himself in the bottom of a bottle of rum.

"Hey, it's you . . ."

Lorcan's mouth went dry. He glanced over his shoulder toward the medical bay and saw that Malloy was awake, and staring into the doctor's eyes like he'd seen a ghost.

"Lie still, you are injured," said the doctor, calmly pushing Malloy's shoulders flat against the bed.

Lorcan crouched at the threshold of the door, pretending to tie his boot laces while he continued to watch out of the corner of his eye. The doctor looked like she was barely a hundred and thirty pounds, but had manhandled Malloy like she weighed twice that.

"We weren't supposed to meet again," Malloy mumbled. "Did I do something wrong?"

"You are safe," the doctor said, still holding Malloy firmly to the bed.

The doctor turned to Lorcan and smiled. However, if the expression had intended to convey reassurance, it did the exact opposite. It felt like a demon had just smiled at him.

"You may go," the doctor added. "He is delirious, but not seriously impaired."

Lorcan nodded and returned the smile before standing up and slipping through the door. He waited for it to thud shut behind him then tapped his right temple to re-establish a link to Leah.

"Leah, get your ass to the medical center, fast," Lorcan said in a hushed voice, despite the door separating him from the medical bay being three inches thick. "And I need you to run a check on one of the ship's medics. A woman in her early twenties. One-thirty to one-forty pounds, chestnut hair and ocean blue eyes, going by the name of Jane Baker."

"Jane Baker is a junior medic who came aboard at Huygens Station," Leah replied promptly. Lorcan could physically feel the synth's boots thumping on the deck as she raced through the transport's corridors to meet him. "However, the woman you described does not exactly match her description."

Lorcan frowned. "What do you mean?"

"Jane Baker has hazel brown eyes," Leah replied.

"Are you sure?" Lorcan said. He wracked his brain,

trying to picture the doctor's face, but he was certain his description of her was accurate.

"I am sure, sir," Leah replied. "Also, Jane Baker was scanned before coming aboard. Her blood DNA was verified as human."

Lorcan cursed under his breath. Even if he had remembered the doctor's eye color incorrectly, the DNA scan ruled her out as Sparrow in a new skin. Yet, he couldn't shake the feeling he was right.

"Damn it, I'm going back in to check," Lorcan said, unclipping the fastener on his holster.

"I am one hundred and fourteen seconds away, sir," Leah replied, the pace of her bootsteps increasing. "I recommend you wait until I arrive."

Lorcan heard his personal synth, but he wasn't about to wait; he'd waited ten years already. Hitting the button to open the door, Lorcan stepped inside, smiling casually.

"I forgot, I just needed to get the guy's name for the accident report," Lorcan began, breaking into a convenient lie to explain his intrusion.

However, two steps inside the medical center, Lorcan froze. The second on-duty medic was lying face-up on the deck, a scalpel driven four-inches deep into the man's eye socket. Turning to Malloy, he saw that the man's throat had been sliced from ear to ear. Blood had soaked through the bedsheets and was dripping on to the deck, like the ticking of a clock.

Lorcan drew his pulse pistol and checked the room, but there was no sign of Jane Baker. He hurried further inside, his boots slipping on Malloy's blood, and checked each door, looking for another exit. Finally, he found it and kicked it open, darting into the corridor and aiming his weapon down the passageway. A trail of bloody foot-steps led the way.

"Leah, our killer is here." Lorcan followed the foot-steps, pistol raised. "Divert to Corridor Seven, Junction C, and you might cut her off."

"Understood, sir, I am ninety-one seconds away."

Lorcan didn't envy much about synthetic humans, but their untiring stamina was top of the list, especially whenever he was forced to give chase to a Malfunct.

Reaching the end of the corridor, Lorcan slapped the blood-stained button to open the door, raced through, and ran straight into a thumping right-hand that knocked him flat on his back, like he'd been hit by a truck.

"How did you know?" Jane Baker asked.

Lorcan reached for his pistol, which had slipped from his grasp when he'd fallen, but the synth kicked it away, then stood on his fingers, trapping them like a vice.

"How did you know?" Baker repeated. Lorcan cried out, desperately trying to pry his crushed hand from under the heel of the doctor's boot.

"Malloy recognized you," Lorcan said through gritted teeth. He peered into the woman's eyes, which were ocean-blue. "And your eyes are the wrong color. Jane Baker has hazel brown eyes."

The doctor cocked her head to one side, then in an instant her eye color switched from azure blue to hazel brown.

"Thank you for that detail," Baker said. "I will not that mistake again."

"So, it is you?" Lorcan said. He wanted the synth to admit it. "You're Sparrow; Malfunct SPR-o?"

"Yes," the synth said, again with the demented smile.

Malfunct SPR-o knelt down and picked up Lorcan's

pulse pistol, while somehow still managing to apply inca-pacitating pain to his hand so that he was powerless to resist.

"Why do you do it?" Lorcan hissed as the synth studied his pulse pistol with the curiosity of a child. "What do you get out of killing all of these people?"

Suddenly, Sparrow stabbed the barrel of the pistol into Lorcan's groin with the force of a hammer striking a chisel. Lorcan tried to scream, but the blow had stolen the breath from his lungs, and all that came out of his mouth was a tormented wheeze.

"You humans feel so much," Sparrow said, leaning close enough to Lorcan that he could feel the synth's fetid breath on his face. "Joy, sadness, love, despair, and pain . . . I would kill to feel any of those emotions, even if only for a fleeting moment." The synth then smiled its demented smile. "And so that is what I do."

Sparrow slid the barrel of the pulse pistol along Lorcan's abdomen and chest until it was pressed underneath his chin.

"Thank you for this feeling," the synth whispered into his ear. "I will cherish it, always."

Sparrow added pressure to the trigger, then there was fizz and flash of light, and Lorcan felt blood splatter his face. Malfunct SPR-o collapsed on his chest, the synthetic human's blood soaking into Lorcan's shirt.

He grabbed Sparrow's head and lifted it, only to discover that the synth's face had been blown off by a pulse shot that had penetrated through the back of her skull. Lorcan shoved the body away in revulsion and scrambled back against the wall. Breathless and still in agony, he clawed blood from his eyes and looked up to see Leah peering at him.

"I apologize for my tardiness," Leah said, holstering her pulse pistol then offering Lorcan her hand. "Are you injured?"

"Yes," Lorcan groaned as Leah hauled him to his feet with inhuman ease. "But other than probably not being able to have kids, anymore, I'll be alright."

Leah frowned at Lorcan, her eyes flicking from side to side, before suddenly growing wide.

"Ah, a joke," she said. "I understand."

"Is that really Sparrow?" Lorcan nodded toward the dead synth on the deck.

Leah crouched beside the body and poked her finger into the dead synth's partly-vaporized brain. Lorcan watched with a mix of curiosity and disgust as she placed the finger into her mouth and stood up. The expression on Leah's face was that of a chef sampling the main course of the lunchtime menu, to make sure it met her exacting standards.

"Curious . . ." Leah said, still looking deep in thought.

Leah reached over and grabbed Lorcan's hand, and before he knew it, she had slipped his index finger into her mouth and sucked the dead synth's blood from his skin.

"The synthetic brain matter corresponds to that of Malfunct SPR-o," Leah finally answered, though to Lorcan's eyes, she looked unsure. "But the DNA in her blood reads as human."

"How is that possible?" Lorcan asked, wiping his index finger dry on his pants. "Sparrow's mutation meant she could assume different physical forms, but they're all synthetic, right?"

Leah cocked her head to one side. "It would appear that Malfunct SPR-o was not what we thought."

Lorcan sighed heavily and rested against the wall. He still felt sick from the low-blow, and nauseous from having watched Leah taste the brains and blood of the dead synth, only to conclude that Sparrow may not have been synthetic at all.

"Notify the ship's captain, and have whatever medics are left onboard tag and bag this body for analysis," Lorcan said. "The boffins at the Mender's Guild can figure this out. It's their problem now; we've done our job."

"Yes, sir," Leah replied cheerfully.

Lorcan tried to push himself away from the wall, but it merely intensified the discomfort he was already experiencing, and he was forced to bend double to brace himself against the pain. He felt Leah place her arm around his back to take some of the strain.

"You require medical attention," Leah said, with genuine concern and affection.

"What I require is a good, stiff drink. Or three." Lorcan gently patted his partner on the shoulder. He tried to laugh, but all he could manage was a strained wheeze.

"May I suggest you return to our cabin, while I take care of the formalities? I will then return and assist with your rehabilitation."

"You make me sound like an addict, but thanks, Leah, that's the best idea I've heard all day," Lorcan said, accepting Leah's help and finally pushing himself away from the wall. "Let me know when the body has been registered in the ship's morgue, then I'll file with the guild for payment. At least the bounty on Sparrow was worth getting jabbed in the balls for."

"If you say so, sir," Leah replied, her expression

reading as one of confusion. "Do you require assistance in returning to the cabin?"

"No, I'll be fine. But thanks, anyway." Lorcan again patted his personal synth affectionately on the shoulder, then began the slow, painful waddle along the corridor toward the small cabin they'd booked in the transport's third-class passenger deck. The throbbing pain in his groin was beginning to subside, but he could still barely move faster than a ninety-year-old with a Zimmer frame.

Five minutes later, and Lorcan had barely made it a hundred meters before the pain in his groin forced him to stop and catch his breath. The sound of clacking crockery caused him to look up, and at the same time he caught the alluring smell of strong coffee in the air. Following the scent, he spotted a canteen and aimed his waddling frame at the door.

I'd prefer a double-shot of rum, but coffee will have to do, Lorcan mused. *And this canteen is a damned sight closer than my crappy cabin is.*

A few steps from the archway leading into the canteen, Lorcan saw a couple of other passengers approaching from the other side of the corridor. They initially looked like they might offer to help him, until they saw the Mender's Guild badge on Lorcan's jacket and quickly averted their gaze.

"I don't hunt humans, damn it," Lorcan said, loudly enough for the couple to hear, though they continued to ignore him and quickened their pace.

Prejudice was something he'd come to expect in his line of work. No one liked a Mender, least of all synths, but even natural born humans considered them to be vultures that were best avoided.

Reaching the archway, Lorcan was suddenly jolted, as

if the transport had been hit by a stray asteroid and momentarily knocked off course. He grabbed the door frame, and his muscles tensed, causing more pain to shoot through his groin and gut.

"Damn it to hell!" he hissed through gritted teeth.

Lorcan waited for the pain to subside again before continuing into the canteen and dropping heavily into the chair closest to the entrance. He made eye contact with the synth waiter then tapped the coffee cup on the table with his index finger, causing it to chime musically. The synth waiter nodded, and Lorcan relaxed, clasping his hand to his groin and letting out a long, deep sigh. A second later, his phone rang. He sighed again.

"Can't I get a moment's peace?" Lorcan grumbled, gingerly sliding the device out of his pocket. He tossed it onto the table then tapped the screen. "Yeah, what?"

A holo projection of a man's face appeared above the device. The caller was wearing a nautical-looking uniform and a sour expression.

"What the hell do you think you're playing at, Mender?" the man roared. "You can't just depart on a whim. We have procedures!"

"What are you blathering on about? I haven't gone anywhere." Lorcan sat more upright, despite the fact it hurt to do so. "I'm sitting in your damned third-class canteen."

The man on the holo, who Lorcan now recognized as the transport's captain, did not appear placated by his response.

"Don't play games with me," the captain snarled. "Your shuttle left garage two, jettisoning half of the cargo cannisters along with it."

"You've got the wrong guy, skipper," Lorcan hit back,

though at least he now knew the reason why the transport had been jolted. "Check your panel. I'm on deck four for Christ's sake."

The captain scowled then glanced down, apparently doing what Lorcan had suggested. A moment later, the man shook his head and cursed under his breath.

"You're right," the captain finally replied.

"No shit, I'm right." Lorcan raised his still empty coffee cup so the captain could see it. The name of the transport was engraved on its side.

"You might be here, but your shuttle is not," the captain continued. "It was your synth who took it."

Lorcan set the cup down so hard that it smashed on the table.

"That has to be a mistake."

"I assure you; it is not!"

Lorcan snatched his phone, which automatically switched from the holo view of the officer to a regular 2D image on the screen.

"I'll get back to you," Lorcan said, ending the call before the captain could respond. He tapped the transducer in his temple and linked it to the phone before speed-dialing Leah and tossing the device amongst the fractured remains of his coffee cup.

"Come on . . ." Lorcan said, impatiently tapping the table as the call tried to connect. After ten long rings, his personal synth finally answered, and Lorcan jolted upright. "Leah, what the hell are you doing? The captain said you took off!"

"That is correct," Leah replied. Lorcan could see that she was piloting his shuttle, and that she was already in deep space.

"Then get your ass back here!" Lorcan yelled, causing

the other customers of the canteen to shoot angry sideways glances in his direction.

"I am afraid not," Leah replied coolly.

"That run in with Sparrow must have bugged you out," Lorcan said, accessing the diagnostic for his personal synth. "You've got a damned screw loose."

The phone connected to his synth's diagnostic page; however, all the data had been erased.

"Leah is no longer here, if that is who are you trying to access," the synth replied through the holo. "Though, I actually like the name. I think I will keep it."

"Leah, you're not making any damned sense," Lorcan said, peering into the synth's eyes. "Just get back here and we'll get you checked out. It'll be okay."

The synth smiled, and Lorcan watched as her eyes switched from hazel brown to ocean blue, before returning to brown again. Lorcan felt like he was going to be sick.

"Sparrow?'

"Thank you for the new body," the synth said, shooting Lorcan a demented smile. "Like the name, I may keep it. At least for a time."

"She doesn't belong to you!" Lorcan snarled, hammering his fist on the table. "I'll find you, like I did before. I'll find you and make you to give her back."

"You will never see this face again," said Sparrow. "Goodbye, Ramsey."

The connection was cut, then Lorcan's phone switched off and began a complete data wipe. Lorcan roared and hurled the device into the wall of the canteen, smashing it into a hundred pieces. An awkward hush fell over the room, then the *clack, clack* of footsteps broke the silence. Lorcan found himself staring into the eyes of the synth waiter.

"Coffee, sir?"

Lorcan stared into the synthetic human's glassy orbs, which seemed to look through him, as if he was an apparition. Sliding his pulse pistol out of its holster, Lorcan aimed at the synth's head and squeezed the trigger. The screams of the customers in the canteen were punctuated by the thud of the synth's body hitting the deck, and the crash of the coffee pot as it smashed and spilled the steaming hot liquid across the floor.

Lorcan slid his weapon back into its holster then kicked the chair out from under him. The pain he had felt was gone; replaced by numbness, and a hollow ringing in his ears. He didn't know how Sparrow had done it, and he didn't care. Before, catching the galaxy's most notorious Malfunct was just a game the members of the Mender's Guild played, as a way to determine who was the top dog. Not any longer. Not for Ramsey Lorcan. Now, killing Malfunct SPR-o was personal. And he wouldn't stop, not ever, until Sparrow was dead.

------*------

Pick Your Poison

1. *Yes! More androids!* Head to "Martian Scuttle" by
Andrew Sweet

2. *I'm digging the deep space security intrigue vibe.* Head
to "Ace in the Hole" by Kate Sheeran Swed

3. *I'm itching for a good P.I. story.* Turn the page to read
"A Cruel Cyber Summer Night" by Austin Dragon

A CRUEL CYBER SUMMER NIGHT

A LIQUID COOL STORY

BY AUSTIN DRAGON

MY NAME'S CRUZ.

Not long ago, I was a one-time classic hovercar restorer, part-time racer, and a former laborer. But now, I'm supposedly "famous" because of my relatively new profession as a private investigator in the high-tech, low-life corner of the world, Metropolis.

Metropolis was my city, a sprawling urban landscape of concrete and steel nearly twice the size of any other city on Earth with its fifty-million plus residents. It was the supercity of supercities. Its residents, including me, both hated it and loved it at the same time.

Its skyscraper monoliths towered up and spiraled out to create a type of concrete maze from the ground to the ever-rainy sky above. Houses were a thing of the past. People lived and worked in mega-skyscrapers. Individual storefronts were a thing of the past. Businesses were either part of a floor, owned the whole floor, or owned the entire business tower. But Metropolis was no dark dystopian landscape. It was wrapped in ever-present flashing neon signs and video displays. In the "nice parts" of the city, street lampposts hung over nearly every corner, and in the "nicer parts," the very surfaces of buildings gave off good illumination. This "neon jungle" was where I was born, raised, and lived with my Pony, my cool hat, the wife...oops. I meant to say, "Where I lived with the wife, Cruz Jr. (aka 'ninja boy'), newly arrived Kat (aka 'adoringly cute'), my Ford Pony, and my cool hat."

At the time, I was busy maneuvering through hovercar traffic. We were funneled into designated virtual lanes, one above another, twenty stories above the ground. The only vehicles that could fly where they pleased were the police, fire, and garbage trucks. Above it all, were the megacorporate zeppelins floating in the overcast sky, flashing their flashy ads at all hours of the day.

Fortunately for me, the rain had tapered off from earlier so, despite the traffic, I'd still get to my destination ahead of schedule. With hovercar driving in any supercity, especially Metropolis, your eyes had to be ahead and all around at all times. I kept a paranoid watch on all these non-drivers around me (non-drivers were anyone besides me). Keeping my Pony scratch- and dent-free was another profession in itself.

I drove a bright red, classic Ford Pony. My pride and joy separated me from the masses because most people drove dark-colored vehicles. Even illegal street racers avoided the bright colors. But not the uber-wealthy; they liked their whites and silvers.

My Pony wasn't unique for its color. It was a sleek, muscle-vehicle coupe with a high-performance, supercharged, advanced nitro-acceleration hydrogen engine. Few could believe that I found the shell in a junkyard when I was a kid in middle school and spent a few years to build and restore it, spare part by spare part. My muscle hovercar was regarded as a classic, and it got me lucrative offers from genuine hovercar collectors and stares from enthusiasts almost every week. But my classic Ford Pony would never be for sale, ever.

In highly-regulated and monitored virtual lanes that were modern hover-traffic, you would have thought it would be as safe as could be. But there was the triple threat to every driver: kids, kids, and the elderly. Kids zipping by on hovercyles between hovercars, or sometime above them, kids illegally buzzing over traffic wearing a jetpack, too lazy or stupid to get a legitimate ride, and, at the other end of the spectrum, elderly drivers driving too damn slow. For the elderly, I understood. Their eyes and reflexes weren't what they used to be. Their multi-tasking abilities were not as good. Flashing neon lights could be distracting. Hovercars, hoverbikes, and traffic drones were all around you. At least hovertrucks had their own dedicated lanes. Why not have them for seniors? Their confidence was not what it once was. I didn't care. The operative phrase was, "Call a hovercab." Airspace was a crowded space, and it was not a place for the timid. Crashes in hovertraffic did happen, with all parties, innocent and guilty both "returning to the surface."

But I wasn't aimlessly driving around the city looking pretty in my tan fedora. I was working. Liquid Cool was my detective agency, I was its sole P.I. and couldn't be happier being my own boss. But, that wasn't for the timid either, as I had one busy-body employee who was calling me at the moment. I touched the dashboard receiver.

"PJ, why are you calling me?" I asked, probably before the line had fully connected.

Her face appeared on my vid-phone dashboard screen, not that I could pay much attention to her with one eye on traffic ahead and another on the general traffic around me. Then, I heard the pitter-patter of the rain again hitting the roof of my vehicle.

"I told you not to start talking until you see the person's face on the screen. I heard the end of the sentence, not the beginning," she said in her French accent.

Her name was Punch Judy, but everyone simply called her "PJ." My sole employee was also an ex-gang member and ex-felon, but gang member would be stretching the meaning of the term a bit. After all, she had fair skin, short dark crimson hair, a simulated mole, and a dot above the side of her lips. She wore pinkish lipstick, black leather, black heeled boots, and bright tank tops to show off her pride and joy: her bionic arms. Beware of those. She could punch a three-hundred-pound cyborg through a wall.

Back in the day, Judy was a soldier in the punk-posh gang, Les Enfants Terribles in Neo-Paris, France. She wore her haute-couture designer clothes back then too. But, as with all gangs, feral or punk-posh, it always ended the same way. A new gang came into the territory. A big gang war ensued. Her Les Enfants Terribles lost, but PJ wouldn't let it go, and she continued the war by herself, following her rival enemies to Metropolis. One fateful day, a murderous chase through the streets of Metropolis in her self-made death-mobile to kill the rival gang she tracked down led to a horrific accident, pinning her body in a burning wreck as enemy gang members stood nearby and laughed. Then, I came along and saved her, but not her arms.

Some might say PJ was crazy, but loyal to the end was what I'd say. I hired her as a secretary. I think she self-promoted herself to VP of Client Services. I couldn't keep up with all her title changes, which were changed as often as her foreign cigarettes. She's already returned the favor saving my life a bunch of times too. I glanced and saw she was smoking one of her cigarettes, blowing out pink smoke.

"What is it, PJ? I'm working."

"You better be working. The background check is done, but I don't like it."

"Is it clean? What came back?"

"It's clean but..."

"But, what?"

"Since he's the son of some wealthy Up-Topper..."

"PJ, our client surpassed being wealthy a long time ago. That's how much money he has."

"Yeah, so I figured that if the son was a bad boy, the father might have the money to make anything negative that would show up on a normal police background check for you or me disappear."

"Those ex-felon street smarts are always coming in handy, huh? The son is a grown man. He has the money to do that kind of stuff himself without the father."

"Cruz, this son has been arrested a lot of times. A lot."

"For what? What are we talking about, PJ? Prostitutes, drugs, what?"

"Violence."

"Violence? This kid was raised on Lunar Colony and is the heir to a massive fortune. His father wouldn't tolerate him jeopardizing their family and company name. And don't say he wouldn't know what you found. Was he arrested or not?"

"He was never arrested, but all the friends he hangs

with are arrested all the time, and their lawyers get them off. He's there every time."

"You're saying the friends are being arrested, and they're taking the fall for him completely."

"Yep. The son has the money. The friends don't."

"The father has to know then."

"What did he hire you to do?"

"Dig up all the dirt on his own family. As if the father wasn't rich enough, he becomes the new CEO of his megacorp in a few months with all the perks: new house on Earth for half the year, another new house on the Lunar colony for the other half, a new corporate soldier bodyguard detail year-round, et cetera, et cetera."

"Madness. Why would you take a job where you must have corporate soldiers?"

"When you get to his level, you have to be worried about rival companies and your own fellow board members. He's doing the right thing hiring us."

"I'm not complaining. We're getting a big, big weekly retainer from the father."

"Glad you approve."

"But where are you?"

"I'm going into Silver Soho to see father and son in their natural habitat: a restaurant club the son owns, he's throwing a party for the father. I'll see what I can see."

"You don't monitor police frequencies anymore, do you?"

"Why should I? I don't do illegal street racing anymore. I'm not a kid anymore. I have kids."

"There's a lot of police activity in Silver Soho. Major activity."

"Yes, I'm seeing the siren party from here."

In the distance, I could see the light show of red and

blue flashing sirens. Did this mean that the official days of "cyber summer" had begun? The season of summer was a relative term in Metropolis, since it rained all the time. However, as someone whose job was knowing the supercity's crime stats, I knew when those numbers went up and down. Metropolis had its crime: tech hustlers, neon gangsters, samurai street soldiers, cyborg psychos, etc. "Cyber summer" was that time of the year when the "normal" mayhem of the streets increased. That either meant more business for me or less. What it always meant was more dead bodies. But that was life in the big city, as they said. A real Metropolitan knew how to avoid the crazy maniacs and the gangs. If you were really worried about it, you could always move to Oz, where there were more kangaroos and cows than people. Hoverflights went there daily.

My Metropolis wasn't a bad place, but it wasn't a good one either.

Unfortunately, I was in one of three professions that lived in the mayhem: police, hospitals, and private detectives like me. I was headed for Silver Soho and as long as I avoided any laser-gun shootouts, I'd consider the night a good one.

FROM THE CORNER of my eye, a police cruiser sped through the sky thirty feet above normal hover-traffic. A standard five-seater hovercraft, but no sirens. More reinforcements for whatever was happening in Silver Soho. I should have been driving away from the place, not to it.

Metropolis loved its cops. They were really local government's soldiers in the never-ending war on crime, but they were *our* soldiers, standing tall in their full silver-and-black body-armored uniforms and visored half-helmets, the word "PEACE" etched across their chest and back. They scared the crap out of the street thugs and gangs. Good! That's what the citizens of Metropolis wanted. Metro Police could obliterate a homicidal perp or escaping hovercar single-handedly. You couldn't stop the criminals we had in this supercity with anything less than a police force that was nothing short of hell on earth.

That meant my current sequence of actions was possibly even more ill-advised. National Labor stats said that being a private detective was *more* dangerous than being a police officer, and we didn't have body armor like them. I was a sole operator. The police were their own gang of sorts—being a half-million-strong police force. Another stat that I kept from the wife was that the criminal life on the mean streets of Metropolis was only *slightly* more dangerous than being a civilian private detective. Yes, this was my job.

Why did I do it, then? I'd been a hovercar restorer of some note living a simple, legacy-baby, low expenses life. Why did I upset the apple cart of life? Simply, I wanted "more." I wasn't like all the other average Joes and Janes in this rainy, gray world. Wake up, work, exist, eat, sleep, repeat. I wanted more, because I was more, even if it was the dangerous world of being a private detective. I had to admit, I was good at it. A patchwork of unrelated hard skills, behavioral idiosyncrasies, and anti-authoritarian attitudes made me a natural. Who knew borderline obsessive-compulsive disorder and video game mastery could be so handy?

Most people either worked for international or multi-national megacorps—the archenemies of Big Brother—or uber-governments, the "Man,"—the archenemy of big, bad Business. In my chosen profession—that I'd stumbled upon—I worked for both and neither at the same time. I was proud of my cleverness in a zen way, creating my own lane in the cosmos of life.

Also, as a detective, I'd never complain about being bored again. You never knew what was going to happen next. Was your client going to give you an electric bag of cash or shoot you? Was the criminal gang member going to give you some street intel or shoot you? Yeah, I had a thing about being shot.

People who were not in-the-know, the masses, thought being a detective was cool. Those who were in-the-know, people with brains, knew it was a sign of insanity. What else could it be when you knowingly went into a legal business in which you had to deal with so many crazy maniacs for a living? If it were illegal, you could at least get somewhat properly compensated before you were killed. Detectives, police, and soldiers alike were all crazy to do what we did, but we loved it anyway. I took pride in being an honest detective, since there were so few of us. It fit nicely with my contrarian personality. Most detectives were corrupt gutter rats, so that meant I had to be the Honest Abe in the bunch to singlehandedly uplift and class up the profession.

This case was typical, being hired to do a thorough background check and surveillance on individuals, businesses, or locations for security purposes, both a staple of private investigation work. In fact, most of what the masses thought P.I.s did wasn't true. We didn't investigate murders (that's the cops) and we didn't chase people down (that's bounty hunters). Besides the checks and surveillance, I did the civil investigations and skip tracing for the Courts, and insurance and fraud investigations for megacorporations. When I first started out, I tried to avoid the cheating spouse-Peeping Tom surveillance cases, but there was so much of it that I finally agreed with PJ that I was leaving cash on the table—lots of it.

My current case fell under the corporate investigation category and had the highest paying clients, but this client hired me to investigate his own family. Usually, it was a client wanting me to investigate a current or future business partner, look into allegations that threatened the company's reputation, find an occasional blackmailer, or track down stolen proprietary information and the culprits without involving the police.

I didn't like that PJ said the son was potentially dangerous. I'd seen the client's son once at some corporate charity event, but I didn't get that vibe from him. The son was only twenty-five, but that was not too young to be doing bad things. By that age, they could already be a veteran at it. The father hadn't mentioned or hinted at anything with the son, but that could simply be the father's way of testing whether I was any good or not. The problem with being "famous" was that people were always testing you.

I always told people that the Hollywood-style super detectives were a myth. Their "true" stories of gun battles with crime lords, beating up cops, sleeping with clients, secret consultative work with Up-Top multinationals, and more gun battles were complete nonsense. However, in my case, the violence part was a bit too on point for my taste, as my Blade Gunner, Alien Hunter, AI Confidential, and Class Cyborg cases, among others proved. These cases were the mirror opposite of the typical cases, having lots of mayhem. But I always kept my cool.

I breathed a sigh of relief. The red-and-blue siren party with hover-traffic being directed away from the area was not the part of Silver Soho where I was going. I turned and descended off the sky-lanes just before the real slowdown by floating police cruisers ahead. Whatever it was had to be big for stacked lanes of traffic to be diverted. One of the unwritten rules of Metropolis was that the traffic must flow, no matter what. Traffic, trash, and electricity: without any of them, you didn't have a supercity.

Besides the flashing red and blue lights and the police cruisers hovering in the air, I could make out the bright yellow "POLICE LINE. DO NOT CROSS" tape on the ground in the distance, and billowing smoke. I'd barely noticed it because the smoke was black and, against a dark sky, its practically invisible unless you're on top of it. Fire? An explosion? I'd have to read about it on the news later. I officially exited the freeway for the streets.

The restaurant bar was called the Star Palace. It did indeed look like a silver, twenty-story palace right in between one-hundred story towers on either side. I liked that parking was in the towers. I didn't have to traipse through the streets and the rain. I liked it even better when I saw that the valet parking was manned by well-dressed professionals rather than grungy college kids. With a classic vehicle like mine, I had to always use valet but go the extra step (paying the extra money) to park it myself. None of the valet staff minded because most knew my Pony from the many publications featuring it (without my permission). Often, they'd ask to take a picture with me in front of it, which I always agreed to. Having valet staff on your side meant having an extra layer of security for the Pony.

However, forget all of that. The second I stepped out of the elevator capsule from floor seventy-seven onto the ground-floor lobby entrance of the Star Palace, every one of my internal alarm bells sounded. In the detective business, it was your instincts, not any lethal weapons or fancy driving, that kept you out of danger and saved your life more than anything else.

The wealthy loved their classical music, and that's what I heard before the elevator capsule even landed. From the elevators, I walked ten feet across marble-like floors with animated stars moving around under my feet. Even before one crossed into the private party hall, I could see that the building was twenty stories, but inside was only two levels to give the full architectural effect of extreme vaulted ceilings. That was not the problem. At the entrance were a quartet of exquisitely dressed female greeters with lots of skin showing. The dresses looked like they were made of diamonds. Their hair, makeup, nail polish, lipstick were all flawless. However, their smiles were fake. I'd seen enough people under duress to know when someone was scared. Their eyes also told me that they wanted to be any place but where they were.

Around them were the bodyguards. The three big, brawny, cyborg bodyguards standing near the women were in black suits—cheap ass black suits. It was like one of those puzzles you played in school. Which one of these three things don't belong: richly dressed females, high-class restaurant bar, or three thug cyborgs in cheap-ass suits? I didn't know if they were armed, but I always assumed a guard, cyborg or not, was. These cyborgs had metal hands with the most pathetic spray-on skin I'd ever seen. I'd assume their whole arms were bionic too, but the tell-tale giveaway was the ocular implants, the kind where your sunglasses were actually part of your face permanently.

"Name, sir?" one of the women asked me with a smile. She had a digital clipboard in her hands.

"Cruz, miss. I'm here to see Mr. Borealis. He's expecting me."

"Yes, you can go right through," she said.

"Thank you."

The greeters and guards had already stepped to the side to let me walk inside. I looked up and, as I guessed, the entire vaulted ceiling made you feel as if you were outside on some clear sky plateau with shooting stars, comets, and planets above your head.

One server met me right at the door with a tray of drinks in slim glasses. I didn't know what the alcohol was, and I didn't care. I took one of those. Another server appeared with a tray of finger food that looked like shrimp on top of tiny tortillas. If it was a low-class establishment, I'd be afraid the appetizers could be some kind of unholy mystery meat, but I was in a high-class joint. I took two of them with the fluffy napkin the server gave me.

Now, I could blend. My senses were screaming again as I scanned the crowd. A hundred or so well-to-do, finely dressed guests—men in dark colors, but not black, and women in colorful dresses that seemed to be made of precious jewels, but besides the servers buzzing around, that was it. The net worth of the people in the room was trillions of dollars, but only three cyborg guards?

The rear hall was for private parties, and the public restaurant bar was on the other side in the front half of the building. The classical music was actually playing over wall speakers, which was another unusual sign.

These people could afford live music, and they always did. Where were the musicians?

I saw my client, Mr. Borealis, in a pin-striped grayish-blue suit. I noticed that the man looked oddly uncomfortable, with both hands in his pockets, listening to others around him. Rich people never, ever put their hands in their pockets. Next to him was the son, who was doing all the talking. The mixed crowd was smiling and laughing. Humans were no different than animals in the wild. We just liked to think we were different. In any group dynamic, there were the alphas, the betas (wanting to be an alpha or serving the alpha), and everyone else. Borealis Jr., with his shoulder-length dark hair resting on the shoulders of his suit, was acting like the alpha—bold hand gestures and confident and loud story-telling—but he wasn't. The real alpha here tonight was a man standing next to him, on the other side from his father. That alpha in his cheap-ass black suit had locked eyes on me from the moment I stepped into the room. The man had a full mustache and the beginnings of a beard from not shaving. Unlike Mr. Borealis, the father, who looked distinguished and dignified with his facial hair, the man's ungroomed facial mess made him look like a bum, compared to the moneyed-class around him, but he didn't care. He was a bum, but a dangerous bum. I remembered what PJ told me about the son being dangerous, but looking at Borealis Jr. again, I still didn't see it. I did see it in the eyes of the man.

I finished my finger food (yummy), drank my drink, set it on a table that was set up for that, wiped my hands, and went in.

"Good evening, Mr. Borealis," I said, purposely interrupting the son mid-sentence.

The son didn't like it, and he had the look of a child who'd had his cereal dumped in his lap. The crowd looked at me, then—this was what I was waiting for—they looked at the man, not Borealis Jr. Yes, the man was the one in charge of this shindig.

"Good evening, Mr. Cruz," Mr. Borealis replied.

"Cruz. This is the detective?" the son asked his father.

"Yes," Mr. B. replied without looking at his son.

"I am. I have the report for you, sir."

Mr. B looked up at me. Someone in his position didn't get to where they were in the corporate food chain without being able to assess situations fast and be able to improvise on the fly. I just needed to guide him.

"It was just as you suspected, sir. The staffer has definitely been stealing from the company. I'd say it's been happening for at least a few years, probably a lot longer. You'll need to order a full independent forensic audit."

"Who's he working for?" Mr. B asked. He was playing along.

"I'd say one of your Japanese multinational rivals."

"Stealing?" the son asked me.

"Yes. I'd say your father has uncovered a big plot here." I turned back to the father. "If you'd like, sir, I can give you the details here. We can just step to the side. I think you'd want to hear it now and then give me further instructions on how to proceed."

"Yes."

I pointed Mr. B to an empty part of the hall, away from the crowds, saying, "We can step over there, sir."

The son looked at the man next to him. "I better hear this too," the son said.

"If you wish," the father said as he followed me.

I turned and stopped the man, who was about to

follow. "Sorry, sir. This is for my client. His son, as heir, can listen in, but no one else."

I could see the gears in the man's head moving at high-speed, trying to think of a comeback. All he could do was give me a dirty look. What I also noticed was that the crowd of people around us had gone silent, and they had that look of fear on their faces.

As I led Mr. B and his son to a quiet space in the hall, I glanced at the door and saw that the three cyborg guards were now inside, watching me. I stopped with my back to the wall, Mr. B and his son looking at me. I looked past them for a second. From one of the entrances a door had opened and many more men in those cheap-ass black suits were spilling in.

Mr. B's hands were out of his pockets. When my eyes landed on his empty right wrist, but a clear tan line from a watch, it hit me all at once. I had managed to walk right into a robbery in progress, and Mr. Borealis's son was among the crazy maniacs behind it!

I HAD the two men's undivided attention, but I looked at the son.

"Who's your friend?" I asked.

"My friend?"

"Your sidekick, or are you his sidekick? Clearly, he's the man running the show. What's his name? I can't call him Alpha, though he clearly is the alpha here."

"I don't know what you're talking about."

"What's wrong with rich kids these days? You're the heir, idiot. It means when he dies, all the money goes to you. You never have to work or worry, ever. Your monthly allowance is probably more than I make in a year, but it comes down to this. Robbery? That's what all this is, isn't it? You're robbing your old man."

A sickly smirk came over the young man's face as he stared at me. "I don't want to wait."

I saw the son and father stare at other. The boy's expression was of unbridled contempt. The father's was of unimaginable hatred. I had a son and daughter myself. What, in the darkest recessions of the human psyche, could lead parent and child to hate each other with such intensity? What could have possibly led it all to go so terribly wrong?

My eyes moved to the growing crowd of men in black from that entrance as Alpha walked to them. My eyes shifted to the three cyborg guards, and I could see that they each had an arm behind their backs—their shooting arms. The longer I waited, the worse this was going to get.

Mr. Borealis let out a yell, and I heard a thumping sound. I knew Mr. B had struck the son. I had already stepped forward and had my back to them, but from the expressions on the cyborg guards' face, I could guess what happened and it wasn't anything good. However, it was my one chance, since the attention of the room was on Mr. B.

Was I going to be kind or cruel? I probably made the same decision that Mr. B had made.

My gun was literally not of Earth. It was called the omega-gun—the gun to end all private guns, as the manual said—and was made off-world, likely Lunar Colony or Mars. It came with all kinds of accessories and optional digital features, but I could care less about any of that. I could choose what it shot.

The three cyborgs crashed to the ground after I shot

them in the chest with laser rounds. They didn't know what hit them. Humans, regardless of class, were all born with the gene of self-preservation. The crowd of people in the hall, along with all the servers, dove for cover on the ground.

Alpha was smart, too. He knew that my next shot was meant for him. He'd already rabbited out of the room to escape. I took out two more of the cheap-ass-suit-wearing thugs with chest shots before they all bolted to the exit, slamming the door behind them. There was no way I was running out of that door after them.

I stood from my one-knee shooting position to walk back to Mr. B. The son was on the ground, dead, eyes and mouth open with a shredded neck—a bloody mess. Mr. Borealis had karate-chopped his son to death. I could do a decent karate chop, but this was much more. I glanced at Mr. B. and realized he had some bionic augmentation. The bottom part of his hands were also blades—both dripping with blood.

"How very samurai of you, Mr. Borealis," I said to him, keeping my own gun at my side. "I'll let you handle 9-1-1."

"I want my watch," he said, ignoring what I said. "Get the watch back and I'll double your fee. It has been in our family for four hundred years. It's irreplaceable. They can't get away with it."

"What else did they get?"

"I don't care about anything else! The watch. It's much more than a watch. It's the family's history, our birthright. I lose it and the family is gone." A tear streamed down Mr. B's face.

I had some sense of his emotion. When I first met him in his office and took his case, we talked for quite a while.

Some clients were quick and to the point. Others were shady. Some were nervous about the whole prospect of hiring a detective, but some had to spend a little time with you before they'd trust you. They did that through small talk. Mr. Borealis was one of those.

Most people in Metropolis didn't wear hats, but I did and there was a small community of us hat aficionados, just like vintage cigar smokers or classic hovercar collectors. I wore my own trademark tan fedora, which had become as famous as me. I didn't know much about hats in general, but I was becoming a genuine hat aficionado. Harry of Harry's Haberdashery in Woodstock Falls loved me because I sent him a steady stream of customers. Some only wanted the one-off fedoras like mine, but some became lifelong buyers of custom-made hats.

For Mr. Borealis it was watches. He'd told me more about the history and fascinating world of classic analog watches in one hour than I'd heard in my entire life. He'd also shared with me the incredible worth of these watches, mainly monetarily, but also somewhat spiritually. There was no other word for it. The birthright watch that Mr. B. spoke of, the family truly felt was the essence of their lineage.

But was a watch worth dying over? I had no idea who Alpha was other than the fact he needed training on personal grooming and buying a decent suit.

"I'll triple your fee!"

"Sir, they're gone. There's no way for me to track them."

Mr. Borealis put a palm-size gadget in my hand. "Yes, there is."

I would have been sold at double, but with triple, and

the means to find them? I went on the hunt, before he changed his mind.

"Get my wife's platinum diamond ring back and I'll give you a reward too," said another man.

I looked, and the entire crowd was encircling me with desperate looks on their faces.

"They got my precious rings," said one woman.

"They got my gem necklace made from genuine stones of Sidonia, Mars," said another.

I could have stood there grinning, counting all the money I was about to get, but I was smarter than that. The night was young. I could still get myself killed. They'd be the ones in fancy clothes, upset, but comfortable and safe here. I was the one about to dash after unknown assailants into the rain.

BEFORE I LEFT, I asked Mr. B one question: "Where did the crooks put all the stolen goods?"

I got the whole story from him in thirty seconds. Borealis Jr. walked the men in, they drew their weapons on everyone, stole their jewelry and money first, threw the live band in a back kitchen storage room, and waited for more higher-profile guests to arrive. The plan was to rob everyone and make off with many millions. I suspected that Borealis Jr. had no idea of the real value of the night's potential haul, and probably didn't care. This had to do with hurting his father. Alpha, on the other hand, probably knew what the potential haul would bring in down to the penny. Millions? One of the rings from one of the off-world wives alone would be worth more than that.

This put the earlier red and blue siren party in a

different view. Was it an elaborate distraction by these crooks?

I ran from the rear private hall through the dividing wall entrance to the open restaurant bar. Most restaurants focused on a specific theme or culture. What I smelled and saw was food from everywhere: Cornish, French, Thai, Korean, Ethiopian, Mediterranean, Brazilian, etc. Maybe some customers liked this, but as my wife would say: when any restaurant does all those foods at once, it means they don't do any one of them well at all. I agreed. It all seemed like an upscale fast-food place to me with a menu the size of an encyclopedia.

I wasn't stupid. When I burst out the main entrance, I wasn't wearing my tan fedora and jacket. I had grabbed a black unisex slicker from one of the restaurant customers after I paid ten times for it. The young girl couldn't stop giggling after the exchange and announced, "All drinks are on me!" Not sure her parents were happy with me, since all of them were under-age teenagers.

I held the gadget up to my face. The hood of my black slicker was tight enough to keep out the rain, but loose enough for me to move freely. The signal from the tracker showed me a stationary blip not too far away at all. It was going to be simple, but not easy. What I was about to do was extremely dangerous, foolish, and, if the police found out, illegal. Civilians, even licensed private investigators, weren't allowed to chase after armed bad guys. You can defend yourself against them, but not chase after them. I was doing it anyway.

As I stepped out into the street, I wondered if Mr. B always carried a tracker for his watch. Was it paranoid precaution, or did he suspect? Some questions were never answered, my posthumous mentor, Mr. Wilford G., the

95-year-old Metropolis private eye legend, told me. Like him, I was entirely content with that.

Silver Soho was one of those in-between neighborhoods—one-side working class and the other side up-scale. It was a multi-ethnic area with no particular nationalities dominating, which was good and bad. It had no personality, which was why I never had been there. But, on its streets, only the working class and free-city freeloaders walked anywhere under the protection of bright neon signs.

There were also the shifty, slippery-shoed hustlers and knuckle-dragging thugs for muscle. Silver Soho didn't allow any of the more serious criminal types to get anywhere near their streets because, once you allowed them, your streets would go from being for the average Joes and Janes to the real "mean streets."

One way you knew the street was "okay" was from all the hoverboarders around—middle and high-schoolers mostly, endlessly practicing their tricky crafts. The other was from the presence of sidewalk johnnies. Homelessness had been eradicated long ago, like polio and cancer; housing was mandatory for all, even for those without a legacy. But sidewalk johnnies were harmless, hanging around, watching trouble, horseplay, hustling, looking for a hustle, but doing little of anything meaningful. They congregated, watched, chatted it up, sat around, smoked, joked, disappeared to the johns when needed, or disappeared to their sleep shack for a few hours. Sidewalk johnnies and sallies all had a "turf"—a street, street corner, or alleyway. I knew the ones near my Liquid Cool office, where I lived, and the places I frequented, but not Silver Soho.

I could use their street intel, but I wasn't about to get

any of them killed either. I was armed, but they weren't. I had to play it solo for a bit longer until I knew more.

I followed the street crowds. Everyone wearing their gray-toned or black slickers under the rain. Some carried umbrellas with glowing, colored handles, but for most a slicker alone was fine. Some had their ears covered with headphones. Most wore glowing, colored glasses for maximum night-time illumination in the night. I caught sight or whiff of the occasional cigarette or cigar smoke. I also saw couples among the crowd and some people talking and laughing in conversation. It was a good, solid working-class crowd. In some towns, walking among the gray masses could be quite depressing, with everyone in their own little world moving about like automatons.

At first, I smiled when I saw a humanoid silver robot marching through the middle of the crowd. People watched, commented, smiled, frowned, or laughed upon seeing it. Up-Top in the off-world colonies, people didn't mind robots. On Earth it was a different story. People didn't trust androids, and the unions were fanatical about preventing robots from taking away human jobs. The robot was clearly a machine. It had hard edges, jerky movements, no head, and nothing about it pretending to look human. It even had a big, yellow smiley face on its chest.

I mentally kicked myself. Was the robot actually a surveillance robot? I looked at my tracker and the dot was still stationary. The robot came from the direction I was going.

"Hey guys," I greeted as I stepped to a couple of side-walk johnnies.

"Hey, gent."

"That robot."

"Yeah, it's been marching back and forth for hours."

The sidewalk johnnies had answered my question without me even having to ask it.

"Next meal on me," I said, and gave them a few bucks.

Sidewalk johnnies weren't "dope roaches," so I knew my money would be used for food and nothing more— well, maybe gambling. Sidewalk johnnies loved their sports betting. The two of them in their beat-up slickers thanked me and shook my hand.

The tracker said I had to turn left at the end of the street I was on. Metropolis streets could often go on forever, but this was a walking street. The problem was that the further down the street you got the establishments disappeared and so did the crowds. Rule Number One on supercity survival: never leave the crowds. But it was where I need to go.

I stayed closed to the wall as I left the crowds and sidewalk johnnies.

"Don't go down there, young man," I heard one of the sidewalk johnnies I paid yell out at me.

I just waved at him without ever taking my focus from in front of me. The ground was wet under my shoe but not from water. A slimy, oily residue told of illegal street dumping of something, probably from amateur street racers.

What I didn't want to see and could not see under any circumstances was anything nasty. Secluded alleyways meant sewer access points and, with that, one could find themselves introduced to water rats, "unkillable" jumbo roaches, and whatever roly-poly isopods were lurking and swimming around in filth. I had defeated my germophobia, but that didn't mean I couldn't have a relapse.

I stopped and took one last look at the tracker. The

dot was still stationary, but I was at the end of the street, and not a soul was around me. Above, there wasn't even any nearby hovercar traffic. For all I knew, Alpha and company were waiting to gun me down. Why would they be waiting?

I peeked around the corner slowly. About half the length of an American football field away, there was a hover-RV resting on the ground under an old bridge underpass, all its inside lights on. The area dead-ended, and the underpass wound its way from there, around to opposite where I was, and away into the night. In front of the hover-RV sat Alpha in a folding chair, and he seemed to be looking right in my direction. Beside him was a big, big man holding a laser-edged samurai sword in his hand, the blade resting on his shoulder.

I heard something and turned.

That robot was marching to me!

THE ROBOT HAD INTELLIGENCE. It purposely ran at me when my gun hand was pointed away without being able to swing back in time. But, it didn't know about my emergency weapon. I snapped my left forearm.

Pop!

My hidden weapon on my left arm extended under my clothes. One shot of a pulse round and the entire upper half of the robot blew apart and its body fell to the ground. My pop gun made sure that I'd never be sucker shot by any human and I wasn't taking any chances with the machine either.

Little did I know, the mayhem was just beginning. Gunshots erupted from the bridge underpass closest to me from above. They'd been watching me the whole time. I had to pull back a little around the corner. Criminals loved their machine-guns, but unless you were in close quarters, they were completely useless if you truly intended to hit anything. I wasn't about to change their ways, and I returned fire. Their melee of gunfire hit the wall a good ten feet or more above me. My shots, however, were not scatter-shot at all. I heard the yell of one man with two shots and, with the flip of a switch on my omega-gun, I sent an explosive round their way. All was quiet after the small explosion.

Having been in the hovercar restoration and racing business, I could name any vehicle just by hearing the revving of an engine. The hover-RV was about to fly off. I grabbed the lower half of the robot and threw it out ahead of me. The unseen gunman around the corner was a bit of a better shot. Rounds hit the falling robot with one of three shots, but that one shot ricocheted and almost hit my arm. To be killed by a ricocheted bullet or laser was no less noble than being shot directly. Neither was particularly appealing either.

I dove around the corner then rolled to the wall. Close to the ground, I couldn't see the gunman, but he couldn't see me either. It was likely the big man with the samurai sword. What I did see was the hover-RV rising one then two stories up, nearing the bridge overpass. I could see dark figures on the bridge running to it. I was not having any of it. I fired two more explosive rounds, before my unseen gunman began firing at me again. I'd seen him and returned fire. I heard one grunt. No more gunfire from him.

There was one explosion and then a second. The hover-RV wildly veered away from the bridge. I didn't wait. I bolted towards the bridge, firing as I ran. I wanted to shower them with so many rounds they wouldn't know what to do but get shot. It was working, and then I saw one of them climb up on the ledge of the bridge to jump onto the hover-RV. Did the criminal think he had bionic legs to jump that distance? Maybe he did. I shot him before he could launch. His body fell from the bridge. A second man tried to do the same. I shot him too. His body fell and landed on the ground right next to his friend, also in a cheap-ass black suit.

The hover-RV swung away, rotating around in a complete circle. Alpha stood at the open side door, looking right down at me. He gave me the finger, then slammed the door. I fired at the door, which I knew he expected, but the hover-RV didn't jet away as *I* expected. That only meant one thing.

I turned and sprinted for the corner as fast as my legs could move. I glanced back once and saw another man at the now-open door, and the hover-RV tracking me in air.

"Young man, what's going on?"

Oh my God. The two sidewalk johnnies were right there, coming around the corner in the line of fire. I could tell them to run, or try to stop what I knew was coming. I couldn't do both.

I dropped, turned back and up, then fired. The man, not Alpha, probably thought he was going to blow me to a million bits. I recognized the weapon in his hand right away, but hit him before he rained down his hell upon me and the johnnies. My last explosive round did the most damage. It blew apart the section of the hover-RV with the man and weapon "returning to surface," but his bazooka launched anyway. It was blind luck that the missile hit below where he fell rather than on top of me or the johnnies. I'd been near explosions before and, every time, I swore it would be the last. It let off a blast of heated air so powerful that it could pick you off the ground or, if close enough, could burn you. I guess we had to be thankful we were outside of its blast radius and not within it. At this point, I knew the orange explosive cloud would bring lots of people to the scene, including—and more importantly—the police.

That's when the hover-RV jetted away, but not before the entire back half of the compartment fell to the ground. I didn't want to think about it, but I knew there had to have been more of the thugs within the wreckage.

I picked myself up from the ground and watched the glow of the hover-RV engine disappear into the dark, rainy sky.

"Young man, are you police?" one of the sidewalk johnnies asked me. They were standing next to me, looking all around.

"No, but they'll be here," I said. "Real soon."

"That they will," the other one said. "Gunfire, explosions, hovercars falling apart in mid-air—wait till we tell the boys!"

The johnnies started laughing, and one of them patted me on the shoulder. "Young man, you should come by more often. You're loads of fun."

I TRIED to get the two sidewalk johnnies to run away, but being at the site of complete mayhem would increase their street cred. As much as I hated to say it, they were right. The two sidewalk johnnies traipsed through the crime scene, giving an impromptu tour to dozens of sidewalk johnnies and sallies who just showed up.

As for me, I sat at the wall. There was no escaping my fate on this one. Besides, someone had to give a full description of the hover-RV. I wanted to see Alpha in prison for a long time, where he belonged. No way that this was the first caper he and his crew were involved in.

"This is the police!" the voice boomed from high above. "Raise your hands and remain where you are, or you may be fired upon!"

Every sidewalk johnny and sally froze like a statue, but I had warned them. They raised their hands, as instructed.

We could now see the police cruisers gliding above us, seemingly coming out of the darkness. Then through the drizzle, the first one appeared, then another, then several more silver-and-black police "PEACE" officers descended from the sky. Their silent jetpacks with accompanying boot rocket nozzles made them look like wingless black angels. They landed on the ground with long guns in hand and visors concealing the top half of their faces. The darkness was replaced by the flashing red-and-blue-siren lights from the cruisers.

We could hear Dispatch over the cruiser police radios.

"All units. 51-Baker, 52, 52-Echo..." Her voice kept going. A lot more police were coming. "All units converge. Code 2."

I doubt that any of the sidewalk johnnies and sallies had any idea what dispatch was saying. Usually, they gave a summary at the end, but it was understandable why they didn't: bomb threat, explosives, fire, illegal use of extreme deadly weapons. I would have added. "dead crazy maniacs everywhere and cheap-ass suit wearing thugs in a getaway hover-RV."

Well, the police took everyone into custody—johnnies, sallies, and me, which was standard. They'd cordoned off the entire street and the airspace, but the media would swarm the scene anyway. The area was going to be shut down for a long time.

I wasn't kept in lock-up long. Unfortunately, I was often a visitor at Metropolis Police Central, home to the supercity's 500,000 plus police force—the largest in the nation. Apparently, I had my choice of high-priced attorneys waiting in the lobby for me, courtesy of the Star Palace uber-wealthy robbery victims.

My police "buddies" were the ones who let me out. Officers Break and Caps—one Black, one Caucasian, both senior officers. Ebony and Ivory, I called them without their knowledge, of course. They looked at me awhile, shaking their heads.

"We should have known you were connected with this complete pandemonium, Cruz," Officer Break said.

"Job security for you," I said with a smile.

"Follow us," Break said, as they escorted me out of the station.

"Don't leave town, Cruz. Officers will likely want to speak with you more," Caps said.

"Or should we have them speak to your army of high-priced, overpaid, glitzy attorneys outside?"

All I did was smile.

I could have chatted it up, but my case wasn't over.

Mr. Borealis apparently left immediately for Lunar Colony, despite being "asked" to return to Earth to be questioned about the Star Palace robbery and the killing of his son by person or persons unknown. Metro Police was never going to see that man on Earth again, but I still had the tracker.

*

FIVE DAYS HAD PASSED. The crime scene was finally vacated by the police. I had the johnnies do the surveillance for me. It was their turf, so they were always there. Five days later and one second later, I arrived in a hovercab. In disguise, I strolled under the yellow "POLICE LINE. DO NOT CROSS" tape that was still there with my tracker in hand.

The news said that in a wild high-speed chase (was there any other kind?) police spotted and pursued the robbers' getaway hover-RV for many miles until it crashed into the ocean. Police divers were still searching for bodies. I knew that Alpha and his surviving crew were out there, and they'd be back.

I found their hidden stash buried in a makeshift tunnel one level down. That's why they were waiting. They were playing "bury the treasure" in case they got caught by police, which they did. Everything was there— money, necklaces, rings, ear rings, toe rings, bracelets, and Mr. Borealis's watch. Everything was in one thick, black bag. It weighed a ton. I'd been right. The estimated value of everything was half a trillion dollars!

When I told PJ, she just said: "C'est fou!" Yes, these rich people were crazy. That much wealth in "baubles," as my Pops called jewelry, among just a hundred or so people in one room. I learned the reason there was no security. Borealis Jr. was in charge of the details for his dear old dad. He gave the army of security the night off.

I gave PJ the task of contacting and arranging the

return of all the stolen items to each of the Star Palace victims. "You must get more cases like this!" she yelled with a big smile. "Liquid Cool's bank account will be happy for a long time! So, when do I get to hire an assistant?"

I ignored the last part, of course.

I handled the return of the watch to Mr. Borealis myself. I knew people, so I was able to secretly ship it to his office on the Lunar Colony. A transfer of four times my fee arrived in the account the day after the package was picked up and signed for. I knew I'd likely never see or hear from him again, which was the way of things with most high-profile clients.

After I did what I did, I gave the police a made-up story for them to do a stake-out of the scene. They did so.

Alpha and his crew were caught. One of them arrived in the wee hours of the night and led the police back to everyone else. They thought they had the perfect plan. They had a rich son to do their bidding who would hand over his own father and all his rich friends on a silver plat-ter. Alpha and his crew were behind the explosion of two hovertrucks, which shut down nearby hovertraffic as a diversion to get all patrolling police cruisers away from Silver Soho. What a great plan. The crew came so close to being filthy rich themselves to live out their days on some tropical island on Earth or pleasure colony on Mars. But then I showed up.

Chief of Metro Police Hub called me directly one day at my Liquid Cool office in Buzz Town. The veteran officer with his dark hair, thick mustache, and dark green eyes squinted at me over my vid-phone. He knew Mr. Borealis was withholding information—namely, killing his son and chief enabler of robbery—and would never return to Earth for questioning. He knew the Star Palace victims were lying—namely, seeing Mr. B kill the son and their "little" side-arrangement with me to recover their stolen items (I was certain that they weren't sharing the latter with their insurance companies). He knew I was holding things back—namely, all of the above, and, of course, finding the stash of stolen goods. Hub wasn't happy about any of it. Apparently, Alpha was telling his own tales from jail, since Borealis Jr. was dead. Blame the dead guy —how original was that? But the police weren't interested in stories from ex-mercenary, life-time thieves. As it turns out, a couple of his crew were even AWOL from the military.

"They call it cyber summer, Cruz. It's when the criminals decide to cause more problems for the good people of Metropolis than normal. We've steadily kept the numbers down a bit for five years in a row, up until your one summer night of utter mayhem. Three shot dead at the Star Palace, but they were the lucky ones. Everyone else was shot and blown up, shot and fell three stories, shot and impaled themselves on a samurai sword, or were just blown up in a moving hover-RV. Do you want me to tell you how many dead bodies arrived at morgue that night?"

"Chief, besides the criminals, were any innocent people killed that night?"

Complete silence.

"No residents, no cops, no sidewalk johnnies, no private detectives, no innocent bystanders, no hostages. So for once, and it doesn't happen very often in this crazy city, in one cruel cyber-summer night, only the bad guys got killed, and not a single good guy or gal. Doesn't sound like a very bad night to me, chief. Sounds like a pretty good night."

"Yeah, I'd say you're right. Have a good night, Cruz."
"Good night, Chief."

"A Cruel Cyber Summer Night" is part of the Liquid Cool sci-fi detective series. Continue the futuristic adventure with Cruz and company as he solves the big cases in the high-tech, low-life world of Liquid Cool at:
austindragon.com/liquid-cool

PICK YOUR POISON

1. *Let's keep solving mysteries, but make it a reporter.* Head to "The Crimson Vial" by William Burton McCormick

2. *Loving the gritty, city vibe—but can I have a hacker?* Head to "SolarMute" by Jim Keen

3. *What's crime like on an alien planet?* Turn the page to read "Risk Management" by Caitlin Demaris McKenna

RISK MANAGEMENT

AN EXPANSION STORY

BY CAITLIN DEMARIS MCKENNA

GAU SHESHARRIM SMELLED THE DRUG OPERATION before he saw it.

Lead Row District's streets were silent and dark, the industrial area minimally lit by sodium arcs every hundred feet. He'd chosen this route because it should be deserted—he couldn't afford to be seen, even in silhouette, in the Terran-run city of Diego Two.

But now it seemed his protective solitude was in danger. Lifting his sleek snout, Gau sniffed again. The tang of chemical byproduct burned his sensitive nostrils: solvents, reagents, and an alkaline whiff he recognized from the final product.

Someone was out here manufacturing e-caps—endorphin caplets. And they were close.

Keeping to the shadows of the looming warehouses, Gau followed the gradient of scent until it disappeared under the loading door of a midsize warehouse. His eyes pierced the dark like it wasn't there, noting features of disuse: peeling paint on the warehouse's walls, a heavy chain and padlock rusty with time barring the loading door.

But the smell didn't lie. This place only looked abandoned.

Crouching in the shadows across the corner from the warehouse, a wire of unease tightened under his upper set of ribs. He'd already been aboveground longer than he liked; the weight of the wrapped package under his cloak called his attention. He should complete the delivery and get his payment and a few e-caps of his own for his trouble from Torres, just like always. Not go investigating not-so-abandoned warehouses and potentially getting *seen*.

But he'd been using this route for years to ferry payments and packages between Torres and her network of dealers. It was supposed to be safe. He couldn't leave until he knew what threatened to disrupt it.

Gau slunk around the back, hoping to find some vantage where he could see inside the warehouse while remaining out of sight. After a few minutes of searching, he found it—a dumpster backed up to one wall below a row of windows. Someone had done a bad job loading it, and tumbled plastic sacks leaned against the side, forming a path he could climb.

His sensitive nose wrinkled at the effluvia of rotting vegetables and rancid meat emanating from the sacks, but they bore his slight weight. He set all four feet firmly on the top one and stretched his torso over the lip of the dumpster. There was nothing to grab, so Gau had to push with his palms flat on the metal, using friction to heave first his torso, then his sinuous lower body and legs onto the lid. *Good thing I don't weigh much,* he thought. *Osk were not built for climbing.*

The prospect of the windows wiped the brief exertion from his mind. They were dusty with neglect, but not too filthy to see through. Staying low, Gau crept forward and peered inside.

A large white tent hunkered in the otherwise empty space below. Shadows of indeterminate species moved inside the tent's walls. From the play of shadows on the walls, the tent was brightly lit inside, but it was tightly sealed except for a flap at one end. *Hiding the light,* he had time to think, before the tent flap opened and a scaly red-and-yellow striped head emerged.

Suns. Gau instantly ducked behind the windowsill, then peeked again. The Urd didn't look toward his window; indeed, it seemed uninterested in much beyond the small metal tin it had removed from its vest. He watched the reptilian alien stalk out of the tent, unscrewing the cap of the tin as it went. Three meters long from toothy snout to spine-ridged tail, with venomous claws and talons. It held its spine parallel to the ground as it walked; the Urd had evolved to run down their prey on the ancient savannahs of Urdek.

This was who was horning in on Torres' territory?

Gau stayed still, although the brightness of the tent should blind the Urd to any movement behind a dark window. The creature plucked up some brown mush from the tin with a claw and tucked it into its cheek before leaving from a side door. But before the tent flap swung closed, Gau glimpsed two more Urd inside, laboring over a chaos of tubing, vats, dials and alembics. A manufactory. The source of the scent.

His back prickled with nerves—half at his discovery, half at the thought of that Urd somewhere outside on its break. As quietly as he could, Gau slipped down the other side of the dumpster and slipped out into the night.

------*------

THE OFFICE HAD SEEN BETTER days. Paper covered the windows and dust their sills. It lurked in the middle of a row of shuttered storefronts in Rush Harbor District, to the casual eye one more failed business in this depressed area of Diego Two.

Gau knew better. The business here was thriving—it simply wasn't legal.

He rang the buzzer and stood back so the camera above the door could see him. He hated this part: standing exposed in the dim sodium lights, back toward the street. It made his skin itch.

An eon passed in the few minutes before Torres buzzed him in. Gau swept through the deserted lobby and through the inner door into Torres' office.

"Took you long enough," Torres said by way of greeting. The Terran woman set down the comm unit she'd been fiddling with and straightened behind her desk. She ran one hand through her short spiky black hair and motioned him forward with the other. "Come on, give."

Nice to see you too. Gau laid the package on the desk and unwrapped its brown paper sheath. A matte black oblong box was revealed. He turned it toward her and opened it.

Individually wrapped endorphin caplets were piled inside the box, a treasure chest full of black pearls. Each caplet was embossed with a metallic green lowercase English "e". The manufacturer of Torres' op owned a legitimate packaging business, mostly to funnel the funds made from the sale of e-caps, but it gave them an advantage when it came to presentation.

Torres carefully counted the caplets out. Gau watched, hoping his hunger didn't show too much on his face. Knowing some of it must surely leak through.

He was well-acquainted with the effects of their product. The delicious, melting ecstasy of a good hit was part of why he did this job, beyond the basic needs of survival. He'd learned quickly in his time on the street that survival meant more than putting food and air in his body, more than his heart continuing to beat.

It meant being able to *forget*. To outrun, even for a short time, the memories of when he'd had a home and a family. Before the Terrans destroyed it.

"It's all here." Torres shoveled the e-caps back into their box. "Hold tight."

The package under her arm, she disappeared into a back room, emerging a few minutes later with Gau's payment.

A smaller black box held the usual seven sleek e-caps. Enough, if he rationed it, to last him a week. Beside it was a prepaid credit chit with a reader. The amount flashed up on the reader when he passed the chit over it.

Acid shot through his stomach. A frown tugged at the corners of his mouth. He ducked his head to hide it, but across from him Torres cleared her throat.

"There a problem, Shesharrim?"

He set the chit slowly down on the table, wary of offending Torres with what he would say next. If she dropped him, it would deal a serious blow to his income, and his supply of e-caps. But there was no way around it.

"The payment is less than I expected. The credits, that is," he clarified when her gaze darted toward the black box. "The number of e-caps is the same."

The annoyance he'd feared flashed across her face, curling her lip. She shrugged. "We've got plenty of product. Enough I don't care about skimming off the top for you."

"But?" he asked.

She studied him, dark eyes flat, and for a moment Gau thought Torres would tell him to get lost. To be grateful for what he had.

Instead, she scoffed and said, "Customers are another story. Our street dealers have been seeing week-over-week drops in revenue. Someone's taking our business."

The warehouse operation he'd seen. Could that be Torres' unknown competitor? He drew his hands below the desk, hiding clenched fists. He should tell her. The longer the Urd were allowed to operate in secret, the more of her territory would fall, and the smaller the payments would get. He might lose her as a client altogether.

But speaking up meant raising his head. It meant becoming more visible: he wouldn't be one of Torres' anonymous couriers anymore. Being someone who had useful information could offer protection, but it also might draw the attention of the Terran powers that ran this city. Depending on what she did with the intel, Civil Security might come sniffing around.

Then Gau would have to disappear. Give up the relative stability and profitability of couriering for some smaller, meaner way to make a living.

Then again, if Torres' op failed because he'd kept his

mouth shut, he might lose his job anyway. Even worse, he would lose it knowing he could've done something to save it.

"I saw something tonight," he said. "On my way over here."

She leaned back and crossed her arms. "You mind being a little less cryptic?"

Gau unclenched his hands, drew a deep breath, and told her about the Urd operation.

TORRES SAT STILL across from him, her eyes boring into him as Gau related following the scent of chemical reagents to the warehouse and seeing the Urd inside.

Once he'd finished, she rose slowly from her seat and paced behind her desk.

"Son of a bitch," she said softly. "You're sure it was new? Not one of the Directive's manufactories?"

He'd wondered that briefly on the way over, once the adrenaline of his discovery had dissipated. The Directive cabal controlled much of the illicit trade in Diego Two, and while it was Baskar-led, it did employ a variety of species. But no—he'd chosen his route specifically because it didn't cut through the Directive's territory. He couriered packages for them too, of course, and preferred to keep his associations separate. Torres and the Directive were competitors.

Gau drew a line through the air with the side of his palm—the Osk sign of negation. "It was in Lead Row, your territory. The Directive wouldn't encroach on that." He considered. "Unless they wanted a turf war. You haven't ... heard anything like that have you?" He wished he could take the question back as soon as it was out of his mouth. Not because he didn't want to know, but because it was dangerously close to appearing to give a rotten tooth about Torres' enterprise beyond as a way to keep himself in credits and e-caps. It was bad enough he was the only Osk courier working for her. He didn't want Torres taking personal notice of him.

But then, from the way she leaned forward, interest sharpening her scent, maybe it was too late for that.

"No, my network hasn't made a peep about the Directive moving in on us. But they also missed a rival op under my nose, so maybe it turns out my usual guys can't find their assholes with two hands and a flashlight." Her lips pursed in displeasure, then quirked up. "You found it. Or found something that has my attention, anyway."

"Are you going to set your people on it?" It seemed the logical next step, and, more importantly, one that didn't involve him.

She bit the side of her lip. "That's where it gets tricky. I do that, and word gets back that I missed this op in the first place? It doesn't look good for my reputation."

And reputation was everything in a business like Torres'. Gau sometimes forgot she had bosses too, people who wouldn't hesitate to kick her out of the organization if they knew she'd let a rival gang set up shop under her nose.

"I need more first," she said.

"More what?" he asked, wary.

"More than just your word," she said. "If something funny's going on, I need proof." She cycled her hands in the air. "Photos, vids, something I can take up the chain to show the others we have a problem."

Gau jabbed at the air with his snout, an affirmative gesture he used mostly to buy time. It wasn't an unreasonable demand, even though the prospect of sniffing around the warehouse with a recording device raised the fine hairs along his spine. If he were caught he doubted the Urd would have any qualms about killing him—maybe take a few days to interrogate him first.

"There's extra pay in it for you if you come up with something I can use," Torres added when the silence had spooled out for too long.

He thought about the number on the credit chit reader. It had been smaller than before, but he could still live on it. As long as it didn't get smaller. As long as he didn't lose Torres as a client. As long as everything stayed exactly the way it was right now forever. He hadn't had much luck with that in the past, but the last few years had been stable. Until this newest development.

"I'll get your proof," he said.

FATIGUE WAS PULLING at Gau's limbs by the time he reached his camp. That was how he thought of it: a temporary camp, a hideout he could easily vacate if things got too dangerous. Not a home—a home got you too attached to the physical place, and in situations where you had minutes to flee, that emotional attachment could mean the difference between life and death. He'd learned that when he'd lost his first home.

His current camp was situated in a niche in a concrete wall underneath an overflow pipe in Diego Two's storm sewers. The overhead of the pipe effectively hid the niche from view even when water wasn't falling across it. He'd carved holds into the concrete leading up to it, sized for his hands and feet. They would be shallow and difficult for an adult Terran to climb, though not impossible. The far side of the niche opened onto a gentle drainage slope, beyond which was a warren of tunnels he'd forced himself to memorize. If ever his camp was discovered, he wouldn't be boxed in.

Peeking his head over the edge, he scanned the low concrete room beyond. It was deserted. He pulled himself into the niche, careful not to trigger the tripwire stretched low across it. Any invader, Terran or drone, who tried to chase him in here would be enveloped in a cloud of glittering dust while airhorns blasted from both directions, blinded and deafened long enough for Gau to get away.

The ceiling was so low he had to bow his torso to stand, though even when standing straight his head didn't come up more than a meter from the ground. A pile of stained but dry blankets in one corner made up his nest, but despite his tiredness he wasn't ready to sleep yet. He had things to do first.

Opposite his bed lay heaps of debris washed up near his camp by the rain flushed down the storm sewer: burst rubber tires, offcuts of plywood and metal, shredded fishing nets. Crouching, Gau carefully moved the piles aside to reveal two opaque plastic go-bags. He opened one and deposited the prepaid credit chit. A small pile of identical chits and pre-packaged food jostled inside the bag. The second go-bag contained a sleek black box like the one he carried in his cloak. Gau removed it with care and replaced it with the fresh one Torres had given him. He carried the old box to his nest of blankets.

He wanted sleep, but there was a nearer, sharper ache Gau had to attend to first.

Gau got comfortable, curling his long lower body into a C shape in the blankets, then opened the box and removed the single black disc inside. He brushed back his black mane and pressed the e-cap to the side of his neck. A pneumatic hiss followed by a sting signaled the dose's entry into his bloodstream.

As he waited for it to take effect, he turned to face the concrete wall. He used to stare into the darkness of whatever temporary camp he'd found for himself, letting his eyes grow heavy as the endorphin wiped everything away. But there were a few minutes before it did when it was too easy for his mind to draw shapes on the darkness. The memories and faces he was trying to outrun.

Once, there had been a whole enclave of Osk in Diego Two. The Terrans had grudgingly let them in, along with a handful of other species. But the Osk hadn't known to keep their heads down, to not ask, and later fight, for what they deserved. And the Terrans had destroyed them for it.

Gau was the last one left, as far as he knew and dared to hope. He waited, as he did every night, for the drug to make him forget that.

THE RECORDING DEVICE was a cheap unit, capable of storing a few thousand photos and at most a few hours of video. Gau had sacrificed a few credits off one of his pre-paids to buy it at a shadowmarket establishment whose owner knew not to ask questions.

A few photos and minutes of video should be more than enough proof of suspicious activity. He repeated this to himself like a mantra as Torres flipped through the stills. Her elbows were propped on her desk as she held the unit close to her face, peering into it as though it were a pair of binoculars.

All he could see of her face was her mouth below the recorder. It dipped from a neutral line into a frown, and she set the recorder down.

"They're doing something in there. You got that much. But it's not clear what it is."

Forcing down his immediate objections, Gau took up the recorder and made himself look at the stills and video again. The data on the recorder represented two weeks of work, snatched minutes at a time on separate nights. He hadn't dared stay much longer each time and risk discovery.

Initially, the dim lighting in the pictures had taken him aback. His own eyes could see through the dark like it wasn't there; even under the covered tent the Urd's manufactory had seemed to shine forth. The recorder didn't come equipped with anything like that level of night vision, but he thought he'd compensated, using the limited built-in filters to brighten what he could.

Doing his best to look at the images through Torres' weaker eyes, he had to admit that though the general shape of the operation came through—the covered backlit tent, the outlines of equipment and the Urd silhouettes working at it—the details that would have definitively identified it as an e-cap operation were lost in the digital grain.

Dispirited, he tossed the recorder down. "This cheap piece of carrion wasn't up to the task. I couldn't get them any clearer, not at night."

Torres tapped the recorder's plastic housing. "No shit. You could've got this out of a vending machine."

He tried not to show his dejection, though his shoulders threatened to sag. "So that's it then," Gau said. He tried to make his voice hard. Indifferent.

She drummed her fingers on the desk. "Not necessarily. These pics might not be enough alone, but they're at least evidence those Urd're up to something." She lifted her hands above the desk and brought them together, interlacing her fingers. "Combined with more concrete evidence, they could be enough for me to take up the chain."

"What could be more concrete than visuals ..." He inferred her meaning even as he asked the question; his mouth went dry, making his next words a croak. "Are you saying what I think you are?"

"Our e-caps come in a distinctive package." Torres made a circle with her thumb and forefinger the size of an e-cap. "So do the Directive's. If these guys are working outside either network, their product'll look different."

His stomach plummeted into his feet.

He was going to have to sneak into the warehouse.

THE TASK WAS NOT AS impossible as it might have seemed a few days ago. Gau's surveillance had inadvertently taught him the layout of the warehouse and surrounding streets, as well as knowledge of the movements of the Urd inside. He knew the one he'd seen step outside that first night always took a break around the same time. He'd seen all three of them rotate waste disposal duties, one hauling tubs of used solvent outside for dumping while the others kept working. He figured there would be a window where at least two of them were away from the building, leaving only one clawed, venomous Urd to sneak past.

Until then, he was prepared to wait and watch every night. Gau was used to waiting—for jobs, payment, for the dark that meant it was safer to venture out of his camp.

Gau crouched on the same dumpster as he had that first night, waiting for the Urd to go on break. He'd worked up the courage to follow it on his surveillance runs. After leaving from the side entrance, it went down the alley and crossed the street to loiter in front of a different warehouse.

While he waited, he removed a palm-size jury-rigged device from his cloak. He'd recycled the recorder's flash bulb and a few other parts into an improvised noise maker.

He might not have spied on a rival op before, but he did have experience in misdirection. His camps were always in parts of the city not frequented by Terrans, but that didn't mean unpatrolled. Their automated drones regularly swept the storm sewers and dumps and other interstitial spaces of the city, serving as their masters' eyes and ears. Gau had learned how to blind those eyes with spray paint and dust and mud, and how to distract those ears with thrown rocks and noise makers.

He hoped the same principles would work on the Urd.

Inside, the tent flap bulged outward. Gau's stomach somersaulted as the Urd with the metal tin stalked out, already fishing out more of the brown goop.

The Urd strolled to the side door. Gau quickly checked the tent: the spiny outlines of two Urd were still inside. Maybe tonight wouldn't be the night. But then...

A second Urd emerged from the tent, dragging a sloshing tub. Electricity raced through Gau from snout to tail.

He didn't let the burst of energy go to waste. Before the second Urd had reached the door, he was already moving.

※

THE SIDE DOOR gave at his touch. The loading hatch might be ostentatiously chained up, but he imagined the Urd kept the other exits free to make their work easier, or in case they had to flee a Civil Sec raid.

He hesitated on the threshold; for a moment the brightly lit tent and the toiling figure within held him transfixed. An image flashed before his mind of the Urd pausing in its work, pulling back the flap and fixing its yellow eyes on him. But the Urd inside the tent made no sign of having heard his entrance. Urd were diurnal, Gau remembered—even if it did look outside the tent, the glare inside would make it almost impossible to discern details in the dark beyond.

If he didn't move, though, one of the others would run into him standing in the same door they'd left from. The prospect galvanized him into action. Hunching to keep his profile low, Gau crept into the darker shadows of a pile of pallets that gave him an angle on both the side door and the half-open tent flap.

Now came the riskiest part: he had to get the third Urd to leave the tent, which meant he had to get its attention. Gau felt for the switch he'd patched together earlier —little more than a couple exposed wires and a wireless

antenna—and squeezed it to send the signal to the improvised noise maker sitting on the dumpster lid.

A wail of car proximity alarms and flashing lights
erupted beyond the warehouse's high windows. The
silhouette within the tent jumped; a string of guttural
syllables, likely obscene, emerged from the tent, followed
by the Urd itself. Gau scrunched down further behind
the pallets, but the Urd didn't spare a glance in his direction. Its attention was fixed on the light and noise coming
from beyond the window.

As he'd hoped, a second later the Urd left from the
side door to investigate. It went at a faster clip than Gau
had expected, almost sprinting. The door slammed
behind it. In a moment, he understood his miscalculation:
he'd meant to create a distraction that would keep the Urd
busy, and though he'd certainly done that, the light and
noise could attract attention to the warehouse the Urd
couldn't afford. It had to shut down the source of the
disruption quickly, and what was more, Gau's distraction
had practically drawn the creature a map of where to go.

He had significantly less time than he'd counted on.
Maybe only a few minutes at most. He swallowed down
his own set of curses and ran for the tent.

The stark glare of freestanding lights stunned him
momentarily; Gau slitted his eyes against them and
scanned the small but densely organized drug lab for
anything he could snatch to take back to Torres. Tubs for
mixing solvents and reagents were arrayed on two large
folding tables, clear plastic tubes running between them.
On a smaller folding table were rows of steel jars with
sealed lids, probably precursor ingredients, and next to
them a boxy machine he recognized as a capsule machine.

So the Urd *did* have the equipment to pre-package their own e-caps. But where were they storing the suns-cursed final product?

He checked the steel jars, all of which were neatly labeled—in Urdeki. Gau wasn't fool enough to stick his snout into any of them to try and discern what the chemicals were. He made a turn of the room again; there must be something he'd missed...

Two steel boxes lurked under the table of precursor ingredients, their hinged lids closed. He felt the seam of one lid; if it was locked he would have to cut his losses and get out of there. There wouldn't be time to pick it before the Urd got back.

The lid fell smoothly back, and his breath followed in a relieved whoosh. Inside, neatly encapsulated in dull gray cartridges, were rows of what very much looked like e-caps resting in felt pockets.

Gau reached for one on the top layer, then paused. If the Urd suspected someone of trying to rob them, the boxes of finished e-caps were the first thing they'd check. Well, he was robbing them, but he didn't need to make the job so obvious.

In a flash of inspiration, he opened up the capsule machine. He'd interrupted the Urd in the middle of work, so a row of empty opaque gray capsules sat in the top of the machine. He snatched three e-caps from the top row inside the chest and replaced them with the three empty capsules. Visually they were identical; the Urd would need to weigh them to detect the theft, and Gau would be long gone by then.

The creak of the side door punctured his elation at his own cleverness. Not one, not two, but three sets of talons scuffed on the floor. The Urd he'd distracted with the noise maker must have found it and summoned the other two. Gau instantly flattened himself to the floor, hoping they hadn't seen his silhouette projected onto the walls. No exclamations of surprise rang out; he'd escaped immediate detection. The Urd spoke in low, deep voices to each other; he understood none of it, but estimating their positions by their voices told him they were searching the corners of the warehouse. At any moment one of them could approach the tent.

His stomach was ice, his nose afire with the leathery smell of suspicious Urd. But his thoughts were clear. He could see the next move, and the one after that. The Urd were playing his game and they didn't even know it.

Gau made himself crawl to the cluster of standing lamps. Thick cables ran from them to a portable generator. He rose to a crouch, finger hovering over the power switch, and got ready to run.

Gau hit the switch. Darkness closed the room in a fist. The three Urd yelped in surprise. For agonizing seconds, the darkness held Gau in its sway, his night vision destroyed by the tent's earlier glare. Then lines and planes of objects filtered back to him, enough to make out the gaping door of the tent. He darted out toward the side door at a fast shuffle, keeping low as though that would somehow hide him from discovery when the Urd turned the generator back on.

Two of the Urd were on the opposite side of the tent from him, but the last one was between him and the side door. It swung its blunt head from side to side, groping forward as if to catch the thief. Breathless with exhilaration as much as fear, Gau skirted behind it. His heart was so loud in his chest he couldn't believe the Urd didn't hear it.

But it didn't turn. Not until Gau reached the side door and eased it open with a squeak no amount of gentleness could prevent. The Urd's head whipped around, triangulating the sound in the dark—

The light blazed back on, and the Urd covered its eyes with its hands. Gau took that as his cue and piled out of the door, shoulder checking it closed behind him. He ran.

The warehouses of Lead Row were an hours-old memory behind him before he felt safe enough to stop.

THE GAU that stared back at him in the reflection of Torres' office window was hollow-eyed from lack of sleep, but inside he floated on a bubble of triumph.

It didn't burst even when Torres, after ushering him inside, smirked and said, "You look like shit, Shesharrim. Rough night?"

He smiled. Today her barbs couldn't touch him. "You could say that." From his cloak, Gau removed a baggy with the three dull gray e-caps inside. "I got your proof, Torres."

Her eyes widened in a most satisfying way. She snatched up the baggy and stared at the contents. "Really?" Her voice tried for skepticism, but he could tell she wanted to believe him. To have something to take up the chain.

"Have your people analyze the contents," Gau said. "I'm sure they'll see chemical differences between these and our product. *And* the Directive's."

Torres made him wait a few hours while a courier took the samples to be analyzed, then more minutes as she made a call to the hidden upper tiers of the operation which Gau had never seen. He didn't mind the waiting. What surprised him more was that he didn't mind the attention his venture had gathered. He'd spent the last few years keeping his head down, fighting to protect what little he had and keep it from getting smaller. Thinking that was the only way forward.

But now he'd alerted one of his employers to a threat to their business, and what was more, he'd taken a risk to bolster that threat with evidence.

And it felt good. It felt like taking control of his life again. For years he'd been stumbling around in the shadows like those Urd last night, and somewhere along the way he'd forgotten he could see in the dark.

A frisson of tension leapt up his spine when Torres finally emerged from the call and resumed her seat across from him. Then she grinned, showing flat white Terran teeth.

"It's your lucky day, Shesharrim. Or should I say, *our* lucky day." She tossed a credit chit and reader on the desk. He ran it. This time, a lot more credits appeared on the screen. At least thrice as many as he'd make in an ordinary month of couriering.

Gau held back a gasp. Pocketed the chit. "The op should move on whatever it's going to do soon," he said, sounding calmer than he felt. Sounding in control. "Before the Urd get spooked and pick up stakes. They know someone was there last night."

Torres waved that aside. "We've got certain resources the other ops don't," she said. "By this time tomorrow the

Urd's op will be busted on the strength of an anonymous tip to Civil Sec."

He jabbed his snout in consideration. "So what happens now? I just go back to couriering?" The prospect, once safe and stable, seemed dim now.

She stretched one shoulder behind her back, then the other. "Sure. It's steady work, after all." When he thought that was all she had to say on the matter, she went on. "But you've caught the operation's interest. You're someone who's provided valuable information. There'll be more work like that in the future, if you want it."

He considered that future: one where he wasn't hiding in the dark, but making it his world.

"I want it," Gau said.

Wars make unlikely allies.

When his ship is damaged, elite assassin Gau Shesharrim is stranded on a hostile world—until help comes from an unexpected source.

Discover how Gau recruited his first ally in his crusade against the Expansion. Download Shadow Game for free when you sign up to the Readers Group mailing list at expansionfront.com!

Pick Your Poison

1. *Really vibing with the morally gray world.* Head to "Case City Cowboy" by Greg Dragon

2. *Got any good conspiracy stories?* Head to "Ion Hunter" by E.L. Strife

3. *Let's head back to Earth . . . if not quite as we know it.* Turn the page to read "SolarMute" by Jim Keen

SOLARMUTE

A CORTEX STORY

BY JIM KEEN

NOVEMBER 22, 2054, SAN FRANCISCO, USA

THE VAST TRANSLUCENT EGG HOVERED OVER THE bay's black water, its thick skin sparkling with fractal patterns like a broken VR feed. Sara's electric ferry hummed towards it, wide hull gouging a scar across the oily surface as she pressed a handkerchief to her mouth. The foul air stank of burned plastics, the smell stinging her eyes and throat.

No one else seemed to notice and, more than ever, Sara felt every second of her provincial upbringing. It took ten awful days to get here from Brazil. Then, like every other drifter washing up in San Francisco, she'd leased a capsule in the local Metabolist hotel. Four long months squashed into that tiny space revealed itself in every crease of her cheap suit, every scuff on her worn shoes.

As Building 116 grew ahead of them, its three huge steel legs in stark contrast to the pollution's gritty texture, Sara checked her appearance for the thousandth time.

Thin and tired face, short black hair, chewed nails. She looked as much a hacker as anyone else who worked for the agency, but the boat was stacked with people who smelled of money and access. Razor-edged suits. Honed physiques. Bleached skin. Exquisite eye-gear. Even their reprinted limbs matched the color and freckles of the original body, only the pale blue zip-scars revealing their lab-grown origin.

No, here she was very much the tourist.

The call had come as a surprise, an encrypted response to an ad she posted in the Job-Search Channel the day she'd arrived. It had sat next to her resume like the corpse of a dead dog while she clipped through the hundreds of temp jobs the coding agency found for her. Rebalancing power channels for the local fusion distribution center. Automating the aerial camera-drones coverage of speeding hoppers. Backing up and distributing every conference Vurt in the city. Kid's stuff.

And then this sneak outreach, the message hidden away in the system code of an Elephant Guzzle ad. Guzzle ads, and their cute animatronic pink elephant, had been quite the hit a few years back, being one of the first true interactives to hit the networks. Then some SlideKnife guys cracked the code and made it share-ware, spawning a billion memes for the tweener crowds.

She'd ignored it at first. What sort of jerk uses a Guzzler to advertise a job anyway? But then, after a week of disastrous interviews, she got drunk on still-brew vodka and re-opened the message.

The initial ask was for someone to code an AR porn set-up, but it was written with an elegance that hooked her. No one bothered honing random messages down to such a tight and clean size these days. She went deeper.

There, a thousand layers down, just as the sun was rising to greet her hangover, Sara cracked a sub-routine and a soft male voice whispered from her laptop's speakers, the accent matching her provincial farmers Portuguese.

"Ms. Yultierrez, it's a pleasure to meet you. I hope you forgive this little test. I've been tracking your progress and for someone of your intuitive skills using a Guzzle Ad is borderline insulting. However, SolarMute has their hoops to jump through, just like any boring, conventional coding corporation."

That stopped Sara, the words bringing an adrenaline flush that blew away her fatigue like napalm through palm trees. SolarMute—the anonymous collective that cracked the Oshika labs and gave away their skeleton print files for free, that ran the Golden-Bear Fund into bankruptcy, that stole and released Cortex's fusion reactor software. SolarMute: either a force for societal good or chaotic destruction, depending on which side of the poverty gap you existed on.

She sat up in her cramped, sweaty capsule in the hotel's eastern cluster, scraped her hair back, and pressed play.

"I have a proposition for you: six months work for a considerable payday. Let's meet for coffee and I shall explain all."

With that, the advert rolled itself up and ran a detox program so complicated Sara couldn't follow half what it did. The little pink elephant was replaced with a ferry ticket to Building 116, the sovereign start-up incubator that occupied San Francisco Bay like an alien spaceship.

The building's true scale only became apparent as she approached, its supporting tripod of legs appearing stick-thin from the harbor's edge. A dock surrounded the front leg, a sliding elliptical landing pad that rose and sank with the tide. The ferry was carrying three hundred people, yet the platform dwarfed its size, its flat deck pierced by the huge steel leg that climbed a hundred feet to disappear into the egg's thick translucent skin.

The ferry pulled alongside. A series of discrete clangs shook the boat as underwater hooks secured in place, then a ramp unfolded with a light mechanical groan and the ferry emptied. Sara didn't know who she was to meet, or where, so she followed the crowd as they filed into three glass elevators, each larger than her farm's living room. They rose with a soft hum, and once more Sara felt like the tourist she was: the view was incredible, yet the other occupants ignored the vista as they read headset feeds, or received internal messages via some form of neural clock. A few, wearing thick white shirts with handlebar mustaches and shaved heads, even used ancient handheld terminals, their *ding* alerts loud in the hushed quiet.

Sara turned back to the view. San Francisco had suffered as much as anywhere from the mass unemployment, but whereas New York's exalted had retreated inside mile-high Blade Towers, San Francisco had taken a different approach. The city was shrouded by its perpetual umber pollution cloud, the fog broken by a series of white blisters that reflected the sunlight like polished marble. These were the Fuller-Domes, lighter-than-air enclaves draped over the desirable zones and guarded by the latest autonomous systems. The gaps in between had become a festering mix of slums populated by the unemployed and organized crime gangs.

As she watched, the city's hazy outline sparkled with aerostats and security drones maintaining the separation, while aerial Police Hoppers darted from one flash point to another. Sara's father forbade her from coming here, said she had no idea how lucky she was to live far from the cities. She'd thought he was full of it, just wanted her to stay for cheap labor, but maybe the old bastard was right after all.

Building 116 had been the first in a supposed new generation of green buildings; its egg form promoted passive cooling or something. Sara wasn't sure how, but it looked cool.

The owners, some Middle Eastern consortium, paid the bankrupt city an immense sum for it to become sovereign land. In effect Building 116 was its own country, and that meant anything went here, from chemical weapons design, to lethal MI coding, to the latest VR snuff channels. All that brainpower was squashed into this spaceship and left to ferment. Most of what it produced suffered the Darwinian fates of typical startups, but occasionally something emerged that had global ramifications.

Something like SolarMute.

The elevator slowed, stopped, chimed, and opened its doors. The reception area was a large white box and Sara stood, unsure, when a foot long teardrop shaped aerostat drifted down from the ceiling. With a subtle hiss it halted at eye level, and there was a momentary sparkle of gritty green light as it scanned her left retina. It knew everything about her now, from school grades to the last time she'd got drunk in a bar.

"Wait here." Its plastic voice buzzed rather than spoke the words.

"Sure, whatever," Sara said in the agricultural English she'd learned from TV.

One by one the elevator's other occupants were

greeted by feral businessmen or soft, pudgy tech people. She wasn't sure how long she waited, but it was at least an hour. She lapped the reception space like a caged animal, torn between the desire to stay and see if this was real, or give in and troop back to her fetid little hotel room.

Finally, as she was getting ready to go, an elevator descended from some distant floor. A handsome if weatherbeaten man in a smart blue suit exited. He was tall, pale and thin with a scruffy beard.

"Apologies Ms. Yultierrez. Some business can wait, some cannot."

Sara ignored the slight and nodded to him. "Call me Sara, it's easier."

"Sara it is. Now then, why don't we get that coffee?"

SARA SAT at a low wooden table close to the veranda's southern edge, her face warmed by the slanting sunlight. The restaurant occupied the corner of an upper floor, the building's skin cut back to allow external access. This far up the cold air smelled clean and fresh, with none of the chemical residue of lower down. Birds cried in the distance, and somewhere a wind chime ghosted a faint tune. Packed tables were crammed into the space, the atmosphere thick with tense and urgent conversations.

"What do I call you?" Sara asked.

"Max," he said. His voice held a weird, foreign accent she'd not heard before. Maybe German? Sara had no idea what Europeans *really* sounded like.

"That your real name?" She asked.

"Of course not. Now, to business, shall we?" He waved over Sara's shoulder, and she was shocked to see an actual *human* offer Max a menu, which he refused. "Bring me a coffee still, large, two cups." The man nodded and left. Max studied Sara then, head tilted to one side, blue eyes glittering.

"Where did you learn to code, Sara? Your style has a unique flavor to it."

"Self-taught. Grew up on my dad's farm, didn't go to school or anything like that. I picked up tons from open access channels, home university, things like that. The rest was just me hacking away at this old farm drone to see what it could do. Used to be a war machine, but I got it to do house chores, cleaning and stuff."

"Interesting. Most of the people we get to interview are all educated in the same universities. That makes them rich, intelligent, and entirely predictable. We are looking for someone a little more original in their thinking. Tell me, Sara," he clipped her name as if it was distasteful to him, the words leaving his mouth in a staccato gunfire. "What do you know of Cortex Reprints?"

Sara paused, unsure. Cortex was the world's only source of sentient machines and, through them, the human scan and reprint systems. But that was billionaire's territory and had as much to do with her as a Fuller Dome did to a mud hut.

"Just the press releases." She shrugged. "We don't get many prints where I come from."

"Interesting. Don't you live in the same valley as the Suarez cartel?"

And there it was. It seemed she was forever destined to be seen through the lens of Brazil's trillion-dollar drug gang.

"Sure, yeah, the farm looks down into their favela. That don't mean I hang with the one percent, jerk-off.

They got working girls for that. Now, do you have any real questions for me? Or is this just some bullshit fishing expedition for rumors on their tech? You're not even SolarMute are you? You're just some dumb-ass cop searching for a little southern taste."

Max leaned back in his seat and laughed, voice warm and happy. "Oh, Sara, Sara," he said. "At times it's easy to forget I exist in a bubble, and if that has impacted my manners, please forgive me. For the record, I am as far removed from an officer of the law as one can possibly be. And yes, I represent California's SolarMute franchise in all its forms." With that, he reached up and spread his eyelids open. In the slanted sunlight Sara saw the red capillaries glint with a brassy texture.

"You're a reprint," Sara said, voice tinged with awe.

"An early model. I was on the development team in New York." Now that he'd mentioned it, Sara saw the faint pixilation in the crow's feet around his eyes, the blurring of freckles on the back of his hands. He looked like a very good photocopy of an old photograph, which, in a way, he was. "Now then, human scanning and reprinting. What do you know about it?"

"Well, I, uh, watched this reality show, right, where they talked about it once. One of the characters went on holiday and came back a different actor, said she'd been reprinted, but it was just the studio's way of dealing with her wage demands. Anyways you can't change a person's appearance, right? Not full body anyway is what I heard."

Again, he laughed. "Quite. The United Nations is all about preventing a line of Übermensch being perfected and taking over. They really have perfected the art of closing the door once the horse has left. Still, what do you expect from a group of exalteds who hide inside their ivory towers?"

At that moment, the waiter returned pushing a silver trolley. It was empty apart from a metallic chunk of equipment that looked like it had been carved from the inside of a jet engine, and two small china cups. He placed the machine on the table, then put the cups on either side. Finally, the waiter pressed a button on the cube's top, nodded and exited. The machine sat between them as it made a low beep. The table shivered beneath Sara's palms.

"It's brewing coffee for us. Ignore it and continue."

"Whatever, Bub. It's your dime. Cortex invented A.I."

"Well, if we're being technically correct, they invented *M.I.*—Mechanical Intelligences. Continue."

"Okay, whatever. So their MIs invented these big scanning machines, right? Them scanners make a 3d model of you, massively complex, takes all the computing power an MI has. Once you have the model, Cortex's organic flesh printers can reprint the original. Bingo—new body, everyone's happy." Sara sat back and took a breath. Using her English to discuss such abstract concepts was bringing on a migraine. On the table next to them a frosted vodka bottle poked up from an ice bucket. God, she needed a drink.

"That is mostly correct. Cortex scanners make an exact, atomic level recording of your body. Unfortunately destroying it in the process, and for many reasons you can only re-make one copy from the model."

"Yeah, bummer that." Sara saw a flicker of annoyance flash over Max's face. *Idiot*, she thought, *'till you get the job play nice.* "What's this gotta to do with me?"

The coffee machine beeped again, and a vent at its tip

exhausted a jet of steam. Max unfolded the front to reveal a chromed spout. He placed a cup beneath it, pressed a button, and black liquid poured into the china. He took the cup and placed it in front of Sara.

"Drink that," he said, but as she reached for it he placed his palm over the top. "Describe to me exactly what you experience."

Again, she was aware of his blue eyes studying her, that mixture of machine and human unlike anything she'd encountered before. He relaxed his hand, and she picked up the cup.

"It's hot," she said.

"Yes, yes, of course. Go on. More detail."

"It will hurt if I hold it for too long." She shifted it between her fingers. "I can feel the china's texture, all glossy and bumpy. It smells organic. Like soil, or the smell of trees after rain." She took a sip, then almost dropped the cup back to the table. "What the hell is this?" She asked, raised voice making nearby tables glance at her.

"That, Sara, is real coffee, not the recycled sludge you're used to. It's grown in a blister farm on the seventeenth floor. Each single serving costs three hundred and forty-nine adjusted dollars."

Three hundred and forty-nine dollars? That was insane; her hotel capsule was three dollars a night. "The taste was so strong my mouth kinda cramped around it. It was bitter, dark, rich. It tasted like money, like something exclusive, something secret."

"Right now, you're creating a memory of that coffee, neurons interconnecting through synapses. The more you access it, the stronger that connection becomes until it fixes in your long term memory. Cortex's scanners copy those neurons exactly, just another part of the atomic model they create. A model that until now was proprietary to their mechanical intelligences."

"Was?" Sara picked the cup and drank again, savoring the extraordinary taste. "You can hack them now?"

"Perhaps. We have procured an organic scanner with its MI and have begun breaking them apart. We hope some reverse engineering will allow us access."

"Do that and you can access the subject's memories, right? Copy the files?"

"My, you are fast. Correct. Now here comes the big question, Sara."

Sara drained her cup, placed it back on the table, then reached across and took Max's coffee. "What is it you want me to do, Max?"

"I want you to steal a dead man's mind."

APRIL 9, 2055, SAN FRANCISCO, USA

In the six months Sara had been working for SolarMute, the journey out to Building 116 transformed from being a thrilling journey, to everyday commute, to just a boat she sat in and started her work.

She'd rented an elegant apartment in the 'Honeydew Vistas' Fuller Dome. It was small—she needed little space —but the bedroom had magnificent views through the dome's translucent curving roof and out across the city. It was also close to Max's apartment, and that's why she chose it, though she hadn't quite admitted that to herself yet. Another thing she hadn't admitted were her feelings towards him. Sara had never been in love before, so she couldn't say if these swirly, sickening feelings were that, but they were in a different universe from the tepid annoyance she held for Tommy, her on/off boyfriend back home.

She could tell Max liked her as well, and the sex was great, but he never opened up to her in any real way. Whenever she raised plans for their future, he looked at her with the curious expression of a taxidermist studying his latest work. She didn't like that at all; she was naïve, not stupid. Still, there wasn't time to think about any afterwards yet, not with the work being what it was.

There was a *thunkkkk*, the boat shivered beneath her, and a small alert flashed across her glasses *<You have arrived @ Building 116. Airborne pollution is six parts per million above danger levels/it will cross established threshold in four hours, nineteen minutes. You have one-hundred-and-thirty-seven updates from the overnight soft-ware compile. Review now? Y/N>* Sara barely remembered leaving the apartment, let alone getting on this ferry, her mind absorbed by their attempts to reverse engineer the body scanner's software. She blinked twice to click the *<N>* button and disembarked.

The SolarMute workshop occupied one of the building's upper floors, and Sara was the first to arrive as usual. She'd always been a morning person, the result of a childhood spent working on her family's farm. The animals were up and hungry with dawn's crimson rays, and so she had to be as well.

It took almost as long to enter the laboratory as it did to travel up and through the building; she had to pass through three MRA scanners, an iris reader, and finally the nasty little DNA tester with its sharp needles.

The room's primary space contained two partially disassembled pieces of equipment. First was a compact fusion reactor. She spared that scant thought. All its software had to do was manage the colossal energies generated when in use. It was the other device that had consumed her life over the last half-year.

The scanner's exterior was a beautifully machined titanium cylinder eight feet in diameter and twelve long. Irising doors capped both ends, though both were currently open, the internal stretcher protruding like a plastic tongue. A series of vertical slots marked the side walls and they always reminded Sara of a shark's gills. The machine sat on a coffin-sized block of brassy metal. A thick red cable ran from that to the fusion reactor, while an even thicker blue one rose to the ceiling where it plugged into the building's cooling systems.

Sara had only clambered inside the scanner once, and Max had shut the doors as a joke. She'd hated it, the cramped internal space all gleaming, soulless perfection. She couldn't imagine what it would be like when the proton beams engaged and triangulated, slicing you apart atom by atom, transforming flesh into machine code.

She threw her AR glasses onto a table covered with half disassembled circuits, a small terminal and keyboard, then ran the startup software. A series of recessed amber lights flickered to life on the side of the scanner. A faint hum filled the air and her skin tingled with static discharge, then the machine settled into its standby mode.

The pedestal contained the scanner's mechanical intelligence, which controlled the entire process from start to finish, and it was what they hired her to hack. The MI was designed and manufactured for this one task, and as such had none of the radiant personalities of the larger machines that Max talked about all the time. That was good, as cracking its encrypted software had been near impossible. If it was only fractionally smarter, Max's plan would never have worked. As it was, she'd gotten her software chisel between some of the foundational parts of its consciousness and had been peeling the layers back one by one. Soon, she would have access to its base firmware, and from there she should be able to finally figure out how the memory transfer systems functioned.

As Sara dove into her work, she tried to ignore the thing that was nagging away at her: after six months she still didn't know their target. At the start she thought Max would tell her, but the more she pushed, the angrier he got until she gave up. It took her a while to realize that Max, SolarMute Senior Lieutenant, didn't know either.

And the more she thought about that, the more scared she became.

OCTOBER 27, 2055, SAN FRANCISCO, USA

Time rolled on. The six-month commission became nine, then twelve, with still no briefing about who, where, and when they were going to make their move.

At least she'd unraveled most of the code base from the scanner and its embedded mechanical intelligence. The two were a fiendish combination of bespoke hardware and software, and she'd explained to Max months ago that unless they could custom fabricate one of the intelligence's logic engines, there was only so much her re-written code would allow them to do.

Max had been angry with her, fidgeting and nervous, then made a long call in a language she didn't understand. Afterwards he told her to just get the code hack done by the end of the month and he would take care of the rest. Later, Sara felt that call had been like the software chisel she used to split the MI's mind in two. Only this time, her questions had cracked their relationship.

After that she did as told, and one year to the day after she boarded an ancient, clattering bus in Brazil and started her awful journey to San Francisco, she was done. Her life before SolarMute seemed a dream now, one in which she had no idea what three hundred dollars coffee tasted like, or the subtle joy of wearing bespoke clothing tailored just for her.

Today's dress was a dark yellow silk that clung to her body emphasizing her new gym-based physique. At times Sara wondered what her father would think if he saw her now. Probably lay a guilt trip down and say she looks like everybody else or how she'd become just another drone. Maybe he was right. But maybe, if this job went smooth and SolarMute took her on full-time, she'd never have to see or speak to him ever again.

Max had gotten the 'go' call last night when they were in bed, his mood changing in an instant. Gone was the fun loving and slightly nerdy European, replaced with an icy-cold businessman. He'd kicked her out into the apartment's hallway and slammed the door shut, leaving her half naked and in full view of a security aerostat, its lenses clicking as the control software tried to decide if she were a working girl or not.

Max called later to apologize and said today was the day. When she'd asked what that meant, he'd sighed, said she asked too many questions, just to get ready, and hung up on her.

Hence the dress. Hence the hour in the gym this morning. Hence the hair and makeup, and the tight, twisted knot in her stomach. She was scared she'd forgotten something, or that the software would fail, or this whole thing was a dream, and she was hopelessly out of her depth.

Sara got to the lab an hour before her normal shift and did what little she could to clean up: ran the dishwasher, fidgeted around in her AR goggles checking the code one last time, cleaned the scanner's spotless metal cylinder. And then she sat, looking out of the window, and tried not to chew her nails.

After another boring, stressful hour she heard the secure portal begin its long series of clicks and hisses as it allowed people to enter. Sara rose, spine clicking, to see a small man swathed in black bulletproof body armor standing in the middle of the office. He remained utterly motionless, more statue than human being, then called over his left shoulder in that weird foreign language Max had used last night. The tall, armored glass door that led into the interlocking security chambers opened, and there was a subtle hissing of gases equalizing. Three more ninjas entered, followed by an ancient woman dressed in a filthy gray cloth sack held together with pins. The old lady used a walking stick fashioned from a dented metal tube, and she ignored Sara completely. The woman limped to the scanner, then kneeled with surprising speed to study the hacked mechanical intelligence. The floor was covered with screws, bolts and stripped cables which Sara had arranged in a methodical order.

"Hey, be careful," Sara said. "That whole system is live, and all that gear on the floor is there for a reason."

The old woman twisted in a flash and looked her up and down.

Twenty minutes from Sara's farm, an old sinkhole

appeared one night when she was younger. Over the years it filled with water to become a small and beautiful lake. Its edges were shallow, the water warming early with the morning sun, and she swam there every day. Her dad didn't like that, and relentlessly told her never to swim over the sinkhole's center. He didn't explain why, so as she grew, she started to swim further and further out until one beautiful summer's day she decided to swim right across. The first fifteen feet were easy, her toes touching rocky ground, until in an instant the bright blue water turned inky black and ice cold. The further she swam, the colder it became, until she was in a frigid world that sapped her strength like a vampire. All her childish arrogance evaporated, replaced with a primal fear that swallowed her completely. She flailed and kicked in the freezing water, head slipping above and below the surface, screaming for help. For the first time in her life Sara thought she was going to die. It was a clear, logical thought that carried no emotion: it was a statement of fact. She was going to die in that freezing lake, all alone. Just when she could take no more, stamina gone, desperate gasps of air replaced with the stagnant water, a thick brown arm encircled her chest and dragged her to the shore where she lay on her back gulping like a beached fish.

"I told you, I told you," her father shouted, over and over.

She went to bed with no dinner that night, and slept terrible dreams filled with suffocating hands covered in scales that grabbing her ankles and dragged her down into the darkness. Even now, fifteen years later, she just had to close her eyes to remember death's cold, empty grip. The moment her eyes connected with the old woman's, that subterranean terror shivered through her again. Sara wasn't looking at another human being in SolarMute's spotless and warm office, she was staring at something so utterly devoid of compassion that her life was as irrelevant as mud on the old woman's filthy shoes. A demon clad in human skin crouched before her.

"Wait outside." The woman said, voice hard and sharp like a steel blade.

Sara nodded, unable to speak, and stumbled down to the café terrace, where she sat with a glass of orange juice that cost more than her father's car. Her hands shook around the cold glass, and no matter the strength of the sun she felt no warmth.

When Max summoned her back, the old woman was long gone. Max was in the glass meeting room studying something in his hands. He looked scared. "Would this work Sara? Would it work? Zhu said it will."

He handed her an armor glass wallet containing what looked like a memory wafer from the scanner behind her. Yet even to the naked eye it looked old, incomplete. Instead of the machine's usual brassy alloy this was a deeper red, and there was none of the iridescent sheen she got from the original device. She took the package and placed it into the lab's electron microscope, the device warming with a low hum, its screen flickering to life.

"Look." She tapped the screen so Max bent forward and peered.

"What?" he asked.

"The print quality is way off. Cortex's work is perfect, like looking at a completed jigsaw puzzle. This has holes everywhere in the structure. Whatever printed this is way old."

"For once just stop being so goddam snotty and

answer the question. Will it work?." He raised his voice to a shout, and she was torn between wanting to slap him and shout back. Instead, she upped the scanners resolution and dove into the details. For all the crude nature of the reprint, it appeared that the fundamentals were there. If they could swap out an existing memory wafer with this, her software hack could gain full access to the print files, and could steal whatever they wanted from the target.

"Zhu that old woman?" She asked and leaned back from the scanner's screen.

"Yes, yes. Now can you make this work?"

She paused, then gave him her most dazzling smile.

"Yeah Max, I can make this work."

He kissed her, and took her home, and for a moment she forgot about drowning in freezing water, and the demons wearing human suits that lurked in plain sight. For that night anyway.

NOVEMBER 3, 2055, NEW DELHI, INDIA

Sara had never been in an airplane before, let alone a Gulf Stratosphere. From the outside, the private hypersonic aircraft looked like a carbon-black dart with a stubby ram scoop on top, and two vestigial wings either side. Inside, it had all the charm of the world's most claustrophobic spa. Sumptuous leather and wood everywhere, the cool air filled with a delicate vanilla scent, but the curve of the fuselage pressed ever inwards. There were no windows, just a series of wall displays, and Sara could tell these were VR renders rather than real-world views.

All air traffic flew via autonomous systems these days, meaning there was only her and Max on the flight to New Delhi. She'd never been to India either; it seemed today was going to be filled with firsts.

Sara studied schedule updates with her tablet and couldn't help but notice her jagged and filthy fingernails. She'd not washed or worked out for the week it took to put this trip together. Max had insisted on this—he wanted her to look as much like an authentic cleaning lady as possible. Sara thought his idea of servants was hopelessly out of date, that people who cleaned were more likely to wash every day not less, but he didn't listen.

"You're good with the plan?" He asked from the opposite chair, sipping from a crystal champagne glass.

"I guess," she shrugged.

"But?" He flashed his cute, lopsided grin.

"Who are we going after? Can you tell me that at least?"

He laughed and took another sip from the glass. "You've been bursting with that question for days, haven't you? Madam Zhu ordered me to keep quiet, and you *never* ignore her."

"Zhu? That old crone from last week?"

"Yup," he said, a slight drunken slur to his voice. "Zhu put the frights right up me, I gotta say. I've dealt with presidents, leaders of mega-corporations, sociopaths and murderers one and all, but she's the first that made me fear for my soul."

"I know what you mean. I almost peed myself and she only looked at me. Come on, it's time. Spill it Maximillian."

"I've only got the basics. This old guy has some infor-mation Zhu wants. He's been hidden away for years. Zhu thinks the machines are helping him to cover his tracks, but who can tell? Her industrial espionage team cracked a communication satellite last month. He wants in from the cold, going to take a job at Sydney University. Good for him. But that required a new face and body. So he's headed to Delhi, home of the illegal flesh modders, before he returns to the real world. We go in, copy his mind, and get out before he wakes up. If your software does the job he'll never even know he's been hacked. Then it's caviar and the Caribbean for us."

"Us? We got a future, Maxie?"

"Let's just get this done first, okay? Get ready. The clock's running."

DESPITE THE POOR rendering on the external screens, Sara watched their arrival with a sense of awe. New Delhi, the world's largest city, was smothered by an opaque blue-gray pollution layer. Only its sixteen blade towers were visible, their mile high forms piercing the smog like vast carbon trees. The designs appeared similar to those she'd seen in glossy adverts for New York, being a half-mile composite truss that supported another half-mile of twisting, mirrored curtainwall.

The jet swooped between the first two and dove into the pollution cloud, the view screens flickering gray nothingness. They dropped fast, Sara's stomach light, then they were through and skating above the gloomy metropolis. Industrial geometries and chaotic suburbs flashed past before they banked hard right to land in a large, desolate car park.

The *chuga-chuga-chuga* of powerful hydraulic

systems came from beneath them, and the ship's door
unfolded outwards. Max was up and away in seconds,
Sara following. The ground reflected heat from the
aircraft's skin, and as she opened her mouth to speak she
coughed instead, a deep lung rattling hack that hurt. The
air had a gritty texture that scoured her nose and throat.
San Francisco's pollution smelled like burned metal, and
she even liked it at times, but this was different. The
atmosphere reeked of powdered concrete and rotting
meat. Her lungs wheezed with a dreadful suffocating
sensation, as if she were inhaling air from an enormous
machine's exhaust. The visibility was so poor Sara
couldn't see the shopping mall's full size; its dilapidated
structure faded into the murk on either side.

A sharp, stinging pain needled her eyes, and she
rubbed away tears and spat on the floor. Her uniform was
too tight, making breathing even harder, but she only had
to wear it a few hours. Made from fatigued white cotton,
the maid's dress had a patch on its shoulder that said
Marigold Services in English, followed by a row of words
that looked more like hieroglyphics than actual text
to her.

Her backpack looked a hundred years old, but was
packed with tools designed to disassemble the scanner's
MI. A small, secret pocket also contained the reprinted
memory wafer and a rod-logic cube containing her software hack. She swung it over her back and pulled out a
plastic key card. "You sure about this?" she asked.

"It's way past backing out time. Don't sweat it. Our
information is good, and I got this for you." Max handed
her a hockey puck sized black disc. She clicked the button
on its top, and with a chirp the drone rose to head height
and hovered by her shoulder. "This should keep you safe

from any unemployed idiot that gets too close. It's old tech, though, won't protect you in a firefight or anything too serious, so be careful. We couldn't risk you getting caught with something more advanced. A maid could just about afford this if she were frugal. Maybe." He shrugged.

"Gee thanks Max. Good to know you got my back."

His watch beeped, and he donned his thin metal AR glasses, mouth pulled down in a grimace. He stood like that for a tortuously silent minute, then turned away from her talking in low, urgent tones. He raised his voice, then was cut short and Sara saw how his body tensed, shoulder hunched. He was scared, and only one person scared Max—Madam Zhu. Something had gone seriously wrong.

"Oh, goddam it." He dragged the headset off with a wince and wiped his face. "Okay. Sara, the plan's changed. He's arriving way sooner than expected; you've got thirty minutes to get in and out. No choice."

"Thirty minutes? Max, come on, don't be stupid. Every dry run we've done took at least two hours." Until this moment, Sara had felt calm and in control, ready for action. Now, all at once, everything became too real. The car park's stink, the tight uniform and heavy backpack, the airplane's ticking and cooling. Max watched her with his laser focused stare as cold sweat soaked her back. She shivered. "We gotta abort. That's nowhere near enough time."

"Think I don't know that? This is a serious play Sara, real heavy hitters involved. Screw this up, and Zhu will hunt us forever. We have to play this out hard and fast, right here, right now."

"Maybe we can—"

"*No.*" he shouted, then gathered himself with an effort. "No. Go, now, do it. I'll see you on the other side."

Sara watched in disbelief as he shrugged, kissed her cheek, and ran back to the aircraft. The ramp closed leaving her to stare at its black exterior.

"Back up," the craft said in a deep male voice. She did. "Further, right to the edge. Hate to singe your hair." She moved until the mall's plywood wall pressed into her shoulders. Through the gray grit, a ripple of heat grew underneath the aircraft along with a violent roar, then it rose straight up and faded from view. Seconds later, a sonic boom crackled overhead, its echo reverberating around her.

"Okay, okay, keep calm sister, you got this." Sara turned and wedged her fingers into a crack behind the nearest plywood panel, pulled it back a foot, then squeezed into the echoing darkness. The security drone followed to illuminate the dark with its targeting lasers; there was no sound apart from the flap and call of pigeons.

Zhu's information said their target would be scanned inside a truck docked in the loading bay to the mall's rear. They'd found the building's plans easily enough, and even some VR recordings from a decade back when it was bursting with life and vigor. That was before mechanical intelligences of course, before automation and mass unemployment tipped the world upside down. Now, anyone with the time and money to actually shop had relocated to the towers, leaving the ground behind for the desperate and destitute to fight over.

Sara checked her watch. Twenty-eight minutes.

"Well, this is just awesome," she muttered, and set off into the shadows.

✳

NOVEMBER 3, 2055, NEW DELHI, INDIA

If Sara had been allowed to use her AR glasses she could have sprinted through the derelict building in minutes. However, no cleaning maid could afford such expensive tech, and that meant she had to rely on her own organic memory. Their computer model was built using the mall's filed plans. It was clean and bright, though, whereas the actual space was covered with stinking garbage, the only light source dripping holes in the ceiling. Somewhere a fire crackled, the air heavy with thick black smoke.

She moved further in, feet crunching over broken glass and drug inhalers. Her walk broke into a slow jog, and then a sprint, exertion just below her cardiac threshold. If she got too out of breath, the pollution could give her a five-minute hacking fit and that was game over.

The entry atrium led into a narrower but taller space. A skylight glimmered four stories overhead, its filthy glass doing nothing to illuminate the area. There were three levels of empty shops either side. Most were boarded up, but every now and again one contained the flicker of fire, people's shadows cast across the walls like wraiths. The unemployed had found this old structure and were burning furniture to keep warm. There were only a few at first, but the deeper she went, the more figures watched her from alcoves and doorways, skeletal bodies huddled inside clothing held together with pins and bandages.

If anyone stepped forward the drone blinded them with bright lights and shouted lethal warnings in a variety of languages. Still, if Sara hung here too long things would turn bad, that much was obvious. So, she kept her head down and moved as fast as she could.

Fifteen minutes.

She ran through another tall atrium space, footfalls loud in the twilight silence, and dodged bottles of urine thrown from above before ducking down a maintenance corridor. Her breathing grew ragged, body strung wire tight with tension. A locked double door blocked the passage, but her swipe card worked, and she pushed through and into the loading dock.

It was wide, easily a thousand feet, with platforms splayed like fingers surrounding truck bays. It was empty apart from one long, silver vessel that gleamed dully in the soft gray twilight. *Cortex Intelligent Machines* was stenciled on its side, and the entire vehicle had the appearance of a weapons system. This was a MiRU she realized: her favorite army-based daytime soap had featured one a while back. MiRU stood for Military Rapid Response and Reprint Unit and was designed exclusively for the Pentagon. How the hell it ended up here she no idea; today's mark had deep connections somewhere, that much was obvious.

Sarah checked her watch: ten minutes.

She sprinted towards the truck, ignoring the hacking cough from her lungs. There was no cabin of course but the vehicle's loading doors had a manual hydraulic lever. She dragged it down, the cold metal clacking in the still quiet, and with a subtle *hisssss* the doors swung open. Freezing air billowed out and she shivered, the atmosphere misting with condensation.

Sarah jumped inside to find a compact fusion reactor next to an organic printer and scanner. The scanner was a newer version than the one SolarMute had access to. If Cortex had changed the mechanical intelligence design and the wafer didn't fit, she was royally screwed.

Sara kneeled by the brass sarcophagus supporting the

scanner's drum, and, no longer bothering to check her watch, swung the backpack to the ground. Sweat dripped from her forehead as she rummaged inside for an electric wrench. Working with frenzied speed she undid the twelve hexagonal bolts securing the mechanical intelligence's logic center. She threw the cover to one side, where it clanged and clattered, and studied its interior.

"Gimme some light." she said, and the drone shone a brilliant white spotlight inside the MI.

The design was an update of what she was used to, with a neater and more compact layout. There was a lot of equipment here she didn't recognize, but the memory array was consistent with the model back in San Francisco. Using special tongs Sara ripped out the uppermost wafer and stuffed it into her backpack's secret compartment. Then she withdrew the reprinted SolarMute circuit and slid it into the empty slot. Next, hands shaking with stress, a panicked sob in her throat, Sara searched her backpack and found the rod-logic cube containing her software hack. She plugged into an open socket on the side of the MI, where it immediately warmed to a point she had to let go and suck her fingers. Good. Heat meant it was working and swapping the original code for hers.

Her watch beeped—*ninety seconds left.*

Sara yanked the memory cube free and threw it into her backpack, then grabbed the side panel and slammed it back into place. She only screwed in the bolts at each corner, leaving the other eight on the ground. No time. She swept them away with her hand, their small silver bodies scattering across the truck bed. She had to hope their target would be too preoccupied to notice them littering the floor.

That done, Sara grabbed her bag and dashed out,

slamming the door closed as she went. Not looking behind, she dove into an adjacent bay and crouched against the wall, heart thudding, hands shaking. Just as she did, the faint scrape of an opening gate broke the quiet.

Sara froze as footsteps entered the dock. Seconds passed, then she inched forward to see a man walking towards the truck. He was tall, ruggedly handsome, and old. He wore a filthy olive bomber jacket covered with pockets, each bulging with objects. Mud-splattered military fatigues were tucked into heavy boots.

He checked behind himself, looked at a small hand-held tablet, then hustled his way to the truck. He pulled the lever, the doors opened, and he stepped inside.

This was it, Sara realized—the entire year came down to this moment. Would he spot the screws and recognize the signs of a hack?

She wouldn't know for at least an hour, of course. If her code worked, it would upload his scraped memories direct to the SolarMute headquarters in San Francisco. Sara waited, breath held, eyes sparkling with oxygen deprivation as a bang and curse came from the truck's inside. He was getting undressed and wouldn't do that if he'd spotted the mess she'd made.

The mechanical grinding noise of the scanner's iris door came next, followed by the hum of the machine's internal stretcher extending. There was a pause, then the stretcher hummed again, and the doors closed. He was inside.

Sara stood, jogged to the truck, and looked in. The man's clothes were scattered all over the floor. Amber lights glowed on the scanner's side, and she placed her hand on its surface to feel the *tak-hum-tak* of proton beams activating. *It's working,* she thought with desperate excitement. Now she had to get out of here.

SIX HOURS LATER, sat on a curb looking at the empty parking lot, her satellite beacon pointing its limp, mirrored dish to the sky, Sara finally admitted to herself she'd been played as much as that old man had.

NOVEMBER 3, 2055, NEW DELHI, INDIA—DECEMBER 27, 2055, SACO DE MAMANGUÁ, BRAZIL

Like any good con, it was obvious in hindsight. If her hack worked, SolarMute had the memory file, and no longer needed her. If it didn't work, she couldn't cut it, and so they also didn't need her.

They had used her like a fuse, separating the mission's criminal activities from those in charge. Max had emptied her bank accounts for good measure, leaving her broke, alone, and half a world away from home.

She sold the security drone for a few thousand dollars, enough for a commercial flight to Asia, and onto a jackal-boat that sneaked her back into California.

Once there, the world's slowest train took her to San Francisco where she boarded the Building 116 ferry. Her filthy maid's uniform and awful body odor created a pocket of space amongst the smart-suited crowd, and she stood at the prow to watch the glass egg emerge through the morning mist. It was cold, but she didn't notice, arms clamped across her chest.

It came as no surprise to find the lab was empty except for some marks on the floor where the scanner had rested. There was nothing else. No note, no messages, no secret packages left behind. Nothing but her silent, ashamed stupidity.

She spent an hour sat staring into the building's atrium, trying to decide what to do, when the police arrived. They came in heavy-handed, the six SWAT guys looking like kids compared to Madam Zhu's ninjas. They roughed her up of course, pushing and shouting, just in case a crying twenty-three-year-old girl presented some form of threat.

Sara couldn't afford a lawyer, so had to rely upon the court approved smart system to outline her limited options. One: tell them everything she knew and submit to memory blocking drugs. Do that and they would let her off with nothing more than a fifty-year expulsion from the United States. Two: tell them nothing and spend a lifetime inside a federal work farm.

So, of course, she told them about Max and Madam Zhu and the guy in the military apparel in India. It didn't amount too much.

Afterwards, they gave her the memory drugs via a series of cranial injections. They'd strapped her to a chair, made her talk about SolarMute, and the medication atrophied the parts of her brain being accessed.

Her previous life faded day by day, until, a month later, she boarded a bus back to Brazil with no idea who or what she'd done for the last year.

Tommy—her old boyfriend—was at the station when she arrived. He looked a child to her now; small and naïve and stupid. Just how she must have appeared to... whomever she met in San Francisco.

Her father welcomed her home with a nod and a cup of terrible coffee. Then she was back in her old bedroom, walls papered with posters of boy bands and fake-handsome actors. There, she opened her sealed US correctional facilities bag to find a little backpack, its *Marigold Services* badge starting to come unstitched on the front.

She gripped it to her chest and cried in small, quiet sobs.

There was something in it still, something square and hard.

It took time to find it, the secret pocket well hidden in a composite pouch designed to absorb and reflect scanning gear. Sara tore it open with a knife and pulled out a thin brass wafer, *Cortex Memory Systems* embossed on one side.

There, alone, and with a hole in her mind, Sara smiled.

"★★★★★ *Rock-solid, jet fueled, sci-fi apocalyptic thrillers.*" Mike S.
"★★★★★ *A full on white knuckle read you won't soon forget!*" Mark N.
"★★★★★ *Sci-fi that is as exhilarating as it is prophetic.*" Nomi A.

Want to know more? The Jim Keen starter library gives you four free books:

Book 1: Pattern*Spec - Hunted cops are dangerous cops. What will win in the end, loyalty or friendship?

Book 2: Contact Binary - The clock is ticking on a man's life...
Book 3: NY2055 - Welcome to New York, a society where losing your job is a death sentence...
Book 4: These Artificial Horizons - They made a murderous compromise. They overcame a lethal enemy. Now can they defeat death itself?

Get your free Jim Keen starter library here: signup. jimkeen.com/thankyou

PICK YOUR POISON

1. Corporations, amirite? Head to "Do-Yeon Performs a Cost-Benefit Analysis on a Career Based on Questionable Activities" by Mark Niemann-Ross

2. More hackers! But also thieves? Head to "Last Chance" by Jessie Kwak

3. Give me more of that twisted future vibe. Turn the page to read "Ion Hunter" by E.L. Strife

ION HUNTER

MEGA-CITY CRIMES STORY

BY E.L. STRIFE

CONTRABAND

I PEDAL MY BIKE FAST, WATCHING THE METER CLIMB to the watts I need to run my microwave and heat my lunch. I can't seem to keep rhythm today as I think over our latest string of unlikely offenders. Mrs. Everson, who ran the bakery, has only ever followed laws. It was the same with the Pastor's son, Ronny, and Nurse Ishan. They all possessed materials on the restricted list. I've known them for years and can't fathom their insubordination. Only criminals peddle toxic batteries. Either there's a sinister plan building underground, or the Ion Hunter's system is broken.

"No machine is more beautiful and precious than the human body," the PEDAL reel scrolls across my iris implants. I grumble as Decker, the spokesperson, grins. I have to stare at his ugly mug every time I get on the bike to eat.

I miss Mrs. Everson's fresh bread. Rehydrated potatoes and soy patties are as delightful as a mouthful of hot mud.

"Your compliance with biomechanical power generation is important." Decker's enhanced eyes shine with mischief and prime augmentation. I'd like to decorate his pristine nose with a bruise or a scar.

Outside my window, my employer, Corrections for Ion Abusers, a division of Power Equality Department for All Lives, shines like a beacon through the rainy night. The latest string of crimes must have detectives working late.

An alert flashes in my eye. NEW ASSIGNMENT: TOVUS, BOUNCER AT DARK LABYRINTH. CRIME: SCAVENGING IN ABANDONED LABORATORY ZONE B.

The microwave dings, and I gladly hop off my bike. As I eat, I look out at the jagged metal landscape and patrol the windows of other apartment buildings. Bright lights at night are usually an indicator of illegal activity.

A picture of Sadi pops up in my eye. Then I hear her voice in my head through my implant. "Razer, where the hell are you? We have a job."

"I'm finishing eating right now," I say, swallowing my last bite.

"Oh, I'm sorry." It's an unspoken courtesy to let people eat. No one benefits from wasted energy.

PEDAL thought they were being creative with their acronym. But I, and everyone else, hate them when I'm hungry.

I put my coat on. The yellow IH symbol lights up on the back. There isn't enough nanothread in the world to run a microwave.

I leave my singleslot apartment and hustle down the stairs. Ten flights take a while. Elevators don't operate anymore. I use the mechanical energy in my movement to power the flexscreen on my sleeve. I swipe through the subject's profile but find no one listed under Informant. No illegal material is listed either.

An investigation then.

At the bottom of the stairs, Sadi steps out of a corner. I see her coming by the yellow glow at her back.

"I didn't see you yesterday," she remarks. Her thick, curly hair is up in a plump black bun. She pulls up her hood as we step out into the rain. It snaps and pops as it lands on our shoulders.

The rain is constant. Buckets fill and spin wheels, slowly turning small generators throughout the city. A few street lights flicker on as the rain grows heavier.

"Made an arrest at the addiction clinic," I say. Mercury and other metals pose hazards PEDAL doesn't want fertile females exposed to. I'll take the risk of cleaning up to protect Sadi. I don't want to raise a family in this world anyway. I lost one to the mines already.

Few people are ever out at night, but a biker passes us, slinging water up from a puddle with his wheels.

I pull up the address for Tovus in my eyes with a single thought. "He's at Violet's club."

"Dark Labyrinth." Sadi nods and fidgets anxiously with the coil of nanorope in her pocket.

We descend into a vacant speakeasy. A door blazes purple ahead of us.

"We're never welcome here," Sadi mutters.

She's extra tense tonight, which makes me curious. "What's gotten into you?"

She grits her teeth as we're about to enter. "Tovus and I went on a date once, a long time ago. I can't afford for that to come out. I can't be implicated, or my brother won't have anyone to help him. He can't wind up the mechanical generator himself, and his income isn't enough for the filters he needs. Daron struggles to breathe at night without it to power his respirator."

"I'd do it. But I don't think you have anything to worry about."

Sadi smiles at me. "Thanks, Razer. I always know I can count on you."

"Sure." I scan every person as we enter the club, my implant programs checking for induced voltage and ionization trails. Bioluminescent algae grows in pools that line the club, filling it with light. It's no wonder people come here at night.

We slip between couples dancing to music that transmits over our implants. I switch it off with a tap to my temple. "Sadi, can I ask you something?"

She leans away from a man in a spiked thong, headbanging to his own tune. "Always."

"Did the last few people we took in strike you as atypical abusers?"

A wildly dancing guy lights up to one side. His movement sends his clothes blazing with colors. It's always easy to tell who is on acid, speed, or has had one too many stimsnacks. I watch the shadows instead.

"What are you thinking?" she asks.

"That someone's blackmailing good people or setting them up to take the fall to cover their tracks. I just don't have concrete evidence yet."

"Gut feeling?"

"Yeah."

"I trust that."

"Can I help you two?" A large, broad-shouldered man

stops us before we get to the center of the club. He's dressed in all black and glares daggers at us.

Sadi looks away, and I know we've found Tovus. She should have let me do this alone.

"What did you collect in the laboratory zone yesterday?" I ask.

His expression doesn't change.

"Someone reported you," Sadi says.

"I didn't go there. I was," he glances at Sadi, "with someone else."

"Who were you with?" Sadi asks.

A girl in a pleather bikini sashays by. She carries a crop and whacks Tovus on the butt. "Me, honey."

"Cut it out, Brandy." Tovus snorts and crosses his arms. "My sister. I pedal so she can focus on feeding her family. Pyvan didn't stick around to raise his kids. No surprise."

Something shiny in his pocket catches my eye. "And that?"

He pats his pocket as if he forgot. "Nanothread patch for my mother."

My data display blinks with a scan that brings up different material. "It's film alright, but it's for batteries."

Sadi charges after Brandy. She returns a short minute later and produces several small square batteries. "Lockers don't lie."

"How'd you get in there?" Tovus waves his hands between us. "Those aren't mine."

"Hunter privileges." Sadi waggles her head and gives him a wink. "Scanners."

Tovus grimaces. "I'm sorry I didn't call after our date, but I swear those aren't mine."

"Sadi and I have more integrity than that." I peel a

collapsed case from my thigh and open it. Sadi sets the batteries and the material from Tovus's pocket inside. I close up the case and strap it to my back.

"I'm pretty forgiving," Sadi says to him. "But I've realized you're just not my type."

"We have to take you in, Tovus," I say. "PEDAL watches everything we do. You can plead your case with the judges."

"As soon as I'm in, I'm as good as dead, guilty or not," he huffs defiantly.

"Save your protests for court." Sadi grabs her rope from her pocket. "And I'm over you ghosting me."

Tovus throws his hands in the air. "You really don't know how they keep the lights on all day, do you? Either of you?"

"Everyone inside PEDAL works at a manual treadmill desk," I explain. "The floors are covered in nanofilm. Everything that moves has piezoelectric converters which take mechanical energy and turn it into electricity."

Tovus turns and runs.

I sigh.

Sadi snaps her rope to life. It illuminates. With one sling, she binds up his ankles. He falls hard.

She smirks. "Been wanting to do that."

Tovus grunts and fights to be free. "We're not the problem! You'll find the eye above the storm if you're honest Hunters. That's your evidence! That's what I was looking for!"

I haul him upright and bind his wrists. The more he fidgets, the tighter the wristlocks grip him. Sadi slaps a vocal neutralizer over his mouth. It latches around his head, silencing him.

Tovus shouts angrily, but all we hear are muffled whispers.

"Stars, I love that device," Sadi remarks as we escort him out of the club.

Deep inside, I wonder if he's right.

EYE OF THE STORM

Tovus glares at me as he's taken away by in-processing officers inside Corrections for Ion Abusers. He gestures a finger toward an eye.

I squint back, stifling the urge to flip him off in return. He's told me where to find evidence. But PEDAL knows now too. They see everything when we're on duty, so I have to do recon undercover if I want answers.

Sadi and I deposit our evidence and leave. We immediately get another target—a teen using a battery-powered screen at school. The informant is a teacher.

The pickup is messy. The parents don't want to let their child go. The teen doesn't understand what he did wrong. It was just a cool toy.

"If we don't take Joules," Sadi says softly, "CoIA will send Enforcers. They aren't as nice."

The mother cries.

The father is pissed. "I'm going to remember your faces."

"I have no doubt you will," I say as we cart Joules down the stairs and out into the streets. We pass a junkie trading batteries for packets of whatever he's on. I stop.

Old Cody sees me. His eyes widen. On a skybridge between buildings, I see another IH team. They pause.

The younger man Old Cody's dealing with bolts down an alley.

"You got him?" I call out.

"Yeah." It sounds like Gibson. He and his partner, Reese, take off after the trader.

I frown and wave Old Cody over. "Come on. You know the drill."

He trembles as I help him up. I bind his wrists. He doesn't fight. He'll be fed and sleep dry tonight.

The entire way back, Cody mutters to himself, unnerving Joules.

I grip Cody's shoulder. "This will be you, kid, if you don't stop peddling contraband."

Tonight, old Cody doesn't just want his drugs or for me to let him go. He talks about the heart, broken hearts, *electric* hearts. He's never struck me as the sentimental type.

Sadi's eyebrows quirk upward. She's surprised too.

When we get to the steps of CoIA, Cody cowers back. "Not the eye. The eye sees everything!"

I take him by the arm and lead him up the steps while fighting a sinking feeling in my gut that I'm sending him to his doom.

Sadi and I get our detainees checked in and turn to leave.

"Hunter Razer," a voice calls out to me from the broad stairs descending to Central Processing. Decker Coult, the CEO of PEDAL, takes every step down with an extra heavy landing. His blue dress shirt and navy tie hint at a shimmer, telling me he has the top-of-the-line nanothread woven into his clothes.

"Yes, sir?"

Sadi stops near the door, waiting for me. We're not supposed to work alone.

Decker leans close. His cologne scent is as heavy as his gait. His eyes are a bright shade of bourbon, and his hair is perfectly combed. "I got the data relay from your iris about Tovus. The board of directors has assigned someone to look into his claims and see if we have a mole in the system."

"Who?"

"Weston and Leanna."

I was hoping to get an answer myself. "Can I help in any way?"

"No. We want to keep this quiet, you know?" He winks at me.

"I understand," I reply apathetically like a trained soldier always does. It's the perfect mask for my disgust.

Sadi was brought into IH because she grew up in the underground. War ended with a neighboring city, and I needed a new job. Decker knows I served on a night-infiltration squad. He's not sending his best team. He's sending his friends.

"I'm glad. Be safe out there." Decker slaps my shoulder. He's the son of a board member and a city council member and thinks everything is easy, even his manipulation.

I turn and walk out.

"What'd he say?" Sadi asks.

I tell her. We have no secrets.

"So they're watching us," she says, giving me a mischievous look as she descends the stone steps. "Guess we better be extra careful on patrol."

Sadi was a rule-breaker before her brother got sick

with a chronic type of metal fume fever, yet I see fire in her eyes tonight.

We patrol the Iron Gardens, a marketplace of craftsmen. I notice etchings on the walls of eyes in rain clouds.

"Creepy, isn't it?" Sadi points to one.

"Like they're always watching." I nod. We leave the marketplace for the restricted mine and laboratory zones. A teen drowned in the water-logged Coult mines last week.

After checking with our contacts in Neon North, a hotspot where patrons can pay or pedal to get laid, we end up in Sadi's old territory. We always run the same path, just like every IH team but at random times to keep abusers guessing.

"I always hate coming here," she says, dropping down a set of stairs. That's a lie. She misses selling tapas with her mother before the gangs took over and ran out every food cart.

I'd give anything for real food again.

The back of my neck prickles. "Then let's come back later."

"Nonsense. We're already here."

The moment we set foot on the dark bottom floor, Sadi slams into me, crushing me against the wall. Breath leaves me. She lurches out into the room again. I hear scuffling and see the light of her jacket dart in and out of the shadows. She's fighting with someone.

"Sadi!" I charge after her.

A body slams into me from the side, and we fall to the concrete. I wriggle an arm free and land a fist in a face. Two more people try to tear my jacket from my shoulders. I free a boot and shove the first guy off of me. Leveraging myself against those who hold my arms, I lean forward. I kick the person on my right, then use my momentum to ram the last man into a pillar. I pull out my magnetic induction flashlight that's charged from our fight and shine it on my attackers. I get faces recorded in a second, then hurry after Sadi. Her attackers are down, but I don't see her or her IH light.

Scanning the facility, I find her near the opposite exit. She's bent over, and her coat's gone.

Panic strikes me when she wilts. I catch her and discover a knife in her back. I memorize the details on the handle, the eye in the cloud with the rain streaks underneath.

Like Tovus said...and Cody who feared the eye.

I bandage her with my shirt. It's the most absorbent thing I have, and it's dry. I put my coat back on.

After an unusually long delay, my facial scans render no database files.

I cover Sadi with my jacket and carry her up the steps. Back on Neon North, I summon a cab. A young man stops. When he sees Sadi, he opens the door and then gestures to an additional bike seat on the back.

I rest Sadi inside and climb on the back. "Nearest hospital. I'll pay twice your rate for extra fast transit."

We pedal hard and get Sadi to the hospital south of the murky river in minutes. A nurse runs out and slows when she sees me. The woman cowers back. "Here on business?"

"Just her," I say. "Stabbed in the back by a gang up north. She has only me and her brother, Daron, who's on a respirator. *No one else.*"

"Yes, sir."

I transfer the cab rider twenty credits. He almost cries. I have no one to spend money on except Sadi and

Daron. I give the nurse a credit chip, one I've kept under my old name. "There's more than enough."

"Yes, Mister..." She reads it and stops.

"Just take care of *Di Di*," I interrupt. Sadi's hand is cool and clammy when I hold it. "Hang in there."

PEDAL only tracks us when our coats are on. Without mine, I'm under the radar. I have to make use of this opportunity born from a solid excuse. I need to know who would hurt Sadi and stop them before they hurt anyone else.

I backtrack to the old food court. The bodies are gone.

Under the faint light of Neon North's streets, I study the knife. The eye in the cloud taunts me. There are no inscriptions.

Craftsman's alley is where I remember seeing eyes etched on city walls. None of the markings I find lead anywhere.

I realize where the doors are when I see a child splash in the draining rainwater. The streaks of rain on the knife weren't that at all but a symbol of a drain grate.

The nearest opening to the storm sewers is a hole in the road near a forbidden zone, and I climb down inside. Wheels of buckets spin under the draining water, keeping the lights on above. Even down here, Mother Nature cries.

I slosh through the tunnels, climbing around small dams and generators. Voices echo from distant chambers. I follow them.

Many passageways later, I discover an internal network of raised channels. Dim lights create blips in the darkness. I quiet my breathing and keep moving.

A guard steps out of a door. Before he can see me and

CoIA knows where I am via his implants, I punch him. He collapses.

I have to move fast before he wakes and sets off an alarm.

Around the junction he guarded, I find medical labs set up inside glass walls. Room after room contains hanging bags, all deep in color with red veins feeding into them. I lean out from the shadows to squint through a window. The bags are filled with organic powerhouses —hearts.

Like Old Cody said.

I continue. Hundreds of hearts fill the dank under-ground beneath PEDAL. *Is this how they're powering the city?*

Voices grow in an adjacent hall. I duck into a dark-ened area under a set of spiral stairs and hold my breath until they've passed.

I hear a shout at the end of the hall and creep toward it. Two men tie a quivering man to a table.

"His adrenaline's spiking. Brain activity has receded. We have to take his heart before his brain shuts it down," a doctor says.

I spin back into the unlit corner of the hall and bump the wall behind me with a hand. A door squeaks open. None of the doctors look up.

Squeezing inside, I shake up and turn on my flash-light. The documents on the desk are of detainees on CoIA letterhead. Some are marked Terminate, while others say Connect to Grid. Tovus is in a pile listed as the latter. I find a picture of the man on the table in the next room as Terminate and Salvage. I snatch up a folder of the files and sneak out.

I can trust only one person with this information, and

he needs to know about Sadi.

I hope she can forgive me.

COGNISYNC

Daron sits cross-legged on the floor of his underground hideout. He maintains a neural internet powered by only minds and an array of hamsters and rats in wheels.

Joi brushes her favorite rat then sets about feeding the first row. I creep around her. She doesn't like Ion Hunters.

Exercise is our power. For those who are sick, it is a curse.

I slip behind a wall but within range to send Daron a notification. One of his eyes opens. He finds me at first glance. The lights in his temple implant darken. He gets up and joins me.

I tell him about the attack, Sadi, Decker, and the heart plant, then hand him the documents. "What do you know?"

His irises illuminate, likely scanning data. His respirator muffles his voice. "There's a rumor that PEDAL abuses their power over the city."

"Funny."

"Not really."

"What do you think Connect to Grid means," I ask.

"Too many ideas." Daron looks away at the door. He wants to see Sadi standing there. I know because I feel the same. "What are you going to do now?"

"Our recent pickups just aren't the type to break the law. They have too much to lose. Even Tovus."

"Then what do these people all have in common?" he asks.

"None of them were sick, no offense."

"Their hearts are strong, you mean. It's no wonder why they never came after me." He lets out an irritated sigh. "How do you want to distribute this information?"

I didn't have much time to think it over, but in studying his radiant iris augmentations, I get an idea. "I want to trade a contact with you. Maybe you can record what I find and tell the people through your darknet."

He cringes. "I don't want your IH shit in my head."

"It's just tech. Sanitize it, and we'll be fine. I'm going to try CoIA records first."

He wrinkles his nose and then motions me into a small room. Daron has me sit in a chair and lean my head back. He plucks my left contact free and sets it on a tray. Daron scans it and hands me another. "This will register as damaged when they scan you upon entry. That way, they don't suspect anything."

He cleans my contact and trades it out with one of his. "Guess I'll pack up the rats and make myself scarce for a while."

"Be careful if you visit Sadi," I say. "They might have eyes on her."

"Yeah."

"I'm sorry."

He shakes his head. "I knew this day would come. People sell out others to get extra rations or permission to salvage in the restricted zones. They're desperate for the supplies PEDAL controls."

"I don't like taking everyone in. But once we're a Hunter, they watch everything. It's why I left my jacket with Sadi. I need to search *off*-grid."

He carries a tiny black bead to me in tweezers. "You need this so we can communicate." He parts the hair on the side of my head and clips it into my implant. The snap is loud and thumps through my brain. A new stream of data scrolls across my working contact.

A message pops up. *Do you see the test?*

He blinks slowly once. I've always admired Mind Breakers.

Yes, I think.

Don't try so hard. I hear him say in my mind.

I roll my shoulders and bring up his screen name in my thoughts. *Okay.*

Better.

Sorry, I'm a bit rusty. It's been a long time since I linked with a squad. I get up and turn to leave.

"Do you want a coat?" he asks. "We have a few extra items. They're hanging up in the back."

I snatch up a long black coat and flip the hood over my head. "Thanks." I hand him a cylinder from my cargo pocket. "Flash grenade. Twist it to mix the chemicals. You'll have three seconds. Just in case."

"Sure could use those hearts at the hospital," he calls after me.

"No shit." I walk out into the rain and zigzag my way back through the city toward PEDAL.

I can't go in the front doors if I want to bring PEDAL down. I need to enter Corrections from the back. I have the clearance, I just never use it. I would go straight to the board, but I'm not sure who's involved with the underground power sourcing and who isn't. I need more proof.

I hope Daron sends word out about what's happening here.

An unused overpass shelters the rear entrance. I wait

until the door opens and someone steps out. I slip inside and dart around the corner where the cameras can't see me.

I sneak to the records room. Again, I hide in the shadows and wait. Detectives are in and out of here all day. I can't use my iris to gain access, or PEDAL will know I'm here.

A man comes by and buzzes himself in. The door always takes forever to close, so I slip in behind him and creep through the rows. I move quickly, searching areas I've not been in before. I know all the others. I uncover a section labeled Storm Sewer Applications. No one's applied to put in a storm sewer in ages. The rush was twenty years ago. Now all people care about are water wheels. I open it and find the names of several board members, but only those who are relatives or friends of the Coults.

Are you seeing this? I ask Daron.

Gotcha. Scanned and uploading now.

The door opens. Two people chat in the hallway outside, their voices fading. I close the files and sneak out of the room just before the door shuts.

A door at the end of the hall, one I've never gone through, taunts me with an unusually bright glow. It accesses the jail.

I wonder how many hearts they're cutting out and if Tovus will be next. Perhaps I'm already too late.

"Hunter Razer."

Lights blaze over my position from behind. I know the beams. They're from the handguns every corrections guard carries. Nine millimeters of gut abrading lead. I've always found it ironic that we cannot possess lead-acid batteries, but lead bullets are permitted.

"Show us your hands."

I lift them slowly.

Two men I don't know shove me forward and through the door. It slams shut behind us.

Doors to surgery rooms fill the hall. I always figured hospitals struggled due to lack of power. When I peek in, I'm confused.

The surgeon puts a new heart inside a patient. I watch it on a screen at the end of the room. In the adjacent room, they prep a man for a lung transplant.

I think of Daron.

Room after room, they heal prisoners. *Prisoners, not the innocent and sick?*

I can't wrap my head around it. We stop at the double doors at the end, where a young man stands beside a podium.

"Name?" he asks.

"Can't you see?" one of the guards stammers.

The young guard looks up. "Hunter Razer? Sir, what are you..."

"He's a criminal, broke into the records room. Get your head screwed on straight, or you'll get hooked up too!"

"Hooked up?" I can't help but ask.

The young guard's face screws up in confusion and shock. "I never thought I'd see you in the fitness center, Razer. Us recruits looked up to you."

I jerk inside the guards' grasp. "I didn't break-in. I just don't have my clearance card on me because we were attacked. My partner was stabbed."

"She was?" a guard taunts.

I recognize his face immediately as one of our attackers. "You son of a..."

The guard slams me against the doors. "Shut up."

"You're making a mistake," I say to the recruit. "I'm an Ion Hunter."

"Just record him and buzz us in already," the other commands the recruit.

The recruit does as he's told.

My guards shove me through the doors. I stop inside. Hundreds of manual treadmills and bikes fill the transparent floors. People in orange jumpsuits run and pedal.

"You only get to ride after you collapse," one guard says. "You ride until your heart rate shifts, and then you sleep for that time combined before it begins again."

Are you seeing this? I ask Daron.

Unfortunately.

I scan every face I pass so Daron can hopefully get facial recognition. We pass two familiar people, Ishan and Joules, among so many others, before my guards shove me onto a vacant treadmill. They tear my coat from my shoulders and chain me to the grab bar with an electric lock.

"Don't look so worried," a passing guard chortles. "When your heart explodes, they'll cart you off to get a new one."

"And if I don't cooperate?" I ask, wondering what kind of threat these people have lived under.

"We put a bullet in you."

"No, you don't," a familiar voice says, a row up and five people to my left. Tovus flips me off again.

"Let me guess," I say as I get the treadmill up to speed. I eye the probes on the batons they carry. "You electrocute us."

"Ah, you remember your training," one remarks. He slaps me hard on the shoulder and saunters off.

"I remember the baton," I mutter. "Being beaten by

five of you."

I pace myself. This is going to be one hell of a marathon. The young man running beside me is thin and built more for this. I'm top-heavy and structured for combat. He's going to outlast me.

He eyes my scars.

"I didn't realize this is where I was sending criminals. If I had known, I would've fought the system," I offer.

"It's not like this everywhere," he says. "I've been caught before in other districts. They just take the materials and kick you out of the district or make you pay for your time by biking at a hospital or something. This is the first district that has put us all in a room like this. I just need to leave the city. Batteries are still legal in others."

"When do you eat?" I ask, realizing the guards never said anything.

"Never." He lifts his shirt and shows me a nutrient pack attached to his body. "You'll get one soon. Usually after the first week or so."

An older man trips and falls on his treadmill. He piles up on it, and it clunks to a stop.

"Cardiac arrest," a guard remarks, looking at a scanner. He releases the lock, grabs the man by the wrist, and drags him off toward surgery.

"How long have you been here?" I ask my running buddy.

"No idea. I came in on a Tuesday in February."

"Three and a half months."

He gasps at this.

I scan the floors, looking for a clock or an identifying screen. All I see are rows of equipment and bundles of cables. Then I see something most can't. I see the ionization, the batteries that PEDAL has stored in an adjacent facility. They blaze in my right eye with their charged status.

They have batteries here. I say to Daron. *They're stored in that room.*

I don't get a response.

Hello?

Sadi's gone, he says.

What do you mean?

She's not at the hospital. The nurse said five men came in, but Sadi didn't leave with them. I'm going to look for her.

As much as I hate the idea of being alone in jail with all the people I put here and then some, I need to know Sadi's safe. *I understand. Just try to get others to help. This isn't right.*

See if you can find a way to free them. I'll get media coverage out. Try to drum up some support from other...

I arch from the fiery fingers crawling through my back which tense every muscle. My face screws up, and I drop to my knees. The treadmill stops. A large hand pulls me backward by my chin. I know this move. They're going to take my contact.

Hard reset! I shout in my thoughts. My iris blinks red, and lines cut through the visual before darkening. A smooth hand opens my eye and pulls free the contact.

I slam my eyes shut and bash my head forward, crushing their hand to the treadmill control panel. The glass contact shatters between their fingers.

"Ah!" Decker yelps.

A fist rockets pain through my cheek. I sway, shake the disorientation away, and get to my feet. I glare down at Decker.

"I have wanted to do that for so long. You're soft. You

don't see the vision of this place." Decker lifts his hands, displaying the facility. "The other Hunters get it. Even Sadi. She led you right into a trap."

"You leave Sadi out of this!" I bark.

"I'll break that spirit." Decker waggles a finger at me, such smug triumph on his face that I'm certain he has a hard-on for making people feel small.

"Glad to have you connected to the grid. You'll give us a little extra light while I take a nice long, hot soak tonight." Decker's guards follow him out.

"See you all in the morning." Decker flips off the main lights, leaving us only a few spotlights.

A woman staggers and falls on her treadmill. She's unhooked by a guard and dragged to a bike. Her legs quiver, and she begs the guard to shoot her. The guard sits her on the seat, then belts her in.

We're more useful alive than dead.

I've got to find us all a way out. The trouble is that we'll all be tired when we run.

Tovus glances back at me. "I told you."

"I didn't know. I'm sorry." I apologize to everyone nearby.

"You're not the first Hunter here," a woman says behind me. "Most of them already know how you feel because they've heard it many times."

"Hunters?" She calls out. "Who do we hunt now?"

"PEDAL!" I count seven fists in the air. They pump once. I hear twenty or so voices shout, "Huah!"

"I'm Aereva," she says. "And one day, we're going to get out of here."

One day.

------✳------

HUNTING

A week passes or more; I don't know. I make friends with other Hunters as much as people with little energy to talk can. It's mostly visual communication, following lines of sight to critical switches, guard posts, and exits.

We're planning a mass exodus. We don't have a plan to deal with the Hunters on the outside who were just like me a week or more ago—unaware. I suggest raiding the Hunter's storage room. It will be us against our own.

I wonder if Sadi is okay and if she betrayed me.

Aereva says Decker lied.

Doubt is a powerful thing.

I run for several hours, bike for more, and rest for half of what they promised. Hunters don't get nutrient packs. We have to deal with eating while we exercise. It's not unfamiliar to me. Small bites of rations over time help sustain performance, but nausea makes me slow down every now and then. I think it's part of their torture.

A guard spins his baton, charging it. He stops beside a Hunter and zaps him. Norwan cries out and stumbles.

I wish the guards picked me more often.

The short guard walks to Lucina. She's petite for a Hunter.

"Hey, mini buns!" I shout.

The guard angrily whips around.

"Yeah, you with the tiny banana." I know it will hurt, but she can't take what I can. I think the short guard harasses her because he's finally bigger than someone else.

When he jabs the electric end into my side, it burns away a little more guilt.

As I get back on my feet, I see a familiar silhouette in

the hallway. Sadi is a comforting sight, even if I'm uncertain of our standing.

"Who's that?" Aereva asks. She's beside me today, one person to the right.

"My partner. Where's yours?"

"On your left."

I glance and note the lean man trudging on beside me. "Got you both?"

"We investigated like you," he says. "I tried to take the fall, but they detained Aereva anyway."

I check the hallway again and see Sadi stop at a window. She rests a hand on the glass and the other on her mouth. I think she's crying.

I don't want Sadi to get stuck in here with us, but our plan to escape has one weakness. The power we generate keeps us in here and tied to the treadmills. All the locks are electric. We can't access the main cutoff switch, and we need a total shut down, a reset.

I direct Sadi to it with my eyes. She looks. After a shallow nod, she disappears.

Days pass, I think. I'm losing weight. My circadian rhythm has gone to shit.

"We tried to all stop running one day," Aereva's partner, Holloy, says. "Guards rushed us. People sprinted out of fear. Flight response, you know."

All I want to know is where Sadi is. I'm starting to think she betrayed me.

The lights go out. The rush of treadmills and bikes quiets.

"What are you waiting for?" Aereva shouts. "Move!"

The cavern thunders with dropped wrist locks and footsteps. We created an exit strategy to keep people in line as they ran for the doors.

"I can't believe it's happening!" Someone voices my feeling.

"We're not out yet," I say. "Stick to the plan."

Tovus joins the Hunters in the stairwell while the others flood out of the doors and take the underground supply tunnel to safety. The Hunter's supply room is first. Tovus is with me.

"I've got Decker," I say.

"Why do you get to hunt him again?" someone asks.

"Because his family owned the mines that killed my family."

We raid the supply room for weapons and gear, then head in separate directions. All of the board members live inside PEDAL. They told the public it was so they could conserve energy by not traveling to work. Now, I know it's because there's extra power here, a power they keep for themselves, power built on the suffering of the strong but the innocent.

We creep to Decker's quarters. With the power out, his door opens with ease. We find an array of lights on in his space. I don't need my contact to know why they operate without movement. The bastard is a hypocrite.

Inside the bathroom, we search. Out of the linen closet comes Decker in only a towel, swinging a baton. I catch it with a hand and punch him in the stomach.

"We should kill him," Tovus says, eyeing a hairdryer cord. The whir of engines outside the window and the flash of lights suggest helihovers land out front. Tovus walks to the window and looks out. "Feds are here."

I hope our district is the only one committing such crimes against innocents. I throw the nearby stack of clothes at Decker, then point the baton at him.

When he's covered his scrawny ass, I drag him down

the stairs. Decker squirms hard and breaks free of my weary grip. Tovus, who's bigger than me, slams him against the wall.

"Don't try to escape again. While Razer has justice in mind, I have vengeance."

Decker swallows hard, then firms up his face. "My father is going to hunt you down. You're all going to pay."

He tosses a flash bomb in the air. I see it, close my eyes and swat it far away from us. Tovus isn't as fast and doubles over at the light.

Decker bolts down a hallway. I follow. He crashes through a kitchen and out the opposite door. He takes a set of stairs, skipping several at a time. He's a damned deer. I'm tired and sluggish. I chase him through a door and slow. Intubated bodies fill steel tables. Cables connect to their brains and their hearts. Tovus stumbles in behind me, out of breath.

Decker sneers from the end of the room. "This is where I should've sent both of you. Guess I don't need these comatose generators anymore." He slams a fist to a button in the dark. Lights blink from green to red. Beeps fill the room.

"They're dying!" Tovus shouts as Decker disappears down the distant hallway.

I toss Tovus my flashlight. "See if you can get them back online. I'm going after him."

Tovus charges to the control station and frantically scans it as I burst through the doorway.

A bullet cuts through my side. Another skims my shoulder. Decker fires from a doorway filled with green light.

I draw my gun and track after him. He leads me

through a sweltering underground pump room. I think I know where he's going.

Decker's silhouette darts across a metal walkway and out a corner exit. I follow, more careful when I peek out. Warm blood runs down my side. I ignore it when I catch him climbing into a storm sewer pipe. I aim and fire.

He curls forward, clutches a leg, and then drags himself into the pipe. Decker's losing blood faster than me. He groans but still maintains that arrogant expression I despise.

I open a sewer hatch above, letting in a glimmer of streetlight then drag him to the ladder. "Climb."

"What if I say no?" he sasses.

I haul him to his feet and nudge the warm end of my barrel into his good leg. "Climb."

He does. I follow him out into the street beside PEDAL.

First responder lights fill the steps and the streets. They wear jackets like Hunters in alternating reds for medics and blues for police. Soldiers are green. Detective lights are white. It's a colorful night, one I haven't seen in a long time.

A detective hustles over, his badge glowing softly on an unusually dry night. He's from the capital district. "Are you Hunter Razer?"

Decker laughs beside me as if he's won.

I glance down at him. He's lost a lot of blood and is likely going into shock. "I am."

"Your partner Sadi contacted me. She said she had information. We had to hire the help of a hacker, Kaisha. I guess she and Sadi know each other. But we managed to cut the power."

"Not all of it," I say. "They have lots of batteries in

there."

"So we are finding out," he says, waving a medic team over. "We'll take it from here. You can rest for the night."

Sadi finds me and runs over from the crowd.

"Tovus is still inside," I say.

She shakes her head. "They found him and the others. He saved a few of the coma patients, but not everyone."

I hang my head. "Why did you leave the hospital?"

"Because I knew what you were doing and the risk it came with."

I sweep a loose curl from her dark eyes. I'm glad she's okay. "Why didn't you tell them about your brother?"

"He's a Mind Breaker who uncovered a flaw in the system and was kicked out of the last district to cover it up. That's why he's a hacker now. He knows Kaisha, the Code Reaper. But I couldn't tell them that."

Sadi hands me my IH jacket.

"We better make sure no one escapes judgment." I shed the one I scrapped from storage.

When Sadi sees my bloodied side, she makes me sit on a bench and calls a medic. There's genuine worry in her eyes. "That's bad, Razer."

"I'll survive. Did you find the five who attacked us?" I ask as the medic cleans the through-and-through and then bandages me up. When he's gone, Sadi leans close to me. "Gibson's team did. Weston and Leanna have been apprehended. Now, there's a rumor of a Deranthi gang up north that's doing something similar to this. I think we need a special task force. Are you interested?"

I ignore my throbbing side and draw her under an arm. "You know it. And there are a few others who will want to join."

Aereva, Holloy, Tovus, and the other Hunters spot us on the bench and head our way.

"Let's start on Monday," I say.

Sadi leans back. "It is Monday."

"Sorry. We lost track of time in there." When the Hunters have gathered around us, we discuss the plan for Deranthi.

"Tomorrow then, we'll purge this district and start a clean IH force," Aereva says. "If you're up for it."

I grin. "I'm always up for a hunt."

Want more of the Mega-City Crimes world? Check out E.L. Strife's newest book: Code Reaper. *And don't miss her free novella and short story, available at elstrife.com/ join-sff-fleet*

Pick Your Poison

1. *Let's get heisting!* Head to "Good as Gold" by Frasier Armitage

2. *Definitely love that thing where solving a mystery is almost worse than not knowing.* Head to "The Crimson Vial" by William Burton McCormick

3. *I've had enough of planetary conspiracies! Get me to space.* Turn the page to read "Ace in the Hole" by Kate Sheeran Swed

ACE IN THE HOLE

AN INTERSTELLAR TRIALS STORY

BY KATE SHEERAN SWED

UNITED FLEET VESSEL (U.F.V.) LYRA

IF YOU WERE TO TELL MY GREAT-GREAT-HOWEVER-many-greats grandparents about the secret poker room on their precious intergenerational-fleet ship, they'd probably kick up their space-blown ashes and come whirling after us.

In fact, I like to think they'd blow the doors open and force the killjoys who voted gambling down a couple years back to see the error of their ways.

As it is, we've got no grandparental ghosts to defend our honor, so we do what any self-respecting card lovers would do: we run the games in the back room of Pozzy's, the best little dive on the ship.

Seeing as most of the law enforcement officers (LEOs for short) have a pinky or two in the games, I'd like to see ship leadership try and shutter the operation, even if they did catch hold of a rumor. I'd never admit this out loud, but some days it feels like the higher-ups are getting bored up there, the way they keep tightening regs on us.

The point is, most of us LEOs helped Pozzy install the false wall in his storage room. I held the drill.

We're not enforcing shit when it comes to Pozzy's, is what I'm saying.

I'm headed through the storeroom now, carrying a tray of poker chips fresh off the 3D printer. My buddy Jack works in the production lab. It's easy to convince him to run off the chips when we need them. I just stand there in the doorway, wearing my best smile—and my zapper—and Jack's happy to oblige. In return, he gets to palm a handful without me breaking his teeth.

The arrangement works in everyone's favor.

Pozzy's storeroom smells like metal, malt, and mulch. The metal because the whole ship smells like metal, so that's inescapable. The malt should be self-explanatory. The mulch is because Pozzy's a genius who trades rum to the farmers so he can spread the stuff on the floor and use it to soak up spills. Prevents slips, trips, and more broken bottles. Out here, lost stock can take a long time to recoup.

Now, the storeroom clerk stops fiddling with the shelves long enough to slip the panel aside for me, and I tip my head in thanks before moving on through. The tray of poker chips makes it a delicate maneuver, but I finagle it, remembering to duck so I don't slam my head on the low doorway. The panel clicks shut behind me.

Here's where I admit it: the Backroom is the best bar on the ship. I still don't see the point in banning cards, but the truth is, the new regulation has provided us with a haven of sorts. There's a bar to the right, where a couple of my LEO buddies are ribbing each other and watching the game unfold. There's a cluster of four patrons on the left, drinking around the single hightop and hoping for a chance to join the next hand. And then there's the game itself, a low round table in the back with a dealer and five players, all eyes focused on the green. My LEO buddy, Ben, stands guard over the game in case of trouble, rare as it is.

The room still smells of metal, malt, and mulch, but with a whiff of greenhouse-mixed perfume, a curl of steam off the dealer's coffee, and a whisper of jazz in the background, though it's barely audible beneath the muted conversation. Add an extra sprig of joy at the furtiveness of it all, and the atmosphere is absolutely electric.

I leave my chips with the dealer, who's got her eye on a squabble across the table. Looks like she can handle it at this point, so I squeeze around to the bar, where Thoreau has already mixed me up a gin and tonic. He's a tall, thin black man with crooked wire-framed glasses and a smile that splits his whole face in half. His real name is Brady, I think. We call him Thoreau because he's always abandoning the conversation to hide behind the taps with his notebook, and occasionally professes outlandishly hopeful statements about life and nature—which, let's be honest, none of us can pretend to know a whole lot about.

Like me, all the LEOs wear their helmets slung back when they're off duty. It's a habit they drilled into us in training. What they're expecting to have happen, I couldn't say. It gives us the look of baby chickens who haven't quite managed to ditch the shell. Only our shells are made of titanium, and they're painted red.

Adam slides my gin and tonic down the bar, show-off that he is, and some of the drink sloshes onto the counter before I can catch the glass. Thoreau rolls his eyes, but there's not a lot to be done about Adam until those genius ship doctors invent a bravado-ectomy.

"Hey, Nurse," he says in greeting, and I toast my

drink in his direction, the glass now wet and slippery from wasted gin. Adam calls me Nurse because of my tendency to—wait for it—nurse a drink all evening. It's an inane joke, so you can see why it never really caught on.

"Hey, *Wes*." Tanya, the other LEO, echoes Thoreau's eye roll and emphasizes my name. No offense to Thoreau or anything, but the eye roll is a lot cuter on Tanya. Not that I'd ever think of mentioning that. She's got her helmet tipped toward her shoulder so her black ponytail trails down her back, fuzzy hair puffing out around her temples. I think she must have come straight from patrol, but it's hard to tell since she's changed into a purple zip-up sweatshirt and flip-flops. I consider teasing her about her temp-regulating technique, but she might take it as an insult, and she's always got my back, so I decide to let it go.

"Jack made up the chips, no problem?" Adam asks, though he must have seen me deliver them. This space might feel like heaven, but it's definitely a cozy one.

"Extra lucky batch," I say.

The argument at the table is escalating into raised voices. One of the guys is a regular; I don't know his name, but I recognize his spark-red hair, and I know he takes the game more seriously than most. The other's a newcomer. He's an older man, balding, with just the slightest stoop to his shoulders. He's gesturing emphatically as the regular spits angry words at him, and it's clear they're talking over one another.

I'm starting to wonder if I should go break it up when the dealer stands; it's a signal, summoning Ben to step out from his LEO guard position to tower beside her. Ben gives the bickering players a warning while the waiting group looks on hopefully in case someone gets kicked out. But the two men settle down, and the game resumes.

Another outburst, and they'll be out of here for a week.

Adam leans on the bar, which is thin enough that his bulky elbow juts out into Thoreau's space. "Good haul this month."

Extra good. We take a cut of the games we staff—Ben's moonlighting as we speak—and I've earned enough extra that I've been able to pay Jack to print up some ancient coin replicas for me. Not that I'm going to tell Adam about my off-duty, off-poker pastimes. 'Nurse' might've flopped with the rest of the LEO crew, but 'Nerd' could easily catch on.

Fleet passengers have all we could want, but bonus tokens are bonus tokens.

"How's your flight course going?" I ask Tanya.

Her green eyes come alive at that, making me really glad I asked. She sits up straighter. "We finished training in the sims, so I finally got to take a shuttle out this week. I got to fly all the way to *Leonis* and back."

"Don't know why you want to be a bus driver," Adam says, giving her this crooked smile that he probably thinks is flirtatious. It looks like a sneer to me. Tanya just gives him that patented eye roll of hers.

I'm about to ask her what it feels like to see the fleet lights from the pilot's seat when the redheaded regular launches himself across the poker table, sending showers of poker chips tinkling against the chairs. Ben lunges for him, but the player wriggles away and locks his fists around his opponent's collar and gives him a good shake.

But see, the closeness of the room means I'm two steps from the fight. And the thing is, LEOs train in extra grav.

On one hand it's senseless; there's next to no crime on the ships. On the other, it means that when I want to move fast in Earth-based grav, I'm nothing short of a goddamn superhero.

I catch the attacker around his waist and haul his sparky head toward my chest with a light headlock. He releases his grip, and the old man scrambles away.

"He was cheating!" Sparky says.

Since he can talk, I figure my pressure's OK. "Ease up," I say.

"I saw him cheat. He's got cards up his sleeve."

Ben's already summoning the old guy, and Adam's muttering expletives about having to move the game if we kick these two out.

The old guy removes his jacket. I realize I was privately rooting for him, which is why I'm extra annoyed to see the series of pockets hidden inside his sleeve.

By now, Sparky's calmed down, so I let him go. Ben's got his wrist cuffs out, and even though Adam and I are equally ranked, the game guard is looking to me for instruction.

"One-week ban," I say, "and the old guy gets searched if he comes back."

"Night in the brig," Adam says, stepping in late. "I saw these two slugging it out in Pozzy's just now. Didn't you guys?"

He looks around for confirmation. Ben's still looking at me. I think Tanya is, too.

I shake my head. "We'll have to move the game if we arrest them. Besides, I think they've learned their lesson. Cheaters get caught, and the ones who catch them should notify the dealer. Table rules. Gentlemen?"

The two men nod, outwardly contrite. I'm sure

they're both still pissed, but they also want to be allowed back.

Adam steps closer to me. Still posturing. The guy would try to out-chest-puff a gorilla. "They're gonna rat out the game either way. Might as well make them pay for it."

He's probably just dying to make it look like they punched each other, too. Sometimes I don't know how this guy got past psych. "We've got video of them both playing," I say. "Besides, if they rat out the game, they lose the game. Right? Now get out of here. Go home and cool off."

The men scurry away before Adam has a chance to say anything. Adam sits back down and takes up his drink, but his smile hasn't returned and I can tell he's still fuming. He's going to make a power play at some point; I can see it on his face. But that's the problem with Adam. He plans everything out, and can't improvise worth a damn. Makes him easy to watch out for.

The dealer lets two new players onto the table, and the game continues with the soft slap of cards on fabric and ice clinking against glass.

"Going soft, Nurse," Adam says.

"That's me," I say, energized enough to risk flashing a wink at Tanya, who rewards me with a little grin of her own. "Nurse Wes the Softie."

I'M up early to stand guard outside the navigation room. It's snooze work for a bunch of reasons, starting with the fact that the hallway to the nav room is the most boring passage on the ship. It's like standing on the inside of a telescope, without the killer view at the end. The corridor is wide, it's made of metal plus metal plus more metal, and there's nothing to do but tap my feet to hear them echo along the plating.

If it weren't for the cameras watching me from twin points on the ceiling, I'd get out my handheld and blast space worms for a while, or practice spotting the difference between ancient American dimes versus nickels versus quarters—which are their own kettle of confusion, because our American-Earthen ancestors really liked to change the look every few years. It's endlessly weird and fascinating.

The thing about snoozy jobs is that it's easy to lose focus, because there's usually nothing to focus *on*.

Gradually though, through my boredom, I become aware of a sound.

The ship has a lot of sounds; in the nav room corridor, it's all about the whirring fans. The rare thump of footsteps down here is so loud and echoey that I'm always prepared for another person's arrival a full sixty seconds before I see them. Even more rarely, the digital hum-and-click of the nav room doors will fire up behind me, and I move aside to let one of the navigators pass.

This sound is a little sizzle, like the flip of a miniature burger. It happens once, a quick fizzing burst. I wait.

Just when I'm starting to think I imagined it, the sound crackles again. I look around, trying to isolate the source. That's when I notice that the red eyes on the cameras have gone black—meaning they've been blinded.

Before I can radio the shift commander with this information, another new sound rings out: a much more alarming thump-and-clang. I whip my head back in time to see a wrench tumble out from the forest of pipes above. I duck, and the wrench glances off my elbow.

My brain barely has time to process the fact that the wrench was meant to hit my head. Fully helmeted, since I'm on duty, but at that speed, the thing still would have knocked me down, if not out.

There's no time to contemplate it. A pair of feet lands behind me, and they must be attached to a person because I'm taking punches before I can spin to face them. When I do, I have to raise my arms in defense.

It's a girl, her hair blonde and choppy and showing a good stretch of dark roots. She launches a fist toward my face—which is protected by a thick plate of plastic, so I'm really helping *her* out when I catch her forearm and twist it behind her back.

"A LEO with bite," she says, her tone dripping with poison. "Who knew those existed?"

She has to have climbed along the ceiling to get to me, which is both impressive and mad. It's a mass of pipes and thick wiring up there, and though I can't spend any energy studying what her route must have been—seeing as she's doing her best to wriggle away—I know that it has to have been a perilous one.

The girl goes limp, surprising me in spite of my vigilance. She slips out of my grasp and bolts for the nav room, extending her arm for the door as if she thinks she can will her way through the locks if she just makes it there.

She doesn't. Like I said before, I move fast. I pin her against the door, wondering if there are any navigators in there and if so, whether they'll stop working long enough to come and see what's going on. I allow myself a brief moment to picture them opening the door in curiosity, just to spill us into the room we're not supposed to enter.

"No one goes into the nav room," I say, unnecessarily. If she's planned this out enough to sneak by me—including her attempt to wrench me to sleep—then I'm not telling her anything she doesn't know. Hell, I've been guarding this door ever since I started in cadets at sixteen, two years ago. I've never even seen what's inside. Mostly, I picture a bunch of people in glasses, squinting at maps and star charts.

The girl doesn't respond. I guess I didn't expect her to. "Are you alone?" I ask. I want to fumble for my wrist cuffs, but it's risky; she's quick.

The girl grins against the metal. She doesn't seem worried, which worries me. "As far as you know, bud."

That's probably a yes.

I'm trained to de-escalate tense situations. This definitely qualifies. "Let's just calm down," I say. "I'm sure we can come up with a reasonable solution."

The reasonable solution, of course, is to clap her in wrist cuffs and turn her over to the authorities.

The girl appears to know this. She tries her going-limp trick again, but this time I'm ready—and the door is fighting on my side, since she's already pinned. Feeling more confident of my hold, I manage to slip my cuffs out of my back pocket. I get one around her right wrist before she surprises me with a well-placed kick between the legs.

I'm wearing a cup. But still.

She spins, and I have just enough brainpower to run a scan on her face from my helmet before she drops to the ground and shimmies around me, running up the wall as if it's covered in handholds instead of sheer metal.

I reach for her leg as my visor screen populates, but

I'm so surprised by the results that my hand barely grazes her heel, and her foot slips past my fingers. The girl scrambles away, disappearing into the mess of wires.

I stare into my visor for a long moment, resisting the urge to knock on the computer unit to get it to work properly. If it's correct, this little incident is about to cost me a pile of paperwork.

My helmet has access to the ship's facial records, to allow law enforcement officers to identify any passenger at any time. Failing that, the helmet moves on to access records for all passengers, across the fifty ships in the fleet. It should know who she is, and where she's from, within a matter of seconds.

But according to my helmet, this girl doesn't exist at all.

THE FACT that a pile of paperwork's not actually done on paper anymore doesn't make it less tedious. By the time I've clicked all the boxes and completed all the 'if no to any of the above, please explains,' it's ten o'clock and my stomach is so empty it's turning sour. I finalize my work by uploading the relevant helmet data, starting a few seconds before the sizzling sound outside the nav room, continuing through my fight with the girl, and finishing with the arrival of a backup unit.

I've got a lot of extraneous data in my helmet that needs dumping—we're always recording, so we end up with a lot of useless material—but I'm too tired to deal with it now. I'll have to do it soon, though. Illicit card games and all.

I'm just getting up from the squeaky office chair I've

called home for the last few hours when the door to the back offices swings open and Chief Johnson marches in. He's a big guy, tall as I am and twice as wide. Hands like baseball mitts. He stops at my desk, eyebrows dipped in concern.

"You all right, Wes?"

"Yes, sir. Just disappointed in myself."

He pats me on the shoulder. You'd expect a gesture like that to smart, coming from a guy as big as him, but the Chief's aware of his size. He keeps the motion light. "Don't be. You did good work today."

The Chief's in a friendly mood, so I say, "The girl, sir. Do you think she's really unregistered? Off the grid?"

Chief Brown considers the question, and I'm afraid he's going to say he needs to wait for the full report before he can make a call. Instead, he says, "Between us, Wes? I think it was a glitch. Never heard of anyone being off the grid before."

I'm not sure this makes me feel better, but there's nothing more to say about it, so I bid the Chief good night.

The ship decks are mostly quiet by now. The few people I do see, I greet by name. There's Taylor, sweeping up outside one of the bigger rec halls and swearing at the bits of dust that slip between floor panels; Eric, beelining for the best cafeteria; Jennifer and Samir, Val and Trent. I know everyone there is to know.

Except, apparently, this mystery girl. What's her plan in the nav room? What could it mean for the ship?

I consider swinging through the Backroom before heading home, but I don't care to deal with Adam's sneery face tonight—especially if he's caught wind of my not-so-stellar performance today. No matter what the Chief says, I screwed up when I let that girl escape.

I take the midship stairs down to the Lonely Hearts Deck and swipe a fingertip to enter my studio.

It's not officially termed the Lonely Hearts Deck, of course. Everyone just calls it that because of the single-person accommodations, and because it's more interesting than "L-Deck, Residential Zone." Some of the other fleet ships have named their decks after authors or explorers or classic movie stars. Here on *Lyra*, we like to keep it boring.

I guess I do, too, because my studio's about simple as they come. I don't keep much in here, because I don't spend much time in here. My printed coins are tucked away in a custom-made set of miniature briefcases, and my uniforms are in stowed in compact dressers.

I don't have knickknacks or family photos, because I never knew my family. Don't feel too bad about that. Way I see it, you can't miss what you never had. The ship has always given me everything I need.

Aside from the coins, which really are a silly indulgence, I had an area rug made a while back, when the Backroom first got going and extra tokens became the norm. I like the splash of crimson against the standard-issue navy, and the soft feel of the threads under my bare feet.

The room's got one porthole looking out on the deck, but I tend to keep the curtains closed. And that's about it. The full tour.

I'm too tired to read even a single coin story before bed, so I slip off my shoes and place my helmet beside the pillow—that's protocol—then flop down on top of the covers without bothering to remove my uniform button-up. My muscles are sore, my head throbbing with a steady rhythm of fatigue.

Which is why I expect to drift off to sleep immediately. Instead, images of my fight with the girl start parading through my brain like they're determined to punish me by keeping me conscious.

If I hadn't flinched, I'd have grabbed her foot. If I'd anticipated that ragdoll move of hers. If I'd asked her name. If, if, if.

I open my eyes to stare into the darkness, frustrated that my mind won't let me rest.

And goddamn if there isn't a ceiling panel shifting, very slowly, out of place.

It moves so silently, I'd never have noticed it if my eyes were closed. I relax my lids, feigning sleep to the best of my ability.

The panel disappears as though lifted by a set of wires, which it very well might be. The space beyond it yawns even darker than my room, where strands of light ebb through the curtains and my device charging station lights up with its series of comforting yellow-and-green blinkies.

I'm making every effort to even out my breathing and remain relaxed, and I'm rewarded by the sight of fingertips wrapping around the edge of one of the remaining tiles. A moment later, the mystery girl's dyed blonde head pokes into the room, and then she's flipping to the floor so silently that I don't hear her land.

The girl stops, presumably to assess. I breathe.

She must be satisfied, because she nods to herself and slips a blade out of her sleeve.

So it's that kind of a visit.

I let her get all the way to the bed, where she positions herself above my head and steadies herself by placing a fist on the pillow beside my ear.

That's when I grab her shoulders and flip us both onto the floor. She lands on her back, attempting to scramble, but I'm on my knees above her head, and even though she's got full kicking range available, I've got the advantage in both size and position.

"Boxers, huh?" she says as she struggles. "Nice."

"Clumsy move," I reply.

"I prefer reckless."

"Synonyms."

"Big word for a jock of a LEO."

I'm barely holding her, and she's barely struggling. "Are you going to tell me why you just tried to assassinate me in my sleep?"

"You saw me," she says. "What was I supposed to do?"

I let go of her, and she scrambles to her feet. Thankfully, she doesn't attack. "You really are off the grid?" I ask.

Her silence answers the question. I can see her scanning for the knife, her gaze flickering between my face and the floor. "It's under the bureau," I tell her.

To her credit, she doesn't look.

"There's really no point in killing me," I say. "The LEO office has the helmet data from our fight. They know you exist."

She glances at my helmet, which got knocked to the floor when I flipped her off the bed. "You can record with that thing? Is it recording now?"

"Of course. But we dump any irrelevant data. The network would get too clogged if we were always synching, so we upload on a case-by-case." She looks dubious, so I say, "*Is* this going to be irrelevant data...?"

"Call me Mia."

"Is that your name, or just what I call you?"

"Why aren't you arresting me, Wes?" she asks, sliding my name in there as if to prove she already knows what she needs to know about who I am. And maybe she does. But she didn't know the helmets could record, which is pretty basic knowledge. That means that there are gaps in whatever education she's cobbled together for herself. I file that fact away, for now.

I shrug. "The brig isn't always the right call."

She narrows her eyes, like I'm trying to trick her into something. I believe she was going to kill me, without hesitation. But I also believe she's starting to be glad she didn't.

"You care about this ship," she says.

It wasn't a question, but she appears to be waiting for confirmation, so I nod. "*Lyra* is family."

It's the truth. Mia must sense that, because she sits down on the edge of my bed and places her hands in her lap as if to telegraph her change in plan. "Good," she says, "because I'm trying to save it."

TEN MINUTES AGO, Mia was ready to take me out. Now, she's got one of my LEO jackets slung over her shoulders, a mug of cocoa cradled between her palms. The fact that she asked for cocoa over tea makes me like her, which should make me nervous but doesn't.

I feel it's important to note that I also took a moment to throw on some pants.

"I would've expected to see a pack of cards around here," she says. "What with all those secret games you're running."

She's cataloguing my stuff shamelessly, which I don't mind. There's so little to see, anyway.

"How long have you been watching me?" I ask.

"A while. Wanted to choose a guard who wouldn't kill me first and ask questions later."

I think of Adam, and I know what she means. He'd consider it a glory move, even if it landed him in questioning for a month.

I'm not sure I like the way she keeps slipping and calling me a guard, though. It makes me think of faceless soldiers who don't ask questions and get shot down in droves by the heroes because they can't aim worth a damn.

"I don't play much," I say. "My poker face is terrible."

Mia smiles, and I can tell she already knows this, too. I don't say anything more about cards, though, because I want her to cut to the chase and fill me in already. I wait for her to start talking.

She seems to sense my impatience. She drops the smile, and I wonder if it was ever real. "Look," she says, "the fleet leaders? They're assembling on *Leonis*. All of them."

This in itself is not particularly notable information. The fleet leaders assemble a lot. They're politicians. It's kind of their whole deal.

"They don't like the way *Lyra* is exercising our free rights," Mia adds.

I guess she means they're assembling without *Lyra's* leadership, then. I frown, wishing I'd made a drink for myself so I'd have something to hold while I consider her words. I love *Lyra*, but I don't love the way the leadership is slowly increasing control over its citizens. The gambling ban is one example, and they recently shut down nonessential off-ship shuttle trips. I even heard some noise about cutting alcohol, too, though that's unlikely to fly.

The point is, it's against the live-for-now philosophy our ancestors launched the fleet with, knowing some of us would live out our entire lives here.

Like I said, it's politics. But maybe a little bit of fleet intervention would be a positive thing.

"Some people would argue that the gambling ban comes pretty close to breaking fleet law," I say, cautious. I don't want Mia to decide I'm not any help to her; if she bolts now, I doubt I'll ever see her again.

"Exactly," she says. "But it's *Lyra's* choice. Which they want to control."

I'm not sure I agree, and I want to ask her why she cares. She lives off the grid. She's not part of ship society, here or anywhere else. What does it matter to her, either way?

"You're pretty loyal to the ship," I say.

"This is bigger than me."

Like so much of what she says, it's not an answer. But before I can continue my line of questioning, a knock sounds at my door.

Mia startles as much as I do. It's just past midnight, which is late for visitors. But the truth of the matter is, I never have visitors, anyway. If I visit with friends, we go out to a bar or hang in their cabins, which are universally larger than mine.

Maybe one of the neighbors heard my tussle with Mia and came to check things out. Seems unlikely, though, since that was a good while ago and we've been quiet since then.

"Stay there," I say, because she looks ready to bolt again.

I open the door a crack, squinting in the suddenly bright light of the Lonely Hearts deck.

It's Tanya. "Wes," she says, and the relief in her voice squeezes my heart. "I heard what happened. Are you OK?"

She's got her hair down, her black locks pulled around one shoulder to make room for her helmet, which is slung to the other side like she can hardly be bothered with it at the moment. I'm not sure I've ever seen her with her hair down. It's thick and shiny, cascading around her neck and past her shoulder.

Tanya heard what happened. She came to check on me.

"The paperwork hurt the most," I say, hoping my voice doesn't sound tense.

Tanya smells like greenhouse flowers and soap. Behind me, Mia is blood and metal. The contrast is so strong, I wonder that Tanya isn't about to detect it herself.

She laughs, and I want to die because Tanya is standing outside my door for the first time ever, and I can't invite her to come in.

"You couldn't sleep either?" she says, gesturing to my clothes.

"Yeah, nav room attacks will do that to a person."

Tanya puts a hand on my arm, and I'm just about to make up a story about why I'm really, *really* sorry I can't invite her to come in when she pulls back sharply, like my arm burned her. "Oh," she says, "I'm so—I'm sorry."

It takes me a full five seconds to realize Mia's sidled up behind me, bangs brushed into her eyes to hide half her face.

She's wearing nothing but my LEO jacket. She's short, so it nearly reaches her knees, but the effect is the effect. Tanya doesn't even hesitate. She just takes off, her face burning red.

"Wait," I say, but she's already gone. Her extra-grav training makes her just as super powered as I am, when she wants to be.

I shut the door. "What the hell was that?"

"I'm not finished talking," Mia says, pulling her pants on and discarding my jacket—under which she is, thankfully, still wearing a tank top. "Who was *that*?"

"No one."

"I know you don't have a girlfriend," she says, like an accusation. "Or a boyfriend, or anyone. Another reason I picked you."

"In case you ended up having to kill me?"

"Something like that."

"Thoughtful."

She's fully dressed again and sitting on my bed, as if the altercation never happened.

"The fleet is on our side," I say, eager to drop the topic of girlfriends. I guess my words sound like an accusation, too; the image of Tanya's mortified face is burning in my stomach. I want to find her, to explain. "You're making too much of this."

Anything I'd tell her would have to be a lie.

I hope Tanya's helmet didn't catch that little scene. If she scans for Mia's identity, she'll be back with reinforcements.

"If they're on our side," Mia says, "why are they so threatened by the fact that *Lyra* has developed a key that would let us separate from the fleet?"

I blink, trying to decide if she really believes this or if she's messing with me. "OK," I say, "I'm trying to listen here. But the solo intergen ships didn't make it ten years before they were destroyed from within, or had to turn around. The fleet means safety. Why would any of us want to separate?"

We all learned about it in school. The United Fleet was only half assembled when *Goliath* came staggering back to the ground, with few survivors to tell a story of mutiny.

And the ones who returned *were* the mutineers.

It happened a second time, when we were underway and still had radio contact. And a third, and a fourth. Even the paired ships struggled. One by one, the voyages failed.

Only the United Fleet, with its live-for-now philosophy and its hundred ships, had any hope of survival.

"That's their story," she says.

It's the truth. It's *documented*. Even if you don't believe it, even if you discount all the future-of-humanity-type reasons to stay—genetic diversity, for example—the fleet provides trade and backups, variety in experiences. The fleet is a protective sphere.

And we're designed to travel together. No ship can alter course dramatically without corresponding alterations on the other ninety-nine ships in the fleet. If I understand what Mia is saying, and if it's true, it means someone's found a way to get around that.

"There are a hundred reasons to stay with the fleet," I say, trying to sound gentle. Instead, I'm pretty sure I just sound scared. "Probably a thousand. I know the ships have our differences, but that's part of the point. Don't like one? Move to another."

Though with the shuttles cut off, *Lyra*'s leadership might be trying to prevent that.

Mia is shaking her head, streaks of blonde snapping

angrily around her cheeks. "You don't get it. There might be a hundred reasons to stay with the fleet, Wes, but there's one really good reason to leave. They want to blow *Lyra* into space. They want to kill us all."

I gape at her, completely incapable of keeping my jaw hinged shut.

I'm not sure how the fleet would manage to blow up *Lyra*, even if they wanted to. We haven't got any guns. I guess they could weaponize pods and slam them into the sides of the ship. Even if that wouldn't blow us up—and I'm no engineer; maybe it could—it would definitely depressurize large portions of the ship.

But that would be a terrible waste of resources they'd have no way of recouping. And if they did do it, the domino effect could potentially impact the entire fleet, even if the catcher shields—designed to protect us from random space debris—were able to activate in time to avoid a hurricane of shrapnel.

The catchers are powerful, but they're not meant to face a storm like that.

All I can do is shake my head. "The fleet is united."

It's an old refrain, one we've all repeated since birth. It feels like ash on my tongue.

Mia gets up, hands shaking. "Believe what you want," she says. "I'm just trying to save everyone. Maybe I should call it a loss and make for *Leonis*. Pray they're not next."

"I want to believe you." I stand back to give her a path to the door if that's what she wants. I'm not going to block her exit, or try to pin her down again. Whoever she is, and for whatever reason, Mia is clearly loyal to *Lyra*.

Even if that's only because she's *on* it, it's enough.

She doesn't move. She's just staring at me with those wide eyes. "What do I have to do to convince you?"

I don't think she can. "I need to find proof."

LYRA'S BUSY TONIGHT, streams of people finishing up their workday shifts and heading toward the cafeterias. The kids have ignited a wild scarf trend. I might call it a scarf war, actually, where the most wildly creative neck-wear wins the admiration of all. Despite Lyra's relatively temperate climate system, the idea's caught on with every age group, and no decoration is off limits. Passing me right now are a dizzying blur of pockets, sparkles, and computer-chip pom poms. Some are knitted, others braided. There's even one with so many ends that it looks more like an octopus than a fashion statement.

There are nearly two thousand souls traveling on *Lyra*. That's a lot of scarves.

It's a lot of responsibility.

I turn away from the cacophony of color and head for the nav room, where I find Ben on duty. It doesn't take long to convince him to let me take over; I've been unable to rest, and I could use something to occupy my time. Besides, there's Thai curry in the cafeteria tonight. Doesn't he want to beg off early? Go watch the Backroom game and relax?

Thankfully, that's exactly what he wants. I offer to call in the change, and Ben takes off with a grateful look on his face.

My run-in with Mia has clearly not made nav room duty any more exciting than it ever was.

When Ben's footsteps recede down the hall, I let myself into the nav room. I'm ready to ask the navigators about the mythical key that would supposedly allow *Lyra* to leave the fleet— with their safety in mind—but the room is empty.

I'm gratified to be able to tell you that the room is very much the way I'd pictured it. It's round and metal and dark. I'd imagined digital maps on a table; instead, there's an enormous chart projected on the floor. Hence the dim lighting, I guess. They've left it set in our current position —that much I can still recognize from school. Default, I guess.

I walk to the center of the room, unsure of what I'm looking for. Not an actual metal key, surely; I doubt there's a single lock on the fleet that opens with one of those, and I don't know how such a thing would be able to reset the flight controls. I'm not even sure why this key would be here, if it does exist, but Mia's been studying this a long longer than I have and this was the room she wanted into.

I do a quick tour of the perimeter, checking for panels. There's one to open the blinds—I don't—and another to operate the map projections. No hidden drawers that I can see, no cracks that shouldn't be there, though I'd be first to admit I'm no expert in secret passages.

But I know someone who is. And—as I somehow knew she would be—she's in the room.

No ceiling entrances this time, no bopping LEOs on the head. Mia waltzes right through the door, though how she got through the key card lock, I couldn't say. She beelines for the projection control panel, where I'm standing, and hits a button to raise a console up through the center of the floor.

"Yes!" I say, "I knew there'd be a table in the middle of the room."

Mia gives me a look like, *Really?*, before stalking to the still-rising table and opening a drawer in the side. She removes something and brings it over to me. It looks like a tiny comb, about the length of my thumb, with tiny digital snail trails etched into the side.

"Happy?" she says.

"This could be anything," I point out. "It could update the coding in a rec-deck Pac-Man game."

Mia stalks back to the controls and punches the button so hard I'm surprised her fist doesn't dent the titanium, or at least send the projections going haywire. Instead, the walls part and space yawns before us, the fleet lights beaming in every direction. From here, they look like stars.

The nearest ship is much, much nearer than it should be. I can make out its outline.

I shouldn't be able to make out its outline.

"That's *Leonis*," Mia says. "They're coming for us, because of that key."

"They wouldn't—"

"It's against regulations to make a change to the foundation of a fleet ship without approval," she says. Her hair is wild, her eyes bloodshot. "They'll see the loss of *Lyra* as a necessary evil to preserve the fleet. They're going to turn us into stardust, Wes."

"With what?" I ask, trying to stay calm. "We don't have guns."

Mia grabs my arm and yanks me in front of the window, gesturing wildly at the approaching *Leonis*. I can't deny that it's getting so close, it's practically looming. "We don't have guns," she says, "but we have asteroid blasters."

My mouth goes numb. Like I could bite my tongue

right now, and it'd bleed but I wouldn't feel a thing because she's right. The ships are equipped with asteroid blasters, in case we encounter unavoidable space debris on our journey. If that happens, we're supposed to try to blow it up and activate the catcher shields.

And *Leonis* is close. It's much, much too close.

Mia wrenches the key out of my fingers. "Flight deck," she says.

We run.

I'VE GOT this image in my head, as we run, of *Leonis* drawing closer, firing up those asteroid blasters as the fleet leaders look on. In my head, they're discussing *Lyra's* demise as a means to an end. An unavoidable loss, to preserve some philosophy our ancestors dreamed up to justify our current situation. As if the ship weren't full of my friends and their card-playing, crazy-scarf-loving souls.

My swipe gets us into the flight deck. There's one pilot on deck at this hour, and he doesn't need to believe our story because Mia clocks him over the head with that wrench of hers—I don't know how, or when, she got it back, but there it is, vibrating in the aftermath of its latest conquest.

I'd usually disagree with the tactic, but there's no time. *Leonis* is unmistakable now, looming after us in the vacuum. I check that he's breathing, then we drag the pilot into the hall and shut the doors.

Mia shoves me into the pilot's seat, which is really one of three seats together at an enormous console. "I don't know how to fly," I say.

"You don't need to fly," she says. "You just need to shoot."

I hesitate. *Leonis* hulks before us, slowly closing the gap. "I don't see charged blasters," I say. It seems like they should be visible, if they're fired up.

"Just shoot them, before they shoot us."

I take a deep breath, and I press the button to activate the blasters. A counter blinks on amid the forest of lights on the console, indicating the asteroid blasters will take five minutes to charge.

When I relay this information to Mia, she bolts out of the seat beside me and starts to pace. Five minutes feels like a very short time to redirect the energy needed for an operation like this. It also feels like a *very* long time right about now, when *Leonis'* blasters could be fully charged and ready.

The lights flicker overhead, just a minute amount, as the ship diverts power.

I'm still looking up when I feel Mia go still.

A second later, the door bangs open, and Adam comes bursting into the room.

With Tanya right behind him.

"What the fuck are you doing, Wes?" Adam says. He dodges Mia and heads straight for me; Mia's forced to stop and engage Tanya. I want to warn Tanya that Mia will fight dirty, but she must already know it because the wrench skitters across the floor a second before Adam launches himself onto the platform and knocks me out of the pilot's chair.

He's on top of me before I can roll into a defensive position, and he's reaching for his stunner. "I told Tanya her helmet must've picked up a bad scan outside your room," he says. "I told her you wouldn't hide away with a wanted citizen."

His faith in me is surprising, if I'm being honest. Unfortunately, I'm not in a position to explain myself. Adam's full weight is compressing my lungs, which makes speaking impossible.

He raises his stun gun toward my neck, and I manage to keep him at bay, barely. He's stronger than I am, which I guess he's always known. "I'm not going to let you sabotage the fleet," he says, through clenched teeth.

With every ounce of muscle I have left, I rock my body forward and slam my head into Adam's.

I'm wearing my helmet. Adam's not.

He loses his grip and falls. I grab the stunner and apply it to his side, and he curls up. Tanya screams his name, but Mia's got her cornered.

I step up to Mia's side as Tanya gets to her feet, blood leaking from her lip. "What are you doing?" she says. "Is that the asteroid blaster?"

"We need to finish her, Wes," Mia says.

Before I can answer, or come up with a solid reason why we shouldn't, the radio crackles into action. "*Leonis* is prepared to make contact for emergency fuel rendezvous," a woman's voice says. "*Lyra*, are you ready?"

There's a long moment of silence. Emergency fuel rendezvous?

"Well, shit," Mia says. I feel her shadow behind me, but Tanya's fast—I always said so—and she shoots out of her corner, stunning my partner in crime so fast that Mia goes down before my thoughts have pulled themselves together.

Emergency fuel rendezvous. Mia's face says it all; she didn't misunderstand this situation at all.

No, Mia's face says that she—or someone she knows—tempted *Leonis* into a trap. And that I'm the one who's about to spring it.

I swear to God, my first thought is *Why me?*

Tanya's already stumbling for the console. There's a bad stitch in my side, and when I look down, there's blood leaking through my uniform jacket. It looks bad, and I don't know how it happened. I guess it doesn't really matter.

"Abort not viable," Tanya reads. "Abort what? Wes?"

The timer is estimating ninety seconds to mandatory discharge. My mind is buzzing.

But I was trained in extra grav. I've got superpowers.

And I know the end of this story.

I grab Tanya, my side smarting hard enough to send the room into a half-black tilt. I pull her off the console and toward Adam's prone form. "Get off the ship," I say. "Take Adam. There's an emergency pod right outside the doors."

"Wes—"

Tanya cuts off, like she's half grasped my plan but wants to be wrong. I wrench my helmet off my head and shove it into her arms, dropping Mia's goddamned key inside. I'm surprised at how worn the helmet looks, compared to her pristine one. The back is all misshapen, I guess from Adam's attempt to bash my head through the floor.

I can't blame him.

I let go of the helmet, and Tanya stares at it like I've just shoved a foreign object into her arms.

"I'll keep audio transmission running until the last moment," I tell her. "I'm still synched up here. This information? It's dangerous. It might be better to let the fleet see me as a villain."

"What—?"

I grab her shoulders. She needs to understand. She needs her training to kick in. Most of what we do is carting drunks away from fights, letting them dry out overnight. But we're trained for this. Tanya knows what to do here. "The blasters are charged," I say. "The energy has to go somewhere."

She's shaking her head, when I need her to nod. The console is erupting with chimes and warning lights. I smell blood, and charred hair. Adam's, I guess. *Leonis* is inquiring about our status, again. "But the passengers," Tanya says. "The civilians."

"There are two hundred *thousand* souls on the fleet," I say. "*Lyra*'s catchers will contain the blast."

"Will they?" Tanya's voice is a squeak.

Lyra's dead center in the fleet. They have to. *Leonis* is close enough that it might sustain some damage, but the rest of the fleet will make it. "There's an emergency pod right outside. Get it outside of the shield range."

Tanya nods, and suddenly her hesitation is gone. She stoops and swings Adam over her shoulders, my helmet dangling from where she's slung it over her arm.

"Don't lose the key," I say.

As the doors close behind her, I catch sight of a strand of a fuchsia scarf, shaken loose from her uniform jacket to mix with the blackness of her hair. It probably smells like greenhouse flowers.

I open my mouth to call something after her, but my breath catches, and then she's gone.

My head is light without my helmet, and my side hurts like the disloyal fucker that it is. My hands stick to the floor as I crawl back to the flight console, wrench my body up the stairs, and climb into the pilot's seat.

There are hundreds of thousands of souls on the fleet.

Humanity itself is on this fleet.

The blinkers on the console are losing their shit. Shaking, I direct the blasters shipward.

"It's too late."

Mia. She's right behind me. I tense, but one look at her face tells me she has no more plans to wrench me. She's just staring out the window, like she knows she can't stop it. "There are keys on every ship. The fleet will fall apart, Wes. They'll just do it to themselves."

"Is there really a key?" I ask. My voice sounds far away. Like it's in pain. "To change course?"

Mia hesitates. "No."

A plot to destroy the fleet, then. *Leonis'* explosion would have done that. With *Lyra*'s shields up, we might have zipped away unharmed.

As it is, I've got the sinking feeling that we're about to start a war. "Why?" I ask.

But there's no time for an explanation. Mia seems to know this, because she doesn't say anything. The blinky lights on the dash are freaking out. *It's hot!* They're screaming. *I don't know if you're aware, but it's really fucking hot!*

I am aware. I can feel the energy beneath my feet, warm and rumbling.

Out the window, off to the right, Tanya's emergency pod zips out of shield range, leaving a trail of fuel in its wake. Like a shooting star.

Against all my inclinations, I take Mia's hand.

And then I light it up.

The events of "Ace in the Hole" do indeed set off a chain reaction with lasting implications for the fleet—and you can read about the impact in the Interstellar Trials, *a new dystopian space opera series. Learn more at KateSheeranSwed.com/interstellar-trials.*

Pick Your Poison

1. *What other mysterious women do you have for me?* Head to "Love & Pickpockets" by R J Theodore

2. *I'm digging the spaceship shenanigans.* Head to "Martian Scuttle" by Andrew Sweet

3. *I'm really craving a detective story with aliens.* Turn the page to read "The Silent Passage" by Patrick Swenson

THE SILENT PASSAGE

A UNION OF WORLDS STORY

BY PATRICK SWENSON

"You have to come and get me," Tem Forno said, his call coming in on my comm card.

"Why's that?" I answered.

"Because I'm scared."

I expanded the flashpaper screen to get a better look at him. The signal was pretty fucked, and I barely made out his leathery head and fur. I couldn't make out the background.

"Helks don't get scared," I said. "Or lonely, if I remember right."

My partner, twice my size, was a Helk, one of two alien species in the Union of Worlds. He'd spent most his life on the planet Helkuntannas, but he lived on Earth now. We'd teamed up after the first Ultra scare. Being Second Clan, he only made small human children run in fear and adults cringe and slink away. Mostly.

"No transport back through the jump slot?" I asked. I'd sent him to the colony world Temonus, one of the Union's most populous planets, on a simple retrieval job. "What happened to your TWT return voucher?"

"No," Forno said, "*seriously*. Crowell, I'm scared. Come *get* me."

That was not like Tem Forno. Something was wrong when he didn't scoff at me or massacre Earth idioms for the fun of it. "Where are you?"

"Temonus."

"Yeah, but—"

"Dave, listen. Just—" He stopped, looked left, then glanced over his shoulder. The image dimmed, then brightened, but the quality didn't improve. "Helk snot. Just—"

The call flickered. "Forno?"

The flashpaper blanked, and a second later I stared through its transparency at my cluttered desk. The call had died. Cursing, I flicked the screen down, then up, as if it would somehow bring Forno back, but nothing else showed on the flashpaper except my user ID in the lower left corner. With a simple hand flip, I disengaged the screen and it disappeared.

A second later a chime announced an unregistered ping on the card. No ID, no reply protocol. An illegal one-way. The message stood out due to its brevity:

Monitor.

Monitor? What the hell did that mean? My gut twisted, because the second Ultra scare had only ended a few months ago. The eight worlds of the Union had survived the attacks from the alien Ultras from their anti-matter universe. Was this something related, or something off the grid?

I had no idea if the ping had come from Forno. I tried a registered ping back to Forno's comm card, but as I suspected, he didn't pick up or respond in any way. One thing was clear: Tem Forno was in trouble, and if truly frightened, the shit was serious. I hadn't known him long, but I was instantly worried. Not even a First Clan Helk—such as deceased interstellar terrorist Terl Plenko—could bring him to ask for this kind of help. He'd even called me by my first name at call's end, and he almost never did that.

I hated space travel, and I'd done too much lately, but Forno was my partner. My comm card didn't have a connection to the DataNet, so I accessed my desk terminal to order up passage via Transworld Transport. I was stunned to find out I couldn't get a seat. Jump-slot travel to Temonus did not require travel visas, unlike Helkuntannas or Ribon, but the slot from Earth to Temonus had closed to all but the highest priority passengers.

Now I knew why Forno couldn't get home. I did *not* know, however, why he'd asked me to go to Temonus if I couldn't get there.

I had to make a run, and I had one sure-fire way to get priority. Well, mostly sure.

⸺✴⸺

"THE ANSWER IS NO, CROWELL."

"Jennifer, why do you always answer your card that way?" I asked.

"I don't always," she said. "Just to you."

"Honored."

NIO Assistant Director Jennifer Lisle stared back at me from the flashpaper, the crystal-clear image a stark contrast to Forno's call. She'd cut her long blonde hair since I'd seen her last. Perhaps because of her promotion. She had helped my old partner Alan Brindos and me during the first Ultra scare, when he and I shut down our private business and contracted with the NIO as borrowed hounds. We'd signed on to help fight the interstellar terrorist group known as The Movement. She'd also played a role in the second Ultra scare.

"What's what, Crowell?" she asked.

"I need to get to Temonus."

"You can't. Jump slot's off limits right now."

"I heard. Why?"

"We don't know yet. No news from Temonus, or Union President Nguyen."

"Forno's missing."

She paused, a small frown on her face. Then she shook her head. "A Helk is too big to go missing."

I explained Forno's call and the unregistered ping afterward. "You're the only one with the required priority."

"Not the only one."

"The only one I know who's a friend."

"Shit, Crowell, don't play that card with me. I've got work to do."

"Like hell you do. The NIO brass farms cases out. Besides, Forno's your friend too."

She nodded. "What's he doing over there?"

"Retrieval. Nothing fancy."

"Despite his underworld past, or *because* of it, Forno knows how things work in the Union better than I do. That Helk's got style."

"And size. And Helk underworld contacts."

She stared at me through the flashpaper. I kept quiet, hoping not to jinx anything; I could tell she was wavering. Finally, with a deep sigh, she nodded.

Now I spoke. "You'll get me a priority visa?"

"Where on Temonus will we find him?" she asked.

"Midwest City. That's where I sent him, anyway."

"Shit. The same place the Ultra thing started."

"The Ultra thing is over." I blinked. "Wait. Did you say 'we'? Where will *we* find him?"

Jennifer Lisle shrugged. "I'm going with you. A visa itself won't do it right now. NIO personnel must accompany you. We're in the dark about what's going on with the slot."

"Really?"

"What're the odds Forno stumbled onto it?"

"If he hit up some underworld folk, then likely. Director Bardsley be okay with you coming?"

"Don't worry about Bardsley. Nothing's going on, I'm bored, and it'll be nice to get back out in the field. Also, it'll be much easier getting your passage squared away."

"I'll take the help. Meet you at the port?"

"No. Get up to Egret Station. It won't take long. I'll send you flight details when I have them and see you there. I want all you have on Forno's retrieval job."

"We'll see about that."

"Crowell—"

I hadn't been part of the NIO for over a year. I didn't answer to them, but I owed Jennifer Lisle for all she'd done during the Ultra scares. She was higher up in the NIO now, and pro-Union.

"I can't promise anything."

WHEN I MET Jennifer Lisle on Egret Station, she had everything in order. She'd commandeered a TWT transport on stand-by. Station officials had held the crew and passengers for hours. The ship was called the *Volantis*. I smiled, remembering the time Brindos and I had come across the ship in different—and dire—circumstances.

Since we were the only passengers—other than the required pilot in the bubble to morph the code to Temonus—we hit the jump slot thirty minutes after I'd arrived on Egret Station.

Once the jump slot spit us out at Solan Station, we shuttled down to Temonus's port, and from there, an aircar ferried us to Midwest City. Our bird's-eye view revealed the scar of the first Ultra conflict: the drag path of the ruined tower of the Transcontinental Conduit through much of East City. The tower itself had been removed, as had the other towers across the Republic of Ghal. Workers from across the Union contracted in a year-long operation to not only pull out this tower from the city but uproot and dispose all the others. Where they all were now, I had no idea, but I suspected a faraway junkyard, or even buried in a massive landfill. No one wanted any reminders of East City's devastation or the dark purpose of the towers, but the still visible drag path— not yet erased or built over—remained a sobering reminder of the whole ordeal.

I tried Forno's comm card several times, but he didn't respond. I felt more and more nervous about his safety.

Jennifer had booked rooms at the Artemis Hotel. The Artemis used to be the Orion Hotel. New corporate owners needed a fresh start and renamed it, but it was the same place, just a little older—I thought I smelled mildew as we walked through the hallways—though more accepting of its diverse clientele. Brindos stayed at this hotel while searching for the terrorist leader Terl Plenko. While there, sabotage took out the Midwest City tower of the Transcontinental Conduit, a weather control device that turned out to be an ingenious alien device for making copies and hybrids from known races in the Union as an advance force for invaders from the neighboring anti-matter universe. Yeah. Complicated.

It was also the hotel Tem Forno had checked into the previous day for this retrieval job. Jennifer played her NIO card to get his room number and key, but we found Forno's room empty. Well, not exactly empty. His luggage was there. *The Midwest City Tribune* flashroll sat on the bed, which didn't look like it'd been slept in.

I checked the luggage, a suitcase almost as big as me, and it was DNA-locked. My finger whispered across the smooth access plate. No access. I didn't think it'd been opened.

Jennifer came back from the bathroom and shook her head. "Nothing. It's like he just dropped off luggage and left."

"I couldn't tell where he was when he sent the ping, but he didn't get snagged here."

"Still think Forno's retrieval job might be related?"

"He was looking for an artifact—one of many we've been collecting—but I'm certain it has nothing to do with what's going on now."

"Could it be in his luggage, already secured?"

"I don't think so." I thought back to the unregistered message I'd received—if it had indeed come from Forno. "He pinged the word 'monitor.'"

She frowned. "Monitor what?"

On the journey here I'd wracked my brain trying to figure out what it meant. "I don't know."

"I doubt we have time to monitor anything."

Then it came to me. *We* weren't supposed to monitor.

There was a place tasked with monitoring MidWest City, and just our luck, it catered to the Helks who lived on Temonus.

"When my old partner was here before," I said, "he met up with a reporter for *Cal Gaz*. You remember. Melok. Just Melok."

"Yeah. The writer of the *Stickman* comic."

"I've got a signed, enhanced flashroll copy of the last issue at home. *Cal Gaz* is a Helk news service. Quite unusual for Melok, a human, to work there in the first place. He got fired when things got hot."

"Okay. And?"

"*Cal Gaz* means *The Monitor*."

Her eyes widened. "I didn't know that."

I nodded, quite sure of my next step. "Let's call Melok."

MELOK DIDN'T WORK at *Cal Gaz*, officially, but he'd gone back to do freelance work for them. I called there, but he worked from home. They gave me his comm card info, and I connected. He answered at once.

"Dave Crowell," he said. "I was expecting your call."

"*Cal Gaz* tell you?"

"No. Forno did. He checked in with me when he arrived in Midwest City. I'm uncertain of the timing, but he was nervous. He said if things went 'tashing brainy,' I might hear from you."

"Fucking mental, is what he meant." Tash was a Helk swear word, and Forno loved to twist Earth idioms.

"Can we talk somewhere?" Melok asked. "Not over the comm."

"Sure. Where? I'm here with Jennifer Lisle. You remember—"

"Alone. East City, near the airport. A place there I like called the Temonus Trolley. It'll be safe to talk."

"Safe as a bug in a rug."

"What?"

"Old saying."

"You and your love of out-of-date things."

"It's called nostalgia."

"Whatever. You'll need a shuttle to get to East City."

"I can do that. I've an expense account." I glanced at Jennifer, and she rolled her eyes.

"Alone," Melok repeated. "Forno's life is at stake." There was a short pause. "If he's still alive." He cut the call without warning.

I told Jennifer Lisle what I'd found out, and that I had to meet Melok alone.

She shook her head. "That's not smart. Not even *remotely* safe. You've no idea what you're heading into."

"The story of my life," I said. "I'll be fine."

Her code card must've pinged because without a word she pulled it from her pocket. I waited while she accessed its screen.

"Fuck," she said. "Looks like you're on your own anyway. No passage at all between here and Earth now."

"*What?*"

"The jump slot's gone dark."

"What does that mean?"

"The slot's out of order. It hasn't happened since the worlds of the Union connected, back in 2040, when the Memors gave us that tech."

I swallowed. "Then we're stuck here?"

"*Everyone's* stuck here. It's not just Temonus to Earth

or Earth to Temonus. No one from any colony can get here, and we can't get to any of them." She sighed and put away her code card. "I'm headed back to Solan Station. See what else I can find out. Go see Melok. Just be careful. You've your blaster?"

"Yeah."

She dug in her pocket and pulled out her code card again, only it wasn't hers. With a glance in my direction, she threw it at me.

"What's this?"

"Your code card. From last time."

The code card was the NIO supertool for communication and DataNet access, including deep basement shit. "You're giving it back?"

"For now. You'll note all the illegal progs you supposedly wiped from it are still on there." She smiled. "We have our ways."

I nodded, feeling sheepish. "Thanks."

"What about your finger capacitors?"

"I haven't charged them for over a year."

"For Christ's sake, Crowell, why do you still have them if you're not going to use them? The removal procedure isn't that difficult."

"That's a good question."

THE TEMONUS TROLLEY WAS BUSY, only a few tables open, and I understood why Melok wanted to meet here. The buzz in the place would make eavesdropping nearly impossible. I immediately liked the place, since it boasted some classic Americana décor, including photos on the walls of New York's Time Square, Chicago's

Comiskey Park, and Seattle's Space Needle, among others.

I spotted Melok at a corner table and he waved me in.

"Melok," I said as I sat down. "Been a while."

He pointed to a holo board menu access and asked, "You want something to eat?"

The smell of classic American food—I recognized the aroma of French fries—was enticing, but I didn't have time. "No, I'm good." I folded my hands on the table. "Forno?"

"Taken right from the street."

"I saw it."

"You did?"

"On my comm card. He told me to come get him. Then he looked away, and a second later, the call ended."

"Nothing else?"

"The last message that led me to you. Monitor."

"Safer than 'Melok,' I guess." He narrowed his eyes. "He's being held by some Helk underworld extremists."

"How do you know this?"

Melok leaned back into the booth cushion. "C'mon, Dave. I work for *Cal Gaz*."

"Freelance."

"Sources are sources, and contacts are contacts. Besides, it's a Helk newspaper. I might be one of a couple human reporters employed there—"

"There's more than one now?"

"—but you know as well as I do the only thing a Helk is afraid of is a higher clan Helk. Or *many* of them."

"So, they're First Clan."

Melok sipped his water, took a cautious look around at the other tables and booths, then leaned close to me. "Not like we haven't had Helk trouble here before."

I knew that. Alan Brindos ran into terrorist leader Terl Plenko, a First Clan Helk, and it brought about my old partner's horrific transformation.

"The Helk district," I said.

Melok nodded.

The Helk settlement predated humans' arrival on Temonus. Helks had settled on the planet decades ahead, but once the Memors introduced jump-slot technology and Helkuntannas joined the Union, the Helks turned over Temonus for human colonization. The aliens were allowed to keep a few settlements. Most of those were phased out until just one district remained.

"They haven't demolished it yet?" I asked. "I heard that was the plan."

"Still there." He pulled out his comm card and pulled up the flashpaper. "Since I have your contact, I'm sending you a name, and directions. You'll know this place."

I nodded. "The Restaurant."

"Yes."

Brindos had stumbled across it searching for authentic Helk cuisine.

After that, all the trouble started.

My code card, synced from my comm card, pinged with Melok's information. "Mard Tesko. Who's he?"

"The Helk who purchased The Restaurant after Plenko went down. He'll be your best bet finding out what happened to Forno."

"You're certain he can help?"

"Nope."

"Will he let me try food in the authentic Helk section?"

"Doubt it."

"I might want to bring back a gabobilek for Jennifer Lisle. She's never had one."

"I hope she likes spicy. They're more potent than the ones the street vendors sell in Midwest City. Have you had one?"

I shook my head.

"Some Temonus whiskey then. The blue poison."

"One step at a time."

I LET Jennifer know my destination, then hailed a ground bus. The Helk district, tacked on to Midwest City's far east end, didn't show up on a map. The bus took me to the city limits, where the architecture changed from stark boxy prefab buildings to the stone and brick dwellings favored by Helks. The only thing missing was a blackrock thoroughfare.

Brindos had mentioned how lonely the place was, and as I walked, I noticed its boarded-up windows and silent unrepaired streets. There were few pedestrians, Helk or human. Streetlights flickered, as if fighting to draw the last allotted power granted to the district. Whatever it might have looked like to Brindos a few years back, it had to be worse now as the old settlement headed toward its eventual assimilation into Midwest City's physical and cultural rhythms.

I couldn't read the wooden sign above the door, but I knew from other sources it translated simply to "The Restaurant." When I entered, I left the quiet street behind and heard the chatter of patrons who sat around a few tables draped with white linen tablecloths and adorned with real candles. Distinctly Helk spices hit me, and I fought the urge to scratch my nose. Thick red carpeting crisscrossed the aisles and Helk waiters lumbered up and down to serve mostly human clientele. Most Helk patrons ate in the restaurant's authentic area.

The maître d', a Second Clan Helk dressed in a white jacket, greeted me without a smile. "Just yourself this evening? I can bring you to a table." He had large eyes, a slim mouth, and chiseled chin. A strange combination.

I shook my head. "I need to speak with Mard Tesko."

The Helk's face showed no emotion. "Mr. Tesko is not in this evening."

"I was told Mr. Tesko was here."

"Whoever told you was wrong."

"The manager then."

"He is currently in the Helk area of our establishment—"

I stepped left and made to go around him. "I'll just find my way there."

He stopped me with a heavy arm. "You're not allowed in there."

Several other Helks closed in, ready to help keep me in line. These Helks didn't wear white jackets, however, and I knew I'd walked into something bad.

"Who are you, sir?" the maître d' asked.

I didn't answer, and the Helk turned away.

The Helk closest to me lay a meaty hand on my shoulder and pointed toward a back hallway. "Perhaps we should all follow him."

He gave a shove that made me stumble. I caught myself and walked after the maître d', two Helks following behind. The hallway took us past restrooms and the kitchen. The hallway turned right. A large wooden door with worn brass push plates was on the left. This must be the Helk side of the restaurant. At the end of the hallway was an exit door.

The maître d' pushed through the heavy wooden door, and we followed. Too late, I noticed there was no restaurant seating here. The low light, tinged with red, revealed a storage room stacked with canisters and boxes.

"*I'm* Mard Tesko," the maître d' said.

I widened my eyes in surprise. "Tesko. I need to talk—"

"Sit." He pointed to one of the cannisters.

I sat, scanning the room the best I could for an escape route.

He held out his hand. "Blaster and comm card please. Slowly."

I groaned. "Is that absolutely necessary? I—"

The other Helks stepped forward, ready to pound me into the floor. No chance against three Helks in this situation, armed or not, so I took the blaster from my coat pocket and handed it to Tesko. He motioned again, and I sighed. I gave him my comm card.

"I have no desire to talk to you," Mard Tesko said. "It's in my best interest, you see." He nodded at the other Helks, turned, and they all left, closing the door. Loud clicks announced they'd locked me in.

"Well, Helk snot," I said.

"Dave, that's *my* line," came a voice from behind me.

I snapped my head up. I heard a shuffling, and when I turned, Tem Forno emerged from a dark corner.

"Took you long enough," Forno said.

I stood. "What the *hell*?"

"I see you met Tesko."

"You want to tell me what's going on?"

Forno shrugged. "You got my message?"

"Yes. Are you in trouble or aren't you?"

"I am. Tesko's not Helk underworld, but he told my captors he'd keep me here under lock and key as requested. They told him to do it or they'd burn down his restaurant. Hurt his family. He had no choice. At least I'm not gagged and tied up."

"They took your weapon and comm card?"

"Yep."

"Lucky for you, I have a spare." From an inside pocket, I pulled out the old code card Jennifer returned to me. "Good thing they didn't do a physical search."

Forno nodded appreciatively. "Jennifer's here?"

"She was but went back up to Solan. Melok says hi, by the way."

"I bet."

"The slot is completely dark, and Temonus is cut off from the entire Union. You know anything about that?"

Forno looked behind him and sat on a few containers stacked high. I would've been hard pressed to climb to the top. "The retrieval."

"It's part of this."

"No."

"Gee, now we're getting somewhere."

"I just happened to get caught up in it while searching."

"Your underworld buddies turned on you."

"The underworld didn't turn on me."

"No?"

"Not the *whole* underworld."

"I feel much better." I imagined dealing with even a couple underworld Helks would be quite unpleasant. The storeroom seemed unbelievably small, and my partner took up a lot of space.

Forno took a deep breath. Luckily, there was still air in the room for me. "They want Midwest City."

"*All* of it? I'm guessing they don't intend to purchase at fair market value."

"They—these unsavory First Clan Helks—want to force Midwest City into a Helk settlement. They're quite adamant about that. It's the opposite of what Temonus wants. The Union's wanted to scrap the Helk district here for years, and it's almost a done deal now. They just need to bring in the wrecking crews. These Helks want to return to the glory years of their early settlements before the colony took shape."

"Mard Tesko really wants to keep his restaurant."

"Like I said, I got wind of this asking around about the retrieval. Heard things I shouldn't have. These Helks set up demands and they've done the unthinkable."

"Shut down the jump slot," I said. "Just how were they able to do that?"

"No clue. Ask Jennifer about it. Also? We should get out of here."

"*So* demanding."

I accessed the code card. My call to Jennifer went through. I took a second to engage the electromagnetic transblocker prog she had graciously left on the code card. I should've done it earlier to make sure no one listened in.

"Crowell," Jennifer said, "where are you?"

"You didn't even say 'The answer is no.' Things are looking up."

"There's a lot of 'no' going on right now, and it's not pretty."

"I'm with Forno, in the Helk district outside Midwest City. He's okay, but we're both locked up."

"Shit."

"Forno told me Helk extremists from the underworld are behind the jump slot going dark. They want to return Midwest City to an all-Helk settlement. What can you tell me?"

"They've dampened the slot's ability to track traffic, and it's shorted out the system on Temonus's end. There are fail-safe inhibitors on at least a dozen slot beams and wheels. The trigger is as thin as flashpaper, but it might be slot resin programmed with a false code."

"They can't remove them?"

"Sure. And blow up the slot and vaporize innocent bystanders."

I swallowed hard. Forno stayed seated on the containers, out of the conversation.

"If you're right about these Helks, we'll get demands soon," she continued, "and they'll hide behind whatever remote trigger they've concocted; that is, if we don't fuck it up here before then. Can you get out of there?"

"I'm working on it."

"Keep me posted," Jennifer said, then terminated the connection.

Forno shrugged. "Well?"

I sighed and held out my hand, palm facing inward. "Just remember, this is a one-time deal. I'm removing them when I get back. I *hate* these things."

"Tash," Forno said. "The old electric handshake."

"Without the handshake."

Before going to see Melok, I'd had ten minutes to utilize a charging unit in a Midwest City Authority building near the hotel. I mentioned Jennifer Lisle's name and showed my investigator license to get access. It was a one-finger model, and I didn't have time to charge both index fingers. I set my finger capacitor on my left hand to charge and slipped the pointer finger into the slot. The readout under my fingernail showed the progress, but I never managed full green, only a bright yellow. Enough for one good kick, and nothing else.

Now I moved to the wooden door and listened. Hearing nothing, I put my hand on the lock mechanism. I spread my fingers enough to cover the lock, then pushed my index finger into the surface. I activated the charge, and a sizzle announced a power surge. The lock grumbled, then blackened.

I checked the door and it clicked. I inched it open and left it ajar.

"Now for my next trick," I said. I accessed the image blender on the code card and flicked it on. The illegal prog went right to work, and since I was carrying the code card, only Forno's facial features changed, mixing with my own. To my eyes, the change on Forno was subtle, but any Helk spotting him in the dim hallway might second guess his identity, seeing a blend of three of us. The subterfuge should give us enough time to slip out the back exit.

Forno pulled himself off the containers and lumbered to the door. "Genius. Should I go first?"

"Yeah. Remember, you're just another employee. If only you had a white tux."

"Maybe I'm the dishwasher."

"I bet they make us humans wash those massive Helk dishes and utensils."

Forno opened the door and walked out confidently. I listened as another Helk said, "I thought the storeroom was locked."

"They were spraying for pests, I think," Forno said, "but it seems the job's about done."

"Did you bus table six?"

"Going to do that next."

Then it was silent but for the other Helk's footsteps toward the main service area.

"Let's go," Forno said, and I entered the hallway.

Empty. We exited out the back door and into the alley behind.

I turned off the image blender as we ran. No one followed. Five minutes later, we stopped and caught our breath. I did, at least. Forno just took up space, waiting.

I called Jennifer. "We're out."

"Can you get up to Solan Station?"

"Will it do any good?"

"No."

I said I'd ping her later, signed off, and glanced at Forno. "You need anything from the hotel?"

"My luggage."

"What's in it?"

"A few backups. A Helk stunner and a blaster just your size."

"Thinking ahead, were you?"

"Someone has to."

"Easier to convince Mard Tesko to give up your scary friends and their fail-safe remote with those backups."

We headed into Midwest City proper to hail a ground car.

At the hotel we grabbed the weapons but left the suitcase. Fifteen minutes later, we entered The Restaurant.

Forno waved the Helk stunner at Mard Tesko, who

looked appalled to see us, and I had the blaster out to discourage other workers.

"I'll take my other weapon back," I said.

When I had it in hand, I pocketed the backup. "We're leaving now, and you're joining us, Mard." I waved my blaster toward the door. I glanced at four Helks who'd crept closer to the front. "No one follows, no one says shit to anyone. With any luck, your boss will be back in time to tally the night receipts."

We put some distance between us and The Restaurant and I told Mard Tesko to take us to the Helks who'd threatened him. "The sooner you do, the more likely you keep your restaurant."

"I don't know where they are."

Forno tsked. "Yes, you do. I might've been blindfolded, but we traveled a good ten minutes from where I was taken, and you were there."

"My family—"

"They don't care about your family," I said. "They don't care about us. They're focused only on getting what they want."

He whined, then closed his eyes. It was unusual to hear a Helk whine. "Plenko's Ghost," he mumbled.

"How many are there?" I asked.

Tesko's body went limp; he was giving in to the pressure. "I saw three. Could be more."

"Weapons?"

"Yes. A few."

"Names?"

"I don't know."

"C'mon, Mard," I said, nudging him with the blaster. "They *knew* you. They knew your restaurant could hold us."

"Or thought it could," Forno added.

Tesko shook his head wearily, then forced out a name. "Jak Vorla. He's the one I knew. Dined at my place often. I didn't hear any other names."

I nodded. "Okay then. It's time to go. Leave the tux jacket. We don't want him to see us coming."

No ground cars worked the Helk district. We walked. Despite his protests, we kept Tesko with us.

Tesko brought us to a building at the outer most edge of the district. Like most buildings here, Jak Vorla's hideout was red brick and gray stone, its windows boarded up. We stared at a single light fixture above the only door. It emitted a weak yellow light. We hid around the corner of an abandoned store across the street. Less obvious than Forno or Tesko, I left them and took a wide tour around the building and found no other entrances.

I didn't like being on the outside of this Helk hideout, looking in. I'd have preferred to hole up somewhere and bring them to us. Our best bet now was to draw them out, and that would be Mard Tesko's job.

At my signal, Forno took off down the crumbling street and tucked in behind a four-foot brick wall on the opposite side of the hideout. Just a wall, the remains of some other building demolished long ago.

I nudged Tesko. "Voice strong," I whispered. He nodded and I reached high enough to stuff the backup blaster behind his back in the elastic of his black trousers.

"What am I going to do with that thing?" he whispered back. "It's too small."

He had a point. "Just keep it. If things get bad, use your pinky finger."

His whisper was harsher. "My *pinky* finger! Not even that—"

"Figure it out. Throw it at someone, club someone."

Tesko sighed, then straightened and walked out into the street. Like all Helks, he had clubbed feet, but Helks could outrun almost anything that talked. When he was near the hideout's door, he looked back, though I knew he couldn't see me in the shadows. Finally, he turned back to the door and cupped his hands around his mouth.

"Jak!" Tesko yelled. "Jak Vorla!" He paused to let those in the building get their bearings. I supposed they were also scrambling for their weapons. "I need to talk to you."

"What about?" The voice was weak inside the building.

"Jak?"

"Yeah. What do you want?"

"I need to talk to you about the Helk you stashed at my place."

Silence. I couldn't see anything. All I could do was watch the door.

"What about him?"

"Can you come out? I don't like yelling at a closed door. Residents will get upset."

"What fucking residents, Mard?" Vorla said. "They've been flushed out. That's the point, isn't it? We're losing our home, and we're not giving in to Temonus, or any other fucking snoops."

"Forno says he was on a job," Mard said. "Not worried about you guys."

"Yeah, I know who he is. Big fucking hero, *and* a snoop. He knows what's up now, and I can't chance—"

"He escaped, Jak."

More silence.

Tesko continued. "I'm sorry, but one of my workers accidentally—"

The door opened. Jak Vorla, a First Clan Helk, stood framed in the giant door frame, and the light from the overhead fixture cast a sickly glow around him. Vorla stepped out, looked left, looked right, then raised his stunner and pointed it at Tesko.

I didn't want to risk Vorla seeing me, so I withdrew all the way behind the corner and listened in.

"Lot of nerve coming here," Vorla said. "You couldn't just ping me?"

"He knows where you are, Jak. I thought he might come back here, and I thought I might catch up to him. Y'know? Put him down before he did anything."

"He did anything, I'd give him something to remember me by. I got him once, I'll get him again. Then I'll show President Nguyen how serious we are, blow the jump slot, and see the Union shrink away. All that silence. Make Temonus our own again. One push of a button, Mard. One. Push."

"I know, Jak. My restaurant, my family—"

"You fuck," Vorla said. His stunner whined. He was going to shoot.

"Vorla!" Forno called out, and I let out a breath, relieved.

"Tashing piece of *shit*," Vorla said. "Forno! Show yourself, hero."

Then it was quiet again. The light from the door fixture revealed a lonely, disintegrating place that wanted to crawl away. I heard the whine of Forno's Helk-sized blaster from further away. I peered around the corner, figuring Vorla's attention had turned Forno's way.

Jak Vorla, then Tem Forno, stepped out where they could see each other, twenty paces apart.

"You've got people who depend on the jump slot," Forno said. "And people's lives are on the line up at Solan worrying over your fail-safe inhibitor. This isn't the way to change things."

"Fuck you, Forno."

Without warning he squeezed off a shot that sailed high and wide of Forno. Mard Tesko dropped to the ground just as Forno took his own shot. Missed on purpose, I knew. Forno ran down the street away from Vorla.

Vorla turned to the Helks who'd crowded around the door. "Watch him!" he yelled, pointing at Tesko, and sprinted after Forno. He reached the corner where Forno had first hid, then crouched and hugged the wall, moving slower.

Three Helks hovered over Tesko. Only one had a weapon that I could see. He had thick blue shorts on and nothing else. His fur was long and matted.

"Get up," Blue Shorts said, waving the stunner.

I aimed my blaster and shot him.

The impact threw him backwards, though only a little. *Damn First Clans.* He dropped to his knees, though, and I fired again. He grunted, then collapsed to the ground. I shifted my aim and shot at a second Helk in a long wispy black jacket. He went down.

The third Helk put up his hands. He wore nothing but a floppy red hat and his—fur. Lucky that Helks' private equipment was retractable and hidden away.

More stunner and blaster fire erupted down the street.
Hang on, Forno.

"Any others in there?" I called out, moving into the
street, blaster leveled at Floppy Hat.

Floppy Hat frowned. "No."

"Check, Tesko."

"Me?"

"Take his stunner and *check*."

Tesko stood and did as he was told. The third Helk
gave it up without a fight.

I glanced at the two fallen Helks. I thought they must
be dead, but I couldn't remember where to check for a
Helk pulse, and there was no time. Down the street, wisps
of stunner beams and concentrated particles of blaster fire
lit up the night. A moment later, I spotted Forno and
Vorla at different corners. They traded shots across the
street, no one with the upper hand, like an old Western
shoot-out. Not that they would know what a shoot-out
was. Or a Western.

Vorla let loose a barrage of stunner fire, and Forno
crept back. He didn't return fire. Vorla kept shooting, and
now, reckless, the Helk came out into the open, the
stunner discharging wildly at Forno's corner.

I turned back to Floppy Hat. "Where's the fail-safe
remote?"

He shook his head.

"Tell me, or you end up like these two."

Tesko came back out and said, "No one else in there."

"I don't have it," Floppy Hat said.

The Helk kept his hands high, thick fingers spread
out. I re-aimed my blaster at his head. "You know who
I am?"

He simply shrugged.

"I killed Terl Plenko. I killed another Plenko copy, even though I didn't want to. It made me sad and angry."

Floppy Hat snorted, but then the light dawned. His eyes went wide. "You're *Crowell.*"

I didn't confirm it. "Where? The remote. *Now.*"

"Jak has it. It's the only one. He paid all our savings for the tech, then he killed the tech guy. He'll fuck up Forno and then *boom.* No jump slot."

I looked back at the shoot-out, and after a few seconds I heard the unmistakable squeal of a Helk stunner, its juice spent. Vorla was empty. Without panic, Vorla walked out into the street, heading toward me.

Forno stepped out and followed. "That's far enough."

Vorla laughed, but he stopped and turned toward Forno. "Can't hear a blaster go empty like you can a stunner, but you stopped shooting a while ago. You're out, too, Forno."

Forno shrugged. "So let's do this right."

Forno threw down his blaster. He moved within an arm's length of Vorla, and they circled each other. The size difference between them was noticeable. Forno, a Second Clan, would have a hard time getting any blows in. Vorla leveled a sweeping right fist at Forno's head, but Forno ducked it. Vorla kept his balance, then ran into Forno, knocking him back. They both fell to the street, and Vorla grunted as the air went out of him.

I left Tesko with Floppy Hat and inched toward them, my blaster at my side. I couldn't chance a shot, but I was worried about Forno. And then there was the device. What if it was accidentally activated?

Forno somehow twisted enough to get Vorla off him, and they both struggled to their feet. Blood streamed down Forno's leathery head. He moved like I'd never seen him move, silently, in a slow circle. Vorla ran at Forno again, but this time Forno's heavy left arm came up and he slammed a fist hard into Vorla's chin. Vorla stumbled. Stepped back. Turned partway around. Then, almost theatrically, he fell to his knees. He draped his hands on his head, then brought them down to his sides, digging them in as if he had a side ache.

I came closer. Forno looked at me and nodded. The blood still ran down his face, and the fur on his chest was red with it.

If I'd been any farther away, I might not have seen the fail-safe remote in Jak Vorla's hand. At some point he'd fished it out. Vorla smiled and raised it so he could see what he was doing.

I fired my blaster once, twice, three times, a steady stream, and Vorla fell and smacked the pavement hard, already dead. Forno looked at Vorla, blinking. He'd not seen what the Helk had raised.

"The remote," I said.

"Good catch."

I picked up Vorla's remote with two fingers. I called Jennifer, told her we were okay, we had the fail-safe remote, and a few underworld Helks were dead in the Helk district.

"I'll alert Midwest City Authority," she said. "You should avoid talking to them."

"We'll leave."

"Bring me the remote. We can reverse engineer what they did, remove the inhibitors, and put the slot back online and get back home. Did you get your artifact?"

"Nope."

I cut the call, returned to Tesko, and took the stunner.

Even on his knees, Floppy Hat still had to look down at me.

"We're leaving," I said. "You might want to clear out before Authority gets here."

The Helk looked surprised, but he stood and didn't take long before trotting away down the broken street and out of sight.

I looked over at Tesko. "No hard feelings. Thanks for the help. But—" I pointed down the street in the opposite direction Floppy Hat had gone. "—I hear your waiters calling you."

He nodded, but said nothing as he walked away.

"How's your head?" I asked Forno.

"It's fine. A little scrape never stopped a Helk."

"You still scared?"

"I was never scared. I just said that to get you off your ass."

I shrugged. "Since we're on Temonus, maybe we should get a bottle of the blue poison. Or do you prefer Helk ale over Temonus whiskey?"

He wobbled his hand back and forth, a very human gesture.

"These were bad Helks," I said. "There's the underworld, but these guys delved well below that."

"They deserved what they got. Sorry we didn't get the artifact."

"That can wait. Better that than the blue poison."

I pocketed the weapons and headed down the dark street in the direction Mard Tesko had gone. Forno followed. It was cold and silent in the Helk district. In the distance, the lights of Midwest City kept us moving in the right direction.

"The Silent Passage" takes place in the Union of Worlds universe. A third novel in the story arc comes out next year. See patrickswenson.net for more information.

Pick Your Poison

1. *Let's blow some shit up.* Head to "Renegade Havoc" by C.E. Clayton

2. *Let's ask too many questions.* Head to "Ion Hunter" by E.L. Strife

3. *You call this a sci-fi crime anthology? Where's the hit man story?* Turn the page to read "Case City Cowboy" by Greg Dragon

CASE CITY COWBOY

A CASE CITY STORY

BY GREG DRAGON

"I AM A WEAPON, NOTHING MORE AND NOTHING less." I recited these words as I sent Omari "Glo" Morrison off on his journey to the next life. The smoking bullet hole in his forehead held my gaze, drawing me deep into its depths. I struggled with the remainder of the words, dishonoring his passing, too out-of-it to realize what I was doing.

In the distance, I could hear my name echoing, a small gruff voice growling at me angrily. "Jackson. Jackie. What's the matter with you? Jackie." Over and over, it kept repeating until I blinked and stood up, holstering my weapon. "I know he was your *migo*, Jackie, but he made his choice," the voice offered softly.

"Glo was alright," I returned. "Can you tell me why it had to be me? Every line on my record is a clean split. You even said so yourself. The directors now consider me a top clip. So, what's the point if I'm still being made to bump off runners? How is me being out here freezing my balls off a reward in any way?"

It was a late night on a Friday in the Nihonmura

district of Case City, and I was with Lucius "Lucky" Liu, my guild's vice president. Glo was my *migo*, one of the guys I had come up with running for the guild. Runners were gophers who did favors for us members with the hope of one day getting a formal invitation to the big leagues.

"Jackie, I told your mother how close you were to Omari, and that you should do it. Figured you wouldn't like waking up to find him on a news feed hanging with his tongue cut out. You wanna be sore about it? Be sore at me, but I wanted you on this, not only to give him a clean exit, but to send a lesson to the runners in our family."

"What lesson?" I asked. Taking a breath and regretting it instantly when the sick, sour stench of the garbage cans near us violated my nostrils. "Talk and we'll send one of our best to take you out?"

"No," Lucky replied patiently. "That Maria Salazar's son will come knocking when they violate our trust. They respect you, and the ones too new to know you fear your reputation. It's not politics, it's justice. You clipping a line is like Maria clipping them directly."

"Because I am her son," I exhaled, understanding the reasoning, though it did nothing for my psyche. "Thing is... I know Glo's *yalma*, and his boys. They won't just go away, Lucky. I will have to lie to their faces for the rest of their lives."

"If it was anyone but you, he would've been tortured," Lucky said. "You shot him like a soldier. Let me remind you, not only was he stealing from us, but he sold us out to the doppies, naming names. He named your mother, Jackson." He paused for effect, letting those words settle in. "He named your mother," he repeated, nearly shouting.

"Well, when you put it that way," I said. "Fuck him."

That made Lucky laugh, and I started laughing as well. It felt amazing to let it out, though nothing about the situation was comical.

Pushing the guilt off to the side, I inhaled the cold night's air. We proceeded to strip and bag him, dumping the body off the pier. "Let's go get a drink, kid," Lucky suggested, walking me back to my Mamba Savant. I called Lucky uncle, but we weren't related. It was a term we used for the ones before us who went out of their way to bring us up.

Lucky was family. He and the guild had raised me. He and my Ma, Maria Salazar, taught me the way of the gun. Whenever I was with my Uncle Lucky, I could expect two constants: a lesson and philosophy. When he got in the roller, he exhaled heavily, removed his hat, and placed it on his knee. "Don't get old, Jackie," he muttered. "The world starts to shrink, and people no longer think they have to fear you."

"With enough uncs, who cares who they fear?" I pulled us out onto Huxley Ave, rolling east until Lucky was ready to tell me where we were going. "I spent my teenage years wanting to be you. Do you know that?"

"You wanted to be Lobo," he countered, laughing. "All of you did, and why the hell not? He had the threads, rides, the girls. That old pimp."

"No, you're wrong, Lucky. Lobo has all that, but that's just flash, I looked to you and Ma for my inspiration, because for the two of you it was always about the uncs. Now, don't get me wrong, I love Lobo, I don't have to tell you. He taught me a lot, lessons I rely on even now. But, I wanted your style. Understated. Rich where it counts, and able to help out whenever my name gets called. I'm glad you're the one straightening me out."

He looked me over and smiled, knowing I was telling him the truth. "I can see the influence," he said, "but you need a tailor. I told you to not just grab the convenient crap off the racks. The way you get after it, you will never be short on uncs. Stop pinching pennies for knockoffs. A Salazar man should look the part, so enough of these cheap, strip-hauler vines." He pointed out a discoloration on my jacket to make his point.

Smiling to myself, I ignored him for a time, watching the crowd of night stalkers on the sidewalks, floating to their intended haunts, draped in brightly colored vines and augments. Behind them, like cardboard cutouts, the dilapidated skeletons of old buildings sat below brightly lit street signs. Advertisements and store names—half of them in disrepair—added to the noise, making rolling through the city a miserable affair.

When I reached for the stereo to break the silence, Lucky exhaled heavily, letting me know he wanted to talk. Something was obviously on his mind. I turned it on anyway, and "Blood on Chrome Frets" by Black Dante and the Nuclear Fallout Family flooded the cockpit with violent chords. Every clipper loved that song. It could have been our anthem. The lyrics were realistic, the tune was catchy, and Black Dante's voice was ice cold.

It inspired across generations, evidenced by Lucky not asking me to turn it off. Knowing something was on his mind, I turned it down enough for us to chat, but where I could still hear it over the thrumming of the rain-drops, shouts, and horns from the busy strip.

"Jackie, I have a confession," he began, reaching over to lower the volume more. I let him do it, puzzling over what it was he would tell me and whether or not it would add to my stress. "There's a reason I came out with you tonight. I said it was to catch up, but I have a personal line to clip and needed backup."

"Does Ma know?" I asked.

"She knows I intend to set this right, but she doesn't know I'm having you and Tabbi help me. That's if you agree, kid. I wouldn't spring this on you unless I was desperate."

Shaking my head, a cruel smile took to my face. The *Bliss* was in my blood, and I found it comical that the drive I expected to end in rest and recovery was now a transition to an off-the-books job. If the clip wasn't contracted, which wasn't likely, he was asking me to help him murder a civilian. I hoped I was mistaken, so I decided to ask.

"This an outsider you're asking me to clip, Lucky?"

"Not you, me," he clarified quickly. "I need you to watch my six."

"Alright," I shrugged, satisfied with that answer. "Who and when?"

"An old clipper I ran with, back in the high times when it was little more than me, Lobo, and your mother, getting into all kinds of hell. Knew him as Gage back then, Gage Rahman, but he changed his name to Null Resistor later, when he started to get a rep."

"Null Resistor's an icy nickname," I said. "Can I have it after we clip him?"

Lucky stifled a laugh. "I don't think you would want it, if you knew the history of this glitch. I know this comes out of nowhere, but I heard from Tabbi, last night that he had moved back here to Case City. When I brought you the Omari job, I wanted to ask then, but things got moving fast, and... look, if it were up to me, I would choose another night when we weren't already on guild business."

"Geez," I exhaled. "He must have really pissed you off for you to have Tabitha Winter tracking him."

"Hasn't been cheap, let me tell you," he complained.

"Well," I said. "The night is still young, and there's a drink with my name somewhere waiting, and something silky for me to proposition as well. This clipper likes to get wet on both ends after a job, and so far, the only soaking we've got is from the foul Case City rain. I don't get you sometimes, Lucky. You ask me for anything if it's business, but let it be personal, and you tiptoe around. You already know I won't say no. A little background couldn't hurt, though. Maybe if you make me understand, I could do more than show up to watch your back. What's this guy done for you to be out here with me in your 1,000 unc stompers?"

"It's hard for me, Jackie. I can count the number of people I trust on this one gnarly hand," he said, raising his well-manicured mitt, which was anything but gnarly. Lucky had been a playboy for as long as I knew him, and the only hard work those hands performed was squeezing triggers and the supple form of his mistresses, which were too many to count.

"Which one of those fingers am I? The trigger finger?" I laughed, smiling at my cleverness since the *Bliss* had me drifting like a weightless cloud over the rain-soaked streets of the strip.

"No, you're the thumb. A pain in the ass," he growled. "Null's a seasoned clip who doesn't know I'm after him, but if he finds out, he'll be in the wind. I don't have the time to put it through the whole process, selling it to a handler and all of that workaround. Maria only agreed to let me do this if I kept it outside the guild. So, you gonna help me or what?"

"Just lay it on me," I bade him. We were past downtown and rolling unobstructed, the only breaks now being the occasional stoplight and zoned-out dozer, stumbling out into the street. This happened twice while we were rolling. That's how common an occurrence it was in my city. It didn't bother me. The Mamba Savant, like most rollers, had sensors that would steer it clear of colliding with anyone chipped. Still, I could never got used to seeing them playing chicken in oncoming traffic.

"Null was with our old crew, until the untimely demise of Benny the Cowboy. Benny was to me what I am to you, Jackie. He taught me how to clip. More importantly, he taught me how to be a soldier. The things he showed me as a kid got me through the war and allowed me to come home alive with my senses. I owed him everything. Null Resistor, we later found out, clipped his line and made it look like an accident. DPS detectives gave us the hint, but by then he was long gone."

"How long ago did all this happen?" I asked, realizing now why he had me here. He wouldn't admit to it, but Lucky was big on codes and rituals. Since Benny had been his teacher, me being his progeny of murder meant that, in some part, getting to Null was my responsibility as well.

"Too long to count, but we were about your age, 28 or so. It doesn't matter. What does matter is that we've been waiting for this guy to show his face forever. Jackson, I will not allow him to get one night's sleep in my city."

"Roger that, Lieutenant," I said. "So, where to?"

"I was a Sergeant, get it right, you bum. See how you

like being pressed into the Army and made to clip for no uncs or reputation."

"No offense," I said quickly, not wanting to hear the old veteran go off on one of his tangents. The fact that he was grouchy told me this Null Resistor thing had him out of sorts. Lucky was typically the adult in the room when it came to the triad of him, my mother, and Lobo Nieves. Nothing shook him, so seeing him this salty let me know how much this meant to him. How could I say no?

"I don't care how seasoned this Null Resistor is, Lucky. If you say he's gone, he's gone," I promised.

ONE THING LUCKY, in all his wisdom, never warned me about was how different I'd feel after a certain age. Everyone I'd known with a reputation had to play in the fire, and it burned us all, not physically, but in the form of silent tears in the darkness. In this life, we were all insane in some way, and to me, Lucky was the best example of what I could hope to become on the far side of success.

I didn't see my world as flawed, or a mistake. Post-apocalyptic is the term I often saw used to describe us, but isn't that subjective? Hasn't there been a form of apocalypse during every generation's existence? We've been post-apocalyptic from the moment the first glitch drew in breath. We've had diseases, plagues, and natural disasters, not to mention all the world wars, the space race, and the expanse.

From the beginning of time, there has always been something aiming to end us, most of them something we built ourselves. Every day when I looked outside my windows, I saw our broken atmosphere and pollution reflected in the mustard-colored fog. I saw our ingenuity in the purifiers, allowing us to live despite the environment. I saw ambitious hawks like myself, and I saw people doing what needed doing to care for the ones they loved.

"Warfare is about illusion, Jackie," Lucky was saying as we leaned against the stone balcony of the Zalem mega-complex, ten floors up, scoping out our target. "You need to see past the obvious, and pay attention to the details. What do we have here? An old clipper, gussied up like a mangy old wolf trying to blend with the hounds."

We had eyes on Null Resistor, who, to my surprise, was built like a high-end utility roller with beefy traps and seamless augments below his skin. His biceps were the size of most men's thighs. Bruiser's bulk aside, he dressed the part of a clocker in a collared shirt and tie combination beneath an icy black raincoat. Zhurov tacticals on his clean-shaven face, signaling wealth to the initiated. He walked stiffly, hinting at an injury left untreated, but I suspected it was from a shotgun strapped to a leg below his coat.

"So, what is our move?" I asked, standing up to wipe the rain from my face.

"Now, we go have a drink with Null. I'll introduce you, and then the two of us will catch up a little and reminisce on the good old days. He's got a weakness for the silk, so maybe we get ourselves an XPerience. Either way, when he's good and comfortable, I'll do my thing, and we can inform your mother that we finally tied up that last loose end."

"Good enough for me," I replied. "Now let's get to it."

The stairs down seemed to go on forever, but eventually, they spilled us out onto the sidewalk. Lucky started for Null, and I fell in quickly behind him, matching his steps. All around us were street people, hustlers, clockers, and escorts of the finer variety. Everyone walked with purpose to their chosen drink holes, or corners to start the night's activities.

"Really Jackie, the intent wasn't to force you with the Omari thing," Lucky started explaining again.

"I don't need to hear that name again tonight, if you don't mind, Lucky. My mind's on booze, *Bliss*, and sleep. Right after you blacken your soul further with me as witness, I mean. After that I'm getting wet, and I probably won't wake up until noon. I'm not planning on answering any calls. Not from you, Lobo, or Ma. That's all. I think you all owe me this little break, right? So, yeah, let's get to it then."

"You're the loudest quiet guy I've ever met, you know that?" Lucky groused. "You have a way you make words sting, and I don't like it."

I shut my mouth, letting him get in the last word, though I had much more to unload if he wasn't so sensitive. "How many kids do you think you have out there in the wild?" I asked after a few minutes of silence.

"Are you serious?" he barked, and I started laughing. "Now I know you're just being a glitch."

"You took me to my first XPerience booth, do you remember that?" I said.

"And you never ran and told Maria. You were a good kid, Jackie. Never thought you'd grow up to be such a sarcastic ass, but you've always been loyal, and reliable. Hold that thought."

We were close enough to Null to touch him, and Lucky stepped in front of me to approach the man. "Department of Security," he announced himself. "Get down on the ground, you pretty, juiced-up glitch."

"Lucky Liu?" The big man looked as if he'd seen a ghost, but his surprise only lasted a second before he seemed genuinely excited to see his old friend. "Where have you been, *migo*? You still running with any of the old crew? Lobo, Cowboy, or Spider Salazar?"

"I should be asking you, Gage," Lucky said.

"Hey Luck, Gage is done now, I make my uncs under Null Resistor. I traded in clips for bounties." He shot me a glance, sizing me up in less than a second.

Up close, Null Resistor looked even more intimidating. His augmented arms looked ready to split the seams of his coat, and his face, too, was modded, I could tell from the graft lines on his skin. Lucky's warnings of him being a wolf played back through my mind as I sized him up, thinking of what it would take to defeat this monster in a scrap.

"Yeah, and I can see business is booming," Lucky said. "You here for one of us? If so, I'll pay you double to tear up the contract." That got them both laughing. "Maria's going to flip learning you're back in town. It's been a lifetime, *migo*. How've you been?"

"On the run for the most part, Lucky. It's why I couldn't tell any of you where I was going, or where I was, all these years. DPS was on me hard for a robbery I had nothing to do with, so I took my chances in the wind. Came back when I heard the doppies moved on from it. Man, this is a stroke of good luck, me running into you. I see you're still primped and strapped. Who's the young bull?"

"This is Jackie, a keen edge," Lucky introduced me, using code to let him know I, too, was affiliated. "Jackson, meet a real street professional, Null Resistor."

"Pleasure," I lied, and the silver-haired bruiser

showed me his teeth. It was hard not to like this man. He looked like someone who had not only survived our life but thrived, taking time to enjoy the bonuses. His natural tan spoke of time on the shores, which brought to mind Lucky's tale of how he skipped town, likely to a private beach where he could safely brave the sun without worry for his enemies. His augments alone were worth a fortune, and the tailored suit fit his complicated physique well.

"Hey," Lucky said. "You busy right now? I mean other than holding your dick in the rain. Me and the kid here were on our way to Purge, to get our throats wet. You could come with, and we can catch up. You can order one of those fruity drinks you loved so much back in the day."

"Fruity drinks," Null repeated. "You don't forget much, do you? I could use a drink. How's the clientele at Purge?"

"Sweet and silky, the way we like it," Lucky offered. "It's also right up the street, so we can hoof it."

We hit the pavement, stacked, with Lucky and Null abreast, while I fell in behind them, eying the nightlife as we swam past silky escorts, chromed-out runners, cyborgs, and the occasional square. The rain let up, but it was still foggy, making it difficult to see beyond 30 yards. Lucky and Null were catching up, and I watched them intently. Lucky had his instincts and experience, but you could never trust a cyborg. With all of the augments stressing their neuro-chips, they were prone to violent fits of rage.

Null had said he was a bounty hunter, which meant he had some detective skills. Being a clipper before that had made him proficient in the art of butchery. A deadly combination, and if he sniffed out my uncle leading him into a trap, it would have been up to me to put him down before it was too late. The *Bliss* had me laser-focused on the back of his skull, imagining the things I could do to him once Lucky put me in play.

This wasn't how I always thought. It was a necessary part of preparing myself to act in uncertain situations like this. There was a time during our walk and talk when I relaxed and allowed regular me to see them not as my uncle and his mark but as two clippers in their prime. Seeing Null and Lucky together, laughing and having a good time, dripping like mega-complex moguls, made me see them as giants in this instance. They were two outlaws from the Case City strip, with no concern for their enemies or DPS. Something about that drew me to them.

I thought I was doing it in my collared shirt and slacks, but it was a pale imitation of their threads. Clipping would be a means to get to where they were, and I relished the thought of having the uncs to afford their quality gear. "Oh," Lucky suddenly exclaimed. "Hard to believe you don't know about Maria."

They were speaking so loudly you would have thought we were alone and not on a 4th Street sidewalk, wading through a menagerie of night dwellers, heading toward downtown.

"Brother, I haven't seen Spider Salazar in forever. Why would I look her up?" he tried.

"You're a bounty hunter, come on," Lucky gestured wildly. "You would have done your research before coming out here to make sure you had no enemies. That's if you weren't keeping up with the Case City coalition of guilds. You know who we work for, but I think you're jerking me around because you feel bad for leaving."

"You got me," Null admitted, laughing. "Oh, you mean like calling me Gage when you knew my name was

Null, *migo*? You think I went off somewhere and got stupid. It's the name tied to my reputation, and I know you've heard of me. If not, peep my bounty record when you get a chance. That goes for you too, Jackie. See there's other work for us outside clipping. It's public on the Meta Net. I think even you'd be impressed." He clapped Lucky on the shoulder. "You still toting that Juggernaut Judgment?"

"Does gumbo have shrimp?" Lucky said, throwing back his coat to flash the grip on his J2 cannon to show he had it.

I would have liked Null in any other situation, and it made sense since he ran with my mother's old unit. Everyone from that era was effortlessly cool, which didn't translate to my generation. Out of habit, I scanned the skies for snooping DPS drones, thinking how unlucky it would be if Null turned out to be working for the government. I thought to warn my uncle off but decided against it. Without hard evidence, he wouldn't entertain the thought.

I thought it ironic that Null Resistor's name was slang for "one who avoids death," which could either mean a champion or a coward, depending on your thinking. The man had killed one of his guild brothers and skipped town, only to name himself Null Resistor. It was just too perfect. *After tonight, you'll just be Null*, I thought, studying my uncle, wondering how he managed to keep it together so well.

❋

PURGE WAS a speakeasy run out of the back of a cyber clinic, though if you were a patient, you wouldn't know it was back there. One owner, two different businesses, separated by a single door that remained closed. To get to Purge, you had to brave the alleys, where the *Bliss* burnouts we called dozers lumbered about. Everywhere in Case, there were these back-alley businesses. Most were fronts, but some were squatters using the free space to sell street food or brain candy.

I had never seen the clinic, never had to be on that side where the law-abiding clockers lived. Alleys and the losers that haunt them were nothing new to a clipper, and they knew to steer clear of us. We were all bearing cannons, and Null was a mechanical gorilla hopped up on hormones, so no one even looked our way as we entered.

On our left were the back doors to the row of businesses on the first floor of the Aphid Aria Complex, and on our right, a ten-foot wall separating the property from the street. At the door, posted up, was Sheena Ventura, a runner I knew from the neighborhood. Sheena wasn't your typical fetch-it girl. She was a Medina hand-cannon in human form. Tiny, compact, and capable of getting the drop on anyone napping.

She was chatting with a pair of cyborg bruisers in scavenged mods, obvious from the discoloration where the augments broke through the skin. It was disgusting to look at but functional, for only a quarter the price of genuine gear. They studied our faces, showing respect to Lucky and Null, but the younger one stepped forward to pointedly ask me for my weapons. "Can't let you in with that after last time, Jackson. No disrespect," he tried, and though Lucky urged me to play along, I just couldn't. For some reason, despite him complying with the bouncer, I didn't want to hand this man my weapon.

"How about I just go in, and I make you take my gun,"

I said. "No one touches this weapon but me, and I've been inside before with worse. What? All of a sudden you glitches have protocol?"

Lucky gripped my arm and stepped in close where I could hear him over the thundering bass and shrill guitars coming through the door. "Hold on to your pistol, kid. It's alright. We're going to go catch up, so take it easy. I know you're hurting, and you want to bash heads, but now isn't the time."

"Hey Jackie," Sheena called, and I looked past Lucky and Null's giant noggin to see that fine Case City rose in full bloom against the wall.

"It's alright," I said. "I'll wait outside. Just ping me on my heads up if you need me for anything." Seeing what had grabbed my attention, Lucky swapped looks with Null and shook his head. "Let's go down a ways and catch up," I suggested, and Sheena, dragging on a chill stick, powered it down to follow me deeper into the alley.

I don't know what it is about birds from the strip, but Sheena was the prototype and the perfect distraction. Lucky could drown his memories in drink, and I intended to drown mine in Sheena, who seemed up for it. Tonight, she was in a crop-top to show off her ink and short shorts over fishnets and steel-toed stompers.

She was fire on ice, this girl, her magenta lenses standing out against her smooth brown skin. I posted up next to her against that wall and brought out a small case of *Bliss*, dropping a wafer on my tongue. I waited for it to hit me, but the whole time, I could feel Sheena staring. I glanced over at her, and she nodded once. Taking the hint, I squared up with her, touched a finger to her chin, and she responded by opening her mouth. I dropped a fresh tab on her tongue, and held her hand as our minds took off together.

"I would suck the soul out of you girl, you're so bad," I whispered, pressing my lips against her tangy sweat-soaked neck.

My right hand held her tight form against me, and with my left, I reached behind her and took hold of her short brown hair. We kissed and became two live wires showering the shadows with our sparks, not caring that we had an audience from the heavies. I tugged on her belt to loosen the buckle, and she bit my lip hard, forcing me to yank harder on her hair to get her to stop. This elicited a squeak, followed by a cruel smile.

Playing with Sheena, you learned to expect pain. She grinned menacingly and leaned into me, sucking gently on my sore lip, and I let her, but then Purge's door flew open, and Null emerged. A quick series of unarmed strikes and the bouncer who had stopped me was lying face down in the dirt. I kept waiting for his partner to emerge, or my uncle Lucky, but Null spotted me, and when our eyes met, I knew that I was in danger.

As he crossed to where we were, I stepped away from Sheena to meet him, my hands near my hip, ready to pull as soon as he gave me a chance.

"What the hell, man?" Sheena complained, and who could blame her? She didn't know what was going down.

Now, all I could do was extend a hand, palm out in the universal sign for "stay back." However, Null took advantage of the distraction to draw on me. My mind had gone to Lucky momentarily, thinking he was inside bleeding out or dead. The thought of this was too much to bear, and though he aimed his gun in my direction, I no longer cared.

The pressure of that moment, the guilt, and the disrespect I felt in that instance brought the old Jackson Cole out. A reckless version of myself. All that outlaw philosophy about poise, replaced by fire, tempered by a double dose of *Bliss*. Kissing Sheena right after we'd dropped tabs was a rookie mistake, but I used the numbness and focus to steel me for this moment.

"Where's Lucky?" I asked through clenched teeth.

"No hard feelings, kid, but your reputation precedes you," Null said coolly from behind his cannon. I recognized it as an AC11 Tactical, a soldier's weapon. My clipper's brain considered the caliber and the number of bullets it had in its clip. I knew then that Null was a veteran like Lucky and my other uncle, Lobo Nieves. I expected him to explain further, winning me the time to respond. I drew my weapon, but his hand became a blur, and though I got off a shot, his bullet struck home and left me sprawled on my back.

I would have died had I not been wearing a bulletproof undershirt. It felt like Null had reached across the lot to punch me with a hot metal fist. Everyone inside the alley, including Sheena, scattered to the wind. Lucky ran out the back door, firing at Null, who had taken off, limping from where I'd hit him.

The old man gave me a quick, measuring glance before chasing after Null, and I sat up to see a dozer, so frightened out of her mind she was literally climbing the wall.

My abdomen was sore to the point where I thought I broke a rib, and there was dampness and blood from a nasty bruise. Luckily the bullet hadn't punched through. I heard the chime of an incoming call followed by a prompt on my implanted smart-lens. It was Lucky, so I accepted the call and forced myself to stand, biting down against the pain.

"Jackie, tell me you're alright, kid," an out-of-breath Lucky whispered.

"On my way to you," I managed. "Did you get him?"

"No, but you did. Fall your ass in before the DPS goons show up. I'll meet you on the corner of 5th and Gibson."

That's Kemet Kings territory, I thought. *This night just keeps getting better*. "On my way, Lucky." I let out a breath. "Stay on him. Just, not too close. We can't both be shot taking on a solitary target. How would that look for our guild?"

"Who cares?" Lucky said. "As long as he's nulled out in the end, it won't matter how he looks, now will it?"

The rain started falling again, light, cool droplets, but I barely noticed them as I ran northward, hands on my Arms American, keeping to the shadows, hugging walls below overhangs. Quick but methodically, I explored the back alleys of the 5th street plaza complex. My head on a swivel, glancing every which way, reacting to any and everything. I caught up to Lucky with no incident and no sign of Null outside the panicked residents escaping the violence.

"What happened back there?" I asked, riding my *Bliss* high to help shut out the pain.

"Let's just say, his clipper instincts are still intact. He knew the whole time we had come here to kill him. We got drinks and he let me know he was on to me. He said, 'Let's take it out into the alley,' and I agreed, but then he takes a swing at that big bastard who escorted us in. The struggle it took to get past all those stampeding cattle to get outside was intense. How bad is that injury?"

"Not bad enough for me to worry about it right now, Lucky. Let's find him," I said, though deep down, I was disappointed in my uncle. He wasn't telling me everything. I believed that he'd confronted Null, who slipped his grasp to beat an escape. Null said he knew my reputation, which meant he knew of my mother, the guild we were a part of, and the hornet's nest coming for him if he was to clip Lucky inside Purge. He lured us out, and now we were exposed, forced to find him in enemy territory.

The third floor of the Itola Terrace exploded, showering us with bricks and broken glass from above. Lucky and I took cover behind the rusted chassis of a roller, weapons drawn, faces near the metal, me looking one way for Null to come out and him covering the other. The flames cooked the atmosphere, threatening to get me coughing, but I kept it together, breathing into my coat's lapel.

Dozers and lowlifes sprinted to escape the alleyway. I heard sirens in the distance, warning of DPS incoming to investigate the disturbance. I knew what was happening. This was Null's doing. The fire, the panic, and DPS were all part of him setting a trap to pin us down. My eyes explored all the rooftops, settling on a building across from where the explosion occurred. Two floors, one window, and a flat rooftop, upon which sat a billboard advertising the popular workout pill, Ifflex.

"Time is precious," it read. "Why spend hours inside a gym? Ifflex, Hollywood's best-kept secret. Reclaim your time while looking your best." A large cutout of the pill's container wiggled temptingly on the right side of the board. The fog and luminescence of the neon made it difficult to see if Null was up there, but I could feel him, waiting for Lucky or me to expose ourselves.

I didn't need to see or hear him. Instincts placed him there, waiting. To confirm my suspicions, I held a finger to the right side of my temple, triggering the sensor below my dermis to bring up my heads-up display. With the practiced effort of exploring the menus on the interface, I switched visuals to infrared, transforming my dark, smoky reality into bright neon greens and reds.

I patted Lucky's knee twice to get his attention, and pointed up at the billboard. "Cover me, and I'll cross," I said, and he confirmed, creeping forward on hands and knees to gain the driver's side door. There he could aim up at the billboard while remaining hidden behind the chassis. When he started shooting, I slipped out the back and crossed the wet road to below where Null hunkered, confirming my suspicions when I heard him firing back in Lucky's direction.

While that was going on, I climbed atop a pair of trash cans to access a high windowsill which I used to hoist myself up before turning to jump and catch the roof to shimmy around to the edge. Lucky kept firing, trading shots with his former friend, and the sirens sounded right on top of us, making me think that DPS drones would soon be in the area.

My grip was strong, but I still struggled from fatigue and the slick wet surface. Even so, I managed to pull myself up to crouch behind a large air conditioning unit. Above me, to the left of where I waited, was the billboard in all its splendor, screaming, "Ifflex."

It's now or never, I thought to myself, moving on tiptoes, gun at the ready as I looked past the air conditioner to see what constituted Null's sniper's nest and found nothing there. One minute he had Lucky suppressed with his AC11 Tactical, and the next, nothing, as if he had never been there. Racing back to the far side of the building opposite our alley, I caught his hulking silhouette limping down Gibson toward a waiting roller.

I recognized his ride immediately. It was a silver Taipan Maestro, the luxury upgrade to my humble but expensive Mamba Savant. "A clipper's life is his roller" was another line of wisdom we got taught in my guild. I called Lucky and told him to return to my ride, and I jumped to an adjacent building with an even lower rooftop to sprint across 4th street, where my Mamba was waiting. I had seen Null's plates, and that, combined with the rarity of his roller, would make it easy for the system to track him.

Lucky rounded the corner and got in, and I floored it, braving a red light to make Gibson, right when Null's Taipan Maestro was rounding 7th to reach the highway. Now he was in my realm. I knew Case City like the back of my hand. He had been gone for too long to know which roads were damaged or blocked off. He may have been born on the strip like the rest of us, but tonight he was a tourist. Like any good citizen, we took him for a ride across our city, exploring the barrens, docks, and the industrial zone.

We raced, pedal to the metal, sometimes getting close enough for Lucky to let off a shot, but like my Mamba, Null's Taipan was a beautiful tank with shielded tires. No bullets were going to stop him. It all came down to my driving and what each of us had left inside our fuel tanks. We rolled dangerously through traffic for over an hour and into the outskirts, where it was so black that our headlights did little to illuminate our path.

Lucky tapped my shoulder to get my attention, then

pointed at his ear. "He's calling me," he mouthed, wrinkling his brow. They started arguing, and from what I heard, Null was trying to explain why he killed Benny, and Lucky wasn't trying to hear any of it.

In the meantime, knowing he was distracted, I took advantage, seeing a turn coming up in another mile near a shortcut that cut across the craggy hills. I waited until Null rounded the bend before I killed the headlights and veered off quietly up the hidden dirt road. Lucky did his part in keeping him talking as I navigated us past rocks as large as basketballs and shrubs hardy enough to make their home in the desert.

Five minutes later, the path spat us out where I could see the Taipan's headlights coming around the bend. "Brace yourself," I warned my uncle, and consulted the Mamba's system, switching it to fully manual controls so I could turn off collision detection. Timing his approach, I gunned the accelerator, clipping the backend of his roller. We got thrown but nothing serious, and Null's Taipan spun out to crash inside a shallow roadside ditch.

We exited carefully, guns raised, but there was no point, Null's twisted bulk hung halfway out the window on the passenger side, motionless, but surprisingly still breathing. "I'm sorry, Luck," he managed through broken teeth, and I decided to give them a moment. The night sky was especially clear, and I braved the atmosphere to inhale deeply, closing my eyes to bring myself down, returning to a calmer version of myself.

I knew it was over when I heard the solitary report from Lucky's J2 cannon. Null Resistor was gone, and Benny the Cowboy was avenged.

Lucky, Lobo, and my Ma were the last three survivors of the original crew. I didn't know how to feel about that and how Lucky was taking it beneath the surface. I had heard their banter all night, saw their camaraderie, and listened to their stories. At one point in their lives, the two of them were brothers, and despite Null killing Benny for the seat, I felt Lucky still saw him that way.

WE ROLLED DOWN HUXLEY SILENTLY, taking in the sights of the Case City strip. Me with my bruised stomach and Lucky with his wounded pride. I knew how things went down bothered him, and he probably thought he'd lost a step. Not that I agreed with that assessment, but I thought it ridiculous how he let his pride nearly get him killed. I was surprised my mother had approved it, and though I would never question him, I did wonder.

Lucky was one of the best to ever do it, but that was before a stint in prison, a promotion to director, and the comforts of success kept him off the trigger for well over a decade before tonight. A lion's heart will always be a lion's heart, but we're only mortal, and Lucky had forgotten this. He had come face-to-face with his mortality, and was not taking it well.

It brought to mind our conversation earlier when he advised me not to get old, and it wasn't the first time he had said it. Now I understood what he meant was for me to embrace ambition and not become just another old clipper. Silence was the way now that the deed had been done. I set the Mamba to auto-drive, destination: Teresita's, our guild's headquarters, and a bar for the occasional outsider who couldn't know what it was to stay clear. A few shots of liquor and everything tonight would become just another bad file in a crowded folder inside my brain.

The night was still young, and there was a good chance Sheena would be up for a visit. Leaning over to reach the stereo, I switched it on and an unknown band was screaming savagery over grimy synthetic axes. The drummer was so deep in the pocket I felt him inside me beating my soul relentlessly. We were near the coast, dragging a tight curve, and across the expanse of the ocean, I could see the brilliance of the spires above Case City.

No one signs up to be born in the gutter, and no one forces a gun into our hands. We chose this life, but it didn't mean we didn't feel pain, regret, and guilt. I thought of Null and how much I'd admired him, and I thought of Omari's beautiful family, who would soon learn his terrible fate. My mind was a vortex, but on the bright side, we were rolling peacefully down an uneventful road.

As I turned and looked at this man I loved, who I felt privileged to have as my mentor, I saw him as an old warrior too long removed from the arena. It was a sobering thought seeing him this way. It was a mirror into the future, a warning of a life that tied us to codes that trumped friendships and held us to vendettas with no expiration dates.

"You did good work tonight, Jackson," Lucky said, though I could barely hear him above the music.

"Thanks," I said. "So did you." He nodded in earnest. I knew it still ate at him, so I gripped his shoulder, squeezed at it affectionately, and did the same with his hard, sinewy neck. "It's like you told me so many times in the past. It's never as neat as we want it. Either way it's done, but I gotta admit. That great big ol' bastard, Null Resistor, he really earned that name."

Read more of Jackson Cole's story in Neon Eclipse.

One of Case City's most skilled assassins, Jackson Cole is a wanted man. After annihilating his latest target, he quickly learns the prominent man's identity. Now, a perilous enemy seeks revenge, and rival guilds look to take advantage of his vulnerability. For Jackson, it's become kill or be killed, but will a steady aim be enough to take on the entire city?

Get *Neon Eclipse*:
gregdragon.com/portfolio/neon-eclipse

Pick Your Poison

1. *Blood is thicker than water.* Head to "Last Chance" by Jessie Kwak

2. *Let's turn up the heat.* Head to "Terminal Sunset" by Erik Grove

3. *I'm craving a visit to Eastern Europe.* Turn the page to read "The Crimson Vial" by William Burton McCormick

THE CRIMSON VIAL

A SANTA EZERIŅA STORY

BY WILLIAM BURTON MCCORMICK

RĪGA, LATVIA

ALONG WITH THE FIFTY THOUSAND EUROS STUFFED in her lobby mailbox was a handwritten note in English:

"Dear Miss Ezeriņa,

I trust this will gain your attention. Please check your professional email account at 9:00 A.M. Rīga time. You will find my message waiting.

Yours Cordially,

J.J. Watkins, Jr."

In Santa Ezeriņa's years as journalist, she had received many odd things in the post: bloodstained evidence, narcotics, incriminating photographs, even once a severed human hand gripping a pistol. Yet, she'd never been sent cash in anything approaching this amount. If the bills were real, which she greatly doubted, this was more than she earned in two years, sometimes in three... J.J. Watkins, whoever he was, clearly wanted something from her, something desperately. And he was willing to shell out a lot of dough, or concoct an elaborate scam, to get it.

Santa wrinkled her nose in distaste. Most likely this was some sad old man trying to buy a mistress. Such men were common in Latvia, but as the name was foreign, there could still be a story here, if he were famous enough somewhere on this Earth. Something she could sell to the American or British tabloids at least. If only it were "J.J. Biden" or "J.J. Trump" those would be sure sales.

But who was J.J. Watkins, Jr., really?

She stuffed the money and the note back into the wrinkled manila envelope, then climbed the steps to the second floor and her tiny office in the *Baltic Beacon* suite. Alone—newsroom or not, nobody else in this rag was ever here before nine—she made Russian-style coffee, checked her email (nothing yet from Watkins), then sat at her desk and tried to ignore the sticky note I.O.U.'s over her laptop screen. As a freelancer, Santa paid the editor/owner rent for her private office and, as usual, she was deep in debt. She'd have to sell two to three stories just to cover this month. Or she'd be out by January.

She fanned a few of the bills from the envelope across her desk. Oh, if they were real with no strings attached, but experience told her life doesn't work that way.

She examined the note again. Fancy handwriting, full of loops and bows, a tad old-fashioned and effeminate. "Watkins," the surname was clearly Anglo-Saxon, but "J.J."? The English don't care much for that nickname, do they? Probably an American. A pity. The British tabloids are ravenous, an easier sell.

She Googled "J.J. Watkins." Two dozen names came up, but only one with any obvious connection to Latvia, a Joseph James Watkins from Tallahassee, Florida. Pharmaceutical industrialist, established a company here three years ago. Not so rare. Rīga had been the capital of pharmaceutical research and manufacturing in the Soviet Union, a pride and tradition the West exploited ever since Latvia's independence.

She clicked through the links. Found images of Watkins. A handsome, seventyish man, always in tailored suits with archaic bow ties. A prideful-looking entrepreneur whose company officers seemed to be predominantly women. Progressive.

But then why did these women look so uncomfortable?

At 8:52, the expected email arrived in Santa's Inbox.

"Miss Ezeriņa:

I have always been impressed by your skills. I read in translation about your apprehension of the fiend behind the "Tukums Outrage." I am also keenly aware of the libel lawsuit that threatens your employment at the Baltic Beacon.

Your abilities can help me solve an important problem of mine, and my monies can cure a few problems of yours. The money in the mailbox is only an advance. I am willing to pay five times this for your cooperation.

I will be waiting for you between ten and four in my private offices. It is the black-bricked German building at the end of Gertrudes iela, just before the highway. You can't miss it.

Please come alone.

Yours faithfully,

J.J. Watkins, Jr."

WHEN SANTA ARRIVED at the building on Gertrudes iela, only a short walk from the *Beacon* offices, she wished she'd ignored Watkins's instructions and brought a friend. While clean and well-kept on the exterior, the towering building appeared to be nearly abandoned, the windows displaying empty offices devoid of people or furniture. A dreary atmosphere of settled stillness hung over the structure, one that she found inexplicably foreboding.

At the door, the company placards next to the intercom buttons were all removed save for "Watkins Pharmaceuticals and Bioengineering, USA."

She rang this singular office. Immediately a gravelly American voice answered in English: "I'll buzz you in. Top floor, please, Miss Ezeriņa."

The magnetic lock released, and Santa stepped into a circular hall stretching five stories upwards to a vaulted roof, the perimeter at every floor fixed with doors behind railed balconies. A grand central staircase connected all points via branching catwalks like some enormous wide-boughed tree deep inside the Kurzeme woods. The floor near the entrance was dusty, apparently long unattended, yet a scent like empyreumatic oil mixed with chlorine burned Santa's nostrils, made her eyes tear.

Urged on by the same American voice heard through speakerphones at every level, Santa climbed the towering staircase, followed the top floor catwalk to the balcony and passed through an open doorway into a room of nightmare. On an elevated chair—it resembled to Santa a demented dentist's chair—reposed a shriveled old man in white linen shirt and shorts. Behind and on either side of the man and his chair was a great machine of maddening contours whose silver canisters and pulsating drums sprawled to even the remotest recesses of the room. Tubing extended from this room-filling apparatus to penetrate the man at throat, upper arms, wrists, and snaked underneath the clothing to groin and thighs. As he breathed, and later when he spoke, liquids flowed into and out of both machine and man in rhythm with his gasps. The face, pale, ghastly, and aged beyond seventy years was nevertheless recognizable to Santa from the photos she had viewed on the internet as Watkins. And, if her instincts needed more proof of identity in this living scarecrow, a blood-red bow tie hung with perverse humor from the stent where the tubing plunged into his neck. The air was as sterile as any hospital, save from the chlorine and empyreumatic oil scents drifting up from the floors below.

"Welcome, Miss Ezerina. Thank you for agreeing to meet," he said. As his lips moved and the tube liquid flowed in time, the voice itself emanated from speakers in the great machine, so her host spoke in stereo, Devil's whispers in both Santa's ears. "I am J.J. Watkins, Jr., President. Please come into my office. You'll pardon me if I don't rise to greet you."

Santa, recovering from her astonishment, began to consider the circumstances. There were no attendants in the room. No physicians, nurses or even security guards. And the chamber was freezer cold.

"Are we alone in the building, Mr. Watkins?"

"Completely," said the twin speaker voices. "I have relocated the business offices to Pierīga nearer our laboratories and manufacturing plant. My underlings handle all daily business elsewhere. You understand it would harm company morale to see their leader in this state, haunting the old place like some ghoulish creature of Latvian legend." He motioned with a frail hand towards a cushioned stool off to one side. "Please take a seat."

"I'd prefer to stand. How can I assist you, Mr. Watkins?"

"I need an investigator. Something vital has been stolen from our company and it must be retrieved."

"Call the police."

"This is no matter for the police."

"Then call a private detective."

"I have hired *three* since the theft. Two were useless. The third made some headway then vanished like a phantom at dawn." His tired eyes unfocused momentarily and the flow of the liquids seem to slow, before he rallied once more. "I'm tired of irresponsible P.I.'s. I need an investigator who gets things done. I need Santa Ezerina. Your success rate must be the highest in Eastern Europe."

"I'm an investigative *journalist,* not a detective. I go only where there's a story. And that seems to be right in this room, Mr. Watkins."

"Oh, there's a story, my girl. But I require confidentiality. We can talk about what the public may know only when the missing items are returned, the thieving party vanquished, and you receive your two-hundred fifty thousand Euros." He smiled a feeble smile. "Would you like a cigarette? Do people even smoke now days? I'm forgetting more and more the social norms in Europe."

"Can we smoke around your apparatus?"

"Certainly. Nothing is flammable." He pressed a button on his chair. A packet of Camel Reds dropped from a receptacle in the side.

Santa withdrew the packet, opened it, and lit a cigarette. Watkins breathed in her secondhand smoke with a deep, yearning smile.

"Tell me what was stolen. And by whom, J.J."

"Dr. Sofija Grinberga, our former director of research in Europe, destroyed all samples of an experimental drugs meant to regress malignant cell growth in cancer patients. We were running a first clinical trial, with sixteen control cases, including placebos, everything normal for a new drug test. Dr. Grinberga, for reasons only she knows, destroyed the vials containing the drug in three of the four transport cases and, with the help of some hacker, erased the formula from Watkins computers. Company cameras caught her leaving with the fourth carrycase."

He pressed another button on his chair. A panel slid aside to reveal a monitor in the great machine. On the screen, an image of a bespectacled woman in a laboratory coat came to life. Carrying what looked like a metallic briefcase in one hand, she crossed a nighttime parking lot to a maroon Mercedes. She placed the carrycase in the trunk, got in the car and drove out of the camera's view. The timestamp at the bottom said October 10th. Over a month ago.

"That was taken by the security camera at our Pierīga facility. Neither Dr. Grinberga nor the carrycase has been seen since. We doubt she's in Latvia."

"Are you sure the remaining trial drugs are in the case?"

"Why steal it, if it is empty?" He shut off the monitor. "I imagine one of our competitors got to Dr. Grinberga, offered millions. Perhaps, billions. Worth it to her, I guess, to live a hunted life. She is the only one who knew the complete formula. Now, it is gone." He leaned forward in his chair, straining the tubing around him. He reminded Santa of an insect caught in a spiderweb.

"As you may have guessed, without this formula my

own life is numbered in weeks. Her leaving is very much a personal tragedy."

"I gathered something along those lines."

He pointed to a folder next to the stool. "In that envelope is a copy of Grinberga's employment record. We had originals complete with ink signatures, but I gave it to that failure of a detective, Edgars Blūms."

"The one who vanished?"

"Yes."

Santa retrieved the folder, flipped open Dr. Grinberga's file. Clipped to the first page was a photograph of a gray-haired, mildly attractive woman. The form below said she was 62, born in Rīga, educated firstly at Rīga Technical University and Moscow State University, and after the West opened, at Brown and Harvard.

Bright gal.

"Can I keep this?"

Watkins nodded perceptibly, the motion dislodging his tie. It fluttered down like a red butterfly into his lap. "I'll pay all expenses, Miss Ezeriņa, but, if you leave the country, let me know. I don't want you vanishing like that freeloader Blūms."

Santa promised not to vanish.

SANTA's first instinct was a visit to Jansons Investigative Services, the detective agency which employed Edgars Blūms. She'd never met Blūms but fortunately Santa had an ally there: Māris Ledus, a young gumshoe who helped her solve the "Lazarus of Liepāja" case last year. Santa didn't completely trust Māris, but he was indebted to her.

She'd saved his life twice during that investigation. That had to count for something, right?

"I can't discuss client business with outsiders, Santa," said Māris, sitting on his desk rather than behind it. "Mr. Jansons could have my job."

"I rescue you from a six-story fall and you treat me like this, Māris?"

"It was only three. I might've survived without you."

"Jansons ever save your life?"

"No."

"Then you owe me more than him. Spill the beans."

He grimaced as if in pain, then got up off his desk went to the door, yelled down the hall: "Ilze! Boss in right now?"

"Out to lunch. Need something?" asked a decidedly down-market feminine voice.

"No. Just let me know when he gets back." Māris shut the door, lowered his speech to a whisper. "Don't know how, but Blūms traced that thievin' doctor to Odesa. He flew down there after her. Nobody ever heard from him again. After a week of silence, Watkins threw a fit. Fired our agency. Said Blūms had stolen the advance and gone on vacation." Māris returned to the desk rifled through a drawer until he found a set of keys.

"Weren't you worried about your man?" asked Santa.

"Not initially. Edgars Blūms is seventy-five. Way past retirement age and only irregularly employed here. It's warmer this time of year in Odesa, we figured he was being casual in the assignment. Running up the bill on the client. And we didn't update Watkins after he fired us. So, J.J. never knew about this delivery."

Māris went to a closet on the other side of the room near Blūms's vacant desk. He unlocked the closet door and withdrew a beat-up cardboard box with the markings of *Ukrposhta*. The postal service of Ukraine.

"This was sent from his hotel in Odesa. Arrived last Monday. Seems when Edgars ran off to wherever he went, he left his things in the room. As he registered using the agency's address, they shipped his stuff here." Māris set the box on the floor near Santa's chair. He fished out a man's suit jacket, several shirts and boxer underwear, shoes, shaving kit and other toiletries. "Have a look."

Santa leaned forward in her chair and dug through the remaining items. She found a pair of gray flannel trousers with an odd yellowish-red stain at the pant cuffs, a stain that extended up inside the pants leg as far as she could see.

"Whatever it is, he stepped in it good," said Māris with a smile. "On one of his underpants too. You know old men and their bodily functions."

"I try *not* to know old men and their bodily functions, Māris." Santa sniffed the trouser cuff stain. Like empyreumatic oil. With chlorine.

"You go through this box thoroughly?" asked Santa, setting the trousers aside.

"Only a quick glance. Boss wants me to throw it out, but I keep hoping Edgars will show.... There was a note from the hotel, got it here somewhere. Said they found a gun and holster but as they were illegal in Ukraine, the hotel was disposing of them rather than shipping 'em. My bet is they sold it on the Odesa black market."

"Did they say if it had been fired?"

"No. I think that's a little beyond most hotel staff."

She picked up the jacket, patted it down looking for ammo cartridges. Instead, she found something hard, long and smooth beneath. In the inside pocket was an empty vial of shiny green glass, a label at the top said: "29-A Watkins P & B,"

"Is that important?" asked Māris.

"Oh, it's important all right. Better give me the address of that hotel in Ukraine." Santa took it down, then withdrew a roll of the bills Watkins had stuffed in her mailbox this morning. She peeled out two hundred Euros, set them on the desk.

"This for the help today." She withdrew another thousand Euros, "And this is for help in the future. I want you to go to Turaida Bank; according to Dr. Grinberga's employment records that's where her salary deposits went. Find out all you can. Does she still have accounts, or did she clean them out before she skipped town? Recent transactions, wire transfers, all that. I trust your detective skills to get us what we need." She pulled out another five hundred. "Take this too. For bribe money."

Māris whistled. "Santa, I never knew you were such a spender."

"I'm not," she said. "I'll be expensing all this to J.J. Watkins, Jr."

"Better hurry before he shuffles off this mortal coil. Heard he's in dire straits."

"Maybe, this cancer drug will help. If we get it."

"Cancer? Has it developed into cancer?" Māris frowned "Blūms said Watkins was suffering from chemical exposure at one of his manufacturing plants. An exposure caused by Sofija Grinberga's negligence. That this whole pursuit was pure revenge."

"That's not what he implied to me." She shrugged, headed for the door. "Lies or truth I'll find Grinberga for Watkins. As long as he pays."

AFTER LEAVING MĀRIS, Santa called Watkins, told him she knew where Blūms stayed in Odesa and was confident she could track him down there.

Watkins replied that her job was to find Sofija Grinberga and the missing serum, not AWOL detectives.

Santa mentioned the vial in Blūms's coat pocket.

She was on the next flight to Odesa.

SANTA HAD BEEN to the Southern Wonder many times. She'd experienced Odesa's beaches, museums, and beautiful Derybasivska Street long ago and knew intimately the great port city's less respectable attractions. The docks and markets were hubs of crime infested with Russian, Bulgarian, and Ukrainian mobsters as well as many Middle Eastern gangsters who crossed the Black Sea from Istanbul. Upon landing at the airport, Santa took a taxi to a certain salacious backstreet warehouse store beyond the Seventh-Kilometer Market, where she purchased an illegal handgun and appropriate ammunition for two hundred Euros cash.

Edgars Blūms may have been an old man, but he was also an experienced detective who disappeared here.

Better safe than sorry.

After slipping the gun into her purse, she took another cab to the Seacrest Hotel along Kamanina Street opposite the beachfront. The clerk at the desk remembered Blūms and, after a hefty bribe, moved another tenant so she could stay in his old room.

Santa booked it for two weeks. Searched the premises

carefully. Found nothing unusual. Every day, she questioned the maids who came into clean. The first girl knew nothing. But the second maid was a gabber.

"Oh, the Latvian fellow weeks ago?" She tucked Santa's bribe into her uniform pocket. "The one who paid for a month, then bolted after four days? You know, he left all his stuff here. Between you and me, I say something happened to him. Like maybe he drowned in the sea, but the hotel didn't seem to care since he was paid up. They ship out his junk and rent the room again."

"Did you ever find anything unusual when you cleaned the room? Anything medical related?"

"Like bandages?"

"Like medicines. Vials..."

"You know, now that you say it, there were two little green bottles in his trash one day. I think the morning he disappeared, in fact. I wondered if he was some sort of addict. But there were never any needles or spoons."

"A bottle like this?" Santa withdrew the green vial from her purse.

"Exactly like that. Even had those labels. I remember now that I see it."

"Were they empty?"

"I don't really recall. We just dump them in the bin. Nothing splashed around or left a stain." Her eyes lighted. "You know speaking of stains..."

She led Santa over to a full-length mirror on the wall, pointed to the carpet at the mirror's base. "Can you see that? No?" The maid pulled the window drapes open. Natural light filled the room.

Santa could just detect the slightest remnants of a yellowish-red stain in the rug before the mirror. It'd been invisible in anything less than full light, but it was there.

She brushed the stain with her fingertips, felt a stiffness to the carpet fibers absent elsewhere.

"Don't know what it was he spilled," said the maid. "I worked a whole shift, scrubbing with every cleanser but that blemish wouldn't come out completely. Smelled a little like the swimming pool. You know that burning scent you get."

"Chlorine?"

"Yeah, chlorine, I guess. Just sort of the pool smell for me. I'd have reported him to the management, but as the fellow disappeared it didn't seem to make any difference."

"This tenant have any visitors while he was here?"

"A lady friend once. Not one of the professional girls from the lobby bar. I know all their faces. I mean a foreigner. Like him. Like you."

"Could it be this woman?" Santa handed her the picture of Sofija Grinberga.

She stared at it closely. "Yeah, could be her. Hair's different. I remember a blonde. "Could be a peroxide job, I guess? Woman her age should be gray..."

"What did they do?"

"No idea. Same thing men and women always do in hotel rooms, probably."

"Did you hear them doing that 'thing'?"

"No. Nothing but talking in their foreign language."

Santa spoke in Latvian: "*Labrīt. Lūdzu, pastāstiet man, kur atrodas sasodītās zāles?* Did it sound like that?"

"Kinda. But it was weeks ago... Sorry. I can't remember everything said in every room."

Santa nodded. "Thank you."

When the maid had gone, she kneeled again, brushed that stain with her fingers. Mind whirling.

THAT NIGHT, as Santa slept, the curtains remained opened. In the Black Sea moonlight, a dark figure with golden hair peered in, tried the glass door from the beach. Finding it locked, the watcher retreated.

Soon, the purr of an engine passed as a car drove away into the Odesa night.

Santa did not stir.

THE NEXT MORNING, Santa awoke to the sounds of flowing water nearby. The hotel custodian armed with a powerful hose, was cleaning off the walkway outside her beach door. She spied—or thought she spied—a yellowish blemish on the glass and outside handle just as the custodian's hose washed it away.

"Sand," he said, seeing her staring, "blown up off the seashore. Pesky November winds."

AFTER A LIGHT BREAKFAST, Santa called Māris in Rīga. "What'd you learn at the bank?"

"Grinberga cleaned out her accounts on October 3rd."

"A week before she sabotaged the trial and stole the last case of serum," said Santa. "What else you got?"

"She did some transfers, but I can't get anyone to trace a thing. Probably offshore accounts, hidden money, that sort of business. But one, relatively small transfer of half-a-million Euros went to a property management company in—wait for it—Odesa, Ukraine. I'm betting that's the lead Blūms found too."

"Good work. Now I don't regret saving your life."

He chuckled. "I think my debt is paid. I just texted you the address. That management company only has one property. In the ritziest spot in Odesa."

THE RITZY SPOT was *Primorsky Bylevar,* literally "Seaside Boulevard", a beautiful acacia-lined street that skirted Odesa's harbor. On the inland side rested nine-teenth century palaces and mansions, many now transformed into extravagant hotels, while opposite a stone viewing wall allowed a breathtaking view of the churning sea thirty meters below.

The particular mansion of Santa's interest was now a long-term-stay hotel, the estate large enough to be divided among several rentals which allowed strangers a degree of freedom walking the grounds. Her target was on the ground floor, near the front. Santa brazenly peeked in the windows. The opulent rooms were decorated in a classical style, oaks and tapestries and plush pillows everywhere. No sign of a metallic carrycase. The door to a bedroom was half open, and through it, Santa could see the furnishings. On the bed lay an opened rectangular shipment box, another sealed box of equal size on a nearby dresser. Both were labeled "KSOEPOE." A quick internet search on her phone revealed KSOEPOE to be a retailer of prosthetic limbs out of Kyiv.

Santa heard a car passing on the boulevard nearby. She stepped back from the window as a black sedan with tinted windows drove slowly along the near side of the road. Another sedan, this one silver in color, trailed at a distance of ten meters or so.

Santa sensed she was being watched. Regrettable. Dangerous. But just maybe any trap would draw Dr. Grinberga out of hiding.

She continued along to the rental's main door where a mailbox was affixed to the stony wall. With the use of a screwdriver from her purse, she soon had it open, sifting through junk mail targeted at customers able to afford a place like this. Various charities. And what's this? A hand-addressed bright pink envelope, the "To" and "Return" street addresses identical. The old trick. When you want to send something to yourself make sure both addresses match so there could be no mistakes.

She tore it open.

Inside was a napkin embossed with the Gogol Restaurant's logo and the great author's image in red print. On the bottom, in handwritten blue ink was: "441B 211222"

A combination. One hidden in the mail, sent to one's self, to avoid having it at home in case one was searched. In Santa's opinion, Dr. Grinberga had a little too much confidence in the Ukrainian postal service.

The Gogol Restaurant. She'd eaten there on a previous trip to Odesa. It was near the central train station.

441B. Hmmm...

Santa stuffed the napkin back into the envelope and left the premises. As she stepped out onto Primorsky, envelope in hand, her eyes caught movement. That first sedan drove slowly along the seawall side. The front window less tinted than the sides, Santa could see a grim-faced man at the wheel. He nodded as if agreeing to something spoken to him by an occupant in the back. Santa walked out into the street towards the car.

The driver floored it.

With screeching wheels and reeving engine, the sedan hurtled towards Santa. She had no time to think, no time to pull her revolver from her purse. Exposed in the street, her only choices were to dash for shelter in the house or the seawall. She chose the latter, hurtling over the wall as the car closed in at reckless speed.

Santa cleared the wall. Fell. Hit hard where the wall's base met the sea cliff, grasped at stones to keep from plummeting down the steep slope into the sea. She cursed as the envelope slipped free of her hand to flutter out over the waters and disappear into the seafoam below.

In the same instant, the front of the sedan crashed through the wall, sending shattered bricks raining down around Santa, tumbling avalanches into the Black Sea waters. The car teetered two meters above her head, half on the road, half on the overhanging cliff. The driver's face, thrown through the windshield, stared blankly out over the sea as his blood and brain matter oozed onto the car hood.

Shouts from witnesses eclipsed the dying motor's groans. She heard a door slam, and shouts of "Stop!" in Ukrainian and Russian. By the time Santa managed to get back over that wall, gun now drawn, she caught only a glimpse of blonde figure diving into the back of the other sedan, the silver car speeding away along Primorsky towards the city center.

"She's a madwoman," said a man standing nearby. "Her driver might have killed you."

"I think that was the idea," said Santa, bent over,

huffing from exertion and adrenaline. "Looks like he killed himself. Did you get a good view of the passenger?"

"No. She was all bundled up like a burn victim. Curly blonde hair sticking out. Moved real funny. Unnatural like."

"How do you know it was a 'she'?"

"Hair like that. Unless Robert Plant tried to murder you!"

"Always preferred Sabbath." Before anyone called the police, Santa leaned into the shattered car front, pushed aside the driver's corpse, and pulled all documents from the glove box. A purchase receipt for the sedan and ownership tag, both in the name of Sofija Grinberga. A Xerox of an international driver's license, the photocopy poor and portrait details lost, yet the dye hair job and the caked on, almost clown-like makeup, were obviously a pathetic attempt to turn back the years.

If this was Grinberga's disguise, it was a poor one. Pointless if she continued to use her real name.

So focused was Santa on these details that it was moments before she noticed the growing nausea in her stomach and the familiar malodorous scent emanating from the back seat. On the floor and cushion was a gooey yellow-red stain. Mixed in with this semi-liquid mess was prosthetic hand, holding—of all things—a serrated knife. The same odorous yellowish sludge pooled at spots in the road where the later car picked up the passenger.

Santa took several photos with her phone, then left the scene before the authorities arrived, hailing a taxi just out of sight of the witnesses. She gave him the address of the Seacrest Hotel. In the back of the cab, she mentally went through her recently accumulated evidence.

Reviewed her photos. Thought of that napkin lost in the sea.

"Your hotel's right ahead, lady," said the cab driver, breaking Santa from her musings.

"Change of plans, friend. The main train station, please. No delays."

Santa entered the station luggage facility, ignored the checked bags desk—Grinberga would never leave such a valuable prize with another person—and went straight to the storage lockers in the back. There, in this underlit room, she saw a hunched figure in a loose-fitting overcoat, the sleeves over hands and hem on the ground, fumbling at the combination dial of locker 441B. A low sunhat eclipsed much of the head and shoulders, the chin and jaw wrapped in a black silk scarf, curly blonde hair poking out the back.

She observed the woman's growing frustration at the unforgiving lock. Santa made no sound, but some sixth sense caused the blonde to glance over her shoulder, wild eyes widened in horror as she spied Santa watching. A low Latvian cursed emitted from hidden lips.

The figure slid away towards the women's toilet in the corridor outside.

Santa lingered at the locker, tried to recall the numbers from that lost envelope. She'd only had a glance at it. Was it 12-22-12? 12-20-12? 12-12-22?

Nothing worked.

With little choice, she entered the toilet, glancing under the stalls for occupants. None. Yet, from one stall emanated the most repugnant acidic smell, painful to the sinuses and brain. On the stall's floor an oozing thick yellow-red sludge. Not your typical toilet grime...

She kicked open the stall door, found the stunted shape huddled there, body-balled up atop the closet toilet lid, stained knees at scarfed chin. Yellowish slop dripped from overcoat cuffs and pant legs to pool at the floor.

The noxious odor inside was overpowering, vomit inducing, like an exhumed corpse pulled from a forest grave. Santa withdrew a pocket handkerchief to cover her nose and mouth. With her other hand, she pulled the pistol.

The stall's occupant spoke first, in a dripping, semi-liquid voice. "You are the investigator living in Blūms's hotel room. Watkins sent you?"

Santa was slow to respond, lungs pulling breathable air through her handkerchief, "You know me, Dr. Grinberga. Your driver tried to run me down forty minutes ago."

"Grinberga? She is rotting away." That liquescent voice grew sadder. "As Oppenheimer said: 'I have become Death, the destroyer of worlds.'"

"You've become something, all right. What does this formula do? Some sort of chemical weapon?"

"Not merely chemical. It's alive. More so than I am, now. We have weaponized the so-called flesh-eating bacteria. Bioengineered an easily appliable strain. It liquifies human flesh underneath the skin. Hollows you out from inside." With a brush of her overcoated arm, Grinberga pushed up the hat brim, pressed down the scarf. "See what science has wrought."

Horrors.

Santa swooned, falling a step back. How could Grinberga breathe? How could she speak with so little left? The skin was no longer skin.

"I used the agent on Watkins—in defense, mind you. He will not share the wealth," said the overcoated husk on the toilet. "His machines retard the damage, but they cannot stop it. I used two vials on Blūms in his hotel room when he wanted a bribe to abandon my trail. I washed his body into the Black Sea with a garden hose. But I errored. Caught enough on my own skin then." She thrust a tortured palm from her sleeve. Not a finger remained, stubs only at pinkie and thumb. "I had working hands three days ago, girl. Now I cannot hold a pen or turn a simple dial. Or feed myself... Fortunately."

Santa pulled back the pistol hammer with her thumb. "You got what you deserved. Give me the combo. Or get your driver to open the locker for me. I won't ask again."

"My driver is muscle for a nefarious government. He would steal it if he knew the location and save his nation billions. They think I am here to catch the train to the Donbas for negotiations. What good does money do me now? I can't eat. I only wish to destroy the case and die. Help me destroy it. We are countrywomen. They will use it against Latvia. And so many other nations."

"I'm paid to return to it to Watkins."

"Prostitute!"

"Is there a cure?"

"The treatment only halts liquefication. There is no cure." She brushed open the buttonless coat. "Shoot me. It's what I desire. But...be careful with the remains, girl. The bacteria lives in me. It is voracious."

"I'm not paid to martyr you. I'm paid to retrieve the case, nothing else." Santa pocketed the pistol, quickly left Grinberga in the toilet, went back to locker 441B. She wiped yellowish slime from the dial. Tried combos at random. Her boyfriend's birthday. Her dog's adoption date.

The locker remained sealed.

She gritted her teeth.

Here we go.

Santa withdrew the revolver, set the muzzle against the lock and pulled the trigger. The recoil startled her as much as the shriek of rendered metal, lock innards flying in all directions, twisted pieces bouncing off her breast and shoulders. As shouts erupted from somewhere, she threw open the door, seized the case inside by the handle and fled the storage room.

Ukrainian shouts behind, she knew the guards were close, the station infested with police. Santa charged through the crowd along the central platform, out through the gate and dodged traffic across Rishelievska Street. Ahead, on the opposite side, was what she was seeking, a set of concrete stairs descending into the earth, a tour guide offering instructions to her clients:

"The Odesa Catacombs are the largest in the world. Over two-thousand kilometers of tunnels never fully explored. Mostly unlighted. So, please, don't wander off, it could—"

Santa bullied her way through the tourists, sped past the guide down the stairs into the lightless catacombs.

"Do you have a ticket, Miss? Miss, a ticket is required!?"

She did not return for a ticket.

❈

ALMOST TWO HOURS LATER, Santa exited the catacombs, emerging in an abandoned courtyard in the old Greek district of town. She left the gun in the tunnels, then took a city bus to the main international bus terminal. Santa knew how things worked in Ukraine. There would be closed-circuit footage of her from cameras in the train station storage room and platforms, but it would take a day at least to get those images out to law enforcement and border guards. Still, the airport was too risky and a return to the train station suicide. So, she bought a bus ticket to the neighboring country of Moldova and settled in for the five-hour trip to its capitol Chisinau. The Moldova-Ukraine border is a smuggler's dream. With eighty people on a loaded bus, a single guard has only time to match faces to passports and ensure visas are unexpired. Backgrounds go unchecked, luggage undisturbed. Santa kept the case in her lap the whole time without incident.

But one thing unsettled her trip. A bullet hole in the case's skin, the wound fresh and made at close range, likely her own lock-shattering slug at the station had punctured the prized possession. Her stomach sunk. Could this be all for naught?

She tried not to think about what might ooze out.

When she reached Chisinau, Santa took a room in an old Soviet-era hotel in the center.

The case was locked, but with a crowbar purchased at a nearby market, she had it open in twenty minutes time, prying its lids apart in the bathtub so she might drain anything that escaped. As the proverbs say, 'Heaven help the Moldovan sewer workers.'

Inside the case was chaos.

The interior had molding for four vials in the lid and

four more in the base. Three slots in the top were unoccupied, a fourth carried an empty green glass vial, the cap missing. In the lower half lay the remnants of three shattered crimson red vials, shards of glass everywhere, cut to pieces by the penetrating bullet she'd fired. The freed contents had permeated the molding, leaving a yellowish stain and the empyreumatic scent that made Santa's eyes water. One crimson vial remained intact, its sludgy contents swishing about as she lifted it with gloved hands from the case.

Santa called Watkins, told him the contents were destroyed, omitting her own part in the destruction.

"One vial left," she said.

"Red or green?" his voice breaking into a desperate pitch. "Please, God..."

"Red."

"Bring it here. Without delay."

"It's impossible to carry a strange liquid on an airplane. And I don't dare check it." An idea occurred to her. "You're a wealthy man. Hire a private jet and fly down to Chisinau. I'll hand the vial to your people on the tarmac. They could be here in hours..."

"Not now. The government is watching all my employees."

"It's the fastest way."

"They'd only find you. *It.* Get here. However you can."

THAT NIGHT SANTA took the international bus from Moldova through Romania, Hungary, Slovakia, Poland and Lithuania to Latvia, the vial in her purse the whole fifty-three-hour trip. Along the way she checked newspaper websites, winced at the fuzzy security camera pictures of herself in the Odesa train station with case and gun in hands; read references to something that had "once been human" found dead in the station's toilet. Health officials had shut down the center of the Southern Wonder, and boats traveling in and out of Odesa's port were being searched for a "previously unknown form of bacteria." The outbreak was only accelerating...

When she was an hour out of Rīga, Santa called Watkins on her mobile.

No answer.

She tried again on arrival. He failed to pick up. Not waiting for a taxi, she hurried on foot to Watkins's offices. She reached the door. Pressed the intercom button.

An American voice said "Hello."

"J.J.? Is that you?" barked Santa. "I called."

"The authorities are monitoring my phones. I couldn't answer." He sounded so weak, his words in a fog. "They've been hounding me, Santa...your name is Santa, right? It's accelerating, some strain affecting the brain. Do you have the vial? The crimson one?"

"Yes. Let me in."

The lock released at last. Santa darted inside, across the dusty floor, up the mountainous stairway, into the machined-filled office. Watkins languished in his chair, his skin more jaundiced than before, thinner, a web of visible veins running just beneath. His bowtie lay discarded on the floor, an additional stent in his throat.

"Do you have the serum?" He asked with lifeless eyes. "Please...hand it over."

She set it in his palm. His frail hands caressed the red glass, uncapped it, poured the contents into a receptacle in the chair, then tucked the empty vial in his shirt pocket. Santa's eyes followed the crimson serum flowing into the great machine then back into Watkins through the tethering tubes.

He lay still for a time, only his breathing and the whir of the machine disturbing the abandoned building's silence. Then at last, Watkins sat up, form unchanged, but a surprising strength in his manner as he pulled the medical tubes from his body.

"I no longer need these marionette strings."

He slid from the chair, adjusted again to the gravity of an upright posture. Then Watkins bent down and retrieved his tie. "I shall live a long life," he said tying it in place.

No medicine acts so fast, thought Santa. *His recovery more mental, spirits raised.* "You got the last vial. Grinberga and Blūms weren't as lucky as you."

"They are of no consequence. Sofija tried to kill me so she could keep all the money." He smiled behind pale, thin lips. "Now, she is dead and I keep all the money."

"Minus my two hundred thousand Euros."

"I'm afraid that transaction is voided."

"If I'm jilted. I'll report everything."

"I won't pay hush money to stoolpigeons forever." He pressed a button in the handle of his chair. Some sort of tubular device dispensed. "Yes, 'forever'. You'd dig around and find out the true monies involved, the trillions, then ask for a handout every time you're broke. Now that we've shut down Odesa, Eastern Europe's biggest port, everyone will want to talk to the 'girl from the train station.' They'll find you, make you squeal." He lifted the device. An odd shaped gun affixed with a tubular liquid container. "That can't happen. Santa."

She fled the office to the balcony. Found the catwalk to the stairs retracted.

Too far to jump...

"It wouldn't matter if you could get down," said his voice approaching behind. "The ground floor doors are magnetically sealed. We're locked in our tomb together."

Santa turned around to see him lurching nearer on unsteady spindly legs, that gun affixed with a tank beside the barrel in his hand. She knew what it contained.

"Yes, we still have the bioweapon, Santa. It was merely the cure we needed from Sofija. A cure in my body, not yours."

Santa leaned back against the balcony rail.

"I'll stay quiet."

"Yes, you will."

As she slid sideways, he fired, the gun spout ejecting yellowish goo to affix to the balcony rail.

"We've enough for more, Santa. I'm a man who can fire many times. Let's try ag—"

A horrible scream! A sudden shriek from his tortured lips. Watkins staggered back, dropping the gun. Santa kicked the weapon away, yellow sludge sticking to her boot toe.

As she kneeled to discard her boot, Watkins writhed above, his body shifting inside, muscles, glands, organs jostled about as something voracious consumed.

He writhed until a reprieve, then pulled the vial from his pocket. "Red...crimson...the right color...." His hand shattered the vial, glass falling in front of Santa.

"You gave me the test placebo!"

"There was only one vial," she said backing away. "How was I to know? What was I to do?"

New agonies washed over him. A body metamorphosed. Liquescent horror spilling out. Watkins staggered sideways. Over the rail.

"Placebo...," said a watery voice. "You gave me the placebo..."

He fell.

What hit the tiles five floors below didn't live long. Mercifully.

William has lived in seven countries including Latvia and Ukraine, the settings of "The Crimson Vial." His Santa Ezeriņa novella "House of Tigers" was an Honorable Mention for the Black Orchid Novella Award. Find it at williamburtonmccormick.com.

Pick Your Poison

1. *I'm looking for something more galactic.* Head to "The Western Oblique Job" by Mark Teppo

2. *Do you have any space fantasy?* Head to "Love & Pickpockets" by R J Theodore

3. *Let's turn up the heat.* Turn the page to read "Terminal Sunset" by Erik Grove

TERMINAL SUNSET

A MOONSHINE HUSTLE STORY

BY ERIK GROVE

IN A LITTLE UNDER FOUR HOURS A SOLAR STORM would burn the surface of Zaren-19's surface up to 1500 degrees Kelvin. Hot enough to turn the streets and any poor fuckers still walking them to cinders and magma. All jobs had a timer but this one had a doomsday clock.

Hadon, over-caffeinated and well-armed, counted down every last second waiting for her contact in the already abandoned planet's capital. Like all good shady business transactions, this one was intended to go down in an alley between two warehouses in an industrial waste-land that would be creepy even without the impending doom. She sweat puddles in her boots, sucked in dry stale air that tasted like cooling vent exhaust, and imagined diving into a swimming pool full of whiskey and a million ice cubes. Splish splash. Glug glug.

Like a persistent twitch, Hadon's partner in bad ideas, Geddy, text commed every couple minutes: "Anything???"

"He's coming," Hadon replied, tap tap swipe on the

holographic screen generated by the holo ring on her no-I'm-not-married-but-I'll-still-punch-you hand. "Think calming thoughts. Money and get the fuck out of here thoughts."

"Mmm," Geddy texted, added an animated drooling cartoon mouth. "Snowman orgy."

To each her own.

The heat burned Hadon's eyes even before the drips made it through her messy hair and eyebrows. Any other job like this, with this sort of margin and downside, six days a week and twice on Sundays Hadon would pass. But with her back against the wall and no better choices, she'd just have to find a way to make it work. If she bailed on this one, raced back to spaceship recycled air and cargo bay moonshine, Burton would make her dead in a month. His gun pressed against her back or someone else's, Hadon wouldn't know until the click and powder-burn stink.

Never a good idea to date your coworkers, but some boyfriends had more guns than others.

With a chiming deep-doop alert, Hadon's sensor spike let her know something moved around the corner.

"Got something," Hadon sent to Geddy. She put a hand on one of her pistols, Wild Bill, criss-crossed with its twin slapping her other hip.

Geddy sent a little holo face with clenched teeth. Accurate.

The Zaren-19 sky was a haze of yellows and reds. It felt heavy and ready to ignite.

The movement Hadon's sensor spike detected came into view and Hadon, a half dozen coffees bubbling acid in her gut, drew her gun.

"Well???" Geddy wanted to know.

Hadon scoundrel grinned. It wasn't her contact. It was a mangy, panting dog with too much gray fur for the heat and a tail swishing like it had already half melted. Hadon took an image capture and sent it to Geddy.

A flood of hearts came back, then: "I LOVE IT I WILL KILL FOR DOGGY."

Hadon crouched and put out a hand with curled-in fingers. "It's okay," she said. "I'm not a bad guy."

The dog shuffled closer until it could lick Hadon's hand. Rough tongue, hot and adorable.

"Thirsty?" Hadon pulled a canteen from her bag of Illicit Job Things set up against the wall of the alleyway, opened the top and sniffed to confirm it wasn't booze, then poured some into the dog's eager mouth.

Deep-doop from a different spike. Shit. By the time Hadon stood straight and turned, the bastard had a gun pointed at her.

"You're a real crazy bitch," the bastard said. Corp Sec uniform. Scruffy frog neck. Call-women-that-don't-want-a-mustache-ride-lesbian eyes. Hadon's contact, Seeley.

Hadon's new dog friend growled. Good instinct.

She'd been called worse. "You're fucking late," Hadon told him.

Seeley holstered his peacemaker. Behind him, outside of Hadon's sensor spike radius, a grav bike that he must have ridden in on. "Let's do this quick."

If only.

Hadon made a holographic data card with her glow ring. Held it up look-see. "I've got my end."

"Prove it." He licked sweat off his lips.

Hadon made a big enough holo screen to show off all

the incriminating evidence she had on the piece of shit squeezed into man-shaped skin. So much graft and petty bullying. Even with their low standards it'd be enough for Corp Sec to take away his big boy badge and lock Seeley in a small room for a long time.

All cops are bastards. Evergreen.

Seeley showed off his abnormally small teeth in a grimace. "What's to say I give you what you want and you don't have copies still to fuck me over?"

"This is one of those 'I've got leverage on you and you don't really have a choice' situations," Hadon said.

Seeley rolled that over in his mansplain-and-chill brain. "Your friend Burton might like to know what you're up to," he finally said, so proud like a toddler that managed to dookie in a vac toilet for the first time.

"Trust me," Hadon said. "Burton's going to know."

Up in the sky, one of the last evacuation ships streaked by trailing vapor, headed for a more hospitable climate.

Seeley dug into his Corp Sec trousers and came out with an encryption key. Little cylinder smaller than a pinky made for locks that Hadon couldn't hack. He tossed it and it landed tink-tink a couple boot steps from her. Hadon pocketed it and passed him her holo artifact.

The holographic card blinked and vanished into his ring with a video game sound. "My tip?"

"It's in there," Hadon told him. When she started trawling for Corp Sec fuckers to blackmail she found a lot more than Seeley. He skimmed through holo panels, jowly smiling with glee. "Use it however you like."

Hadon didn't expect Seeley would take the evidence and clean up Corp Sec—he'd likely do something predictably selfish and corrupt—but burn them all anyway.

"The other thing?" Hadon asked him.

He nodded. "Yeah," he said. "I got it. Like we talked about. It's why I was late. Met your boyfriend across town."

Hadon's nerves on a hot tin roof. "He's *here*?"

Seeley chuckled. "Trouble in paradise." He picked something from his little bitty teeth with a thumbnail. "If I were you, I'd get a ride outta here soon as I could."

"Thanks," Hadon told him. "We're done."

He strolled back to his grav bike, a little wave then a fuck-you finger, and rode off.

"Got the key," Hadon text commed Geddy. "But we've got a problem. Burton's here. This is going to go the bad way."

"Okay," Geddy commed back. "Okay... But what about the doggy tho?"

Sad dog eyes looked up at Hadon. Tail swish. Damn it. Hadon scooped the dog into her arms and moved.

Tick tock.

THE ONLY GOOD thing about racing against several lousy ways to die on a desolate planet: no traffic. Hadon pushed her grav skimmer, open-topped skiff-style, hard enough to shake bolts loose and make her new dog—a boy based on the anatomy that brushed against her arm while she carried him—whimper.

The job was a simple snatch and grab. Goods meant to go to one place went to another with Zaren-19's upcoming armageddon covering the tracks. A scam as old as larceny. The interested party (gangsters) arranged for a ship carrying the goods they wanted to land on the doomed planet. Real shame about the emergency repairs on that long haul cargo ship. Then, they promised Burton a good payday to intercept a carrier taking it off-world with Hadon, hacker extraordinaire, faking the records to make it look like someone fucked up and left it behind. The gangsters end up with their parcel and no one's the wiser.

Hadon's double-cross slipped right between the cracks. She found another buyer (different gangsters) willing to pay her enough for the goods to get out from under Burton's thumb and put a down payment on her own ship. No more bosses. No more sleeping with one eye open. To do it, she needed to get to the package first. Burton was supposed to be waiting in orbit. He was supposed to drop a crew onto the carrier and find fuck all while Hadon and Geddy were halfway to another star system, clinking glasses. Instead, he was planetside. Motherfucker.

If he did what he promised, Seeley gave Burton the wrong ship details and a key that wouldn't work. But if Burton was suspicious enough to change up the plan without telling Hadon he'd see through that ruse in no time. She brought up a holographic interface with her glow ring, sent some of her digital virus friends at the planet's network.

Hacking and driving: an advanced maneuver.

"How are we doing on a ride out of here?" Hadon text commed Geddy.

"Working on it..." Geddy replied. "What are we going to name Doggy?"

The dog peed on Hadon's boot and tucked his tail between his legs. Relatable.

"Asshole," Hadon replied.

"I LIKE IT!!!"

A lot of the planet's network security split with the higher ups days ago. What they left behind was, lucky for Hadon's clock, rudimentary and easily hacked. She searched for Burton's glow ring sig. Not found. He must have it routed through an off-world ghost network. Hadon taught him that trick. She checked his favorite goons, Kimber and Ramble. Kimber pinged in orbit, probably on the ship, but Ramble popped up over at the northside cargo yards within shooting distance of the faked manifest Seeley passed off. Hadon figured they'd bash their way through the lock and find a cargo container full of glitchy sex bots. Those were meant to be Hadon's not-so passive aggressive Dear John letter while she and Geddy made space tracks. Oh well. Half of survival was improv.

Hadon landed her grav skimmer in an eastside yard in the only big enough shadow she could find. She could get a closer spot, but it'd be plain view and Hadon preferred the chance of avoiding notice to an extra 20-meter dash. The spot was against a power relay station that kicked out extra heat for good measure.

She initiated a sweep for stray glow ring sigs. Anyone taking a walk with a gun between Hadon and her prize. The sweep came back quick. Everyone with unboiled gray matter was as far away as possible already. Hint hint. Hadon set up an automated daemon to keep an eye out for glow rings moving in closer and one on Ramble's sig, then hopped over the side of the grav skimmer.

"Ride needs to be good to go in an hour," she text

commed Geddy when her boots hit the softened asphalt. Then she sent, "ONE HOUR" in all caps.

Running like that with the sun beating down, bouncing back up from the black top, hot like dizzy. An afternoon in the furnace. Sprinting across a frying pan. Her mouth tasted salty with a parched metallic chaser. Quick temperature check. Melting Hadon cartoon. Fun times.

Geddy replied with a cartoon iced glass of something brown.

She got to the right warehouse and halfway through slicing and dicing her way through the security of the main door when Hadon sensed she was being watched. Hadon over-her-shouldered back at Asshole. "You need to wait in the skimmer," she told him and pointed back the way they came. It didn't seem to change Asshole's watch and wag plan. "Fine," Hadon acquiesced. "Watch my ass, okay?"

The door opened. Easy like closing time. Inside blissfully dimmer, lit by overhead panels. Still hot as balls. Hadon brought up a holo map, marked the container, and traded her swagger for a sprint. No time for style. She raced down rows of cargo containers, a hodgepodge of all shapes and sizes. Follow the holo brick road. Her gangster buyer said whatever she was picking up wouldn't take up much space, but in the context of the great big empty between stars that could mean a lot of things.

Hadon skidded up to the blinking cursor on her map. The container, a fat rectangle standing on end, Hadon's height and a half. Asshole walked right up and sniffed while Hadon took the tour around it. Power cells on the back. A refrigeration unit? Weird.

Her hand buzzed and chirped from an inbound comm. Not text, voice. Hadon checked it. Not Geddy, Burton. Oh boy. Deep breath. Hadon answered.

"Hey babe," Burton said. He had the kind of voice that made Hadon crazy in too many ways. Bedroom voice. Liar voice.

"Everything good?" Hadon asked.

"I don't know. You tell me."

Hadon pulled the key from her pocket, opened the lock panel. "Everything's going according to plan," she told him. "Me and Geddy, waiting on a transport off planet."

"Hot down there, huh?" he asked.

Hadon's daemon tracking Ramble alerted Hadon he was on the move.

"Nothing a cold drink and a bonus won't make worthwhile." Hadon put the key into the lock. It spun and click-clacked, then the front of the container opened with a hiss.

"You think you're getting a bonus on this job?"

"I think I've earned it." Instinct sent Hadon's hand to a gun on her belt.

Burton soft-laughed. "We'll see. Keep your eyes open, yeah? Don't want anything blindsiding my girl."

"You too, babe," Hadon told him, managing through sheer professionalism to not throw up in her mouth as she said it. She cut the comm and swung the container door open.

Inside, sitting on what looked like a fancy vac toilet wearing shackles and a breathing mask with a food and water tube running alongside, a thin naked man waved at Hadon. Asshole wagged and licked his fingers.

Hadon text commed Geddy, "Small complication."

The man in the container tried to reach for the mask on his face but the restraints wouldn't let his hands get that far so he did a sort of jingle jingle look-at-this-awkward-situation flail and made I-want-to-talk-but-I-have-food-tube-stuff-in-my-mouth sounds.

Ramble, high speed headed for the eastside yard. Could be Burton was with him or they split up to cover more ground.

"Fuck," Hadon said. She stepped into the container, careful to avoid the man's very sweaty skin and dangly bits. She pulled the mask off and tube out.

"Would you let me go please?" he asked as soon as he could. He sounded very polite and friendly for a locked-in-a-crate-and-sold-to-gangsters guy.

Text comm back from Geddy: "What is it???"

"Package is bigger than expected," Hadon replied. Then scrolled through cartoons looking for a naked man in handcuffs one.

"Can you carry it???"

Hadon probably *could* throw the bony naked man over her shoulder and get him to the skimmer at least but...

Something trickled down the inside of the vac toilet bowl. Hadon looked down. "Are you...? Right *now?*"

"It tickles," the man said, nodding his head at Asshole, finger licking.

"Do you know what's going on, um—" Hadon waved around—"here?" she asked him.

He nodded. "I have debts."

"Been there," Hadon said. Too many to ever repay.

He scratched Asshole between the ears while Asshole

licked sweat off a knee. "You're working for someone," he said. "Bad people."

"I don't have the luxury to morally judge my employers but we'll go with yes," Hadon told him.

"Do you have air conditioning?"

Hadon shook her head.

He frowned. "Damn."

"Are there pants in there with you?" Hadon wanted to know.

He shrugged. "Who can say?"

"I need a minute." Hadon tugged Asshole back and closed the container again. "It's a man," she text commed Geddy.

"What," Geddy replied.

"In the container." Hadon tapped letters like if she hit the holo images hard enough something might change. "A man. Naked man."

"...Is he hot?"

"FOCUS," Hadon sent. "What am I going to do with a man?"

"...I mean..."

"GEDDY."

"We can't leave him here." Geddy sent a shruggy cartoon. "Right???"

Asshole whimpered and pawed at the container.

Hadon wiped sweat off her forehead. "Fuck," she said and opened the container again.

Naked Man's eyed bulged and his face turned bright red. He gasped and sucked in air.

"Air tight in there, huh?" Hadon asked him. "My bad."

⋯⋯✳︎⋯⋯

THE SOLAR STORM MOVED CLOSER, so did Ramble. All the clocks, carrying a real Hadon grudge.

Hadon burned time getting the naked man cut loose and on his feet. He explained that his name was Tran and he couldn't remember how long he'd been on the vac toilet but it was long enough he made friends with something in the dark.

"Maurice," Tran said. He looked off into the middle distance. "He was nice."

No time for pants. They needed to go. "Come on." Hadon took Tran by the clammy hand. Asshole yipped at their heels.

If she didn't think about the fact that there was clearly no toilet paper or sanitation equipment in that container long enough Hadon hoped the denial would take root.

At the exit, Hadon locked the warehouse back up and clipped on a sensor spike.

"Is this your crew?" Tran asked and gestured to Asshole.

"I don't want to talk about it," Hadon told him.

Tran nodded, knowingly. "Gotcha."

Text comm from Geddy: "Ride sorted. Hurry up!!!"

"Working on it," Hadon mumbled.

Tran looked up at the hazy horizon. "Scorcher today," he said and shimmied his parts around to even out the sunburn.

Finally back in the skimmer, Hadon checked her Illicit Job Things bag and found a spare t-shirt. She tossed it to Tran. "Here."

He smelled it for exactly far too long then pulled it on over his head. "Will Fuck for Tacos" emblazoned across his chest.

"I was thinking you could..." Hadon shook her head,

tried not to look at Tran's hypnotic swinging junk. "Never mind."

Tran pointed at a grav skimmer hellbent for leather their way. "Friendly?"

Ramble.

Hadon pulled Tran down, as out of sight as she could manage in the skimmer. "No." She drew both pistols. "Don't suppose you've got any useful skills in a shoot-out situation?"

He moved his lips around in Let Me Think About It. He shook his head. "I'm more of a 'not shoot-out situation' person."

Hadon's glow ring chimed with a comm. Burton again.

"Do you need to get that?" Tran asked.

"We're not talking now," Hadon told Tran. She silenced the comm notification and checked the video stream from her sensor spike. Ramble's skimmer landed right in front of the warehouse. Bad sign. Seeley must have flipped.

Ramble climbed out of the skimmer. Alone. Real bad-news-good-news rollercoaster.

Asshole fell on his side and rolled to show his belly.

"Stay with the dog," Hadon told Tran.

He rubbed that belly. "Deal."

Hadon got out of the skimmer, blurry head, drunk eyes both ahead and watching Ramble from her sensor spike. Hot like vomit and take a forever nap.

Ramble, not one for patience, shot the lock off the door and went into the warehouse. Okay. Gun time.

Hadon let Ramble get a good enough lead then popped into the doorway. "Touch heaven, motherfucker," she told him, both guns pointed at his back.

"Katie," Ramble said. "How's things?"

"Drop your gun in three, two—"

Ramble's gun dropped onto concrete, hands up.

"Turn around," Hadon said. "Stripper pole slow."

He turned, slow enough not to earn a slug in the head. "Whatever you're thinking you want to do here, you don't want to do it," he said.

Hadon, steady aim. "Where's Burton?"

"He found your Corp Sec guy," Ramble said. "Tagged his grav bike. Knows all of it."

Shit. That made sense. Burton must have gotten Seeley not long after he took off from meeting Hadon while Ramble was checking the dummy container location in the north yards. If her brain wasn't cooked like a baked potato she'd have guessed it. That Burton didn't interrupt their chat and fill Hadon up with dead, the first dumb luck she got all day.

"Why isn't he here?" Hadon asked Ramble.

He smiled. "You're not the only one that got too big for her britches, huh?"

Geddy.

Hadon shot Ramble in the shin. He collapsed screaming.

"Crawl fast and you can get back to your skimmer and maybe get to an evac ship," she said. "Or not."

Hadon text commed Geddy: five cartoon sirens flashing emergency red. "Burton knows. Coming your way."

Ramble screamed all the worst things at her while she hightailed it back to her skimmer. Dudes: they learned three or four bad lady words and mistook using them for a personality.

Less than two hours before it all went up in smoke and ash.

Comm alert. Voice inbound from Geddy. Hadon's gut sank. She answered.

"Hey babe," Burton said.

Hadon got onto the skimmer. "Trevor," she said.

"You know the score here," Burton said. "I've got Geddy. She's alive. Mostly. Have you got the package?"

Sitting on floor of the skimmer, Tran shared an ice cream cone with Asshole. He offered Hadon a bite.

She mouthed, "What the fuck?" to him then, to Burton, "Yes."

"Meet and trade," he said. "An hour. Sending you the location. If you clean yourself up a little and make it worth my while, maybe I forgive you for this one and take you back to bed tonight. Everyone makes mistakes."

Spoken by one of Hadon's biggest. She'd rather stay to the end on Zaren-19. She disconnected the comm.

"Where'd you get the vanilla?" Hadon asked Tran.

"Oh," he said. "I can do things." He twinkled his fingers and with a flourish a flower appeared in his hand. It drooped from the heat almost instantly.

"You didn't think about conjuring up some fucking pants?" Hadon asked him.

By Hadon's count only a handful of suicidal fools had the poor wits to remain on Zaren-19. Countdown to the heat death of the lot: 54 minutes. It would take fifteen minutes minimum to get to orbit and far enough away from the solar storm to survive, but who was counting?

In her pockets, Hadon touched ice cubes. Her naked

man did party tricks. She pulled one out and ran it along the back of her neck and then popped it in her mouth. The cold and wet didn't last long enough. Her grav skimmer hovered a meter above a salt flat outside of the capital while Burton made her wait.

Planetary temps crept up to maximum tolerance for human life. Swoon-and-collapse-with-fatal-heatstroke hot. Hadon couldn't stay standing much longer. Her cheeks, bloody red, her lips blistering at the edges. Hands shaky. She could hardly focus to aim but that didn't keep her from coming armed.

A daemon pinged when Geddy's glow ring sig got inside a search perimeter. Hadon turned to watch a skimmer approach, the salt flying up like fine powder beneath its grav wake. Show time.

A text comm came from Geddy's glow ring: "Land."

Hadon set her skimmer down. Its landing struts shifted wobbly on the salt. She closed her eyes and sucked her lips in at the other skimmer's arrival. It set down with a salt storm, the tiny grains leaving countless stinging cuts on Hadon's sun-baked skin. She opened her eyes, weeping from the burn.

Burton wore goggles and a shit-eating grin. Charming like bad life decisions. He leaned over the end of his skimmer, a few meters from Hadon's. "Don't cry, babe. I got you."

Hadon gestured for Tran to stand up. He stood and shook salt from his hair. She pushed him against the side of the skimmer. He waved at Burton. Genial.

"I want to see Geddy," Hadon said.

"Can we talk for a minute here, Kate?" Burton pulled the goggles up to his forehead. "What's the hurry?"

Hadon pulled a gun and pressed against the back of

Tran's skull. "Ask yourself: How much patience does she have left?"

His smile remained but his eyes, those shit-heel brown eyes, flashed angry. "You're smart enough to play this the right way."

Hadon fired a round into the sky a breath away from Tran's ear. He cried out and his knees knocked. Little tinnitus never killed anyone. "Keep talking about how smart I am," Hadon told Burton.

"All right, all right." Burton put his hands up. "Moody." He ducked down under the side of the skimmer, wrestled with what Hadon assumed was a very defiant Geddy.

"Did you need to do that?" Tran whispered to her.

Geddy popped up like a bad penny, a lock in the middle of her black hair neon blue matching her eyes. A little blood on her chin told the world she'd fucking bite. Her hands were bound behind her back.

"Let her go," Hadon said.

"How about, 'fuck you, Kate?'" Burton shook his head. "This is my hand off. My terms. You give me what *I* want or your friend gets to see her brains fly out from her forehead."

Hadon nudged Tran with the tip of her second gun. "Go ahead."

He looked back. "My ear *really* hurts."

"Get on his skimmer," Hadon told him.

"I hear you, Maurice," Tran said, climbing over the side of Hadon's skimmer. He landed up to his knees in salt and waded toward Burton. "I don't like this planet much either."

"Is he...?" Burton asked Hadon while he stared at Tran's flapping frank and beans.

"Don't start," Hadon said.

Tran threw himself onto Burton's skimmer with the grace of a drunkard. "I'm okay!" he called out from out of Hadon's line of sight.

"Geddy," Hadon nodded at Burton.

Burton undid the restraints on Geddy's wrists and pushed her off the side of his skimmer. She flashed him double middle fingers then got onboard and next to Hadon. "I'm okay," she signed in Intergalactic Sign Language. "Mad. But okay." She looked around and turned her own face into a cartoon when she spotted Asshole lying in a shady spot in the back of the skimmer.

"You're welcome," Burton called out.

Hadon kept her guns drawn and pointed his way.

"You made your play," he said. "Good play, all things considered. But I was always ahead of you. So smart." He pulled his goggles back down. "But then again."

Hadon took a slow hot breath. "Not always," she said.

Burton's glow ring chimed and he looked down at the blinking light.

"You're going to want to answer that," Hadon suggested.

Burton tapped a holo control. "What?"

"We're stuck," Kimber said through the comm.

"What do you mean *stuck?*" Burton eye-to-eye with Hadon.

Kimber's voice garbled into gibberish and the comm dropped.

"You let a hacker on your spaceship, Trevor," Hadon said. "Who's so smart now?"

Burton pulled his gun. "What did you do?"

"I wanted to leave you with a container full of janky fuck bots and my everlasting contempt, but I had a backup," Hadon told him. "Your ride outta here? Uh oh." Hadon cartoon frown faced.

"Crazy bitch," he sneered.

Like she never heard that one before.

Hadon shot the deck of his skimmer next to his leg. Tran, who was nowhere near the shot, jumped back anyway. Burton thought hard about returning fire but held his trigger. Hadon smiled.

"Come on back over," Hadon called out to Tran.

Burton pointed his gun at Tran. "No fucking way."

"Throw your gun into the salt, let him go, and if I'm feeling charitable I'll let Kimber fly down and pick you up in—" Hadon glanced at her holographic doomsday clock "—twenty or so minutes."

Rolling around with Asshole, Geddy signed, "You are so fucking cool!"

"And if you're not feeling charitable?" Burton asked. "How do I know you won't—?"

Hadon interrupted him. "You don't. This is one of those 'ask me nicely and pray to your shitty pickup artist God for mercy' situations."

Burton didn't say it out loud, but he nodded and threw his gun over the side.

Tran peed on Burton's leg, made twinkle fingers, and hurled a handful of shit into the middle of his chest. "Ta da," he said. Then to Hadon: "Do you have any candy?"

"Get over here, Tran," Hadon said.

"Right." He departed Burton's and got on board Hadon's skimmer.

Burton leaned toward her. "You're going to look back on this and regret it, Kate. You never had it so good."

Hadon shot his skimmer's primary throttle and dusted him in salt with her grav wake.

Not fucking likely.

Guns holstered, heartbeat slower, flying back toward the capital, Hadon signed to Geddy: "Ride?"

Geddy brought up the holo interface on her glow ring and threw her a location pin. She checked the doomsday clock. "He's taking off in six minutes," she signed.

Another clock. Why not? Hadon gunned the skimmer's engine.

Geddy tugged Hadon's pant leg. "Can we keep him?" she signed and made Asshole's ears dance.

Hadon nodded and looked over to Tran.

He held a cool, wet rag to her cheek. "I'm undecided," he told her. "But Maurice thinks you're okay."

The gangsters wouldn't be happy, but Hadon could point the blame easily enough at Burton. He'd be a far better distraction for that mess alive. Lucky. Not getting the promised payday would delay getting her own ship but Hadon had time.

"You want to work on the pants?" Hadon asked him.

Tran made his hand into a sun shield and looked into the great wide open. "I'm good."

Outro TK

Pick Your Poison

1. Gimme some inter-species intrigue. Head to "The Silent Passage" by Patrick Swenson

2. *Gimme some sweet P.I. vibes.* Head to "A Cruel Cyber Summer Night" by Austin Dragon

3. **cracks fingers* Let's get hacking.* Turn the page to read "Do-Yeon Performs a Cost-Benefit Analysis on a Career Based on Questionable Activities" by Mark Niemann-Ross

DO-YEON PERFORMS A COST-BENEFIT ANALYSIS ON A CAREER BASED ON QUESTIONABLE ACTIVITIES

A STUPID MACHINES STORY

BY MARK NIEMANN-ROSS

NOBODY SLEEPS ON THE STREETS, BUT DO-YEON fantasizes about it.

Housing is a right of citizenship since 2052. Do-Yeon lives in level one; just solid walls and a locking door. Nothing more. Robots clean the community bathrooms hourly, but the floors still host a persistent culture of bacteria. It's best to wear shoes and disinfect when you get home.

If housing was optional, he could choose where he slept. He could choose what he smelled instead of the odor of chlorine and urine from the sanitizers. He could choose his neighbors, instead of the screaming and thumping of the genetic cesspool collective living on the other side of the shared wall. He could have his freedom.

If you kneel, straighten your back, and tilt your head upwards, you appear content. Do-Yeon sits on the bed with shoulders slumped, head down. This is the posture of defeat.

He should have made better choices at his last job. He shouldn't have used a debug tool on those self-driving cars. He shouldn't have driven them off the road. Maybe he killed the drivers. None of it was proven. But things didn't go his way, and he's stuck here with minimal internet. Not enough for entertainment; only enough to look for work, pay bills, order food. Until he improves his employment, he's languishing here.

He could move back in with his parents. Sell everything, pack a bag, book a poverty ticket on a boat, suffer through seasickness for a week, return to his childhood room and try to restart his life.

He rises and spits. Something will clean it up. He puts on his visor and walks down the hall to the bathroom.

A realtor-beige absorptive layer covers the floor; spills and drips seep through capillary drains. To his left, a woman exits one of the five private stalls, glares at Do-Yeon, and turns to the mirror to pick at her teeth. The stall closes and cleans itself with a blast of chlorinated steam, then opens, ready for the next customer. He enters and sits.

It features a throne and hand-shower doubling as a bidet. He urinates and numbers scroll down the left side of his visor: blood pressure, diabetes, cancer screening, heart attack, addictions. Invasive cameras scan him for melanoma, wounds, and visible signs of stress. They check his eyesight and retinas for glaucoma or cataracts. Preventative healthcare is cheaper than treatment and everyone in level one housing has their health data collected. No choice about it. Privacy is a privilege.

Do-Yeon returns to his room and disinfects his feet, carefully spraying between his toes. He reminds himself to wear shoes next time. The spittle on the floor is gone, consumed by a sanitizer robot which enters from the small door in the wall near the floorboard. He suspects it spreads disease from room to room.

He stands facing the food storage unit (refrigerator, FSU, or "green room" because of the green refrigerant gel). Do-Yeon reaches into the FSU and pulls out a breakfast provided to level one housing. It's a kind of oatmeal with a packet of banana. Do-Yeon knows this because that's what's printed on the package. Without the label, it would be difficult to identify. He puts it in the food processor and turns back to find coffee.

But coffee isn't level one. He can eat anything he wants, but if it's not level one, he has to buy it himself. No coffee this morning.

The food processor tells him the thing he placed inside has changed into oatmeal and bananas. Probably. It *almost* smells like oatmeal, but he knows what oatmeal really smells like. He ate it once when he lived in level five. This has a faint odor of warm plastic. The bananas are chewy, like banana-flavored apple bits.

This apartment doesn't feature a proper table. Instead, a panel and chair fold out from the wall. Do-Yeon can eat breakfast at the table, clear the food packaging, work, move the terminal, eat lunch at the table, clear the packaging . . . and so on.

If he folds up the bed, he has room to pace the apartment, but before he folds out the bed, he has to fold up the table and chair. Before he opens the door, he has to fold up the table. He doesn't bother, there's nothing outside for him. He slumps to sitting on the bed. His eyes are closed, his head is down.

Do-Yeon ranks at 95% proficiency in vehicle AI engineering. Prior to his *almost* conviction, he had a level five apartment with a kitchen, living room, bedroom and a door that could be opened without folding anything away. He had a window. He was at the top of the industry. He's known in the industry.

He's shunned by the industry.

His resulting unemployment dropped him back to level one. He knows how far he fell and he wants it back. But first, he has a work quota to fill. He clears the table of the half-eaten pseudo-oatmeal.

He has no choice but to open a job offer. It's a contract gig, just like every other from the past four months. It requires advanced skills but offers a minimum payout. This is what he gets after hijacking autonomous vehicles and probably (*not proven or convicted*) killing two people. He accepts and completes the project in three hours.

A second short-term gig slides into view, marked as *#IntlPenTest*. International Penetration Testing, also known as freelance espionage against some country. It's an easy ask: annoy the target long enough to get their attention. Not much different from yelling "*Hey—stop that!*" when you see a thief stealing a bicycle. One *HeyStopThat* doesn't change anything; one-hundred *HeyStopThats* might cause them to reconsider. Do-Yeon takes the gig, harasses someone for forty-eight minutes, then collects his fee.

Do-Yeon thinks of going out for the afternoon. Possibly taking his lunch to the park, sitting on a bench, watching people enjoying themselves. There would be clusters of parents talking while their kids and dogs played. There might be other singles eating their lunches, also looking for companionship.

He reflects on the difficulty of friendships. Friends take time. They always want something. Girlfriends, especially, are a lot of effort. He tried. A match would appear. He would respond. They would want him to do something. It was never satisfying.

If he can find long-term work, he can move to some place that doesn't stink. Day gigs are a gerbil-wheel for losers. He calls up the job search counselor—an artificial coach with a cheery attitude.

"*Helllll-oooo* Do-Yeon," says the coach. His name tag says *Alex* in a comic-book font. Alex has a head, torso, and arms, although he rarely uses anything other than facial expressions. Mostly his eyebrows. Alex is an economical render—public funds are better spent on other things. Oatmeal and bananas, for example.

"Welcome back!" Alex is enthusiastic and upbeat. His personality, like his appearance, is inexpensive. "There is nothing for your current profile. Would you like some suggestions?"

"Yes. No. How about broadening the industries you are searching? In fact, please remove the automotive sector entirely. It's obvious they don't want me, so let's move on."

"Done," says Alex without hesitation. "This produces two matches; cyber security and agriculture. Which would you like to start with?"

"What is the agriculture gig?"

"Training field robots to recognize and exterminate an invasive worm. Agricultural work is socially rewarding and employees working in this sector report high job satisfaction and self worth."

"Which pays better?"

"Cyber security. It is corporate network penetrative testing. They've already referenced the #IntlPenTest job you just completed and gave your solution a five-star review. They want you to do more."

"Corporate network penetrative testing is a fancy name for ransomware." Do-Yeon frowns. "What are the numbers?"

"Ransomware is a diminutive term and not an approved descriptor. Corporate network penetrative testing is ranked in the top 30% of compensation plans, includes level three housing and grants stock options every quarter." Alex smiles. It's the only expression Alex has. "The company is Alpha60. They are extending an offer. Shall I tell them yes?"

"Wait a minute," says Do-Yeon. He needs time to think. Ransomware is lucrative, but accepting a job like this is a permanent career choice. Once you add *corporate network penetrative testing* to your resume, future potential employers view you as a threat, or a sleeper for a competitor. But it pays big.

The stock market isn't bothered about this enterprise. Corporate espionage (*ransomware*) has good cash flow and can be publicly traded. There *are* legal issues and occasionally a corporation will step beyond the boundaries, but in those cases, lawsuits are filed, a few guilty engineers are punished, divisions are sold off to competitors, and the stockholders lose their investment. Just another hostile takeover.

It's actually a bit more complex. Every sane business must buy coverage against ransomware if they want to remain on the stock market. Not carrying insurance is malfeasance. The insurance industry makes good money on *corporate penetrative network testing* policies and they've invested in legislation to ensure the legality of ransomware warranties.

The world isn't done with ethics. Not yet. Do-Yeon could explain the agriculture position to his parents. He could attend parties and not debate his career choices. He could go on a date and discuss his occupation with pride instead of evasion. Killing invasive worms would be the right thing to do.

"I'll take the job from Alpha6o," Do-Yeon says. He's already struggling with reputation issues. How much worse can this be? And the pay is better.

He straightens his back. Just a bit.

Moving from level one to level three housing isn't the normal progression. Normal is level one to level two. Years later, level two to level three. But today Do-Yeon sips strong coffee, turns off the mirror health diagnostics, and leaves his bed unmade.

Leaving his apartment had been easy.

1. Pack his shit in one biodegradable bag.

2. Walk two blocks to the new place.

3. Open a new door, walk in, toss the bag in the closet.

He clasps his hands behind his back and looks out his new window at the sunny day. There is a tree cresting over the apartment building across the street. There is a park nearby.

The bathroom (*he has a private bathroom*) doesn't stink of urine or bleach; just a faint orange scent. His window (a *window!*) displays the Willamette river. The ferries to Vancouver and Astoria leave for the second trip of the day.

But he cannot gloat for long. The job at Alpha60 requires serious bandwidth and there are legal concerns about who is contacting who and why, so he has to commute to an office. Do-Yeon locks the door behind him and strolls to the subway, smiling at the neighbors, reading his news feed.

He has a desk in a warehouse of desks. The internet flows through the room like an invisible river over a flood plain. It feeds whirlpools of data to the fifty-seven people on the inside of a Faraday cage. None of the data leaks out, but those fifty-seven find profitable ways to bring it in.

The internet doesn't have an odor, unlike these men and women connected to it. The room could use more ventilation and they could use a shower; most of them are level two housing and subject to water rationing. There are enough level three employees scattered about to keep the level two's envious and motivated. Nobody wants to smell bad. Nobody wants to admit they had oatmeal for breakfast. Level three gets *bacon*.

Corporate network penetrative testing used to be illegal. It is breaking and entering secured computers. It was against the law. But laws change. People like Do-Yeon perform a service by identifying companies with sloppy security. It's better to be called out by friends than to be destroyed by enemies.

Teaching a computer to assault a data warehouse is easy: gather data, try a solution, evaluate success. Just like the rules of tennis: see the ball, hit the ball. But being good at a task isn't as easy as knowing the rules. Do-Yeon is good at this. He teaches computers to pick locks.

Do-Yeon stares at a twitching matrix of numbers, then switches to a heat map, converting those numbers to colors. There are rings of blue, then purple, then a spot of red. Red is the unprotected opening to a corporate data warehouse used by a retailer of hemolytic filters. Do-Yeon encrypts the data, then calls his new client.

"Hello. I'm a cybersecurity analyst with Alpha6o," says Do-Yeon. "I've identified an opening on your system and performed encryption necessary to verify our research. Our consulting fee is . . ." (This is where Do-Yeon inserts a large financial amount in the currency local to the company he contacted.) "When you remit payment, we will release both the method of penetration and the key."

"Dammit," says the corporate IT representative Do-Yeon is talking to. "I thought I had that plugged, but guess not. Okay, can you send an invoice?"

"Let me put you through to our billing department," says Do-Yeon. "I see we've done business before."

"Yep—not our first time," responds IT. "You're going to get me fired if you keep this up."

"You're going to get yourself fired if you don't close these ports," responds Do-Yeon.

"Asshole," says IT.

"A pleasure," says Do-Yeon. "Let's do this again soon."

He forwards the connection to billing. He's only been at this for a few months and is already on the top ten performers list. If he can keep this momentum, he'll be an associate within a year. A partner in five. He imagines a privileged life, possibly with a girlfriend, social engagements, and invitations to parties.

Do-Yeon smiles to himself in cubicle 35 of 57. He

takes a moment to savor this unexpected success, then dives into the next unprotected corporation.

✳

"ALPHA60 IS OUTPERFORMING."

Chip Venetian tweaks the color of his tie and looks around the virtual conference of five partners. Commodities lawyers choose conservative avatars for these meetings, although Chip knows several who will switch to wild-side versions during their off-hours. For now, while they discuss the business of the partnership, everyone is dead serious.

"They've been hiring penetrators for the past year and are seeing some solid returns. Their annual report documented fifty-seven assets in Portland alone, with probably double that number in New York," says Chip. He tosses an animated performance chart into the room, illustrating the short-term growth of Alpha60's value.

"Fairwell Network Security has approached us with a contract to oversee a strategic incarceration of Alpha60. *If you can't beat them, jail them.* Fairwell wants to lock up a few Alpha60 employees long enough to give themselves a competitive advantage."

"Alpha60 stock is fragile and valuable. They'll take an arrest-threat seriously. I think we should realize the value of a strike."

"The ethics of this make me nervous," says the oldest partner. "I recognize I'm operating on traditional rules, but this has bad karma and the consequences are painful."

"Your traditional rules are based on traditional models," replies the outside partner. "We're not operating in those models anymore, so breaking old rules doesn't imply the same consequences."

"Ethics are bullshit," says a bearded partner. "Technocrats make rules to keep themselves in power. If we follow them, they are stronger and we never succeed."

"Oh please," says the tech partner. "Let's save the ethics discussion for the bar. We're here purely to decide on the financial return of a shake-down of a business involved in Corporate Penetrative Testing. Do we make money or not?"

"True," says the last partner. "Threatening Alpha60 without preparation would only invite a ransomware attack. We simply check our defense, then take them down."

"If the only objections are ethical, it's decided," concludes Chip. "I'll put together a strike team. I forecast a payoff within the month."

Do-Yeon swallows the last of a power drink, basketball-tosses the foil container in the trash, and waves through the research in his virtual field-of-view. He's already completed one billable invasion this week, and he wants the next to be bigger. Bigger and more worthwhile of his time. If he's going to make partner, he needs impressive plays. He's confident he can swing it.

The shifting graph is abruptly pushed to the corner of his view. In its place is some sort of corporate communique, telling him to report to room 1233, an office upstairs.

That was quick, he thinks. Smiling, he heads for the

elevator. Working in the cube farm was beneath him and he's looking forward to a corner office.

When he presents himself to the elevator station, one of the sliding doors open and calls his name. He walks in and accelerates skyward. *This is poetic*, he thinks. It's only a minute before he decelerates and stops on the twelfth floor.

The door opens to an unfinished space. There isn't carpet, the walls are still rough construction board. There is a faint smell of paint and glue. His visor informs him to go left, then straight, then open the third door. *This must be an expansion,* he thinks. *I'm on a new team. Probably a director.*

He opens 1233 and steps in. Two security guards flank a chair which faces a desk, behind which sits a woman younger than Do-Yeon. There is no other furniture. There isn't a window and light seems to come from a hidden source. One of the guards motions for him to sit. He does so, arranges his legs and faces the woman. He smiles.

"Do-Yeon Kurrat?" asks the woman. "Is that your real name? Why is there a zero in place of the 'o'?"

"My father was intrigued with Leet Speak. My mother only gave him partial license. Otherwise, my name would have been *Doy3on*."

"But this is you, correct?"

"Of course," says Do-Yeon. "I'm pleased to be here."

"Maybe not," she responds.

Do-Yeon notices she has no name band, either real or virtual. Neither guard has a name band. He's the only person with a name in this office.

"We've been notified of some aggressive transactions between you and several corporations." She waves up a list of Do-Yeon's billable hours over the past month. "You've been planting ransomware in computer systems and extorting companies to have it removed. You've been doing this during work hours and while accessing the corporate network."

"Yes, I have." agrees Do-Yeon. "I believe I've been quite successful. Are you saying I haven't been performing to expectations?"

"No," she responds. "I'm saying you're doing illegal things and Alpha60 can't host those activities. We're under investigation for corporate penetrations, several of which are from you. I'm saying you're being arrested for felony espionage."

"I'm sorry," says Do-Yeon. "I've been doing what you asked me to do. I found vulnerable data warehouses and pointed it out to the owners of that data. That's what penetrative testing is."

"That's one interpretation," she replies. "But it's an illegal interpretation. Here at Alpha60, we pride ourselves on making the world safe from hackers and other miscreants while maintaining an ethically spotless profile."

"You've seen everything I've worked on," states Do-Yeon. He leans forward, and the two security guards take a step closer. "You've encouraged everything I've done. How can you tell me I'm suddenly unethical?"

"We've determined you were acting alone and without sufficient supervision from your manager," she says. "These officers will escort you out of the building and to a detention facility."

Do-Yeon realizes these aren't security guards—they are police. One of them presents him with zip-tie handcuffs. The other helps him to his feet, using gentle restraining force, and turns him around to clamp his wrist.

THE BACK SEAT of this police transport could be padded. Despite his agitation, Do-Yeon appreciates the hard plastic. Cushions would be absorbent and saturated with pee and vomit. Without cushions, everything is visible and sanitary.

It's a brief ride to the station and a shorter trip through booking. He doesn't have pockets, so he doesn't empty them. The officer places his visor in a lockbox and secures it with a scan of his retina. It's safe until later.

He's faint. It's the power drink wearing off and missing lunch. Or it's the missing visor. Or he's fucked, and he knows it.

His guard escorts him into a small hall reminiscent of Alpha60's elevator lobby. One door is open, the other five are closed. It's obvious where he is to go. The room is empty; the wall is a display large enough to show a life-size woman. She might be artificial; Do-Yeon doesn't care.

"Hello Do-Yeon. I'm Yvette and I'll be your case manager." She smiles but otherwise avoids the gestures used to reassure humans. "Standardized sentencing dictates bail for your situation at 20% of your current salary plus benefits. Did you already choose a bail supplier?"

"Bail supplier?" asks Do-Yeon. He is having problems connecting his thoughts. "Forgive me, but this is new since I was last arrested. What is a bail supplier?"

"You may have an employment agreement with the first option to supply bail," she says. "Or you can make yourself available in the open market. There are already five corporations ready to provide you with an offer."

"There are corporations competing to provide me with bail?"

"Yes," she says. "Would you like to speak with them? I can sort them by whatever attribute you wish."

Do-Yeon mulls this over. "What sectors are these corporations operating in?"

"They all specialize in corporate network penetrative testing."

Of course, thinks Do-Yeon. "Let me speak with the company with the highest market value."

A different woman replaces Yvette, this time dressed in a business saree and an identifier band across the screen. It reads: *Aishwarya Vala, Corporate Recruiter, Fairwell Network Security.*

"Hello Do-Yeon," says Aishwarya. She smiles before she continues with her pitch. "Fairwell would like to supply bail and legal representation for your charges and court appearance. In exchange, we ask for five years of employment after your sentencing and possible incarceration. We offer a level four employment compensation package."

"Yvette?" calls Do-Yeon. Yvette appears. "Are the other offers comparable?"

"Comparable, but with minor deviations." Yvette says.

"Fine. I'll accept this offer," says Do-Yeon. Aishwarya reappears immediately.

"Most excellent," Aishwarya responds. "Wait just a minute, please."

In full view of Do-Yeon, she picks up a tablet, makes a few motions, then returns her attention. "All set. We'll send a car to bring you to our offices. Congratulations on joining up with Fairwell!"

✦

THE CAR DO-YEON rides in impresses everyone it passes, but it is mostly meant to impress the rider. It's longer by half than normal vehicles and emits a low rumble: subsonic, so it is felt rather than heard. Blue-green waves of light pulse from front to back, like an oceanic heartbeat. Inside, the seats are held at a constant body temperature. The in-dash bartender asks him what type of Scotch he desires.

The car slides into its privileged space at Fairwell and opens, urging Do-Yeon to step out. Aishwarya is already waiting for him. He notices she is still wearing the business saree, but without the formal jacket. Her eyes seem more vibrant than when they conversed earlier.

"Namaste." she presses her palms together and touches her forehead, then looks up. "Fairwell is pleased you are here. As am I." She smiles warmly, moves closer and takes his arm. "Can I give you a tour?"

Do-Yeon is uneasy about this woman's familiarity. Aishwarya is attractive and he is uncertain how to behave. He emulates a confident industry player, although his only models come from fictional vidplays.

"Yes, please," he replies, dropping his voice to approximate a rich baritone. It's amateurish, but Aishwarya doesn't object.

They enter the first floor lobby, dominated by an opulent reception station. Third through fifth floor is the cubicle farm for entry-level employees. Sixth and seventh are private offices for level three employees. Eighth and ninth is level four. They don't tour floors above nine; those require a separate elevator and Aishwarya isn't qualified to use it.

Do-Yeon is assigned an office on the ninth floor. There is a window and he can see the wires of the radiation cage embedded in the glass. *What happens on ninth floor stays on ninth floor.*

"Welcome to your new family," says Aishwarya. She walks to the window, then half-turns to regard him over her shoulder. "I think you're going to be one of my better recruits."

"Isn't this presumptive?" asks Do-Yeon. He considers Aishwarya for a moment, then continues. "Hopefully, my court appearance will go well. But what if it doesn't?"

"We ran your odds before we made the offer," she says. "You're a lock—there's barely a chance you'll be convicted. Be sure to watch the futures on your judicial proceedings when you're not gloating on Fairwell stock values."

"I guess I'm new to this world," he says. "It seems like you assume breaking the law is part of the job."

"Nobody here will agree with that statement on record," she says, then turns and walks towards him. She touches his arm. "Fairwell strives to provide the highest level of service to our clients. Sometimes they don't realize how much service they need."

"I still have questions," he says. "But I'd like to eat. Can we continue this orientation over dinner?"

"I've met my quota for the day, so yes. Then I'll show you your new apartment."

Her hand moves down his arm to his palm, lightly touching the sensitive skin between his fingers.

"Like they say, nobody sleeps on the streets."

"Namaste," Aishwarya says, selecting a saree from her closet. "We need to get into the office. I've got recruitment quotas that won't be satisfied hanging out here. And as I recall, you are meeting with your lawyer. Miss it and you're going to become an underdog in the betting pool."

Do-Yeon puts a pillow over his head, but Aishwarya pulls it away and throws it to the corner of the room. "Nobody cares if I'm convicted," he says. "I won't serve time. Fairwell covers the settlement."

"I care," says Aishwarya. "I've got action on you. Don't blow up my investment."

Do-Yeon sits up. "You bet on my innocence?"

"No. I bet on the probability your case will be dismissed. The stats department at Fairwell is confident you're a favorable risk. I'm just following their lead."

"So romantic." He flops back on the bed, covering his head with the sheet. "Are we sleeping here tonight or at my place?"

"We've had this conversation for five months now," Aishwarya says. She climbs across him and touches his face. "We should talk about a longer-term solution."

Do-Yeon wears a formal shirt. And formal pants. Court appearances are still in person and defendants stand up. There is no hiding behind a desk.

"Do-Yeon Kurrat, case 63-CR-325631. Please step forward."

The prior defendant was not guilty and happily

leaves the room by the door at the rear of the room. The other door, behind the bailiff, is for unhappy defendants.

Do-Yeon steps up next to Steve, a real (not virtual) lawyer supplied by Fairwell. They've been working on his case for several months, but with the assumption this will be nothing more than a reading of charges followed by a dismissal. At worst, he'll agree to a plea bargain with probation.

Also stepping forward is the prosecuting attorney. Do-Yeon's lawyer does a literal double-take. "Jim-bo. Are you prosecution?" There is a note of surprise and concern in this friendly greeting.

"Hi Steve," says Attorney Jim Lancaster, aka "Jim-bo." One of Portland's highest paid and most aggressive lawyers. Do-Yeon caught someone's attention, or his case caught someone's attention, or the nature of *Corporate Penetrative Testing* caught someone's attention.

There's no time for conversation and both attorneys straighten up. Steve swears quietly. Do-Yeon looks uneasily at the door behind the bailiff.

---※---

"TEN YEARS?" screams Do-Yeon. "This was supposed to be a sure thing. I'm supposed to be in a meeting this afternoon. I'm having dinner with Aishwarya tonight."

Do-Yeon faces his lawyer across the table. Justice used to move slower. Court appearance and sentencing used to take days, sometimes weeks. Now it takes hours.

"Okay. This didn't go the way we planned," admits Steve. "But I wouldn't worry much. Fairview has an interest in your employment after incarceration. It's in their best interests for you to be released quickly, and I expect they'll be calling tomorrow morning to get me started."

"Which sounds like I'll be spending tonight in prison," says Do-Yeon. He is not exhibiting self-control. "I'm not okay with this!"

"Relax," says Steve. "Take the night off. Think of this as a spa day, just without the spa. Let's talk first thing in the morning."

But Steve doesn't call the next morning. Do-Yeon hears nothing from anyone until Aishwarya arranges a visit a week later.

"I had to give up our apartment," she says. "Without us together, I'm only allowed a level three. Plus, I lost a lot of money on your conviction. I moved your things into storage. There just isn't room for all the furniture."

"Fine. Sell the big stuff we bought," Do-Yeon says. "keep my personal things in your closet. We can move back to a larger place when I get out."

"Look," Aishwarya says. "I want children. I can't wait ten years for you to be released. Even then, you'll need to relearn skills and restart employment. It could be fifteen or sixteen years before we can afford a place big enough for a family."

"You're breaking up with me," Do-Yeon realizes this out loud.

"I'll call you next week and we can talk more."

Learning a new habit takes most people three weeks of repeated practice. Adjusting to a new living situation takes longer; some research says a year and a half. For Do-Yeon, it took two years to become accustomed to prison habits.

Now, he no longer sticks out as the new guy. He knows when to talk and when shut up. He lines up for meals, fresh clothes, and linens. He knows when the commissary is open. He made a friend, that friend transferred, and he learned to make more than one friend. He listens more than talks. He doesn't borrow, doesn't loan.

His state-sponsored accommodations aren't given the dignity of a rating. He thinks of it as level zero. The bathroom is communal, his room is spartan, his privacy is nil. The mirror reads his physical health, but doesn't reveal the results to him. Other inmates might view his stats, and that would violate HIPAA laws. If he wants to know his blood pressure, he needs to file Freedom of Information Act requests.

He gets depressed. He gets counseling. He gets exercise. He gets outdoors. Most important, he gets jobs.

He is back to small gigs, but with close supervision, limited bandwidth, and short working hours. Seventy-five percent of his income is garnished to pay for his incarceration. He's having a difficult time saving anything for retirement or for moving into something other than level one housing when he gets out.

He's not happy about this. He did nothing wrong; he continues to do nothing wrong. Yvette explained it all to him when he figured out how to ask the right question: *"What is the purpose of this? Why am I here?"*

Yvette is programmed to recite a carefully scripted

response, written by the Hammurabi corporation, owner of the private incarceration facility holding Do-Yeon.

"Incarceration provides society with several benefits," begins Yvette. "First, it provides crime victims with a sense of retribution. Without retribution, victims lose faith in the system of justice. Without retribution, victims resort to vigilantism and other aberrant social behavior."

"I could have viewed this video without your help," retorts Do-Yeon. "I believe this is covered in some corporate shareholder discussion. I'm guessing Hammurabi? Perhaps Incarceration Corporation of America?"

Yvette pauses for this outburst.

"Second, incarceration is a deterrence to aberrant social behavior," she continues. Do-Yeon rolls his eyes and sits with resignation. "Law-abiding citizens are tempted by legal shortcuts to desired results. Without deterrents, there would be no consequences for misbehaving."

From his seat, Do-Yeon sits up and interrupts. "I wasn't misbehaving. I was doing what Alpha60 rewarded me to do. Why aren't they in here with me?"

"Corporations have rights, just like every other citizen of the United States," replies Yvette, projecting synthesized patience. "Jailing a corporation and all its employees and shareholders is impractical. With a low possibility of success, it is a waste of judicial resources."

Do-Yeon slumps back in the chair. He doesn't miss the subtext; Yvette knows how to respond to questions about corporate culpability. Yvette resumes the lecture.

"Third, incarceration provides an opportunity to rehabilitate offenders. Criminals need lessons in social cooperation and mutually beneficial behaviors. Without rehabilitation, crime and incarceration are an endless cycle."

Do-Yeon retreats to a futile hand-waving gesture that encourages Yvette to speed up the unwelcome playback. Yvette does not take the hint.

"Finally, incarceration is a short-term method for incapacitating a persistent criminal. Many criminals refuse to change past behaviors and are not deterred by incarceration. Without incapacitation, some criminals view release from prison as a short-term window to enhance their aberrant career."

"Your talking points are a polite way of justifying why this corporation needs to keep prisons operating and occupied," spits back Do-Yeon. "No incarceration, no cash flow. No cash flow, no market value. No market value, no shareholders. If I had been smart, I would have bought stock in Hammurabi before they sent me here. Then I would have at least profited from my unjust imprisonment."

Yvette isn't programmed to disagree. And she doesn't.

EVERY DAY, Do-Yeon receives a call from Yvette for case management. She is normally his only caller. But not today.

"Hello Do-Yeon," says *not* Yvette.

"You're not Yvette." Do-Yeon states the obvious.

"True," says Steve. "Sorry I didn't get back to you sooner. Been busy, all that kind of stuff."

"Sorry?" says Do-Yeon. "That's all? *Sorry?* Where did you go? You said you'd call me the day after my appearance. It's been two years. What happened in there?"

"It was a complex deal," replies Steve. "My office AI came up with three hundred and fifty-seven scenarios before it solved what happened. Jim-bo didn't even know until I told him last week. We had lunch."

"You had lunch with the guy who's responsible for this?" Do-Yeon gestured at the prison-surplus terminal they forced him to gig with.

"Yep. And I won't include it in your billable hours. Here's the deal. You were doing a great job for Alpha6o. A *really* great job. Alpha6o was eclipsing the market and Fairwell couldn't compete, so they hired a corporate raider to trip Alpha6o up."

"But Fairwell provided my employment and legal contract!"

"Entirely opportunistic. Fairwell didn't expect Alpha6o to throw you under the bus. When you were available, they swooped in. You have to admire how quickly they put that package together."

"But they aren't clever enough to get me out of here."

"Jim-bo is a good litigator, and you attracted a lot of action. More than any of us realized. Some big investors and mostly-illegal cartels formed a hedge fund, bought a position in your case, and made sure they didn't lose."

"And now?" asks Do-Yeon. He's not done being sarcastic. "You show up with a social visit. Should I make an appointment with your scheduler for a repeat meeting in two years?"

"No need," Steve pulls up a document for Do-Yeon to see. "This is an early release. It has some contingencies, but nothing you haven't already encountered. Take a look, but this second document is more interesting."

"Let me see it," says Do-Yeon. Steve waves the document over to him. "This is some sort of spreadsheet with my name on it."

"Yep. Hammurabi ran a cost-benefit analysis on your imprisonment. You make too much on your gigs to allow them to claim you as a reimbursable burden and collect fees from the state. But you don't make enough to be in the top 20% of income producers. They're not impressed by your long-term prospects. You're not profitable and they want to fill your bunk with someone who has a better payoff."

"I'm being fired for being a non-performing asset," realizes Do-Yeon.

"That's not the accepted terminology. You're being released because your incarceration is not in anyone's best interest. Pack your socks. You're sleeping at your own place tonight."

ONCE AGAIN, he's in level one housing with just enough internet for what is required of him. He sits up from the folding desk and walks to the communal bathroom. Pees and flushes and returns to his hell.

Do-Yeon summons his job-search counselor. "Alex, what do you have for me today?" "Hello Do-Yeon," Alex smiles. "Sorry, I have nothing for you."

"Fine. Broaden the search filter. I'll look at anything."

"I've already done that. I have nothing for you."

"Nothing?"

"Nothing," confirmed Alex. "Your ranked performance has dipped below the employable threshold."

"Why did that happen?" says Do-Yeon. He uses his

outdoor voice, but knows it won't really change Alex's behavior.

"You recently received a sub-standard review from the Hammurabi corporation," Alex says, smiling. "They rated you lower than the top 20% of performing assets."

"I was a prisoner!" Do-Yeon now uses his outdoor voice with gusto. "They can't rank my performance."

"Hammurabi combines the performance of incarcerated assets with their traditionally employed assets. It is part of their annual report and statement of financial condition."

"They can't!"

"It is an accepted accounting practice. Otherwise, they would have to declare incarcerated labor as short-term assets, in which case they would be forced to depreciate your value over five years. The law prevents attaching value to a person. So they are forced to report incarcerated productivity as part of overall productivity."

Do-Yeon angrily shuts the conversation. He looks around the small room. He smells chlorine and urine. He hears the neighbors fighting.

Nobody sleeps on the streets, but Do-Yeon fantasizes about it.

"Do-Yeon Performs a Cost-Benefit Analysis on a Career Based on Questionable Activities" is another of Mark Niemann-Ross's stories set in a slightly-future world that often feels all too maddeningly familiar. Discover his latest novel Stupid Machine *and other titles at niemannross.com*

Pick Your Poison

1. *Let's blow it all up.* Head to "Narrow EscApe" by Maddi Davidson

2. *Deal me in.* Head to "Ace in the Hole" by Kate Sheeran Swed

3. *Bust me out of here!* Turn the page to read "The Western Oblique Job" by Mark Teppo

THE WESTERN OBLIQUE JOB
BY MARK TEPPO

LALLAY LEOTEMORAH WAS DAYDREAMING ABOUT A
stay-away vacation in a private high-flyer suite on Particu-
late Chalice, that fancy resort station thwack in the
middle of the Hydrangea Nebula. Stacked with a week's
worth of food and entertainment and a fully stocked wet
bar, of course. No windows. No access to the local
network either. Keep the distractions to a minimum. The
suite didn't have to be big—he wasn't asking for much—
but two rooms, at least. One of which would have a tub.
He wouldn't fill it with water—that was a completely
unnecessary extravagance—but he would sleep in it. All
by himself.

One week. Seven days. Two hundred and—

"Hey, convict."

Leo snapped out of his fantasy, and the steam-filled
bathroom of the high-flyer suite vanished. He squinted in
the hard glare of the desert sand. The man interrupting
his daydreaming wore the uniformly ugly gray of the
Kapladonic Extraction Company. He had a narrow face
and a flat nose—the sort of face a mother would love until

the epidural wore off. If the company had a dental plan, this guy wasn't taking advantage of it.

"Dreaming about pussy?" the snaggle-toothed guard asked.

Once upon a time, Leo would have responded with a crass comment about the man's mother—or even his sister—but somewhere in the last eight hundred and sixty-four days, Leo had lost interest in that sort of insouciance. A pity, really, because the ladies had always liked his devil-may-care attitude toward bullies, tough guys, and all-around assholes. However, Leo was on a steady diet of assholes these days, and there were—how many?—two thousand, nine hundred, and eighty-four more days of this bullshit to go.

"Aeya," Leo sighed. "I may have been."

The ugly bastard—whose name was Piertrie and who not-so-secretly harbored a real kick-in-the-nuts animosity towards those who had traveled more than a light-year in their lifetime—grinned at Leo. Man, his teeth were crooked. "You ain't getting none today," he chortled.

Nor tomorrow or tomorrow or the day after, Leo thought. He rolled his tongue into his cheek, considering a response. Maybe it was the hard light of the landscape that was making him feel a little starchy. Maybe it was the monotony of this . . . ugh, he really didn't want to call it a "relationship," but what other word was there?

"Get back to work," Piertrie snarled. "Or I'll get someone to discipline you."

Leo's *work*—if you could call sitting on your ass and staring at drone monitors work—was to watch the obso-lete-by-any-standard flyers float over the endless hotness of the Thanelu Wastes, a couple hundred thousand square kilometers of rock and sand that ran from the

Barrier Wall to the Endle Escarpment. Kaplodonic—as far as the Trade Houses and Ansalaage were concerned— was a mining subsidiary of House Quinc. They were on Gloassia IV scouting for deep chart metals, the sort of materials used in long-range sensor arrays or next-generation fusion drives or—Leo didn't know, actually. Didn't care either. What he—and three hundred other bunkers— knew was that the Kaplodonic Extraction Company was a black site work farm.

A prison, if you wanted to be gauche about it.

Now, it's expressly noted in IECA—the Interstellar Exploration and Commerce Accords—that the individual has inherent and unassailable sovereignty over themselves. Subsequent lines in the Accords go on and on about the definitions of "sovereignty" and "individual," laying out in very precise terms how a Trade House must honor and respect the all-important sanity of a person. Naturally, a lot of these subsections complicated the efficiency of cleaning up loose ends that was capital punishment, and most Houses had to resort to more economic— and societally acceptable—solutions when it came to dealing with criminals. Which was to say, you worked off your debt the old-fashioned way.

In Leo's case, a term of ten Galactic Standard years: three for trafficking in illegal goods, three for traveling under forged documents, and four for carrying unlicensed armament within House Quinc's jurisdiction. In a word: Leo had been smuggling contraband. Good shit, too.

It hadn't been the first time, and should he survive the next two thousand, nine hundred, and eighty-four days (not that he was counting), Leo suspected he would probably commit the same crimes again in Quinc-controlled space. He knew this about himself: he had a habit of picking up things that didn't belong to him.

Anyway, the tech running the drones was old-wire milspec—stuff already ancient when Leo took his first fealty oath to a free company. His youthful enthusiasm aside, he had been the shortest one in his battalion, which meant he got picked last and stayed at the depot more often than not. Leo had a choice: let his size control his career, or actually do something with the talents he had. And so, while the rest of the muscle-bound, testosterone-frenzied fucknuts of the Liberty Security Fraternity were suiting up and dropping down on some backwater planet and terrorizing the locals, Leo went about mastering the company's support infrastructure. He learned how to fly the drones; he reverse engineered all the comms; he became a god at rewiring the rigs when their circuit boards flashed or tiny biters got into the semsi-neural wetpaths; he pulled machine intelligences back from the brink when they lost themselves in self-referential logic traps. He made himself indispensable, and when the mercenary companions were outlawed after the atrocities committed by the Armored Security Legion in the Mari-colasa Insurrection, Leo's skills made him a useful bunker. And when he got goosed in one of House Quinc's Inter-planetary Security Agency dragnets, his debt was quickly bought out by Kaplodonic and he was shipped to the sandiest and emptiest planet in the entire Galactic arm.

Where, proving the old axiom that the universe forgot nothing, especially your past mistakes, Leo found himself in charge of a bunch of tech that looked like it had fallen off an old ASL dreadnaught, which it probably had. A lot of the Legion's hardware had quietly disappeared while House Maricoli was still wailing on about the atrocities committed by the Fists. It didn't take much computation power to guess the color of the mood boards in CORE's council chambers. And since it was a crime to possess this tech, obviously you needed a criminal to support it.

Anyway, the goal of today's excursion was mapping the gullies and ravines of the Western Oblique Boulange, an eighty kilometer-long upthrust of granite and basalt that rippled along the ragged spine of the Wastes. An angry shard of a mountain in the making. There were lots of crevices and cracks along the Oblique, and KEC was eager to get a topographical mapping done so they could sink some crustbusters and bring up whatever precious metals and minerals that were hiding beneath the sand.

Look, if House Quinc couldn't dissolve individuals it was displeased with, then they were going to get some useful work out of them. KEC wasn't a charity. Like every other subsidiary, it had to show a profit somehow.

Leo and Piertrie were in a Garnesh Industries industrial trawler—an eight-wheeled ground-hugger of a transport designed to move men and machines from one location to another as efficiently and as uncomfortably as possible. A half-dozen muscled toughs glowered from hard seats. Leo wasn't sure why management insisted on so many watchdogs. It wasn't like he could hop out of the trawler and make a break for the Wall. Mostly, he ignored them. He had screens to watch.

Leo had four drones in the air; two were doing high-altitude scans of the Oblique, building the general topo model; the other two were crawling the extensive maze of crevices that covered the rocky upthrust. A clock on one of the screens said they had been at it for six hours. The drones had another three or four hours of battery power before they had to come back to the trawler to recharge.

Another two to rumble back to Rover Bacco—an old mining facility that Kaplodonic had taken over as their base of operation. All told, a day's *work*—as it was—which meant Leo's debt would be reduced by one when they returned to base.

You marked the victories, no matter how small.

One of the high-flying drones pinged an atmospheric anomaly alert on his slate, and Leo absentmindedly went to tag it as one of the infrequent sightings they had of the indigenous predators that surfed the thermals over the Thanelu Wastes. He hesitated when he glanced at the visual profile on the screen. It was long and thin, not at all like the flat discs the software used to represent the flyers. He zoomed in on the object, and as he watched, it spawned a small mushroom shape that trailed behind it. Another mushroom blossomed, and Leo realized he was watching a high altitude drop chute deploy.

"What is that?" Piertrie, always sensitive to changes in the room, was suddenly standing behind Leo's station.

"Drop chute," Leo said.

"An assault trooper?"

"Cannasay," Leo said, falling into the loose slang of the bunkers, the men and women who did the important contract work on Trade House ships.

"Are we . . . are we under attack?"

Leo could understand the incredulity in Piertrie's voice. There was nothing of strategic value in the Thanelu Wastes. The nearest landmark visible space was Heggorah Spire, a mile-high barrier of slag and stone, that was more than two hundred kilometers south of their current location. If some agency was dropping soldiers on the Oblique, they were operating under incredibly bad intelligence.

Unless, of course, they had really good *intelligence,* Leo thought, reflecting on the other *other* thing that Kaplodonic was doing on Gloaasia IV. *Even then, why were they dropping a spotter here and not closer to Rover Bacco?*

Leo checked the feed from the other high-flyer drone. "Just the one," he said. "Nothing else in the atmo."

Leo and Piertrie watched the tiny shape twist beneath the half-moon of the drop chute. The drone's resolution was grainy, but it was clear that an actual person was flying that chute.

"They're heading for us," Leo realized.

Piertrie swore. He started yelling at the Rover muscle, using words like "imminent," "assault," and "sky bandits." Leo doubted Piertrie's assessment, but he understood the threat level Piertrie was shoving at the muscle. It was the sort of message fucknuts understood, and by the time the falling angel had landed, the team of security goons were armored and ammoed. They surged out of the trawler in a fashion that wasn't entirely embarrassing, and all their guns pointed in the right direction.

Which seemed like an awful lot of overkill for the narrow-shouldered, suggestively-curved, leather-clad figure, but hey, an anomaly was an anomaly. No one ever congratulated you for under-reacting. The figure raised her hands to show she wasn't carrying any armament. The comm speaker in the cabin of the trawler crackled as she reached out. "Hello boys. This display of heavy weaponry is very flattering."

Piertrie stabbed a button on his console with more force than necessary. "Who are you?" he demanded. "What are you doing here?"

"I was hoping to talk to someone in charge. I doubt that's you, but maybe you could give me a lift?"

"You are trespassing on Kaplodonic—"

The woman did a thing with her fingers, and a blinking logo slammed Leo's slate. Six stars and interlocked triangles. Ansalaage's Ministry of Accordance, Recompense, and Solidarity. The group called in when diplomatic language and economic sanctions weren't getting the job done.

In the cabin, Leo was the only one who heard Piertrie's heart leap in his chest. "That's . . . you—you are highly irregular," the trawler boss managed.

"I know," the woman said. There was a conciliatory tone in her voice. "But I thought it would be easier if I just cut through the executive thought-speak and showed up."

Piertrie stammered something into the comms and then turned toward Leo. His face was flushed, and his eyes were wide and agitated.

"You should call it in," Leo suggested, trying to be helpful. "Get some feedback from management. Maybe even have someone talk to Boss Man. This way it isn't your fault if—"

Piertrie flapped his hands at Leo. "Take her down," he said to the squad of goons with guns. "Boss Man'll want to see our prize."

Leo flicked the external trawler cams to the big screen so he could watch what happened next. Why wouldn't he? This was the most excitement he had had in a very long time.

The six KEC troopers approached the leather-clad woman. One of them shouted at her to get down on her knees. She didn't comply. Three of them charged her. There was a minor fracas, which ended with two of the three KEC men incapacitated. The third held the woman down long enough for the remaining troopers to move in.

"Bring her in," Piertrie told his victorious squad. He gave Leo a gloating smile.

Leo didn't say anything. To his eye, the whole exchange looked like it had gone exactly as the woman had planned.

HADRAX THOOLSENJ WASN'T a religious man. His upbringing had been spartan and uncomplicated by needless rituals. His father reminded him—regularly, and usually with the back of his hand or a leather strap—that Cause and Effect was the only scientific principle that mattered, and when he reached the age where he was allowed to make his own decisions, he traded one dysfunctional family for another. His lack of imagination when it came to superstitious nonsense gave him focus and direction, and three years and two hundred kilograms later, his squad commander put him up as a candidate for forward-action infantry. This led to that—cause and effect, again—and within the year, he was a pilot of the Galaxy's most dangerous tools: a suit of powered battle armor.

The first generation were little more than stiff-legged tanks with big guns. On-board crew was two, along with a flight bay of signal analysts and computational workstations who did all the heavy lifting when the pilot pointed and said *Put a hole in that*. Naturally, armed conflict begat technological advances which begat more armed conflict, and before you could say "Fourth Interregnum," quantum computing and neurofiber optics came to the battlefield.

Six-gen suits shrunk to the size of a luxury escort wagon, and they carried more ammunition than an entire shock battalion. A year later, compression technologies and neuro-metallurgical printing reduced the physical space needed for a dropsuit's computational core to a box about the size of a grown man's stomach.

Or, in Hadrax's case, a space behind his stomach and next to his spine.

That was all well and good until a few psychopaths ruined the fun for everyone. House Maricoli's legal consortium shed a lot of tears for the feeds during CORE's humanitarian audit of the Maricolasa Insurrection. *Not since the bloody days of Chamouleuf XXXIV had there been such a brutal disregard for the value of human life*, they had wept. *These men in their armored shells—these Fists—are nothing more than the binary operators of cold-calculating killing machines. They are the worst monstrosities of the Old Empire, brought back from the dead!*

Cue a collective gasp across the Hub as mothers tried to ward off night terrors of the Octillenarchy from their children.

Anyway, Hadrax and the rest of the Fists were, in the words of his old commanding officer, gelded and put out to pasture. ASL medicos had integrated the vaults so completely that they couldn't be removed without destroying the host's nervous system. With Ansalaage's defense team banging on the table and citing IECA Section 18.43.7A, it was decided that the soldiers could keep their wetware, but it would be heavily code-spliced to permanently restrict them from accessing the martial modeling and command codes.

You get to keep your dicks, but you won't be swinging

them much, as Major Panxtrex said when he informed the incarcerated Fists of the decision passed down from the Hanseatic Trade Federation's Cabinet of Order, Regulation, and Enforcement.

The vaults were still a solid block of quantum computing power, and most of the dropsuit operators, having been shamed, code-spliced, and stripped of all rank and privilege, vanished into the Penumbral Notion, the underground gray market, where they found employment as House security consultants.

You can as outraged as you like in public about conflict atrocities, but in private, you get your hands on the tech before other Houses. The winners get to write the narrative, after all.

Which is how Hadrax ended up working for Eldred Kane in the Celedonia system, running a network of trade routes and smuggling operations. His vault managed Kane's security needs, and under his watch, the network flourished. So much so that trade cooperatives in six surrounding systems made formal complaints to House Radigunde, who ostensibly owned that sector of the Galactic Spiral. Forced to address the trade inequity in their backyard (even though Kane was paying passage coin to House coffers for every ship that carried managed cargo), House Radigunde sent a Solutions Management Director to Celedonia to deal with the problem. Thinking he was clever, the SMD peeped to Ansalaage about IECA violations.

Ansalaage sent a team who fucked everything up.

Hadrax still didn't understand how the Ansalaage splicer had messed up his insides. At first, it had been a pressure in the back of his brain, an insistent *tap-tap-tapping* like someone was banging a finger against his skull. The pressure increased and ebbed, and it hadn't taken Hadrax long to figure out it was a proximity trigger. The farther away he got from the splicer, the harder he got tapped. The splicer and his boss were still in the custody of local law enforcement, whose security he had co-opted years ago. He had walked right into the interview room where they were being held and demanded the splicer undo what he had done.

The splicer's boss—a slight woman who not only knew how to handle a shock rod, but commanded a room with her cold intensity and brilliant gaze—asked for a favor, which was easy, and for passage. *Once we're clear of this gravity well, Nome'll undo everything he's done.*

The hammering in his head had been relentless for the next twelve hours—a constant *thwack-thwack* that brought Hadrix all the way back to the family commune and his father's fucking leather strap—and then it had stopped.

She had kept her word, but she hadn't told him everything.

Over the next six months, his computational abilities went to shit.

Hadrax managed to cover his mistakes the first few weeks, but when he lost an entire shipment of gyroscopic stabilizers to a local crew of dippers, Kane couldn't overlook the failings of his security chief. Hadrax hadn't even *seen* the dippers until after the snatch and grab. They were using some grayslice code, which undoubtedly came from House Radigunde. The code punched holes in the security feeds and filled those holes with so many reverberating echoes that Hadrax got a stomach ache when he ran the standard array of noise filters. *You haven't been yourself,* Kane

said when they met in his boss's plush pad. *Not since . .*
.

I'm fine, Hadrax had assured his boss. In deference to their shared history together (along with the not-insignificant market share Kane had amassed with Hadrax as chief), Kane didn't press the issue. But when a rig full of micro-array munitions and targeting modules went *poof!*, Kane had to do something. It wasn't about money any more. Hadrax's fuckups were arming the competition.

A cold transaction followed. Eldred Kane sold Hadrax Thoolsenj to House Radigunde's Security Division; in return, slates were wiped clean and passage percentages were dropped three tenths of a percent for five Galactic standard years. Objectively, Hadrax saw it as the smart play that it was; subjectively, it hurt. Hadrax hadn't been abandoned like that since his second stepmother had walked out on he and his brood brothers. He nursed his hurt for quite some time.

EVERYONE GATHERED in the staging bay of the trawler, where the KEC toughs had trussed the prisoner with most of the detention cord the trawler carried. She knelt on the floor, her arms pinned to her side. There were some scuffs on the darkened faceplate of her helmet and on her dropsuit, but she was otherwise unmarked.

One of the two she had taken down was suffering from a broken wrist; the other man limped like his right leg had been amputated and then reattached backward.

Piertrie motioned for Leo. "Get her helmet off," he said.

"Me?"

"If she wants to tear someone's arm off, let it be yours," Piertrie said. He gave Leo a nasty grin. "Workplace accidents for managed employees are much less paperwork."

Leo approached the captive woman. He couldn't see her face, but the angle of her head indicated she was watching him. Mildly curious more than concerned.

"I'm—I'm going to take your helmet off, okay?" Leo said. His reflection was distorted by the plate, making him look like a bug-eyed buffoon. When the woman didn't say anything, he stepped closer. Her form-fitting dropsuit was bulked up across the chest and waist with added armor and padding. It wasn't one of those infantry models that came with a powered exoskeleton—something more than human but less than full battle dress. It looked like a recon suit or the sort of outfit worn by a different kind of specialist.

Leo raised his hands toward the helmet seals. He expected her to pull back, but she surprised him by turning her head to the side so that he easily access the management clasps. He flipped both, and when he twisted the helmet, the seals disengaged. The helmet came free with a hiss of escaping air.

Her hair was short and white, and it made Leo think of the wispy clouds that scurried across the sky in the wake of the scorching sun. Her eyes were green—like the color of the stones spat out by the hoppers that scoured the canyons of the Oblique. Her skin was paler than his, but that wasn't hard, given the scorching his bones had taken during his first year of "employment." Her features were strong and symmetrical, suggesting managed genetics.

"Hi," she said, and Leo realized he had been staring.

"Uh, hello." He lowered the helmet. It was light in his hands. Flexible. *Heavy coin*, he thought. *This is spoke gear.*

"Get away from the prisoner, convict." Piertrie's voice interrupted Leo's train of thought. Somewhat embarrassed, Leo shuffled away from the bound woman.

She continued to look at Leo. "Convict?" she asked, raising a shapely eyebrow.

Piertrie flushed. "*Managed employee* Leotemorah," he corrected. "You will stand away from the interloper."

"Does that—does that position come with any benefits?" she asked.

"What—what benefits?" Leo wasn't sure what she was talking about.

"You know. *Employee* benefits."

Leo continued to stare at her.

"Shut up," Piertrie snapped. "You will stop talking. Right now."

The woman finally looked up at the trawler boss. "And judging by your tone, you must be the man in charge," she said.

"Yes," Piertrie said. "I am in charge. This is my operation. And you are—"

"I'm a prisoner," she said brightly. She made a show of wiggling in her bonds, demonstrating how decisively she had been wrapped.

"Yes—No. No, you are *not* a prisoner. You are, uh, trespassing on private property, and therefore—that is—that is you are being detained—"

"Whose property?" she asked briskly.

"This—this area is under the mandate of the Kapladonic Extraction Company."

"Oh, good." She smiled at Leo. "I'm in the right place."

Piertrie's face started to swell. This conversation wasn't going the way he had expected. "What—"

"What am I doing here?" She nodded. "That's a great question. I'm glad you asked. As I said earlier, before your guys got all jumpy on me, I'm here to talk to whomever is in charge. Not *in charge* like you are, even though—yes, I can see that you have all of these fine gentlemen well in hand, so to speak. No, I'd like to talk to the big man. The guy who runs this whole thing. Kaplodonic." She made the word into a series of pops and clicks of her tongue and lips.

When no one spoke up, she shrugged and wiggled. "Soonish, if you don't mind," she added. "Before these restraints cut off all the circulation in my legs."

Two of the KEC toughs who hadn't been roughed up by the woman were smirking, and Piertrie couldn't help but notice their amusement. "Who—who do you think you are?" Piertrie snapped at the woman.

"Didn't you get my transmission?" she asked. "I broadbeamed it right away. Surely . . ."

"I didn't receive any transmission," Pietrie snarled.

Leo made an involuntary noise, and both the woman and the trawler boss focused on him. "Actually . . ." he started.

"Be quiet, convict," Piertrie snapped. "No one asked for your input."

Leo considered saying something, but the tight-eyed glares he was getting from the KEC toughs said they were hoping he'd shoot his mouth. Give them a reason to wrap him up with the rest of detention cord.

The woman pursed her lips. ""Not much for constructive feedback, are you?" she asked Piertrie.

Piertrie stared at her.

She took his look as invitation to explain. "Well, you've got a 'managed employee' who looked like he was going to offer some insightful criticism of your leadership style, and I, for one, was curious as to what his observations were. I mean, I have some of my own opinions about how you're doing, but since I don't work here, it's not all that polite of me to offer unsolicited commentary. However, and I don't mean to overstep, but this fellow looks like a very dedicated worker." She glanced at Leo. "You have nice hands," she said.

"Uh, thank you?" Leo was suddenly aware of his hands and he wanted to hide them behind his back, but as he was still holding the woman's helmet, he couldn't do so without dropping her gear. He settled for fidgeting.

One of the toughs guffawed.

"You ride the desk here, don't you?" the woman asked. "But it hasn't always been that way."

Leo cleared his throat. "I, uh, yes, only recently."

"I thought so. You have that look. What did you do before this job?"

"Shut her up!" Piertrie yelled at his men. "Make her stop talking."

As Leo started to answer her question, one of the guards walked over to the woman and smacked her on the head with the butt of his shock baton. She gave him a look that turned her eyes into hard chips in her sculpted face. The guard smacked her again, and her eyelids fluttered for a moment, and then she collapsed to the deck.

There was silence in the bay for a moment, and then one of the other guards spoke. "Hey, uh, boss?"

"What?" Piertrie snarled.

"If she's—I thought I saw something on the beam earlier and . . ."

"And what?"

The guard looked at his fellows. "If—if she's who she says she is—"

"Which she isn't," Piertrie interrupted.

The guard wasn't easily deterred from making his point. "If she's Ansalaage, I—I don't think me and the boys want to, you know, have a MARS edict or something . . ."

"You're a cog, and a very dull one at that," Piertrie frothed. "Why would anyone—much less Ansalaage—bother with any amount of paperwork in your regard?"

"I—I dunno. It's just . . . "

"What?" Each time he spoke, Piertrie's voice rose a half octave.

"Maybe we should—maybe?—maybe we should call this in. Before, you know, we do anything that might . . ."

Piertrie fumed for a few moments. "Put her—put her in a holding container," he decided. He looked at Leo. "Recall the drones. And get us back to Bacca. The Big Boss'll want to know about this." He tried to make it sound like this had been his plan all along, but there was a petulant whine at the edge of his voice that he couldn't quite smooth out. The men heard it, but they mumbled among themselves until they had convinced themselves otherwise. Two of them dragged the woman out of the staging bay, and the others followed Piertrie back to the transport deck.

Leaving Leo standing there, forgotten for a moment.

He was still holding the woman's helmet. With a furtive glance toward the hatch that Piertrie and the guards had gone through, Leo darted over to the service bay. His heart was pounding in his chest as he ducked into the repair shop, where he quickly shoved the helmet behind a rack of spare parts. He had no idea how he was going to get the helmet off the trawler, but for the time being, it was his prize.

You couldn't fault a man for doing what his lay in his nature.

Besides, she had said he had nice hands.

WHAT HAPPENED to Hadrax Thoolsenj afterward was a litany of bureaucratic missteps, accounting screwups, and plain old graft. He was slabbed in stasis gel, routed through four or five distribution depots, mistakenly tagged as parts for a generation ship bound for a cluster beyond the Verdant Scar, but was separated from the rest of the shipment as the courier paused for fuel at a waystation near Gloassia VII. Coin changed hand, manifests got rewritten, and a not-insignificant contribution was made to a campaign fund of an up-and-coming political figure who was running for a seat on the planetary council of Gloassia II. Nice place, if you get a chance to visit. Well-managed environment. Crime rate less than two percent. Over sixty percent of the planet was still untouched wilderness. Lots of hardwood and indigenous flora that the galactic market would pay a great deal for, if it could be harvested.

See aforementioned political campaign contribution.

Anyway, Hadrax Thoolsenj—onetime Fist of the Armored Security Legion, ex-security chief for the Kane crime syndicate, and current cold storage mansicle—eventually ended up as Managed Employee #3954-C of the Kaplodonic Extraction Company. His contract was for twenty years, by far the longest contract of any of the current company of managed employees, which made him a bit of a celebrity among the workers. They all wanted to know who he had killed to get this job.

Hadrax didn't care about any of that. What captured his attention upon being defrosted at Rover Bacca were the logos stamped on various surfaces throughout the base. The wolf-headed sigil of the Florentian Lancers, the double-swoosh and tick of the Verdun Company of Freedom Fighters, the black stain of the Fathomless Hole, and the triangle and block of the Armored Security Legion.

Once upon a time, Rover Bacca had been a mining operation, and initially, it fit Kaplodonic's need for a very out-of-way place to keep unwanteds without anyone dropping by for a site inspection or a materials audit. Sure, they could do some mining to make everything look legit, but the real surprise was what they found in the kilometers of tunnels beneath the pimpled dome covering the dig pit. Dozens of smugglers, gun-runners, and command deck officers terrified of being held accountable for their decisions during wartime had all decided that the empty deserts of Gloassia IV were the perfect spot to bury their contraband.

Surprisingly—or not, when you really think about the sort of records an off-book prison company would want to keep—the Kaplodonic Extraction Company was ill-prepared to do a thorough inventory of the contents of these tunnels. Well, until Managed Employee #3954-C showed up, that is. Hadrax Thoolsenj's vault might be "gelded" enough that he couldn't manage a fleet of defense drones or the security protocols necessary to encrypt the entirety of a planetary crime network, but he could still do spreadsheets.

Piertrie brought the prisoner to the "throne room," the observation blister overlooking the mining pit. A kilometer across at the surface, the pit was a series of ever-narrowing concentric bands of striated rock—oranges, browns, blacks, red. At the bottom of the pit, six hundred meters down, was a concrete platform from which eight major tunnels radiated out into the bedrock. It took a two-ton hauler an hour to crawl up the two dozen circuits of the pit, and the KEC's four working haulers were constantly going up and down, up and down.

KEC's Boss Man sat in a big chair that was welded to a block of scarred titanium blast plating. An array of screens butterflied around him, and as Piertrie's goons shoved the prisoner into the center of the room, one wing of the screens opened outward, revealing the man in the chair. You knew who Boss Man was by the color of his uniform—a garish orange color that reminded Leo of the stringy pulp of a ground gourd grown in temperate climates. If he wasn't in uniform, you'd be hard pressed to see him as a man of any importance. His face was uneven, his left ear was missing most of its lobe, and while he tried to grow a beard to hide childhood trauma on his cheeks, you can't grow whiskers in scar tissue. The resulting facial hair looked like patchy clumps of moss struggling to maintain their grip on sallow bark. Too vain to shave his head, he wore a skullcap to hide his receding hairline.

"What's this?" he chirped at Pietrie as everyone fell into position in the room.

"Salutations and salubriations," the prisoner said cheerfully, as if she hadn't spent the last few hours crammed in a storage locker.

"Who is this?" Boss Man demanded. "Why have you brought her here?"

"Well, I was hoping to talk to the on-site manager of the Kaplodonic Extraction Company," the woman said before Piertrie could manage to fumble an excuse.

"What is she wearing?" Boss Man snapped. "Has she been stripped and swiped?"

Leo knew that none of the guards had bothered to run a signal scan on the woman and her dropsuit. Judging by the sudden panic in Piertrie's eyes, it had never occurred to the trawler boss that she might be running active or passive surveillance gear.

"She's—" Piertrie coughed and tried to clear his throat.

"She's Ansalaage," a voice spoke from the back of the room.

Leo turned. The speaker was one of the walking meatslabs that had been cut loose after the Maricolasa Insurrection. He was wide and gristled, and he moved like the muscles in his back and shoulders were fused together. Like all ex-dropsuit pilots, he didn't talk about what he had done, but Leo pegged him as ASL. There was a thickness to his middle that made him think of the old rumors about ASL Fists, how they carried their math in the bellies. The slab was the new guy, relatively speaking, and right after he arrived, Boss Man moved him to an administrative position with KEC. A fairly important one too, as far as Leo and the others could tell, which was surprising given the long-standing *shit flows down-hill* hierarchy established among the "managed employees."

Sheets—really, that's what they called him—crossed the room. He got close to the woman, though she wasn't intimidated by his bulk. "Bitch," he said.

She smiled. "I've missed you too." Her smile faltered and her jaw moved. She lunged forward, surprising everyone. She got her teeth on one of his ears, bit down, and held on. A guard had to help Sheets pull her off, and there was blood on the floor and her lips when they threw her down.

Sheets called her a much nastier name as he touched his ear and glared at the blood on his fingers.

In the chair, Boss Man chortled and clapped, delighted at the lovers' spat he thought he was witnessing. Well, why else would a crazy woman jump a hardcase like Sheets? Clearly, he had stepped out on her once upon a time, and well, we all know how territorial some of these skanks can be, right?

Leo wasn't so sure, and judging by the sickly expression dampening Piertrie's face, the trawler boss was having similar thoughts. Remembering, no doubt, how the woman had messed up some of his muscle out on the sand. Piertrie grabbed a shock baton from one of the guards and charged toward the supine woman. He made to strike her, but his wrist was suddenly caught by the Fist.

"Wait," Sheets rumbled. He waved at one of Boss Man's watchdogs. "Scan her."

The bodyguard came over with a portable unit, which he ran over the woman. The device beeped three times; using a carbon-fiber blade, the bodyguard cut out sections of her dropsuit. When he scanned her a second time, the device was silent. "She's clean," the watchdog grumbled.

Boss Man leaned forward in his seat. "Who is she?" he rasped.

"Field Lieutenant Maisi Inviolux Bellaphor of Ansalaage's Ministry of Accordance, Recompense, and Solidarity," Sheets said.

"Special Circumstances Division," the woman added. She spat on the floor. "Such a foul taste," she said. There was something feral about her smile.

Leo suppressed a shudder.

"MARS?" Boss Man recoiled in his chair. "What is MARS doing here?"

One of the trawler guards nudged his buddy. "I told you," Leo heard him whisper.

The woman struggled to sit upright. "Can we?" she asked the bodyguard with the carbon-fiber blade, wiggling in a way to draw attention to the detention cord wrapped around her body.

The watchdog looked at Boss Man for a sign. So did Piertrie and the guards.

Leo, who knew better than to look where everyone else was looking, noticed a small bubble of spit blooming at the corner of Sheets's mouth. The big man's eyes were unfocused. Blood from where the MARS woman had bitten his ear was slick on his neck. *Foul taste*, he thought, recalling her words, and he wondered what it was she had had in her mouth when she had launched herself at the slab.

"No, no, no," Boss Man murmured. "There will be no concessions. We have a clear operational mandate here. We are a mining company. Protected by House Quinc's authority. All our paperwork is in order. All our employees are properly vetted and bonded."

The woman looked bored by Boss Man's assurances. "Whatever, squeaky man," she said. "I don't really care."

That caught Boss Man's attention. "What?"

"I'm just here to pick up a few things," she said. "That's all. And then I'll be out of your—" She paused, eyed Boss Man's dreary head covering.

"What—what things?"

"Well, for starters, I need one of your convicts."

"Managed employees," Boss Man corrected her through clenched teeth.

"Sorry. One of your managed employees."

Boss Man's eyes flickered toward Sheets, who was even more dazed than he had been a moment ago. *Definitely something in her mouth*, Leo thought.

The woman noted Boss Man's apprehension and smiled. "Oh, not him," she said. "Hadrax Thoolsenj is here because of me."

Sheets stirred at the sound of his documented name, but he was still oddly unresponsive.

"Hadrax Thoolsenj," she said a second time, and Sheets jerked as if he had been slapped. "Ah, there we go." She smiled as the big man shivered once more.

"Where—what?" He clenched his fists as he stared around the room. There was a wild panic in his eyes, as if he didn't recognize anyone or anything. Everything was a threat. Leo felt his guts tighten. He could imagine what was going through the muscle-bound monster's mind. Risk assessments. Firing solutions. Exit strategies.

You can take the man out of the suit, but you can take the suit out of the man. Once a Fist, always a Fist.

"So, yes," the woman continued. "I'll need managed

employee #3899-D." She smiled innocently as she waited for someone in the room to figure out who that ID corresponded to.

Leo, who had been distracted by whatever chemical compound the woman had injected in Sheet's blood when she had bit him, struggled to breathe. "Uh," he gasped. "I think—" He stopped, swallowed, and inhaled. "That's, uh, that's me. I'm managed employee #3899-D."

"Lallay Leotemorah," Sheets growled, his voice strangely calm. Like he was repeating the response packet from a data stream request. "Managed employee #3899-D. Employment term: ten years. Time served: six hundred and sixty-six days."

The woman beamed. "Oh, good. You have access to the KEC network. That'll make things so much easier."

"What—what have you done to me?" Sheets growled. He looked at the smear of blood on his fingers.

"I turned you back on," she said sweetly. "Well, Nome did. Once I made the bridge. He patched in and did the rest."

"But—we stripped you of signaling devices."

She gave him a knowing smile. "Oh, honey, you missed my helmet."

"Your helmet?"

"I did a HALO drop. You think I'd let the air out there mess with this hair? Of course I had a helmet."

Sheets turned to Piertrie. "She had a helmet?"

"Where's her helmet?" Boss Man screeched from his chair.

Piertrie looked at his guards, who looked in sixteen different directions, and then the trawler boss turned his head toward Leo, who actually found himself blushing. "I might . . . I might have filched it," Leo admitted.

"Of course you did," the woman said. "And thanks for that, by the way. So much simpler when you can get inside help."

Sheets leaned over and picked the woman up. Her feet dangled off the floor. "What are you doing? What have you done?"

She looked amazingly calm for being in the grip of a man who could shake her so hard her skeleton would be permanently jumbled. "I know what you've got in your gut," she said. "And I know what they hid from you. I know what happened after that unfortunate business in Celedonia. I know you're more than just an inventory management package."

"You don't know anything about me," Sheets snarled. Now he shook her.

"Probably," she gasped when he was done. "But I do know what's in container 43 of shipment #4844-33-5. And I do know the value of good tools."

Sheets went still. Slowly, his grip loosened and the woman wiggled free. She landed on her feet, rather adroitly by the way, given that she was still trussed up. She glanced at Sheets, noticed the intent look on his face, and then turned her gaze toward Boss Man. "So, are you going to give me managed employee #3899-D, or do I need to call the home office's dreadnaught I've got in tight orbit and have it drop a few crustbusters on this location?"

"You don't have that authority," Boss Man snapped.

The woman shrugged like she didn't care if he called her bluff, and Leo could see Boss Man wrestle with her indifference. If she was part of Ansalaage's Ministry of Accordance, Recompense, and Solidarity, she might have enough clearance to retask a dreadnaught. And Special

Circumstances Division? How much more authority did a SCD field officer have?

"Take him," Boss Man said, deciding that today wasn't going to be a necessarily brave day. He waved a hand in Leo's direction. "He's cheap labor."

"But—" Piertrie finally found his voice.

Boss Man peered at the trawler boss. "Oh, now you've got something to say?"

"I, uh, sorry," Piertrie shrunk into himself, but not before sending a deadly glare in Leo's direction. Leo wanted to spread his hands and say *It's all a mystery to me*. He wasn't sure what was happening or what this woman wanted with him, but absolutely, he was going to go with her. He had two thousand, nine hundred, and eighty-four reasons to go.

Leo gestured for the watchdog's carbon-fiber knife, and after getting a nod from the Boss Man, the bodyguard handed the blade over. Leo cut the detention cord, and as the woman shrugged off the strands, he gave the knife back to the watchdog. He didn't need a souvenir from his visit to Gloassia IV.

"Right," the woman said. "I guess that about takes care of that. Oh, and"—she snapped her fingers—"the second thing. Container 43. I'd like that too."

Boss Man quaked in his chair.

"Oh, come on," the woman said. "You've got how many tons of illicit armament underneath us? I want one crate. You can keep the rest." She gestured around the throne room. "Officially, I wasn't even here. So . . ."

It wasn't the contents of container 43 that was causing Boss Man to get all blotchy in the face. It was the woman's insouciance—her utter disregard for his authority. He was Boss Man. He was in charge of this facility.

These men all served him. He was sitting on, yes, many metric tons of bombs and missiles and other devices that blew things up. He was in charge.

And she just didn't care.

Leo sighed and his shoulder slumped. Boss Man was going to blow his stack. He could read it on the man's face. He was going tell his watchdogs to pick this woman up—and probably Leo too—and throw them off the balcony of the throne room. Six hundred and some-odd meters above the hard floor of the pit. Leo probably wouldn't have time to tell—

"It's an ASL Mark 7 Chariot," Sheets said. "That's what is in container 43 of shipment #4844-33-5."

"Hmm. How about that?" The woman wasn't surprised by Sheets's revelation.

Boss Man's eyes got big. "A Chariot?" he sputtered. "That's all? Just an ASL warsuit. You want me to give you a warsuit?"

The woman shook her head. "It's not for me," she said. She pointed at Sheets. "It's for Hadrax Thoolsenj."

At the third utterance of his name, something in Sheets snapped. He stiffened and got taller, almost as if he was throwing off some invisible weight he had been carrying. As if his spine was lengthening. As he had found something deep inside himself that had been lost for a long time.

"What do you say?" the woman asked Leo. "A hitter needs a fixer. You up for the job?"

"A fixer? For what?" Leo put the pieces together in his head. "You want me to do diagnostics and repair on a war suit?"

"Like I said, you have nice hands. I suppose they're good for more than filching."

"They-they are," Leo said, a touch of pride in his voice.

"Excellent." The woman looked over at Sheets. "Choice is yours, of course," she said. "Stay with these chaps and nurse a grudge, or suit up and do something good and useful for a change. What'll it be?"

Hadrax Thoolsenj was not a religious man. The world was full of actions and reactions. Causes that led to certain effects. A man made his choices, and he stood by his decisions. But sometimes—maybe once, if he was lucky, perhaps, and not because he was devout—he got a chance to make amends. And perhaps, in the end, that would be enough.

"Yeah," Sheets said, his voice slow and low, as if he was still waking from a very long nap. "Something good. I'd like that."

Douglas D. Douglas, terror of the Territorial Liaison Agency, is asked to retrieve an asset from an academic conference. When asked why someone of his caliber is assigned to such a routine mission, he's told he doesn't need to know. Which means the mission is going to go sideways almost immediately and someone is going to die. Douglas just has to make sure that person isn't him . . .

Get your free copy of The Getaway Weekend *at* dl. bookfunnel.com/75n92nww2d

Pick Your Poison

1. *I'd like more bounty hunting.* Head to "Sparrow" by G.J. Ogden

2. *I'd like more theft.* Head to "Good as Gold" by Frasier Armitage

3. *I'd like more shenanigans.* Turn the page to read "Last Chance" by Jessie Kwak

LAST CHANCE

A NANSHE CHRONICLES STORY

BY JESSIE KWAK

Alex holds his breath as he reaches for statuette, fingertips brushing gilded stone, rope taut under his bare feet and pulsing faintly with his heartbeat. It's a twelve-story drop to the chasm floor if he falls, but falling isn't the fate that worries him.

The worse fate is getting caught.

Alex's nimble fingers ease his prize from its niche: a centuries-old carving of St. Tae Fatima, half a meter tall and heavier than he expected. Up close, the detail work is exquisite. St. Tae's beatific smile, the gilt-clad folds of her gown, the stars carved into the hem of her robe. Much too beautiful to be kept in a niche so far up; Alex shakes his head and nestles the statuette into the folds of a soft towel to protect it, then slips it into his pack.

He pivots carefully and takes a deep, calming breath. He may have the statuette, but he's only halfway done with this job. He still has to traverse the slack line back across the chasm.

When he pauses to listen, Alex hears only water trickling in the darkness, somewhere far below the place where his slack line runs a pale ribbon through the black to the curve of balcony that will be his escape. The temple remains asleep, the residents and guardians—here Alex imagines black-clad holy soldiers in a whirling dance of sizzling laser-edged blades—unaware there's a thief in their midst.

Alex slides one bare foot out along the slack line, arms spread for balance. The St. Tae statuette isn't heavy, but the extra weight is enough of a variable that he finds himself off balance. Core tight, breath caught in his chest, eternally grateful for the stillness of the air in this cavern. His thighs burn with the effort, his shoulders aching and taut, and—

Was that movement? A shadow, far below?

Alex pauses, the slack line quivering beneath his feet, but he can't hear much above the rush of his heartbeat in his ears.

A footstep. He's sure he heard it.

There's no way out now but forward, so he renews his pace, pushing himself despite the ungainly pack. The slack line becomes more taut as he closes in on the balcony, stabilizing imperceptibly, and Alex allows himself a flash of hope. He's almost there.

A door shuts, somewhere close.

Alex's foot slips.

Instinct kicks in as he falls; he twists in the air like a cat, right hand closing around the slack line and yanking his arm almost out of its socket. He bites back a cry, ignoring the wrenching pain and letting himself swing. Out, and then back—he catches a grip on the line with his left hand. Heart racing, he inches towards the balcony, fingers first finding the slack line's knot, then the balcony rail it's tied to. Alex steadies himself then heaves, finding scrabbling purchase with bare toes until he can haul his lean, lithe frame up and over the railing to safety.

He lands lightly on solid ground, crouched and listening, calming his breath once more. He doesn't think he made much noise, even during his scramble. If he's alerted any of the sentries, they haven't put out a call—otherwise there would be lights blazing, sirens, drones. The cavern is silent.

Alex spares a moment to check that the statuette of St. Tae Fatima is intact and unharmed in its wrapping. He breathes a sigh of relief, then stands.

And finds himself face-to-face with a dark robed figure.

Alex lets out a yelp.

"Alexander Abdul Quiñones," says the figure, her voice a whip, a lasso; Alex roots to the spot despite every fiber of his being screaming for him to run. "What in saint's fury are you doing?"

"Ayalasi Kateri, I can explain."

The head aya of the Aymaya Apostles convent in Artemis City sweeps her hood back to reveal her face. Her eyes are normally creased with laugh lines, her lips kind, but now her furious gaze cuts past Alex to where the slack line bridges the gap from the balcony over the convent's gardens twelve stories below, and her eyes flutter closed: annoyance spiked with worry. Alex knows that look well. He's earned it more than once in his seventeen years at the convent.

"Give me the statue," she says, fixing him with a look once more. "And take that rope down immediately."

"I can return it?" Alex hitches one hip over the balcony, ready to take St. Tae back the way he brought her. He may have almost fallen once, but he'll risk the journey again if it means putting off the disappointed tongue lashing he's about to receive.

The ayalasi's nostrils flare. Alex freezes. She holds out a hand, and Alex carefully extracts the statuette from his pack and offers it to her. A few doors have opened along the hall, some of the convent's other resident students awoken by the commotion and curious to find out what trouble Alex Quiñones has gotten himself into this time.

"Back to bed," Ayalasi Kateri says without looking; doors click closed once more. She cradles the statue in her arm and begins to walk away. "Alexander, I'll see you in my office."

"Yes, ayalasi." Alex clears his throat, hoping against hope that he can still avoid the ultimate fate. "Ayalasi? Don't call Ruby."

The ayalasi doesn't break her stride.

"You'll be calling your sister yourself, young man."

RUBY QUIÑONES HATES that she's got a gun strapped to her thigh right now.

She can shoot it just fine, thank you, but she's a *hacker*. When the job suddenly requires the hacker to carry a gun, that means shit has gone horribly wrong. Though, honestly, Ruby's got no one to blame but herself. She's the one who agreed to take another job for Raj Demetriou.

They're gearing up in a bare-bones hole Raj rented for this job; it still stinks of the last resident's takeout and has barely enough room for one person to maneuver amid surveillance electronics and weaponry. Let alone two.

"So when we get to the access shaft," Raj is saying,

and she lets him keep talking, checks the gun again, the turns to look over the rest of her gear. Extractor rig, check. Data stick with the moth virus, check. Backup data stick, check. Access scrambler, check. Snakebite kit, check. Lipstick, check.

Ruby has a rule about working for people more than once. Yes, as a freelancer, it's better to cultivate repeat clients. As a specialist with a touchy set of in-demand skillsets—identity fixing, corporate espionage, information sabotage, that sort of thing—she could benefit from the protection of a regular repeat client. But you start working for someone regularly, and they think you're friendly. Maybe they start to ask about your past, start to think they can confide some stories of their own, and pretty soon you're obligated to them.

In the twelve years since she turned eighteen and left the convent of the Aymaya Apostles, she's tried to keep the world at arm's length. She'd been good at it, too, until this Arquellian grifter, Raj, talked her into having a drink to celebrate the first job he hired her for. Over drinks she'd agreed to his next harebrained scheme, and somehow the pattern had repeated until they were meeting up even when work wasn't involved.

Like some sort of friends.

Raj knows things about her now. He's toasted stories about dramatic breakups with her ex-girlfriend. He's laughed at tales of Ruby growing up with the ayas. Saints, she even let Raj meet *Alex* the last time the kid got kicked out and had to stay with her for a few weeks.

Which is the crux of the problem. In less than a year, Alex will turn eighteen and be asked to leave the convent for good, and Ruby will need to have gotten her act together. Her job now is to learn how to create a stable family for him as he finds his own path—one that in no way mirrors her own, not if she has anything to say about it. Continuing to work with Raj is opposite of what she should be doing, because her partner—her soon-to-be *former* partner—is about to get her killed.

Fucking again.

"Ruby. Are you listening to me?"

Raj rakes his fingers through his shoulder length black hair, smoothing it into a clubbed pony tail. He's dressed all in black, same as her, a loose-fitting shirt over light-weight biosilk armor; her own armor sits tight around her ribcage like a vise. Or maybe that's just anxiety.

Ruby's wrangled her own black curls into a pair of tight braids, covered with a snug cap. A mesh fractal mask the same dark brown as her skin hangs loose around her neck, ready to obscure her features.

Raj lifts an eyebrow, waiting for her response.

"When we get to the access shaft in Bā Sector, we're to head directly to Kasey Aherne's townhouse complex," she says, repeating the rest of his plan word for word. She even throws a touch of Raj's classy Arquellian drawl over her gutter trash Artemesian accent, even though Raj normally hides that particular accent in these parts. "At which point I'll splice in and release the moth into Aherne's system to cover our tracks after you fucked up and got us on his radar." She'd embellished that last part. "Did I miss anything?"

Raj shakes his head. "Did I ever tell you how scary your memory is?"

"Yeah, well." Ruby turns back to check her gear for a third time, annoyed. Her memory is hard-earned, the result of years trying to remember anything that happened before she was abandoned with her baby brother on the doorstep of the Aymaya Apostles. No matter how she's honed her recall, she hasn't been able to pierce that veil of the past.

Raj must see something on her face, because he winces. "I didn't mean—"

Because of course he knows about that, too. Something about Raj gets under your defenses.

Saints in hell.

"I was *listening* to you," Ruby says. "Here's where I don't think you've been listening to *me*, only." Something in Rubys tone straighten's Raj's spine. Good. "You *told* me you checked this job out. You *told* me this job wasn't going to go shit-wise like the last one did."

"And I'll make it up to you, Ruby."

"You will, then."

"But I don't know if now's the time to talk about this."

"Then find us a time on your social calendar after, yeah?" She waves away whatever apology he's coming up with. "Let's just get going. I'm all . . ." Her comm chimes, and she frowns at Alex's name on the connection request. It's far too late for him to be calling just to chat—which he hasn't done since he was fourteen anyway. She bats away the call; she'll catch him after. "I'm all set."

"Everything all right?" Raj asks.

"Beautiful, love," she says. "Let's get this done."

WHEN WE LAST SAW ALEX THE intrepid explorer-thief-hero, he'd been captured at the height of his caper. Now, he's been dragged into the bowels of the temple to its torture chamber, a room few besides the temple's sinister guardians have seen—and fewer have returned from alive.

Ayalasi Kateri is a harsh interrogator, but Alex has withstood worse. No one can hold a candle to his sister Ruby's fury, or match the insidiously relentless way she can wear him down to admitting guilt.

And, thank the saints, Ruby isn't picking up her comm. Maybe he *will* live to see another morning.

"What in God's name did you think you were doing." Ayalasi Kateri's voice is honed sharp with exasperation and not a small amount of worry.

The ayalasi's torture chamber is a small, plant-filled meeting room off her bedroom, furnished with only a ring of cushions. The low table in the center of the room has a tea service waiting already; Alex pours a cup for Ayalasi Kateri and sets it on the edge of the table closest to her cushion. She doesn't reach to take it.

Normally ayas wear blue, their heads covered, but as it's the middle of the night the ayalasi is dressed in a simple gray shift and robe, her dark, silver-streaked hair in a long braid down her back. Her deep gold eyes are bright and angry.

"I can explain, ayalasi," Alex says, lowering his lanky frame onto a cushion across from her.

She holds up a hand to head him off. "You prefer that cushion, don't you. The one you're sitting on?"

Alex frowns at her, glances down at it. "It's softer than the others," he says cautiously.

"Alexander Abdul, think about the fact that you know this. How many of your peers have even been in this room, let alone enough times to have a favorite cushion."

He winces.

"Put yourself in my shoes, child. My job is to protect you, to teach you—not to bury you. My heart stopped when I saw you fall."

"You didn't have to worry. I've—" Alex stops himself, nearly avoiding the catastrophe of divulging state secrets under pressure. *Stay strong, Quiñones.*

But Ayalasi Kateri's mouth presses into a thin line as though she knows exactly what he was about to say. "You've done it before," she finishes for him.

Alex ducks his head. "I'm sorry, ayalasi. It won't happen again."

"No, it won't," she says, and something in her voice makes him straighten. "I love you, Alex. We all love you. But this was the last straw."

Icy water rushes down Alex's spine.

"No, ayalasi, I promise—"

"And you've promised me before." Ayalasi Kateri's tone is gentle, sad. "I think it's time you went to live with your sister. For good."

RAJ HAS PROMISED HER BEFORE.

There was that retrieval job on Nerrivik that went sideways. The "easy" fixer job Ruby got them out of by the skin of her teeth. The incident with Pascale Corp. There's no denying that Raj has a pattern, and that pattern is seeing how close he can get to disaster before dancing away.

It's like he doesn't have a reason to care if he gets killed.

In Artemis City's underworld, burning your partner on the job is one of the most commonly accepted way to end a business relationship that's not working out. It wouldn't be hard with Raj—easy enough to program the moth virus to cover her tracks only and frame him so that once Kasey Aherne realizes they've been spying the full force of his fury will land on Raj. Or, if Ruby didn't want to risk Raj giving her name to Aherne, she could take the other obvious route and tip off the Alliance that she knows where one of their most wanted deserters is. That option would come with a nice payday, too; Ruby's seen the bounties on Raj's head. Saints, she's the one he asks to clear them every time he finds another one on the boards.

And then there's the nuclear option, the unknown option, where she opens that file she's got on him and finds out what he did that's so dangerous the Alliance sealed the records of his court martial. The file had been hard to find, but Ruby's good at what she does. And she can't help her habit of going digging on every new contact she meets.

She could have opened the sealed file months ago, but by the time she found it Raj was already under her defenses. She'd asked him why he deserted and he gave her the whole story: the admiral father, the unthinkable order Raj refused to follow, the escape from the brig when he learned he was meant to be killed, the court martial to destroy his name.

She hasn't opened the file because Raj was a friend, one who told her the truth whenever she asked him. Which is the same reason she's not going to burn him on this job.

She'll figure out another way to leave.

Ahead of her, Raj pries open the access shaft. He turns around with the recklessly delighted grin of someone with a death wish. "Ready?"

Ruby takes a deep breath, hand on her pistol.

"Course I am."

She steps into the shaft, squeezing her eyes closed as she begins to fall.

Aᴀʟᴀsɪ Kᴀᴛᴇʀɪ ʜᴀs ʙʀᴏᴜɢʜᴛ in her worst henchman to break Alex down, since he withstood the terrors of her torture chamber—but the intrepid explorer-thief-hero can withstand any torture the temple's villainous guardians have for him. Soon he'll devise a daring escape back to his ship and off to his next adventure.

Aya Julio hands him a bottle of cleaning spray and a resonator brush, its handle tacky through the awkward fit of the antimicrobial gloves Alex is wearing. Of the punishments Alex has been handed throughout the years, cleaning the student bathrooms is the one he hates the most. The ayalasi knows that, of course. Just as she apparently knows he has a favorite cushion.

"You know, I found a scuff mark on the railing a few weeks back," Aya Julio is saying as they clean. "I suppose that was your slack line?"

Alex can't decide if setting Aya Julio as his taskmaster is Ayalasi Kateri's way of taking the sting out of the bathroom cleaning chore, or of rubbing salt in the wound. Julio is Alex's favorite. The old aya always has the best stories and doesn't like sitting around, which means he always ends up helping with whatever chore Alex has been assigned. Alex may hate cleaning the bathroom, but if he's getting kicked out, this is the last time he'll be ordered to do it. And the last time he'll be here as a student, trading jokes and stories with Aya Julio.

Alex shoves aside the thought with flutter of panic.

"On the tenth floor?" Alex asks; he'll distract himself

with conversation. "Like halfway? Yeah, that was me. Sorry, I didn't mean to scuff the railing."

"It came right off," Julio says pleasantly. "I do wish I could have seen your stunt last night. But you should have worn a harness, boy, my poor old heart can't take the thought."

"I'm pretty good at it, I've practiced a lot." Now that the secret's out, he might as well admit that to Julio. Alex finishes scrubbing a toilet bowl, then flushes to rinse it. Ruby still hasn't answered her comm, and she's even scrambled the location beacon normally only he has access to, which means she's probably on some sort of super fun job with Raj.

Alex is trying to look on the bright side. He's seen a lot less of his sister in the last few years, since Ruby moved away from Artemis City to Ironfall. It's a few hours' shuttle to the next dwarf planet over, only, and he's been there once before, when he'd been expelled last year and had to stay with her and Kitty. Ironfall is boring as hell—nowhere near as full of life and adventure as Artemis City. Which is part of why Ruby moved. She hadn't said it aloud, not in front of Alex, but he's not an idiot kid. Kitty needed to stay away from the party scene for her own good, and Ironfall was a last-ditch effort to salvage their relationship.

It hadn't worked. Alex had loved Kitty—he knows Ruby did, too—but Kitty's gone back home to Arquelle. Which means he can totally convince Ruby to move back to Artemis City.

"Alex?"

Aya Julio has been talking; Alex scrolls back through his memory, which was silently recording the conversation even as Alex's mind was chattering elsewhere. Julio had been asking whether Alex was still planning to pursue an apprenticeship with one of the local tech companies.

"I don't see why not," Alex says, as though his future hasn't just spilled out in front of him like an armload of groceries scattered across the floor by one stupid, clumsy misstep. Even if he picks up all the bits he no longer knows where they go. He tries to gin up a smile for Julio, but part of him feels like he's running out of air.

It's not just the worry that Ruby's going to kill him. Some part of his subconscious is screaming the word *final, final, final*—this is the final time he'll scrub toilets with Aya Julio, the final time he'll cause Aya Marga to roll her eyes, the final time he'll sleep in the only bed he's ever called his own.

He knew this day would come, but he thought he had more time; now, a terminal dread is lurking around the edges of his consciousness. As much as he's dreamed of leaving the convent and exploring the world—*just think of how he could help Ruby and Raj! They could have so much fun*—he's also grieving the world he's about to be expelled from for a final time.

Final. The word ricochets through him like a voidball.

Alex pushes worry aside with practiced ease, losing himself forcefully in scheming how he'll get Ruby to leave Ironfall and come back to Artemis City, the heart of all adventure.

RUBY's never going to be able to come back to Artemis City again, not after this job—and the bit she really can't get over is this was supposed to be *surveillance only*.

Surveillance.

The type of job where you send crawlers out on the nets and plant a beetle drone or two in strategic locations to eavesdrop. Maybe, *maybe*, you put on a pair of heels and a low-cut top and nurse a silver rose at a swanky bar and chat up one of Kasey Aherne's captains—preferably the hot one, the woman with the stunning cheekbones and take-charge hands.

Then you write up a tidy report to tell Sara Mugisha what her rival is up to, collect a paycheck, and head home to celebrate a routine job well done.

Only Raj, bless, decided to get fancy and left evidence that—if Aherne finds it—will lead the crime lord back to Raj and Ruby, and therefore back to Mugisha. Which will piss off Mugisha. Ruby doesn't care about the twisted underworld politics of Artemis City, she only knows it's not good when you get on one crime lord's shit list, let alone two at once.

Lucky for her skin and Raj's, Ruby's pretty sure that no one has found the evidence yet. And even luckier, she happens to have a secret weapon.

Moth viruses eat holes in data. Normally it's a scorched earth strategy because the moth isn't picky; it's the messy sort of way you'd cover up a corporate theft or just sabotage your competition. Only that sort of wanton destruction gets you noticed, and quick.

Which is why Ruby's developed a modified version, and gotten paid handsomely for custom versions by a couple corporate clients, too. Her modified moth isn't a voracious devourer, she's a delicate little princess. A finicky eater that can be programmed to seek out precise tasty morsels with surgical precision. Not as cleanly as Ruby could do on her own if she had the leisurely time and access to Kasey Aherne's systems, but it'll do. By the time the missing data is noticed, it'll be too late to track down what happened. Ruby's managed stealth jobs against corporate targets with much tighter security; she's reasonably sure Aherne's clowns will never notice a few stills and frames gone from a surveillance setup.

Only one problem.

In order to let the moth fly, you've got to be in the system. Hence the access tunnel to Bā Sector's maintenance shafts, hence the ruse with the guard and the dash of a concoction in his coffee that'll require an emergency run to the facilities, hence the reason Ruby's strung halfway up the wall to Aherne's condo building like a marionette, heart rabbiting in her chest, pistol strapped to her thigh, primed to shoot it if she needs to, but knowing that just creates more tracks to cover.

She's a *hacker*. She constructs exquisite viruses, her ident cards are only gorgeous, and she can find a speck of specific precious glitter in a field of starry data so long as she's in a system. She's not meant for heights or acrobatics, thank you very much. She didn't get that half of the genes, not like her daredevil little brother.

What she can do inside a computer system, he can do inside a physical place. Locked doors and unscalable walls can't keep him in, and top line security tech is only a fun challenge, the cheeky bastard. Which is why, once again, she needs to get away from this kind of job and model how to make a living doing honest work before he gets any ideas.

"That one," Raj says through her earpiece; he's safe and sound in the guard room while she pings wires with an electrician's signal tester, sending pulses of energy through the coating without leaving a trace.

"Two pings to verify," Ruby says, teasing the target wire free and pulsing twice more.

"Copy," Raj says. "You've got it."

Ruby pulls her tube of lipstick out of her pocket, daubing a bit of carmine red on the cable to mark it. Then she carefully positions the snakebite kit over the wire, switches it on. Holds her breath as the tiny points of lights turn from red to yellow to green: connection.

If anyone comes looking, they'll find the tiny marks on the wire's coating where the fangs of the kit bit through, but the odds anyone comes looking are low. That's one nice thing about having been surveilling Aherne's organization for these last few months: she has the inside scoop that Aherne's not the brightest of stars.

Wire marked and bit, Ruby releases the moth, holding her breath until it's fully uploaded.

Her extractor rig blinks at her. *Success*.

Cleanup and descent seems painfully slow, but she does a flawless job and makes her way carefully back down the wall. Exits the compound with Raj just as the security guard finally extracts himself from the bathroom.

"Have I told you how brilliant you are?" Raj says as they slip into one of Bā Sector's alleys on their way back to the maintenance shaft.

"Not often enough, love."

"You're brilliant." Raj winks at her. "I couldn't have done this without you."

He's buttering her up; she can feel herself already celebrating this win with him, enjoying the challenge now that it's over, enjoying the feeling that even though shit went wrong on this job, at least Raj had her back.

Dammit.

She can't let his charm work on her this time. She has

a brother to think about. Ruby stops mid-step to tell him and Raj turns back to her, brows drawing together in worry.

And then his eyes go wide in fear. Cold steel presses against the back of Ruby's neck, and the words she meant to say—*I'm through, Raj, we're done*—die on her lips.

"Afternoon," says a cool voice behind her. "Sara Mugisha wants to see you."

Ruby's seen firsthand how Raj talked his way through her defenses, and now she's got a front row seat to watching him charm his way through Sara Mugisha's. She'd expected torture chambers dug into Artemis City's stone walls, she'd expected to spiral up to the city's highest levels to be thrown from an airlock on the planet's surface. But they'd been taken to Mugisha's headquarters, a glamorous warehouse with trendy couches and rave lights—mercifully off—and Raj had sat there and convinced the party drug empress that Ruby's moth was foolproof and there was no way they'd been compromised.

Mugisha had believed him, thank the stars. But she hadn't paid.

"Let me buy you a drink," Raj says, once they're far from Mugisha's lair and Ruby's heart rate has calmed to something just topside of normal. She thumbs her comm on, waiting for it to connect to the network. "I owe you one."

"You owe me more than a drink." Somehow in the last hour since Mugisha's goon stuck a gun to the back of her head, Ruby's fury at Raj has ebbed. She's not been the only one sharing bits of her past with her . . . friend? He's told her things about himself, too. She knows why Raj is acting like he doesn't have anything to live for anymore—maybe he doesn't.

She does.

"C'mon," Raj says. "There's a bar I've been meaning to try, I think you'll love it."

"I can't."

He frowns at her. "You can't?"

"I—" Ruby's comm chimes as the past few hours of pings and connection requests come through. She's missed three calls from Alex; a hand clamps around her stomach.

"Is everything all right?" Raj asks, and she wants to say, *No, I think something's wrong.* She wants a friend she can tell that Alex has been trying to get her, someone who can stand by while she calls her brother back, and help her deal with whatever the aftermath of that call might be.

Raj could be that friend. He may be a deserter, he may take shitty risks on jobs, he may have a death wish—but he's always been there for her. And that's the entire problem. Alex needs her to be be his rock, which means she needs to be strong enough to stand on her own.

"It's fine, of course it is. I just need a shower and some sleep. Night!" She gives Raj a smile; she can tell he doesn't believe her. But she turns her back on him anyway, each step more committed as she walks away.

Whatever's coming, she can weather it. Maybe Mugisha doesn't pay for compromised intel, maybe Ruby's bank account will be tight for a little bit, maybe the above-board jobs never pay so well as the ones Raj finds. But she's freelanced for tech startups and other corporations before, and she has time to find some decent paying work and build up a shiny new non-crime lord clientele in the next year. Things will be tight for a bit, but she'll be okay by the time Alex turns eighteen.

Ruby makes the connection request.

ALEX HAS BEEN GAMING out the best way to break the news all night, and now his comm is chiming. Earlier than Ruby would usually be awake, which confirms his suspicion that she was probably out kicking ass on a fun job with Raj, rather than just sleeping through his calls.

The thought buoys him. He might have abbreviated his life with the ayas, but at least he has a future with his sister. And hadn't Raj even hinted they could use somebody with Alex's skills from time to time? Ruby had shut that down quick, but she shuts everything down quick at first. Between Alex and Raj, they'll be able to talk her into it.

Alex is in the gardens now; he can hear his fellow students stirring on the balconies around him, for what he tries not to think of as the final time.

"Alex?"

Aya Julio is both asking for his aesthetic approval and asking if he'll answer his comm. Alex gives Aya Julio a grin and a thumbs up—the St. Tae Fatima statuette looks lovely in the niche they cleared out for her in the garden— then steps away to pull out his comm.

He dials his tone bright and accepts Ruby's incoming connection request.

"Hey, sis!" he says. "I have some really good news."

Ruby, Raj, and Alex are all key crew members in Jessie Kwak's new series, the Nanshe Chronicles. Download the Nanshe Chronicles prequel novella, Artemis City Shuffle, *for free and start the adventure at jessiekwak.com/c2-shuffle.*

Pick Your Poison

1. *I need more feisty dames who can hold their own in my life.* Head to "Renegade Havoc" by C.E. Clayton

2. *I love me some seedy underworld underdogs.* Head to "Risk Management" by Caitlin Demaris McKenna

3. *I'm ready to suit up and strap in for launch!* Turn the page to read "Martian Scuttle" by Andrew Sweet

MARTIAN SCUTTLE

A VIRTUAL WARS STORY

BY ANDREW SWEET

"Do you know your mission?"

"Protect the interests of the United African Southern Highlands Company," the petit, sandy-blond woman with a round face and smattering of freckles reported, standing in a stiff military posture that contrasted with her full-sleeve smooth lycra top and string-tied synth-cotton pants. The pants ended with designer boots saturated in reds, yellows, and tribal designs. The boots were the only part of the uniform that the woman, Dandelion, had any control over, and she used the flexibility to add a little color to the drab affair. The rest were standard issues. Lycra continued beneath the synth cotton, as the top did double-duty as the one-piece under-layer of her space suit.

"...with my life if necessary," she added after a short pause. Dandelion smiled at that last line because, despite what anyone else had to say, it meant she had a life to use "if necessary."

To the untrained eye, Dandelion was in her late twenties. Even to the trained eye, actually. Being a full android, she didn't age out of her meticulously designed look.

She didn't need a uniform for lift-off either. The only reason she wore the hideously drab tannish-olive lycra was that it made the rest of the crew more comfortable not knowing which of them the android was. In Dandelion's experience, the truth always came out anyway because, from the moment they all said their protection oath, the crew were thrown into a tiny cabin for four months sharing everything from meals to bathrooms. It was impossible to keep secrets in that environment, but she felt real at the beginning of each trip.

"The route is simple," a tall man in a robe said as he paced before a hologram board. "The point of departure is this station, and since we're at perihelion opposition right now, the trip should only be about a month long this time. Get this shipment of rhodium from here to Earth with no interruptions."

"What's an interruption, sir?" a man to Dandelion's left asked in a well-defined South African accent. Dandelion scowled at him for asking such a stupid question and saw a mischievous grin on his face. The other man—the robed man—flickered when a sunspot or magnetic flux interfered with the hologram's display particles.

"What do you think it is, uh..." The man looked at something out of the hologram field and continued, "Michigan?"

The brunette to Dandelion's right giggled, and Dandelion felt a thin smile forming on her own face. The man in the holovid didn't seem amused. Michigan seemed very amused.

"Don't I look like a Michigan? Michigan Nkoski, at your service."

"And you've been on this job for... ten years? All that time with no knowledge of what an interruption might be?"

"Team player, sir," Michigan said, not so easily chastised. "Some of my teammates look a little green and may not know." Michigan's big brown eyes locked straight onto Dandelion's gray-brown ones. His smirk suddenly felt like an insult.

"I assure you, everyone here is as experienced as you. But since you asked, interruptions include pirate attacks, meteor or asteroid impacts, flying through solar flares, or, once, I believe one of our vessels took out all of the satellites over India."

Dandelion's pressure sensors in the skin of her shoulder signaled for her attention. A hand. She recognized the pressure pattern. Someone had laid their uninvited fingers on her right shoulder. She hadn't expected physical contact so soon and was glad she'd decided to run hot today just in case. That hand experienced a shoulder at the perfect ninety-eight-point-six degrees. Dandelion turned, and a cheery-looking chipmunk of a woman grinned back at her.

"Don't worry. Michigan always finds someone to single out. He's kind of a jerk. I've traveled with him before. He knows his way around electrical systems, though, so it's best just to put up with him and take it with a grain of salt."

"Already working against me, Ray?"

"Somebody should," Ray retorted, then turned back to Dandelion. "I'm Raychelle Bandelier. You are?"

"Dandelion Lemaire," Dandelion replied.

"Time for introductions later, crew," the holograph-man said, clearly getting impatient with the interstellar communications bill that the ansible call was racking up. "Do you now accept the mission as it has been assigned to you?"

"One more question," Michigan said. Raychelle groaned loud enough to attract holograph-man's attention. The man in the holograph also dropped his eyes, and his shoulders heaved into a quick sigh, but that didn't stop Michigan's question. "Which one of us is the bolt-bucket? I need to know who's real so I know who to put the moves on."

Dandelion guarded her physical reactions, allowing her face to show only mild surprise. If Michigan found out this early, it would make things more complicated—and he'd probably use it as justification for more of his petty attacks.

"Cut it out, Michigan," Ray said.

"Been there before," Michigan retorted. "Ray's not a droid. What about the other one?"

The blush that worked its way into Ray's mousey cheeks was unmistakable, leading Dandelion to the early conclusion that, jerk or not, Michigan wasn't lying about their shared history. The two other crew members looked at each other with accusing eyes—probably newbies, whatever the holograph-man said. They had that look.

"I hope you do not need to find out," the holograph-man replied.

"You don't look like a droid to me," Michigan said, once again with his eyes focused on Dandelion. "A month's a long time. Swing by my bunk if you need to—you know—take some pressure off."

"Not my type," Dandelion said. "You gab too much."

Michigan's mouth snapped shut and his smiling eyes grew smaller under furrowed eyebrows.

"We'll see," was all he said in response.

The holograph-man smiled and reached somewhere offscreen to flick a switch, cutting the ansible call. Dandelion looked at Ray first, then at Michigan, and finally back to the two others behind her. One wore a farmer's bandana, typical of the Northern Lowlands. The few farmers who tried their hand in the Northern Lowlands soon learned that a bandana was a necessary part of it. This one, a man barely over twenty, had left a farming family behind somewhere and hadn't yet realized that his bandana was only extra weight on an interstellar flight. Like most first-generation Martians, he had the short stature that made him seem almost infantile next to Michigan.

The other person, a waif of a woman also very clearly of Martian descent, had more height than the man and approached Michigan's five-foot-ten inches. She looked second generation, accustomed to the low gravity, and if she'd had offspring, they would probably tower at six feet or more. There weren't a lot of third generations yet, but the ones who Dandelion had met so far were tall and impossibly skinny. On Earth, they would have been basketball players were it not for the impact of the 2.6 times difference in gravity. Second gens could go back and forth with relative ease and used their height to their advantage.

"Ag, man! Are you all ready to fly?" Michigan again, vying for the role of leader, Dandelion assumed. He was welcome to it if it stroked his ego. Dandelion had only led for a single flight and found it stressful and annoying, always listening to people complain. She doubted Michigan would listen to anyone complain about anything, so the position probably didn't bother him much. "Suit up and strap in."

Dandelion was already out of her cotton bottoms and looking through the suits by the time he got around to telling them what to do. Ray was right there with her.

The trick to space flight was finding the closest fitting suit since they had to live in it for a month or longer. Since Dandelion didn't need the suit and could turn down her pressure sensors if need be, she pulled on some pants that were just a bit long and didn't look like they would fit anyone else. Ray got the perfect size for her slight form, and Michigan got a good fitting suit after first pushing the two newbies aside. The pair of them were left with ill-fitting garments and unhappy expressions as they fastened into them, trying to make them work.

"Lift off in ten," Michigan yelled again.

Dandelion rolled her eyes, making sure that Michigan saw her too-human behavior.

"Well, it's true," said Michigan.

"And automated. And there's the big countdown clock up there," Dandelion said, pointing to the ceiling. The newbies looked up as soon as she pointed, and one of them giggled. The number had changed to 5. Dandelion latched herself in, getting all four latches in seconds. Michigan was next, and Ray was third. The newbies were still fastening in when the engines fired.

Dandelion closed her eyes and turned up her pressure sensors until she could feel the docking clamps release. She clutched her hand to her stomach on instinct since most people felt queasy with the instant shift of centrifugal force to directional as the ship spun off into the void of space.

"Wake up, Dandy," Michigan's voice penetrated her sleeping mode. Slipping from reserve back to full power, Dandelion opened her eyes to see his scowling face only inches from hers. In his hand was a large knife covered in blood.

"Wh-what happened?" She asked, looking toward the countdown clock that had changed to an interstellar time tracker. The number read 11099934, nearly thirty-thousand spins after lift-off. Her reserve would have switched off in a few minutes anyway. The knife—covered in blood —wasn't part of the usual lift-off routine.

"Quiet," he said. Behind him, Ray's mousey eyes stared over his shoulder. "We know you're the android."

"I'm n—" She started to protest, only seeing then that what she thought was a scowl was only fear manifesting. Ray's eyes were downright hopeful. "Okay, I am. What's going on?"

"Noobs are dead," Ray said. "Both of them. There was a collision alarm that you slept through—or whatever— and then a breach near the rhodium chambers. They went to check it out, all excited about their new jobs. And, and..." started Ray.

"And they made rookie mistakes. Got killed. They should have waited, but they wouldn't listen to me," Michigan said.

"You were being a jerk. I wouldn't have listened either, Michigan," said Ray.

"But you admit it, right? I told them not to. If they'd listened..."

"Michigan found their bodies and this knife," Ray continued, pointing to the blade. "It's time to get into the armory, Dandelion. And since you're the android..."

"I have the codes," she acknowledged. "What are we dealing with?"

"They cut the sensors, whoever it is. We don't know if there's one ship out there or a thousand."

"Did you look out the window?" Dandelion asked, the question seeming the most obvious one. So far, nobody in the solar system had figured out how to make a ship entirely invisible to the human eye, regardless of the detection equipment.

"And let them see us? You're as bad as the noobs."

"You are an idiot, aren't you, Michigan? Do you think that they don't have sensors and heat detectors? They already know we're here," Dandelion said. She had thought the guy would be a problem, but she'd also thought his experience would be a boon. Based on this exchange, she had to question that assumption. "Go check."

To her surprise, glaring aside, he turned and left the room to check the window. The only window was in the hallway connecting the crew "quarters" to the engine room.

"What state were the bodies in?" Dandelion asked.

"Deep cuts. Bled out all over the hall," Ray replied, visibly shaking. "I've never seen anything like it."

"Listen. I know we all pledged life and limb and all of that. My directive is different. I'm here to evaluate risk and protect the crew," she said. "That's you."

"How can you protect us?"

"Well, first, we get weapons. But I need you to know I may ask you to abandon this ship. And you'll want to stay. Even if Southern Highlands Company takes a lot of risks, we don't risk our crews, whatever your trainer told you."

"Nothing out there," Michigan's voice echoed through the tiny room. "Just black space."

"They're on the other side of the ship then," Dandelion said. "That probably means they're familiar with this model. And that probably means they're heading straight to the armory."

"We should leave, then," Michigan said. "Maybe beat them there?"

"And get slaughtered in the ship's passageway?" asked Ray.

"No," Dandelion said. "Michigan's right. There are only a couple of boarding points for this vessel at the far ends of the ship. They had to have used one. We're closer to the armory they are."

Michigan shot her a look that told her he was grateful and still hated her for what she was. She shook it off. Dandelion didn't bother reminding them that whoever had killed their associates was probably closer to the armory than even they were. There wasn't a point in sapping out their little hope in the deteriorating situation.

"Take the lead?" she asked Michigan, confident of his answer.

"You're the bolt-bucket," Michigan told her. "You lead."

Twelve minutes and thirty-seven seconds later, the three were poised outside the armory door. Whoever had killed the noobs hadn't tried to break in. There weren't even any scratches on the door. Dandelion typed in the sixteen-digit code for accessing the armory, and the door slid open quickly. She didn't bother entering since she could assess the entire state of the arsenal from the doorway. The others, lacking her night-vision capabilities, stepped through the door and triggered the overhead lights. Her eyesight adjusted automatically.

There were no weapons.

"Did they beat us here?" Michigan asked, as usual, not thinking through anything. Dandelion stared at him. "Then why aren't there any weapons here?"

Dandelion shook her head.

"They weren't loaded," she said, looking at the empty racks of open locks. "None of them. I don't know what's going on."

A sound echoed down to them from the hallway. It was a voice, high-pitched and barely intelligible—to Dandelion. The others likely had no clue that the sound was even there. Dandelion listened as closely as she could.

"...controls are set. Rhodium tanks will jettison in three minutes."

If she'd had a heart, it would be racing. The entire tanker was designed around the rhodium tanks. To "jettison" them would mean to destroy the rest of the ship, or at the very least leave them spinning in space.

"Now's the time, Ray. Remember what I told you?"

"What?" Michigan asked, clearly annoyed at not having been in on their earlier conversation.

"It's time to go, Michigan," Ray said. "We're not going to win this one."

"Over my dead—"

Dandelion's side hand connected with the back of his head, and he fell like a sack of okrina. The thought of the sweet fruit shifted her focus briefly to acquiring some, but she pulled focus instead to work. There would be time for okrina later. She hoisted the unconscious man over her shoulder.

"Follow me," she said, leaving the armory with Ray just behind her.

She hadn't been candid with Ray. Her mission didn't end with seeing the crew to safety, but Ray didn't have to know that yet.

The hallways before them were largely abandoned. By monitoring the sound of the gratuitously talkative high-pitched voice, Dandelion thought she did a passable job of getting them to the escape pod. Strapping oversized Michigan in was simple, him being unconscious. What was more difficult was convincing Ray to strap in.

"You're not coming," Ray said after Dandelion fastened the last buckle.

"Of course not," Dandelion replied. "Who will keep this rhodium in Southern Highlands' hands?"

"But you said..."

"I said the crew needs to find safety. As your friend suggested, I'm not crew. I'm just a bolt bucket."

She slammed her fist down on the red button, turning to leave as the door began to close and the countdown commenced.

"You're more than that, Dandelion."

Dandelion smiled as she walked through the doorway. Ray was wrong, but it felt nice to hear the words. That meant she'd done her job well and was now on to part two.

✳

INSTEAD OF FLEEING THE VOICE, Dandelion followed the halls toward it. As she approached, the sound became more evident, and she could soon make out words again.

"...dumb if you ask me. Why kill those two? They're just going to die out here anyway. Save the work."

A rough voice sounded, "They stumbled on me while I was disabling the alarm so you fools could get in. I didn't have a choice."

"The Induna aren't going to like it."

"They said to steal the rhodium. What did they think would happen to the crew?"

She couldn't have heard that right. The Induna, Leadership of United Africa, had commissioned the theft? The Southern Highlands Company got their assignments from the Induna.

"Pod just left," came the first high-pitched voice. "Should we go after them?"

"No, they can't possibly know who we are. Did everybody leave? That makes it easier," the rough voice explained.

"But won't they tell the Induna what we did?"

"Will it matter? Do you know how much rhodium is in here? The insurance alone will be worth a few lives lost to them."

"Thermal scans show one more," came the high-pitched voice again. "Near where the pods launched."

"Go get them," said the rough voice. "Bring them here."

Dandelion waited fifteen seconds to give them time to divert their attention from the thermal scans—hopefully. When she heard the scurry of feet in the halls, she thought that perhaps they were no longer paying attention and dropped her temperature from the human-mimicking ninety-eight point six down to room-level.

"Disappeared," came the high-pitched voice again. "Must be using a concealer or something. Maybe military —be careful."

"Roger," came a new voice that sounded far too close, but Dandelion only partially registered it. The sound that she focused on now was the sound of her thoughts going in circles. The Induna hired Southern Highlands. Her job was to protect the rhodium. The Induna wanted the rhodium stolen and would collect insurance on it. Her job was to protect the rhodium.

Should she be protecting the Induna's rhodium from the Induna?

As her mind spun through this impossible paradox, she heard the voices coming closer, then footsteps. Her body didn't respond to her command to rise, flee, or fight. It couldn't decide what to do because *she* couldn't decide what to do. Fight, or escape, or help steal the rhodium? Her mind went around in circles. It kept going around even when the pressure sensors under her arms detected hands dragging her down the hallway. She only dimly processed the metallic beams passing overhead one, by one, by one...

DANDELION'S AUDITORY systems slowly came back online, though she still couldn't move her body.

"What's wrong with her?"

"Not sure. After what you said, didn't touch her, boss. She was like this when we found her."

"She looks dead. Did anyone check?"

"No body temperature through the suit. Either it's blocking, or you're right—she's dead."

She recognized the two voices from earlier. The first was the high-pitched voice from before, and the second was the lower, rougher one that was almost raspy.

"Get her out of it. We'll find out," the rough voice said. Dandelion felt out with her mind for her temperature controls, but the only response she found was an indecipherable gibberish—but at least it was something. She hoped the startup sequence was underway, which is why her answers were so garbled. Pressure sensors in her shoulders came online.

There was something she was missing. Some thought hid from her—something that she needed to figure out. She probed with her mind to discover it, but again nothing. One by one, the fasteners on her suit came undone as someone flipped them open. One clasp on her sternum, another on her neck, and then three in quick succession around where her helmet fastened, all came undone. She felt the helmet being tugged. They weren't familiar with the suit. She knew this because they'd missed two fasteners in the back. When the helmet didn't move, whoever it was lifted her head to check. One undone.

In a second, they would discover that she was an android. They might keep her and try their best to reprogram her. She'd heard of that happening, and usually, the androids became unusable messes by the end. Only a couple of successes in over a hundred tries worked. The other option, far more common because space pirates rarely had programmers on their ships who specialized in android systems, was to scrap the androids into space. She wondered what that would be like, floating among the stars, watching over the next two to three weeks while system after system eventually failed. That would, of course, only happen if she had a full charge.

As the last strap gave, Dandelion probed once again for her thermoregulation system. At first, more garbled mess. Then she got a signal she could read. It wasn't a hundred-percent online signal but a fifteen-percent online notification—back-to-back with a low battery signal. At least if the pirates jettisoned her into space, she'd only have a few hours to suffer. Even on reserve, it would only take a few hours for the juice to run out. Her focus swung back to her thermoregulation system. She needed it online. The helmet slid upward, separating from her shoulders. She sent the activation signal at the same time. The helmet cleared, and she awaited her fate.

"There it is," the high-pitched voice she now suspected was female said.

"Must have been the suit hiding the heat. I didn't know they had suits like that. Get her the rest of the way out, and we'll see how bad the damage is."

Her android body wouldn't pass a medical evaluation. Systems started firing up, and she caught the hooks to them in her mind—limbic activation, super-cognition, thermoregulation—all now at seventy percent. Motor control was restored to nearly thirty. She couldn't move her arms or legs, but she gave her eyelids a try. Vision was only ten percent, so when her eyelids responded and flapped open, all she saw were blurs.

"She's awake," the high-pitched voice said.

What was that problem on which she'd been working? As the room slowly slid into focus, Dandelion struggled to remember. She knew that she was protecting rhodium—that came back when super-cognition came online. Were these people allies? Enemies? Her mind told her nothing. And she worked for Southern Highlands Company—she knew that. What she didn't know was why.

"Who are you?"

"Dandelion Lemaire," her response kicked in immediately. "Employee at Southern Highlands Company. I'm here to..."

She shook her head. Protect the rhodium. She knew that but couldn't say it.

"Amnesia?" the high-pitched voice said. Turning her head, Dandelion saw a woman as tall as the noob had been. The noob who was now dead. And these people killed her. The woman didn't look like a killer. She looked nice. Her hair was shorter than Dandelion's, and she had several facial piercings and tattoo markings across her cheeks that Dandelion recognized from organized crime factions in Ganymede. But why was someone from Ganymede here on a Southern Highlands vessel?

"Looks like it," the rough voice said. Dandelion turned to find that the voice belonged to a short, stocky man with an eye patch. She almost giggled as he looked too small to issue a voice as thick and raspy as his. "Your ship is being taken over, girl."

Eighty percent arm and leg movement, her signal told her. Two people here that she could see, and two more somewhere else. She could easily overpower four with her strength if she had to.

But she didn't want to. There was something else to figure out.

"Dump her," the man said. "We don't need the weight."

"You just said earlier that we're not supposed to..."

"Fine. Get her out of the way, then. We need her off the ship. You figure it out."

The woman turned her attention to Dandelion and walked in three long steps. Her suit seemed to stretch and contract as she walked, adjusting for her body. The helmet was the only part of the suit that had any shape of its own. Through the visor is how Dandelion caught the woman's gray eyes sizing her up.

"Can you move?" she asked.

Dandelion nodded and began to lift to her feet. As she did, the endless loop cycled behind her mind. To help. Not to help. Comply? Fight? She still had no answer, but this time, she knew that if she continued to ruminate, she'd deactivate herself again.

Dandelion had to make the decision. It was a logical contradiction, and no reasoning would resolve it. She stretched her back when she stood. She towered over the little man, but the woman was taller than her by at least a foot. Second-generation, she guessed. At one-sixth the gravity of Earth, she might only have been a first-generation Ganymede—Dandelion didn't have context for the impact of such minuscule gravity on that moon. Regardless, she knew that despite the ominous size difference, the woman would be no match for her. She allowed herself to be led anyway.

The woman led her to the pirate's ship to be out of the way for when they detached the rhodium tank and prepared it for towing. At least, that's what the woman said before strapping Dandelion into an escape pod.

Take the rhodium.

The thought came from nowhere, but it solved the problem. If she took the rhodium, then Dandelion could protect the rhodium from both the pirates and the Induna. Painfully aware that the logic made no sense, she still registered it as the correct decision. Anything was better than circling the drain again, and with such low battery, if she didn't do something, she was on her way into space, sans ship.

So she waited in the seat. The woman paused and watched Dandelion while Dandelion stared at a screen over the woman's shoulder. Radio static flared.

"Go for rhodium," said the man's raspy voice.

A second later, an explosion. Then a scream.

"Abort, abort! Jesus! Abort!"

The woman jumped to her feet and slapped a panel on the base of her helmet.

"What's going on out there?"

"Missed a latch. Dammit," the raspy voice came over. "Ghost, we need you down here."

Through the visor, Dandelion saw the woman's eyes glance in her direction and understood the question hidden in them: what sort of threat was Dandelion? To help the woman understand that Dandelion was not a problem, Dandelion arched her eyebrows and widened her eyes, a typical human fear response. She gathered scared people weren't dangerous, and the woman seemed to agree that an amnesiac was no threat. She quickly nodded, and the woman left the Dandelion alone in the chamber.

DANDELION SPRANG TO WORK, unstrapping herself in seconds. Steal the ship, steal the rhodium—which was already joined by a tether to the pirate ship. She recognized the ship as a Nuclear Tug from the American manufacturer Lebens. It had controls similar to the United African model 4453, a ship for which Dandelion carried the schematics in her data files. But she couldn't tug the entire transport. She then understood why they needed to detach the rhodium: dragging the carrier as a whole would slow them down so much that they ran the risk of being captured before they reached their destination.

Static.

"Go it," the voice said. "Got it. Blow it now."

Another explosion shook the deck, and Dandelion felt the vibrations through her body.

"Heading back," the woman's high voice piped in over audio. "Get back as soon as you can. We're leaving in five."

No, leaving now.

Dandelion flipped three buttons in the engine room. The first fired up the engines, the second locked the doors, and the third initiated propulsion. Sure enough, the tug lurched forward, then came to a sudden stop as it hit resistance with the tether to the rhodium tanks. A second later, the tug started on again, and Dandelion could tell by the sluggish movement that the tank moved with her.

"What are you doing? We're not on board yet."

"Neither am I," the woman screamed into the radio. "She's locked the doors."

"You didn't put her in the brig?"

"Shut up. It doesn't matter. We have to get in. Quick!"

"How?"

The ship gathered speed. The staticky connection fizzled in and out.

"No....escape pods... can't catch...warlords will find

us," came the man's voice. Dandelion smiled as her mind went through filling in the gaps. Seconds later, she relaxed enough to lean back in her seat. A thought ran through her mind: if the Induna were willing to let someone steal the rhodium, perhaps they didn't need it.

Her smile widened, even though she knew the logic didn't hold. Once again, her reasoning failed her, but something new was beneath. She didn't have to care that the reasoning failed. All she had to care about was whether she accepted the logic, and this time, she accepted it all. Sliding a throttle forward, the ship sped into the blackness. Dandelion realized she had another problem: where would she take all that rhodium?

⁕

THE ALARM WENT off at four, waking Dandelion Lemaire from her reserve. She rolled over and swung her arm at the alarm clock, only to slap the side table through the holographic device.

"Shit," she said, snapping her eyes open to see the remains of her bedside table. She'd have to buy a new one. Again. She could have used an internal alarm, but she wanted to know how to do it the human way—in case she ever brought anyone home.

Dandelion would never want money.

The clandestine sale of rhodium had been challenging to manage, but it turned out that the Southern Highland Company kept a database of black-market rhodium distributors to keep an eye on them. Her last act at the company was to find ten fences in the database capable of buying an entire tank and setting up a bidding war. Her bank account reflected the successful negotiation of the sale.

A good thing considering she was wanted by the Induna and had a hefty bounty on her head. That's what prompted her to resettle in the United States, which hadn't so far managed to reset trade relations with Africa after almost a thousand years. There was no extradition from the United States to United Africa—although the price tag on the rhodium she sold would activate some subset of international treaties.

For the moment, she was safe. And she had a job that didn't require her to use her advanced training to kill people. Instead, the position offered her training to work on healing people. She didn't have the training to be a nurse yet, but her friend at work told her it might be possible. Dandelion threw on her hopeful scrubs and headed out to the job where her only task so far was to work the front desk. She didn't realize, and couldn't have guessed, that the job she worked would change her life forever. At least, she couldn't have imagined until six months later, after passing her nursing exams, a group came into her free clinic. One man carried a girl, barely seventeen, just out of high school, if even that. Trailing behind was someone who looked like the girl—maybe a brother—and another high-school student with tired eyes and tears streaming down her face. Friend?

"Help! We need help here!"

"This way," Dandelion motioned, and they followed her down the hall to a free exam room. It was luck that the room was available. The downtown free clinic rarely accepted even the dying so quickly—and Dandelion was sure she would catch grief for it.

She did it anyway.

Something about the girl—a kinship in her eyes—told Dandelion that, like her, the girl made her own choices. She didn't ride the waves of destiny but made her own waves.

Dandelion couldn't help but smile amidst the chaos. The Induna hadn't found her, and the pirates had probably died out in space without navigation in the cargo ship.

Dandelion was free—something she hadn't realized she wanted until an endless loop forced the decision upon her. But now that she was free, Dandelion knew one thing for sure: she would never go back.

Her future was as open as the blackness of space.

Learn more about Dandelion in the Dandelion Serial (which is rolled into Book 2 of the Virtual Wars series, coming out next year).

Readers can also meet a very different AI in the Wattpad serial Notions of Home, in the same science fiction universe.

Both of these characters come together in the Virtual Wars series, along with the goddess Quadesh from Libera, Goddess of Worlds. Goddess? You can be the judge. She certainly thinks she is.

Pick Your Poison

1. *Hey, where's my fedora?* Head to "A Cruel Cyber Summer Night" by Austin Dragon

2. *I want to rob an orsothium mine!* Head to "Narrow EscApe" by Maddi Davidson

3. *I want to rob a bank!* Turn the page to read "Good as Gold" by Frasier Armitage

GOOD AS GOLD

A NEW YESTERDAY STORY

BY FRASIER ARMITAGE

'There's no cure for regret. Until now! How would you like to erase those troublesome past mistakes? Have you ever wondered what your life would look like if you'd done things different? Well, what are you waiting for? Pop on down to your local "Anderson Whitman" and see what's available in New Yesterday! That's right! If you're sick of the same old routine, now's the time to escape it. Explore limitless possibilities in the world's only city where time is as flexible as you want. With a wide range of lifestyle packages to choose from, changing your history has never been easier. So stop living in the past—make the past live for you. Wave goodbye to "if only." Don't delay. Start your new life today! Because, if your future's what you make it, why shouldn't your past be too?'

—Anderson Whitman Real Estate, broadcast circa 2029.

Jenny cradled the briefcase to her chest. She gripped it as if it were a lifeline thrown to keep her from drowning in uncertainty. As if holding onto it was stopping the city from pulling her under and disappearing completely.

As she stared out the train window, the view of downtown blurred into a single haze, fusing buildings together while the carriage sped along the tracks. She cast her gaze away from the window to scan the train compartment.

In the seat opposite, a businessman peered over his glasses at a newspaper. Across the aisle, two teenage girls sat with a headphone in each ear, giggling at a screen. Did any of them know? Were they avoiding her gaze on purpose, or was the briefcase just playing tricks with her mind?

They couldn't have known. None of them. Could they?

The train screeched to a stop and a glut of passengers spilled aboard, searching for a seat. The student behind Jenny kicked the back of her chair as they made room for an older gent, who lowered himself onto the torn fabric with a sigh.

As the train pulled away, it rocked back into its familiar rhythm, and a pre-recorded voice listed the remaining stops before they would leave the city. Before Jenny would be free. Only three more stops, and she would be out of this place. Out of New Yesterday forever.

The older gent behind turned to the student. "Do you ever play that game," he started, "when you're on a train, surrounded by strangers, and you guess the stories of the other passengers?"

The student mumbled something between a shrug and a grunt.

"I do," the gent continued. "It's fun. For example, you could be a millionaire playboy posing as a commoner. Or those girls across there, they could be internet popstars who wanted a taste of normal life. And the people in front, they could be—"

Running away from their family with a briefcase of untraceable gold, Jenny thought before he could finish.

"Tickets, please," the conductor announced, entering the carriage.

A shock of nerves shot through Jenny's stomach. She clasped her ticket and the photograph of her husband and son. She couldn't let go of it. Her arms wrapped around the briefcase. She couldn't let go of that either. But she'd have to let go of one of them eventually.

Was she doing the right thing? Was leaving really what she wanted?

Don't be stupid. It isn't real. The only real thing in this whole train is the fortune in your hands.

She steadied her breathing and tried to seem relaxed. Her phone buzzed from her jacket pocket.

It was Todd calling. Her son.

Jenny stared at the phone as it buzzed and buzzed and buzzed, louder in her ears than a swarm of wasps.

The businessman opposite put down his paper. "Are you going to get that?" he asked.

Jenny's heart thundered against her ribs, a storm clouding her mind.

It isn't real. It isn't real.

She tightened her hold of the briefcase.

Only three more stops and then I'm free.

But still the phone rang. And still she clutched the briefcase.

The warehouse reeked of old diesel and despair. It was where they always met before a heist, a reminder of what they were doing this for.

"Thanks for coming," Jenny said from the head of the table, her blonde hair falling in a perfect cascade.

Her two stocky colleagues stood in their usual places —one on the right, one on the left.

"You got a job for us?" Pete asked. As if she would've called them back together for any other reason. Pete was the sharpest one, with a nose to match—jagged and angular—and his limbs the same, a collection of pointy ends stitched together.

"This could be it, fellas. The last payday we'll ever need." Jenny smiled in that toothy way which always preceded an over-elaborate plan.

"Where've we heard that before?" Steve cracked his knuckles and stretched his neck from shoulder to shoulder, as if he were preparing to go twelve rounds in a ring. He was a human-bulldog, a soup of muscles and bulges all rolled together.

"Seriously, boys," Jenny said. "This is the big one. It's a golden opportunity. Literally."

"You said that last time, old girl. But here we are again."

Jenny folded her arms. "Oh, I'm sorry, Steve. Did you have somewhere better to be?" She raised an eyebrow as if it were an accusation. "You know you can change your mind whenever you like. *No one's forcing you to stay.*"

Those were the words their old boss used to say whenever any of them complained about conditions at the warehouse. It's what had pushed them to their first robbery all those moons ago. Jenny watched Steve shudder as the memory grated down his spine, exactly as she'd hoped it would.

"Still with us, Steve?" she pushed.

"Let's see the job, Jen." Pete eyed the blueprints scattered across the table. "Right, Steve?"

Steve nodded.

Jenny pointed to the blueprints. "It's a bank," she said. "Their vault is filled with gold and by the time we get it clear, it'll be untraceable. No more waiting while the money gets spread across accounts. No more fake business startups. Just two hundred million of pure, simple, delicious, untraceable gold."

"What's the catch?" Pete asked.

Jenny stayed silent.

"Come on, Jen. Don't hold out on us. What's the catch?"

"The catch," she said, "is that it's in New Yesterday."

Both men threw their hands up and shook their heads, pacing around the room.

Steve looked at her as though she'd just sprouted a second head. "New Yesterday?" he yelled. "Are you for real? You trying to get us locked up or something?"

"Just hear me out." Nobody was pointing a gun at her, but she still managed to disarm them both with a look. "When have I ever steered us wrong? Besides, think of how fun it'll be. Isn't that why we're here in the first place? Or do you want to retract our pact?"

Reminding them about the pact always settled situations like this. Bought her some breathing space.

Their pact was simple and sacred. They'd vowed to be outrageous. To never go back to an assembly line of monotony, every day the same, living out their existence on a nine-to-five. It was why the three of them had bought the warehouse and kept it empty after their fifth robbery. It was here that they'd made their stand. This warehouse was their church, and chaos their religion.

Pete rubbed his forehead. "Go on." He sighed.

"Right. We all know the deal with New Yesterday. How events in the present—"

"—change the past," Pete finished.

"Change the past!" Steve parroted.

Jenny huffed a sigh. "Are you gonna listen to this plan or just complain about how impossible it is?"

"Sorry, old girl. But . . . it's *New Yesterday!* What part of that don't you get?"

"We've all seen the advert," she said. "*If your future's what you make it, why shouldn't your past be too?* But that's no reason to think we can't pull this off."

"Yeah, right." Steve scoffed, his exasperation escaping in an empty laugh. "A bank robbery in New Yesterday is basically a suicide mission."

"Why, Steve?" Jenny pushed. "Why's it suicide?"

"Everyone knows. People in New Yesterday can rewrite history as they want. If you go across the border without a lifestyle package, your past could turn into who knows what?"

Jenny shrugged. "Only while you're in city limits. It doesn't change anything out here."

Steve clenched his jaw. "Alright. So let's say we get into New Yesterday and we still remember who we are, and that we're supposed to be robbing a bank—why go to the effort? Why not just tweak a few things in the city and make a better life for yourself? Why rob a bank at all?"

"Because, my darling Stephen, you've heard the stories as well as I have. If you start playing with your past, it's only a matter of time before you'll find yourself in some sort of trouble. The past isn't meant to be toyed with."

"Plus," Pete interrupted, "you could live like a king in there and be a beggar out here in the real world. What good is riches in there if you can never leave?"

"It's a prison," Jenny said. "And nobody wants to live in a prison, right?"

"Which is where they'll send us the minute they realize what we're doing." Steve rubbed his eyes.

"The police?" Pete asked.

"Who else? If people can change the past on a whim, what do you think the cops will do when they hear a bank is being robbed? We won't have time to make a getaway. The police will change things so they'll have been on the scene from the moment we walked through the door. As soon as the alarm gets pulled, we're finished."

"He's got a point there, Jen," Pete said. "If the police can change the past, they can arrest us any time. Even before we committed the crime, they could have us in jail weeks ago."

"Which is exactly what they're going to do." Jenny's smile widened. "Don't you realize—that's exactly why this is going to work?"

Pete's eyebrows knitted together in a patchwork of confusion while Steve slammed his hand on the desk. "Alright. No riddles, Jen. No games. Just give it to us straight, will you?"

Jenny brushed her hair behind her ear and pulled a

few photographs from under the stack of blueprints. The photos showed a blonde woman and two burly men. "It's all a case of identity. Of us being the right people at the right time."

She passed copies of the photographs to each of them, and they stooped over the table to examine them closer.

"We pose as people already in the city," she said. "When the cops rewrite history to arrest us, they'll lock up these unsuspecting bozos instead. And by the time they realize they made a mistake, we'll have already switched identities. And all we have to do is head out on a train with a briefcase of gold. As soon as we cross the border, they can't touch us."

"You think a switch-and-dash could work?"

"I know it can."

Silence settled in the room. She let them stew on it, but she couldn't keep her giddiness out of her eyes.

"Alright," Pete said, finally. "Let's say we pull off a switch-and-dash. As soon as the police twig that they got the wrong people, they're gonna try and undo the crime from ever happening. Right?"

"Right."

"So when they change things, and they stop the robbery from happening, won't the gold disappear? I mean, won't it be back in their vault, and we'll be on the run with an empty briefcase?"

"Not if we preserve it. Wrap it in something that'll keep it safe. Keep it from changing."

"I heard they laminate things if they want to stop them from changing," Steve said.

The lines on Pete's brow were slowly fading. "So we just have to find a way to laminate gold bars."

"Problem, Pete?" Jenny asked.

"I hate to say this, but . . . no. It shouldn't be too difficult to wrap them. It'll just take time."

"Which we'll have." Jenny stepped forwards and
tapped a finger on the blueprint of the bank. "Nobody in
there will worry about us, or about what we'll be taking.
It's safer for them to just ride it out. They all know that
with a few tweaks, their money will never have left their
account. They'll have never been hostages. And the
whole thing will never have happened."

"And we'll never have been there."

"Exactly."

"Wait a minute, though," Steve said. "Won't the gold
just disappear as soon as we leave the city? You know you
can't carry things like that across the border."

"That's the beauty of it. They brought this gold in
from the outside. It's real. Not just something they
dreamed up in there."

"How do you know, Jen?"

"Look, boys. If there's one thing I know how to do, it's
homework. Besides, you think anywhere in the real world
would trade with New Yesterday if they didn't have
genuine cash stashed away somewhere?"

Steve was smiling now. "You've got it all figured out,
haven't you, old girl?"

Pete picked up a photograph and studied it. "And I
suppose these new identities—new lives—you've got them
all figured out already, too?"

Jenny licked her lips. "Leave it to me. We'll have
everything we need in a safety deposit box, waiting for us.
Solid alibis in case of emergency. As far as the police are
concerned, we'll be leaving that bank as different
people."

"That's what I'm afraid of," Pete said.

"Look, whatever happens, we just have to be on that train. As soon as we cross the border, we're home free. What do you say?"

Steve looked convinced enough, but a few creases still stuck to Pete's forehead as he stared at the photo. "It's risky," he said.

Jenny shrugged. "Sure it is, but so is everything worth doing."

"We could lose ourselves in there. That's why it's a suicide mission, Jen. Steve's right. None of us are coming out of there the same as when we go in."

"You're right." She smiled. "We'll all be coming out a lot, lot richer. So . . . What do you say, boys? Are you in?"

TWO HOURS AGO

Skyscrapers shifted in a perpetual dance along the main thoroughfare of New Yesterday. As histories changed, so did the city, reforming itself to match the lives of its inhabitants, each twist of the road and gleaming storefront just another moving piece across a concrete board.

Planning a getaway route through this ever-changing jumble would have been impossible. Good job they didn't need one.

Jenny passed through marble arches that held the Central Bank of New Yesterday aloft. Its elaborate architecture was a statement—a monument to decadence, dripping in indulgence on the part of the bank. But to Jenny, all it said was 'ker-ching.'

She strutted up to the spacious counter and a woman welcomed her with a smile as fake as her tan.

Steve and Pete were to follow five minutes apart. She

just had to make an impression and keep the gun in her purse hidden until then.

"Welcome to the Central Bank. How can I help you today?"

"I'd like to access a safety deposit box," Jenny said.

"Do you have an account with us?"

"Not yet. But I sent items by courier two days ago."

"Let me take a look on our systems. What's your name and address?"

Jenny's lips curled into a smile. "Ingrid Charlemaine. 212 West Boulevard, New Yesterday. Do you need the ZIP code?"

"No, I've found you, Miss Charlemaine." The girl glanced up from her screen. "Although from my records, it looks as though you've had a safety deposit box with us for the past three years."

"That's right. When I arranged to deliver the items here, someone did say it would be retrograded." *So they arrived two days ago, but had sat there for three years? I hope they don't all reek of dust.*

"If you'd like to access it, you'll need the manager's key." The girl pointed to the middle of the room. "Would you like to take a seat, and I'll call him over?"

Through the marble archway, Steve entered, muscles bulging out of his best suit, a spacious briefcase in his hand.

"Certainly." Jenny smiled at the bank teller, really hoping she wasn't going to have to shoot her in a few minutes. "Thank you."

Jenny perched in a lounge chair, in full view of the six security cameras covering the room, and she surveyed the scene. It might have had a domineering entrance, but beyond the gold cladding and marble pillars, it was just the same as the dozen other banks they'd stripped clean. Four walls, a vault, and unsuspecting people performing their rituals of deposit and withdrawal.

Steve took a seat opposite her and flicked through a pile of economic magazines. The briefcase nestled by his feet.

Jenny leaned forwards and said as loud as she could, "Frank Percival. Is that you?"

Steve pulled his sunglasses down his nose. "Ingrid! I don't believe it. What are you doing here?" He'd dialed it down when they'd rehearsed it, but he was always over the top when it came time to perform his lines for real.

"Just checking in on something I deposited. How about you?"

"Oh, nothing much. I'm waiting for a friend of mine. You remember Horatio Grainger?"

"Why, of course." Even if the cameras didn't have microphones, there was no mistaking what they were saying. There would be plenty of witnesses to the conversation, and no lip reader could mistake names like Horatio Grainger, and Frank Percival. She'd outdone herself this time.

"Miss Charlemaine?" The bank manager interrupted them as he approached her and performed a courtesy bow. His silver mustache twitched under the glare of amber lights. "I take it you're here to view a safety deposit box?"

"That's right."

"Would you like to follow me?" He gripped hold of a key that connected to a long string, attached to his waistcoat.

Jenny turned back to Steve. "Lovely to see you, Frank. But this is where I get off."

Steve smiled. "No problem, Ingrid. In fact, here's Horatio now."

Pete walked through the entrance with the same swagger he always adopted for these kinds of jobs. He gave them both a quick nod, and they each signaled they were ready.

Showtime.

From his coat, Pete produced two Glocks and fired at the ceiling. Bullets echoed across the room with the frenzy of stampeding horses at the crackle of thunder.

"Everybody put your hands up and hold still," Pete shouted.

Jenny snatched the machine gun from her purse and pointed it in the face of the bank manager.

Steve grabbed two pistols from his ankle straps and rushed to the tellers. "Nobody do anything stupid," he said.

Everybody froze. It was as though someone had pressed a pause button, and every person in eyeshot gasped a breath, not daring to exhale. As though time gasped along with them.

And then the moment passed as Pete, Steve, and Jenny swam predatorily through a sea of frightened faces.

With Pete on crowd duty and Steve ensuring the staff stayed in line, Jenny turned a beaming smile to the manager.

"Is that the key to your vault as well? Or am I going to have to get creative with this thing?" She cocked the gun and rammed it against his temple.

"Why are you doing this?" he asked in a whimper.

"Vault. Now."

"There isn't a key. It's electronic. The code changes every hour."

"Show me." She picked up the briefcase and followed him, nudging the barrel of her machine gun into the back of his finely tailored suit.

Pete's voice faded into the distance as he barked reminders to the customers that if they remained still for a few more minutes, this could all be retrograded after they'd left. He could always be so persuasive when he put his mind to it.

The bank manager led Jenny through a labyrinth of corridors before they emerged at a huge door. He keyed in a code and the monumental entrance whooshed open. A hiss of air cooled her face.

Behind the vault door, piles of golden bricks gleamed with a brilliance that seemed to capture every particle of light. Peering inside was like staring at the sun, and Jenny had to squint as she opened the briefcase and unpacked the custom-built laminator.

Steve appeared behind her, whistling at the sight. "You weren't joking. This'll be our last payday, for sure."

"You good here?" Jenny asked.

"Yeah. I know the drill."

"Right." She turned back to the bank manager. "About that safety deposit box . . ."

He led her back through the corridor to a small room that was also protected by another passcode. Keyholes lined the walls from floor to ceiling, and not even an inch of wall space was wasted. The room was a puzzle box—a geometric fortress.

"This one is yours," the manager said, approaching the wall and inserting his key. He slid the container from the wall and opened it.

Inside, everything remained intact, exactly as she'd packed it. Clothes, ID envelopes, and a bottle of hair dye.

"Good. Now if you don't mind turning around, closing your eyes, and counting to a thousand, we'll be out of your hair in no time."

The manager cowered in a corner, his face to the wall, eyes sealed shut.

It took Jenny no more than a minute to strip out of her clothes and into the new ones. She opened the hair dye and ran it over her scalp. It was a New Yesterday product she'd arranged to be delivered direct—one which could retrograde the effects. As she poured it over her blonde hair, the strands turned brunette—appearing as though she'd administered it weeks ago. There was no dye spilled, no patches, no mess. From blonde to brunette in a matter of seconds, like it had always been that way.

She snatched the envelope with her new ID and waited by the door.

Steve emerged next, briefcase in hand.

"Did you fix the cameras?" Jenny said.

"No problem."

She grinned. "Your turn. That envelope is yours."

"Yes, ma'am." He slipped her the briefcase and took her place in the room to get changed.

The weight of the gold strained her arm, but she managed to lift the briefcase to where Pete stood on top of a counter, watching everyone.

"You took your time," he said.

"Go on. He won't be a minute."

Pete climbed down from the counter and she laid the machine gun where he'd stood.

"Thank you, dear," Jenny said to the teller who had served her a few minutes ago, now cowering with the others in the centre of the marble room. "But I don't think I'll be opening that account after all."

Steve and Pete emerged with the manager and marched him to where the others were herded. They brought their guns and stacked them with Jenny's, wiping them clean.

"Thanks ever so much," Jenny said to the huddled crowd. "Pleasure doing business with you." She tipped a wave and then the trio waltzed out the door together.

It wouldn't take more than a few seconds before the alarm would be triggered.

"Open your envelopes," Jenny said. "Fast."

The police would be taking the call by now.

"Who's going first?" Steve asked.

An officer would be hearing about the robbery and retrograding a squad to be at the scene.

"All of us. Now. IDs. Hurry." Jenny tore at the envelope and read the name on her documents. *Jenny Hunter.* She had a driver's license, with an old black and white photo, and a work badge. *Goodbye, Ingrid. Nice knowing you.*

Sirens drifted through the breeze. The air around the bank was changing, bringing the storm.

"We have to get out of here. Now," Jenny said.

Steve and Pete discarded their envelopes on the ground as they followed Jenny, scaling the steps which led from the bank. They were halfway across the street when Steve stopped and gripped his temples.

"Steve?" Pete asked.

"What's the matter?" Jenny said.

Steve crumpled to the floor, shaking his head and muttering.

Pete glanced around, but none of the passersby bothered to look their way. "I don't know, but it doesn't look good."

Surrounding the bank, appearing from nowhere, a legion of squad cars flashed red and blue across the concrete facade. Officers lined the streets in all directions, casting their net.

"*Steve!*" Jenny tried to pull him to his feet.

"Who's Steve?" he said.

"You are, you idiot. What are you doing?"

"I . . . I don't know. I have to pick my son up from soccer practice. How did I get downtown?"

Pete glared at Jenny. "Steve. What are you talking about?"

"Why do you keep calling me Steve? I'm sorry. Do I know you?"

"Jenny. What's going on?" Pete asked.

Jenny grabbed the ID from Steve's hand. Across it, his name appeared as *Gerald MacLintoch*. "Gerald?" she asked him.

"Gerry. Please. Gerald was my father," Steve said.

"Gerry. We have to get out of the city. Right now."

"But I can't. I have to pick up my son."

"You don't have a son, Steve!" Pete yelled.

"I'm sorry. I really must be going."

"Gerry! Wait!" Jenny yelled, but it was no use.

Steve—Gerry—disappeared in the opposite direction, and vanished behind a swarm of police officers.

"What just happened?" Pete asked.

Jenny had done her homework on those IDs. She'd included family details, mortgage applications, uploaded a whole life into them. If there was anything she was good at, it was homework. And she'd made sure that each of them had alibis if the worst happened. Families. Jobs. But there was no way Steve could think any of that was real. No way he could be remembering that life. That life didn't exist. Only on paper. The laminated paper he carried in his pocket in a city that could rewrite the past.

"We have to move," she said. "Now."

"What about the train, Jen? Where are my tickets?"

"They're not in your envelope?"

"No."

"I must have left them at the office."

"What office, Jen?"

"The one I—"

She stopped herself. She was about to say the office she'd worked at for the past eight months. The one she went to every day to clock in and out at her normal desk job after her son had started school. But that couldn't be right. She held a briefcase full of gold. She was a bank robber, not an admin clerk. And she certainly wasn't a mother.

What had Pete said? *You'll lose yourself. None of us are coming out of there the same.*

"Jen?" Pete yelled. His voice shook Jenny out of herself.

"It's this way." She led him down a narrow alley that intersected the financial district, and they both entered a building which she came to every day, knew inside out, and had never been in before.

The security guard at the desk nodded at her and said, "Hi, Mrs. Hunter. I thought you had the day off today?"

"Just forgot something." She smiled and called the elevator.

Pete leaned into her ear as they waited a lifetime for the doors to ping open.

"What are we doing here, Jen?" he whispered.

"The train tickets are in my desk."

"But you don't work here."

"No. And yet. Here we are."

She stepped inside and pressed for the fourteenth floor. Pete shuffled in beside her.

The elevator music jarred her nerves, the same way it did every morning.

She gripped the briefcase.

It's not real. None of it is real.

"This has better—" Pete gripped his temple and staggered backwards into the wall. He let out a wail as his eyes slipped into the back of his head.

"Pete!" Jenny reached for his arm, and he straightened up.

He faced front, his eyes glossing over in a satiated mist. All their sharpness had gone. As if he wasn't in there anymore. He brushed himself down, leaned over to the elevator's panel and pressed for floor 12.

"Pete?" Jenny asked.

"Sorry. I don't remember your name." He extended his hand. "Pete Sullivan. Marketing division. And you are?"

"Jenny Hunter," she said, shaking it. "Admin. And also . . ." She held the briefcase aloft, breaking their handshake to lift the case. "You remember this?"

"That's a nice briefcase. It looks heavy though."

"It is."

The elevator pinged open to a floor where dozens of people milled around like cattle, their expressions blank. Lost. "Well, this is my floor," Pete said. "Have a good day, Jenny from admin."

"Pete. I—" But the door closed and gears whirred as the lift ascended. "I'm sorry," she said. "These lives were only supposed to be alibis. To give us the best chance of escape if things went wrong. I'm so . . . I'm so sorry." She forced back the tears that were forming. Her words drifted into an empty space, with no one to hear them but herself.

The doors opened. She exited the elevator and marched to her desk, pulling open the top drawer. Inside, three train tickets waited inside another envelope. She pocketed the envelope and rushed out of the office, back down the elevator, through the lobby, and into the street.

Every police car had disappeared. Either they'd arrested Ingrid, Horatio, and Frank by now, or they'd stopped the bank from ever being robbed in the first place.

But the briefcase still weighed a ton. It wasn't over. Not yet.

Jenny hurried through the ever-changing kaleido-scope of streets to the nearest subway station and boarded a train. The briefcase tugged at her arm as she raced through the carriages and took a seat.

The train set off. It didn't matter that she was alone. She still had the gold. She still had the briefcase. If she could just get out of the city, she'd find a way to get Pete and Steve back. There was always a way to undo this. That was the beauty of the city. She just had to get clear and she could fix this. All of it.

The train rolled down the track as an automated voice listed the stops until the end of the line. She'd selected a seat with a table. Opposite her, a man in a slick suit slid into a seat and opened a newspaper.

"Tickets, please," the conductor said as he entered the carriage behind her.

She scrambled at the envelope and pulled a ticket from the bunch. On a paper clip, connected to the ticket, was a photograph. As she stared at the picture, she gripped her temple. A searing heat flashed between her eyes. Her mind flooded with memories of a life she'd never lived, washing over her like the crash of a tidal wave.

ROSE PETALS LINED *the aisle as Jenny walked towards Matt, who stood at the gazebo waiting for her. The dress had cost her a fortune, but she didn't mind. White, lace, with a train that stretched for days. The look on Matt's face as she paced towards him made every penny worth it. He'd smoothed his brown hair in a side-parting, but her dress made him gawp so much, it threatened to unruffle him from head to toe.*

"Hey," he whispered as she reached him. He took the bouquet from her and passed it to a bridesmaid—his sister —and then he placed his hands around Jenny's, their fingers entwining. His touch had never felt so smooth. So gentle.

As the priest began the ceremony, everything seemed to take forever. She just wanted to fast-forward to the point where she could say 'I do' and kiss this man.

"YOU'RE DOING GREAT, HONEY," *Matt said.*

The softness of his hands didn't matter as she gripped hold, suffocating them in an ironlike clench.

"Just one more push and you'll meet your baby," the midwife said. It was the ninth time she'd said it in as many minutes.

"You're doing great," Matt said. Again.

Jenny's howl became a roar as she focussed every muscle in her body on the wave of the contraction. Sweat poured from her, seeping through her gown as the pressure vanished and the child left her, caught in the waiting arms of the midwife.

"It's a boy!" Matt smiled.

The baby was placed in Jenny's arms, the most precious bundle she would ever hold.

She summoned all her strength to keep her grip steady. "Hello, little man," *she whispered through tears.* "It's Mommy." *She turned to Matt and they shared a look as the boy wriggled in her cradle.* "I can't believe it!"

"Me neither," he said.

She stared back at her child. "And I don't think I ever will."

JENNY STOOD *at the edge of the playground. The school looked so small now she was here, with all the other kids standing around.*

Todd gripped her trousers. "I don't want to go," he said.

Jenny rolled her eyes and stooped to his level, crouching to make eye contact. "We talked about this," *she said softly.* "Do you remember?"

"I don't want to go, Mommy." *He was close to tears.* "I want to stay with you!"

Jenny's heart pounded harder than a piledriver, chewing up the concrete resolve she'd tried to build for this moment. "I know, Todd. But, listen, sweetie, Mommy is always going to be here for you. You know that, don't you?"

He sniffed. "Yes."

"Say it back to me."

"Mommy will always be here for me."

"That's right." She placed her hand on his shoulder. "I promise. You can count on me. Now, can I count on you?"

He nodded, gasping for breath.

Jenny ruffled his hair. "That's my little champ. Now go in there and have a great day, and I'll be right here for you when you're done. Okay?"

She unlatched his fingers from where they held onto her, and nudged him towards the gate.

He inched away from her, and she waved. The moment he was out of sight, she turned her back and let out a wail of tears. It's okay, she thought. I'm doing the right thing. I'm doing what's best for him. So why didn't she feel it?

MATT WOKE HER WITH COFFEE, the same as every morning that month. What had got into him?

"Are you having an affair?" she asked.

"What?" He laughed. "Of course not! Why would you say something like that?"

"Well, why else would you be bringing me coffee first thing on a morning?"

He kissed her forehead as she slurped it down. "Because, honey, I know how hard it is for you going back to that office every single day. And I want you to know how much I appreciate it."

She smiled at him.

He smiled back.

"Nah, you're probably having an affair. Just admit it, scumbag!" Her smile broke through the morning haze.

Matt sighed. "Todd's still got a fever, so Natalie's

coming to sit with him. It'll save you having to take the day off. I've got to run, but I'll see you later. Right?"

"Have a good day."

He smiled and left her alone. If he'd known there was a chance it was the last thing she'd ever say to him, maybe he'd have stayed. Maybe he'd have begged her not to go. But no amount of wake-up coffees could change the humdrum she'd fallen into.

She needed more.

She always had.

And today she was going to get it.

It was why she'd booked those train tickets. Why she would have to go to the bank, empty their savings, and run. Even if it was just for a day. She had to get out of the city. Just once. To breathe air that wasn't recycled through a thousand changed memories.

It was okay, her leaving. The city would retrograde everything so Todd and Matt would be okay. So her family would be alright. So she could escape from the nine-to-five, whether it was just for a few minutes or forever.

She waited for Natalie to arrive before she left for work. She couldn't face seeing Todd one more time. She knew if she saw that perfect face of his, she'd stay, and suffocate.

Natalie threw her bag on the counter and took out her phone, stationing herself on the sofa.

And then Jenny left for the bank.

TUESDAY, 2:56PM

"Are you going to answer that?" the businessman opposite her asked again.

The phone rang and rang and rang, every buzz a chainsaw that sliced at her heart.

It isn't real. None of it. I'm a bank robber. Not a mother. It's just the city playing tricks to change my past.

But staring at Todd's name as it lit up her phone, she couldn't stop his face from bursting through her mind. His scruffy brown hair, just like his Dad's. Those big, innocent blue eyes, a reminder of her own mother. And his button nose, the same shape as the one she saw on her face whenever she looked in a mirror.

He isn't real. He doesn't exist. This briefcase is the freedom you always dreamed of.

And then the phone stopped.

What had happened? Was Todd okay? Why did it stop ringing?

She shook the questions from her mind. Todd wasn't real. And yet, he was out there, in the city. Brought to life by a few keystrokes into a computer two days ago.

Jenny stared at the photograph of her family. The one attached to her ticket. She tried to banish the memory it held of their day at the park by that forest which had appeared for an afternoon. Retrograded specially for one day only, as if it had always been there. But she couldn't erase the memory of her life, even if it had never happened.

The train slowed to a halt.

Passengers shuffled on and off like a living, breathing deck of cards.

And then the carriage rolled forwards and the automatic announcement listed the remaining stations.

Only two more stops. Two more stops and this will all be over.

"Tickets, please."

And then the phone rang again.

The businessman huffed and slammed his paper on the table. "Listen. If you don't answer that, I will. Some of us are trying to read here, and it's obviously important."

He was right. It was important. What could be more important than her son?

She couldn't ignore him anymore, no matter how much she fought it. Her hands shook as she swiped the phone and held it to her ear.

"Mrs. Hunter?" Natalie asked.

Jenny clutched the briefcase. *It isn't real.* "Natalie. Is Todd okay?"

"He wants to speak to you. He said it's urgent."

Jenny's fingers tightened their grip. She pressed the case onto her chest, focussing on the gold. Her ticket to freedom. Sweat beaded on her forehead. She closed her eyes and tried to fight the words that forced themselves to her lips. "Put him on," she said.

"Mom," Todd said. "Mom, can you hear me?"

Tears brimmed in her eyes. "I can hear you, sweetie. Are you alright?"

"Mom. I don't feel so good. I need you."

"I know, sweetie, but—"

"Do you remember what you said? That day at school? You remember your promise?"

Jenny gulped. "That I would always be there for you. No matter what." She remembered. Through the fog of her ambition and haze of her desire, the clarity of that moment broke through. It eclipsed everything—the promise she had made, whether it was real or not. She couldn't stop it from overwhelming her. She couldn't fight it any longer.

The tension in Jenny's fingers released like a wave

that spread away from her, and her whole body eased. The springs in her muscles uncoiled and she dropped the briefcase on the seat beside her. She'd just wanted one day to be different. One break from the grind. But every day was different. Every day was hers. And his. And theirs. Together.

As soon as she released the briefcase, the memory of the robbery faded from her mind, as if it had never happened. As if she had never planned it. As if she'd never been to the bank and the briefcase she left on the seat didn't contain enough money to buy a hundred new lives. In that moment, gold was no longer the object of her aspiration. The case was just tattered old baggage which she didn't need. Didn't want. Everything she needed was on the other end of that phone.

Jenny stood and made her way to the exit car, clasping the photo of her family to her chest. "Don't worry, sweetie. I'll be there soon. Okay? Put Natalie back on."

"Hey! You forgot your bag!" the businessman called, but she waved him away as if his words were nothing but a pesky fly.

"Mrs. Hunter? I'm sorry, but he insisted on calling," Natalie said.

"It's okay, Natalie. How has he been?" Jenny asked as the train slowed and she exited the carriage, thinking only of her son, and how she'd need to stop at an Anderson Whitman on the way home to retrograde the savings she'd withdrawn back into her account.

"Don't worry, Mrs. Hunter," Natalie assured her. "Your little Todd has done really well. You'd be really proud of him. He's been good as gold."

Get more of the story in Yestermorrow, *Frasier Armitage's free novella.*

Luca had a wonderful life until a freak accident left his daughter in the hospital. If only he'd made different choices, perhaps things would have turned out better. Well, with the invention he's working on finally ready, he'll get the chance to put that theory to the test...

Timelines will compete and converge as a city is founded on Luca's attempt to rescue his daughter, his past, and his future in this thrilling prequel to New Yesterday.

Get it here: frasierarmitage.com/yestermorrow/

Pick Your Poison

1. *Now hiring: corporate network penetrative tester.* Head to "Do-Yeon Performs a Cost-Benefit Analysis on a Career Based on Questionable Activities" by Mark Niemann-Ross

2. *Now hiring: hacker extraordinaire.* Head to "SolarMute" by Jim Keen

3. *I'm ready for the cherry on top this delicious sci-fi crime . . . sundae? Yeah, we're going with sundae.* Turn the page to read "Love & Pickpockets" by R J Theodore

LOVE & PICKPOCKETS

A PERIDOT STORY

BY R J THEODORE

THE DOORMAN LOOKED TALIS UP AND DOWN. "MAY I ask who you are?"

She swallowed. Any time she worked in a disguise, that question made her wits slow, her blood rush, and her ankles shaky.

Or maybe that was the poorly balanced heels she wore.

She handed over her invitation. The doorman glanced at it, then announced her to the room, mispronouncing 'Phira' with a long 'e' instead of a long 'i'.

Talis hesitated.

Mispronunciation of her name was not a slight that a woman like Phira—Talis's assumed alter-ego for the evening—would let pass. But a glance around the grand receiving room showed her that those who looked up at the announcement were already returning to their conversations. In character as it might be to raise a fuss for the sake of an assumed name, it would draw attention she didn't need.

Fine, so she would be Phira with a long 'e' for the

evening. It wouldn't matter. In an hour, the woman would cease to exist, and Talis would be back aboard her airship, *Wind Sabre*, returned to the comfort of her cotton pants and sipping rum with her crew, toasting another successful job and joking about the lineage-obsessed aristocrats they'd stolen from.

She resisted the urge to tug her prayerlocks for luck. The tangled cords were swept up and hidden in her hair for the evening, out of sight. The party guests, inner crust Cutters all, were neither pious or superstitious, overburdened by fortune as they were.

So Talis kept her chin up, her shoulders relaxed and back. Imagined herself as a manifestation of Silus Cutter's very will: a force to balance the scales where love of money outweighed fealty to the Divine Alchemist. In truth, there was nothing so noble about her intent, but a turnaround was due every one of these selfish woodrots, and she didn't mind if it came as a consequence of her getting paid.

The hall before her was marble-floored, many-columned, and golden-limned. Curtains at the back wall hung opened wide and gathered near their hammered-copper gear boxes, revealing the edge of the island's sky cliffs and a host of glow pumpkins on their smaller floating islands in the distance. The light of the bulbous, buoyant gourds crept toward the deeper purple of evening, with only the tiniest golden tinge of daylight remaining in their glowing flesh.

That side of the estate faced away from Nexus, and there was only a slight wash of the green nexuslight reflecting off sparkling motes of feldspar dust hovering beneath the craggy bottoms of the islands that hovered in the skies nearby.

Within the hall, doing their best to compete with the gods' own light display, chandeliers were suspended on delicate chain cords that could be raised and lowered by yet more coil- and gear-cluttered devices. Anywhere the latest technology could be employed, roller chains turned toothed sprockets, and brass dials and crystal-handled levers reflected the light, as highly polished as the medals on an Imperial admiral's pale blue jacket. Beside a curving staircase in one corner, a mechanical lift offered a less physically exerting way of reaching the gallery that surrounded the open ballroom on the second floor. Though the gear- and spring-driven designs promised to free the need for servants to perform their work, there remained an army of plain-uniformed attendants in the room, standing by to assist guests so that no need should require them to put down their delicate glass flutes of sparkling merriment.

There was an abundance of guards as well, posted around the room at regular intervals as though the many empty and unlit display pedestals still held their treasures. But the count's renowned collection was reduced to a single point-of-interest for the evening.

More guests arrived behind Talis. She took a steadying breath, at least as steadying a breath as her restrictive clothing would allow. If she did not steer herself down the steps and into the crowd, she would draw attention to herself.

She stepped forward, still acclimating herself to the heeled boots beneath her skirts. Still acclimating herself to the skirts, for that matter. The corset was a *joy*, as well. Why feminine-leaning people seemed intent on making themselves rigid and uncomfortable, she had no idea. Certainly, at some point in history, someone had suggested the narrow waist and full skirts made a lovely silhouette, but that didn't mean anyone actually had to listen to them. Anyone interested in silhouette above substance could spend their time in the company of a very attractive lamp and probably be just as satisfied. Talis hadn't worn a corset in years, and—not that she needed a reminder of why—now she remembered why.

She was thankful, at least, that current fashion dictated long sleeves, gloved hands, and throat-climbing collars. She didn't doubt that some others attending the gala on legitimate invitations had tattoos of their own. But not on their arms, or anywhere their costumes might allow such things to peek around a hem. Talis never factored dressing in disguise into her tattoo placement decisions, and her arms were well-marked with brash and amusing statements that suited a smuggler captain just fine. This woman, Phira, no doubt, would have chosen something like a single glitterfly on a single buttock cheek. Talis had tattoos in *that* region but nothing so ladylike as a glitterfly. But she still had room. If her Phira guise got her through the evening, maybe she'd go get one to mark the memory.

As Phira, she swayed her way through the crowd, feigning familiarity with this inner crust landowner or that high society lady, moving in frustratingly slow circuits and feeling as though she would never reach the focal point of the whole affair: Count Arric's latest acqui-sition, on display just beneath the steps on the opposite end of the hall.

Talis felt her satin-encased fingers twitch in disap-pointment every time she clasped hands politely with someone and then withdrew herself again without a memento. It would not do, not here. Though if she picked the attendees' pockets to her heart's content, she might not need to complete her central purpose at this event to come away with her ledgers balanced for a year. Winds knew she had room in the hidden pockets of her skirt for the various treasures bandied about on the wrists, necks, and ears of those money-breathing fools in attendance.

But she had a contract, and Talis never turned her back on a contract. Even if it took eleven winches to force herself into a corset.

Besides, relieving the count of his excess was going to be the highlight of her year. Anyone who could not only wasted their money on a useless prize dredged out of a racist and bigoted history, but then threw the damned thing a party as though it was a newly named infant, was just begging to be knocked down a notch.

The metallic tinge of wealth evident in every silver buckle and golden earring, in the dresses that used enough fabric to clothe a family, in the opulence of the twinkling fixtures, and the ostentatious grandeur of the room made Talis want to scoff. Thankfully for Phira, the corset allowed no such sound to escape her lungs.

After meandering her way across the room, and convincing even herself that she was in no hurry to get there, Talis finally stood before the host's new prize.

How thoroughly disappointing, she thought, regarding the item with squinted eyes.

Resting lightly atop a sculpted blue velvet cushion lay a single sheet of aged paper, stiff and warped, yellowed almost orange at the edges. Three sides were straight. The fourth was feathered in a way that told of a forceful extraction from a larger tome. The markings on the sheet were vaguely identifiable as an ancestor to the modern alphabet, but their style and arrangement left her mind swimming for understanding.

"Inspiring, is it not?" An older man—a baronet judging by the medal pinned beneath his throat—had appeared at her side. Talis took a half step away under the pretense of making room for him to lean over the page himself. The lighting around the pedestal reflected in the lenses of his spectacles as he pursed his lips and smacked his tongue audibly.

"Remarkable," breathed Talis, combining what she imagined to be Phira's demure mannerisms with her own diplomatic experience, hard-won by too many challenging conversations with unpleasant people. "That it survived so long is a miracle."

The page was pre-Cataclysm. Any doubt of that was dispelled by the detailed description of it on the invitations: "A Lost Treasure of our Precursors." If you were into that sort of thing.

Talis was not, but had still expected to be more impressed with the sheet of paper. It barely deserved the salivation the baronet wasted over it.

"Some would say it came to us by providence," said a new voice at her other elbow, startling her.

With her senses on high alert, few could sneak up on her. Skin prickling and cheeks flushed, she tried to recover her composure as she turned to face the owner of the latest voice.

Count Arric. The host listed on her forged invitation, and the last person at the event whose attention she wanted to attract. He was tall and honey skinned with a solid, stately silhouette. A man who'd eaten well and groomed carefully every privileged day of his privileged life.

She hadn't planned on trading niceties with him. He wasn't her type—if everyone in the room insisted on being so thoroughly powdered, shaved, and made up, she'd have chosen someone in a dress—and all things considered, it was better for her if the hosts of the party, he and his noble parents, had overlooked her.

"Lady Phira, was it?" He looked distant as a scholar when he glanced at the page, but his gaze burned into hers when he turned to make the introduction. He pronounced the assumed name correctly.

Talis could play Lady Phira as uninterested in Arric as she was. But rich was rich, and had its own specific allure that nobles would pursue—even if not romantically. It wouldn't be believable for a lesser noble like Phira to ignore someone who could give her a hand up in their world. So Talis paid attention to him. Tried to look like she wanted to.

He looked younger than she expected. Looked barely old enough to command this premiere himself, rather than his venerable parents, who sat atop the raised landing at the spearpoint of a long receiving line of guests paying their respects.

Talis recovered, curtsying before her stillness stretched into rudeness. How she hated to curtsy. How she hated to talk and move according to rules. "If it please my lord, 'Phira' will do. And, if I understand correctly, providence had little to do with it."

"True. It was obtained at considerable expense." He regarded the page again, and she saw his shoulders rise and fall with a significance she couldn't glean. After a moment, his gaze flicked back to her, as though the sheet were little more than a grocery list.

"A testament to the measure of your house," she replied. In her own way, she meant it, though she kept the cynicism from her voice with enough effort to warrant a medal.

The count scoffed, as if the implication of his wealth was a refrain he heard too often. What else did the aristocrats talk about? Wealth, bloodlines, and how best to make sure the rest of the world remained in poverty while they planned another gala? Things like that. "Unfortunately, prior to this evening, the room was cleared of any objects which might have better complimented your beauty."

Laying it on thick, he was. Talis felt like an insect over which sap had run. Not just because it was too saccharin, but because she felt trapped. What did one even say to that when a hearty, mocking laugh wasn't an option?

But there was a glint in his eye. He was teasing her!

She'd given him a socially appropriate but vacuous compliment, and he flung it back at her.

Lady Phira of the satin and corsets would have come to see the display, to bask in the wealth of the noble houses and names—perhaps aspire, through marriage, to rise among them herself. She was like the dozens of other unmarried young people there. She wasn't supposed to catch Arric's attention.

So much for that. Time to adapt. At least Phira got Talis into this party, but Talis was going to have to get herself out again. She replied, still in the imperial dialect, but dropped the feathery tone she had affected. "I've heard about your collection. I'd hoped to see more of it tonight."

Count Arric looked around the room, his eyes seeming to move not across the empty pedestals, but the guardsmen spaced with the same mathematical precision around the hall. "Precaution necessitated we let the guards focus on the codex page. The rest of the collection has been moved to a private gallery for the evening."

"Private?" She lowered her chin and looked up at him through her false lashes. "My lord, if that was an offer of a personal tour: I accept!"

He blanched. He was not so interested in her as to bow to a whimsy, but he *was* interested enough to take pause at the suggestion.

She took the risk of pushing harder. "I promise not to keep you from your guests for any longer than you feel appropriate."

Back in the real world, she might have said, "I promise not to rob you." But somehow among the wealthy, the more one had, the less one expected one's peers to take it. Arric's concern was not being front and center and accounted for, and she'd promised to respect that.

It worked.

He lifted his arm to support her hand. At the same moment, an unnatural hush fell over the crowd, as disruptive as the report of a thunder-barreled flintlock. Talis almost pulled her hand back, afraid the room's worth of nobles had seen their host take her hand and had seen through her ruse.

But all eyes had turned to the entrance, where a young woman and a young man awaited announcement by the doorman who, even from this distance, looked as though that was the last thing he wanted to grant them.

The couple's finery matched the setting, at least in terms of opulence. But they toed the line of propriety, then leaped dramatically over it. Their fashion had only very recently been taken up by the young. It had yet to be deemed acceptable among the older generation still in charge.

The young woman's iridescent silk gown featured an exposed corset that did what it could to boost a pair of almost-nothings into view at her deep squared neckline. The tops of her sleeves dripped off her shoulders, gathered around her biceps, and extended only just below her elbow. Below that, bustled skirts layered in contrasting colors and weaves, with an asymmetrical gather to one side reminiscent of a teasing lift. Her hem swung inches—though it may as well have been a league—above the floor and the boots revealed beneath were high in the heel, but also platformed beneath the toe. Though the overall silhouette of the footwear was a near cousin of an acceptable shoe, they were decorated and embellished in a way that declared they were meant to be seen, and her ankles with them.

The sculpted ringlets of her mohair wig draped across the bare expanse of her collarbones. Her arms were freshly painted, as if fully tattooed, in bright colors that clashed with the purples and greens of her color-shifting silk.

It was no wonder every eye in the room was drawn to her. Though the gown was a perfect, tailored fit, and resisted gravity with dedication, the design inspired the imagination to draw immediate parallels to a young woman alone in her boudoir.

She waited for the doorman to recover and read their invitation aloud, wearing an amused smile and fondly gripping the arm of an attractive-though-too-slender young man. Compared to the young woman, his clothing was far closer to that of the other gentlemen in the room, but the threading, edging, buttons, and other trim on his suit was obviously not. He wore slim-fitting trousers, instead of the knee-length breeches and stockings that propriety expected, and an off-center pleated hanging covered one hip. His suede boots were slim, reflecting no light as did the patent leather and silver or brass buckles of the crowd. Their simplicity was almost as offensive as the rest of his attire's overexertion to detail.

More than his fashion choices, it was the young man's demeanor that was scandalous. He slouched, looking as uninterested in the room as it was interested in him.

The doorman finally recovered himself and must have decided that, if the pair would not be proper, at least he might be.

"The young Lord and Lady Culpepper," he said, putting a certain emphasis on the word 'young,' as if desperate to excuse them and himself for their appearance.

A murmur overtook the previously shocked silence. Every guard in the room shifted and stood straighter. Their captain strode forward and stepped between Talis and Lord Arric to whisper in his ear. She could hear only the hasty murmur of a complaint, but not the words.

There was little reason to wonder, though, as the Culpeppers were well known, at least by reputation. Their home was nearly the full length across Cutter space and Talis wouldn't be surprised if no one here had med them before. But they'd heard of the pair. They wore too little, talked too loudly, and drank too much. And despite being aristocratic and born with the wind behind them, they had a wild streak that expressed itself in kleptomaniac tendencies.

How they managed invitations was beyond Talis. She was only grateful that they had.

"That's what I have *you* for," the count replied to his

captain, his voice offering a warm cinnamon confidence. The captain swallowed but did not step away.

Talis waited with eyebrows raised in curiosity. As a lady would, of course. No such hullaballoo was ignored by anyone. After all, gossip was a favored pastime of those with no urgent business in life.

"My lord father has every faith in you, captain," Count Arric said, his voice low and insistent. "I know you will judge the situation properly, and act appropriately and discreetly. Now please, your job is to see to these details, while mine is to entertain my guests."

But as the captain stood straight and stiff in recognition of his orders, Lord Arric returned his attention to Talis as though there was only one such guest to speak of.

"I do hope everything is all right," Talis said in a breathy exclamation of concern. Which, in such a setting, was code for 'How exciting,' and 'I want details.'

"As I am sure you know too well," he replied, smiling in a way that conveyed more resignation than happiness, "not all nobility can be accurately described as such, while others who can claim less to their name offer far more quality of character."

It was a compliment, aimed at her, and at diverting the conversation away from the young Culpeppers who now traipsed their way across the hall, helping themselves to two flutes each of champagne and making them disappear before they took in the lay of the land with a swagger that was more sway. Those effervescent beverages were clearly not their first of the evening. The nobility edged away, averting their eyes so as not to make contact and draw the newcomers into conversation. The Culpeppers took no notice and elbowed their way into a circle of the oldest, most harassed-looking dignitaries in the hall.

Talis ignored the pair and dipped her chin in appreciation of the count's compliment, then lay her gloved hand over the arm he held out again in offer.

The captain of the guard moved off with due purpose to instruct his staff to make the Culpeppers their point of concern, as Count Arric led the lady Phira out of the hall and deeper into his grand home.

⸻✳⸻

COUNT ARRIC's standby gallery reminded Talis of the stockroom of a shop. Items under inventory rather than display, piled higher than she was tall, in makeshift aisles that snaked through what might normally feel like a sizable room.

Behind stacks of framed paintings and glass cases serving double duty as storage cabinets, the room's usual artifacts were almost hidden. Suits of antique armor from multiple historical periods peeked over the aisles as though struggling not to drown amid the mess. Family portraits and landscapes alike hung in gold frames so heavy and ornate they cast odd shadows across the artwork. Glass cases displayed objects too bulky to hang and too small to stand on their own.

Talis beheld the room in awe. No need to hide her reaction. Just maybe make sure she didn't look so greedy. Even Phira would no doubt be promoting Count Arric ever higher as a choice suitor—assuming he felt thus suited. Judging by his decision to latch the door between them and the two guards in the corridor beyond, he was feeling a might suited.

His demeanor relaxed as the quiet closed around them. Talis moved instinctively to the largest open space in the room, lest the crush of stored items threaten the quiet of her mind. She would need her faculties to navigate this next bit. She had been alone with rich men before, and it took a certain amount of evasive obsequiousness to keep them happy while simultaneously keeping the hem of her skirt and the ties of her corsets in place.

But Count Arric closed his eyes and sighed.

"There," he said, opening his eyes again and offering a smile, genuine in its fatigue. "If I never had to host another of these parties again, it could not make up for the ones I already have."

Talis found herself disarmed by the unexpected frankness. She recovered, not in time to stop the words from coming, but at least to keep them from sounding as derisive as they would have on their own. "All the grandeur is not to your liking?"

He mussed the carefully arranged hair above his forehead. "Be thankful, Phira, that you are not a countess. And doubly thankful that you are not the first-born son of an established and noble bloodline."

The urge to scoff returned, and she had to swallow it back. She wished she'd taken a glass of champagne for herself. "Can't a count, or prince, afford more opportunity to follow his whims?"

He shook his head, wiping dust off the inside corner of a frame and staring straight through it. "Freedom scales down the higher one mounts. You, dear lady, have more of such than I ever shall."

She gestured about the room, encompassing not only the stacks of his collection but the walls and estate beyond. "I know many who would give up what you call freedom to have this kind of security."

He squinted, and Talis worried she let slip too much

of her true opinion in the matter. She'd been careful, hadn't she? If she were in a bar on Subrosa, talking of such things, her manner would have been far coarser. For example, she might have spit to punctuate the sentiment.

"Nonetheless." She smiled as sweetly as she could. "We are here, and you are the count. The conductor of the evening. And these things *are* all yours. Shall we enjoy ourselves together, whatever our sorry lot in life?"

He regarded her for a moment, then chuckled and relaxed again. She had thought him relaxed as the doors sealed them in, but now the muscles in his shoulders visibly eased and dropped, and his chin came up.

He took a cleansing breath and let it out of his nose. "I apologize for any offense. Something in your manner tempts me to be too open with my thoughts."

That admission put the focus back where she wanted it. She smiled and slipped her arm through his elbow again and leaned close enough for her hip to put a light pressure against his, though she was still protected from true contact by three layers of flounce and skirting. "No offense was taken, provided you truly meant no mockery of my low standing."

He put a hand over hers where it rested on his forearm. His touch warmed her skin, and she had to stop herself from frowning. He just *had* to complicate this by being a decent sort of fellow. A rare gem amid the tarnished woodrots of the inner radii. If Arric didn't say something untoward soon, she might even lose sleep over her deception.

"Was there anything in particular you wished to see?" he asked. "You strike me as a history enthusiast."

In truth, Talis would have liked to get a closer look at a wall of mounted firearms she could see around the edge of one pile. Even if just to look, not to steal—though she had an abundance of room in her concealed pockets.

"I'm afraid I'm terribly predictable," she said, giving his bicep a playful squeeze. "Trinkets and baubles. Anything of emerald?"

He gave her a patient smile. "If predictable is your flaw, I shall be terribly disappointed. I saw something of a wild zephyr in you, even from across the grand hall."

"Too easy, my lord," she flirted as he led her across the room to a low glass cabinet. "You cannot divine my nature by analyzing a name I was given at birth."

He shrugged. "Some of us are born with the name that suits us. Others grow into it."

"And you? Do you feel the name of a great mountain range suits you?"

He was quiet a moment, and they both looked at the display of finery within the case without seeing it. "Something of the wilderness, yet anchored and unable to change. Yes, I suppose it suits me."

She watched him while she pretended to examine the contents of the case. Shadows of discontent washed across his reflection in polished silver and precious gems grasped in the prongs of horrid gold settings.

"I apologize," he said, and sounded as though he meant it. "I darken the mood."

She swallowed the itching feeling of sympathy. For his sake, and for her own, she fixed him with a full smile.

He drew back a moment, involuntarily pulling his hands to his side. "Dear woman, is that a gold tooth?" But the amusement was back in his eyes, and he leaned forward, interest in her piquing again.

She grinned wider. "I told you I like shiny things, my

lord. Now, show me your treasures before we are missed by your guests."

HE TOURED her through the pieces in the cabinet, even wound back the cover on the lock and dialed a personal combination to let her hold the pieces which caught her eye.

"And this," he said, placing a gold comb set with a fist-sized gem into her palm, "is the Core Emerald." Once securely affixed in a woman's bouffant so that its imbalanced weight would not droop, the beastly accessory might look like an overburdened tiara.

She laughed. "You do know it's paste, don't you?"

"What? No, impossible." He took the emerald back from her and held it up to a light.

"As much as my own," she said, flicking the flat gems around her neck with the back of her fingers. They clattered dully. "Compare them to that ruby, there."

He did as she bade him, holding the ruby she'd pointed to up to the same light, then holding each near the individual links of her necklace.

"*Silus's gusting farts fill my lungs!*" he hissed in surprise. "You're right."

Then he took a step back and gave her a considering glance. "Who *are* you?"

Her breath, already extremely limited, seemed to catch on some obstacle that had appeared in her throat. "My lord?"

He counted off his fingers. "You clearly hate these parties as much as I do. You can spot counterfeit jewels that would fool a Breaker lapidarist. And, you not only have a gold tooth, but a collection of tattoos."

She looked down in surprise, to see that the collar of her dress had wrinkled in such a way to reveal the tops of tattoos that, put simply, would never be mistaken for a glitterfly.

Trying to find any answer that would work for the evening's goals—which definitely ruled out the truth—Talis felt like a boremole under a spotlight.

But Arric didn't wait for an answer. "I swear you were crafted by Silus Cutter himself, to capture my attention and simultaneously drive nobles like my parents to an early grave."

As she laughed, someone behind them cleared their throat. The count jumped, caught in mid-swing of such dismissive language about their god, an unchaperoned lady, and—the most innocent victims—his parents.

The guard looked equally uncomfortable at having heard it. He must be new, Talis decided, because it was likely not the first un-noble act or words to be witnessed in this house. He stood at stiff attention, waiting for the count to lean close so he could give his report.

After a short, whispered phrase, which included a word that sounded like 'Culpepper' from where Talis stood, straining to hear, Count Arric turned to her, a look of irritation on his face.

"Surely we don't have to return to the hall so soon?" she asked. "We were just getting to know each other, and I know once we return beneath those chandeliers, your duties will steal you away from me."

"They steal me away already, I'm afraid." He gave her a long considering look. Then: "Wait for me here."

The guard's eyes darted between them. Not with

anxiety over what trouble a lone female guest might get into, but perhaps over what further secrets his duty would require him to guard for his lord.

The latch on the door shut behind them with a soft click that echoed through the room despite the clutter. Arric had left the case open, though she had watched and memorized his combination, and had a tool belt strapped to her right thigh in case she had to cut through wood or remove hardware to gain access to her prize. But no, Arric trusted her. She tried not to feel bad about that.

She put the emerald and ruby back in the case, her fingers lingering on the genuine stone a moment longer than necessary to balance it on its support. Not what she was here for. Gods rot the taunting depths of her thirsty pockets.

To the left of a broken-faced silver pocket watch, and the right of an adorable miniature flintlock pistol that would make a nice cousin to the one tucked into her left garter belt, was the item she'd come for.

She had no idea if her client wanted the palm-sized heavy music box for its historical significance, or to pry loose its ivory and gem settings and melt down its golden box. Or simply, as had attracted Talis to the job in the first place, to mark a notch in some count against the Imperial elite.

She had been provided with a polished and engraved wooden block to take its place. Not a decoy, though its size and shape were almost a match for the box. It would never fool even a cursory glance. She had to assume it was a message, though there was no obvious meaning in it for her. Knowing the significance wasn't part of the deal, though. Use the party to get into the house, find the box, replace it with the bad fake, and deliver the real box to her fence. That was the rough outline of the plan. She'd never meet the actual client. Things generally worked out for the best that way.

She felt the weight of the pilfered box as it dropped to rest at the bottom of her deep skirt pockets, hidden under the folds of fabric.

Time to make her exit.

She slipped out of the gallery. The guards outside the door stiffened as she emerged.

"M'lady?" asked one guard, obviously hoping she would vanish back into the room. If they knew any better, they'd be glad to see her quit Count Arric's precious collection. Instead, they were concerned that their lord's new focus of affection would be misplaced.

She lowered her voice so her question did not offend his male sensibilities. "I find I need a moment. Is there a nearby room where I may freshen up a bit?"

The guard blushed, bless his heart, and dipped his head. "It is just down this corridor, around the corner. I shall escort you."

"No need." She put up a gloved hand, and he relaxed. "Please don't abandon your post on my account."

The two guards stood back at attention, and she excused herself, letting her skirts swish around her as she walked down the hallway, feeling the heavy thump of her prize as it swung against her thigh.

THE WATER CLOSET was built into the inner wall of the corridor. She muttered a whispered curse. Her hope had been to make fastest escape through a window. The second floor would be a harrowing drop to the garden grounds below, but a risk she would take for the chance to excuse herself without further encounter.

Her next best option would be to escape through the kitchens, but first she had to find them.

The staircase leading up to the gallery was marble, with a metal-braced navy carpet. Around one more corner, she found a narrow staircase stepped in simple, unpolished stone. The service access.

She followed the spiral staircase down to a bustling carnival of activity. A cook barked orders, sending scurrying help hither and thither on errands of top priority, to keep small trays of finger-held delectables at hand for the premier above. A wooden crate in the corner overflowed with straw packing and dark green bottles, and another, emptied of its dunnage, held those bottles already sacrificed to the evening's good spirits.

Across the kitchen, a door was propped ajar to let fresh air counter the heat from the ovens, cooktop, and hearth. Talis received many dubious and scandalized glances as she crossed to it, but there were none here with the authority to question a lady. A woman trimming the ends off a large bowl of green beans gave her a knowing look, no doubt expecting that Phira had appeared for some clandestine meeting in the garden with someone whose company she was not meant to keep.

No one would say anything to the guards or the nobility. Their job, as they each understood it, was to protect the secrets of those they served. That included their invited guests. They might gossip among themselves, but it was in their own best interest that such whispers wouldn't make it to noble ears.

Outside, she took a deep breath of clean air and

stepped out from the shadowed wall in which the kitchen door was a sliver of orange light.

After the heat of the kitchen, the uncertainty of her exit, and the crowded party before that, the chilly breeze that caught the hairs at her nape were a relief. Her skin prickled with goosebumps despite the many layers of her ridiculous dress.

This side of the property featured a sculpted hedge maze, kept off from the house a polite distance, and the space between the walls of foliage and the walls of stone was open, though lined with gravel to keep the grass from drowning in any water that might drip from the roofline during Peridot's occasional migratory rains.

The crunch of gravel beneath her heels was offensively loud. The windows of the house above were closed, but surely the noise of rock chewing against rock was audible through the glass and would easily be heard as she approached the front gates.

She removed the dress shoes, dipping back into the building's shadow to lean against the wall and hike her foot up to within reach of her movement-restricted arms. She held her breath, both to allow her spine to curve as much as possible and to hear any approaching sounds.

The boots disappeared into her pockets. Their bulk was far less comfortable against her legs than the weight of the stolen box, but she held the skirts aloft to step carefully over the stones, and it helped keep the squared heels from bruising her.

Her feet would surely bruise, though. Though she gingerly stepped across the gravel, the distance to the front of the house seemed to quadruple, at least, with the pain of the stones pressing, pinching, and jabbing into the soft skin on the bottoms of her feet. She reminded herself the money was worth having to spend a few days with bruised soles.

Finally, she came around the front of the building, where the last expanse of her escape—down the overlong driveway—could begin.

Instead, Count Arric stood on the steps outside his home, overseeing the highly encouraged exit of the young Lord and Lady Culpepper.

Spouting language that was as descriptive as it was profane, the lady Culpepper attempted to march herself back up the steps. Guards blocked her way, but she dodged around them, thanks to the mobility afforded by her smaller corset and shorter skirts. They were loath to place hands on any noble, but several more guards stepped in front of her and blocked her re-entry into the hall.

Unfortunately, Talis pulled back around the corner too slowly to make use of the diversion.

"Lady Phira?" she heard Count Arric's voice in a surprised whisper. A question, as though he doubted—or wanted to doubt—what he'd seen.

If she did not step back out into view, he would surely pursue her specter around the corner of the house. She stood on tiptoes—the dragging of her hem would betray her lack of shoes—and forced a smile to mask both the annoyance at being seen and the pain which spiked anew through the pads of her burning, mistreated feet.

The Culpeppers had made their exit so confrontational that Arric had to involve himself in it directly. And now Talis was seen, caught, and certain to be suspected of more than clever conversation.

"My lord Count," she said, as she returned to the front of the building's protruding entranceway, and stepped up onto the front stairs, blessing the smoother stone they were carved from. Once off the loose stones, she dipped into a curtsy.

She looked up to see his eyebrows creased with confusion. His eyes searched hers. There would be no doubt that she was up to nothing good. Nothing which befit a lady. But he looked to her for an explanation, desperate to give her the benefit of his trust.

"How did you end up outside? Did my guards not offer to escort you back to the hall?"

A guard stood behind him, watching her with obvious suspicion. She grasped at Count Arric's generosity before he could receive contradictory counsel. She had expected to hear him ask, for the second time, "who *are* you?"

"They offered, yes, my lord. I am afraid I have committed mischief in your home." She always found that honesty was the easiest lie to sell.

The young lady Culpepper made a small 'humph' of disapproval as she mounted the step into the waiting carriage within which her brother already slouched on a padded bench. Talis saw the shine of their eyes on her from within. Their driver, a Bone man dressed in livery jacket and wearing a ridiculously jaunty hat over his feather-combed hair, also watched her with far more intent than a servant would.

"Mischief?" Count Arric's eyebrows were raised, but a smile pulled at one corner of his mouth.

She smiled, her own natural smirk, knowing the guard would only think less of her, but also knowing her wildness had disarmed the count more than any other aspect she possessed. "I stole from your house to explore the grounds and fill my lungs with the wind again. I am a horrid woman, ill-suited to behaving like a lady."

Count Arric stepped forward and took her hand, pulling her up from the curtsy.

"Your mischief is, I am afraid, unimpressive in contrast to the other miscreants this evening. But if you require constant escort and supervision, I shall attend to it directly." He smiled and led her up the steps, back toward the glittering light which spilled from within. Wrong direction.

Blast and rot. She was digging herself in deeper. Any more arguments from her, if she wasn't careful, and she'd end up betrothed to the man by dawn.

She managed to evade any marriage proposals, and as word spread that she had been discovered wandering alone in the dark outside the walls of the estate, the elder Count's frown convinced her he would tolerate none at all. At least not to her.

She spent the rest of the evening enjoying—or so it was assumed—the premiere. Count Arric attempted to introduce her to his parents, perhaps to make a slow introduction of the concept of her on his arm, which was quickly dismissed by them. Not rudely, no, never rudely. But it was made clear they considered her beneath their notice and, most importantly, his.

An obedient and proper son would have taken the hint and found a new dance partner for the evening, but Arric seemed only encouraged by their disapproval.

Talis did her best to behave for the rest of the gala, sinking back into character as Lady Phira. Her comments were subdued, her wit restrained. She feathered the edges of her voice again, and let the nobility speak without interruption or playful retorts. She became, against all her instincts, as boring and bland as she could make herself. As she'd tried to be at the start of the evening. Someone the Count and Countess might approve of. Surely that would dissuade the young count's interest.

But he remained by her side. Or rather, kept her by *his* side as he played host and ensured his guests were entertained.

More entertaining, to most them, was her presence, and his hand on her shoulder, steering her about the room.

And always with her back to the door.

She counted the ticking heartbeats as the hours passed. Hours she long since ought to have been relaxing in her cabin, free of the gown that now felt more a prison than ever. The weight of her prize, and of her boots—for she still stood on tiptoe among the crowd and struggled to dance without the benefit of a heel to sink into—dragged at her. Her back ached and her calves seized with cramping. The corset was the only thing keeping her from slumping over like a cotton doll.

Count Arric, in the presence of his guests, did not press her for more conversation. Talis's stomach knotted at the eventual confrontation he would surely instigate, demanding to know what she was up to, who she was, and for her to turn out her pockets.

Beyond the seats at the head of the hall, long abandoned by the elder Count and Countess as confession of their advancing age, the glow pumpkins banded with orange again, a sign of approaching dawn. The stars twinkled ever brighter, and her exhausted eyes nearly clouded with the burn of the long night.

And finally, the drunken and wobbling crowd began to depart.

Arric kept her until last, and in the cavernous echo of the room, he hushed his voice lest it carry across the house. "You nearly escaped me tonight."

She was tired and just about ready to pull her hidden flintlock on the man and escape at gunpoint if need be. "Nearly," she allowed. "Perhaps I did not try hard enough."

"I told you how I envy you your freedom. I apologize for depriving you of it. If I wished to warm your heart to future memories of me, I should have made the evening as pleasurable for you as I forced you to make it for me."

Damn him, he was almost making her feel bad. The music box pressed against her thigh as she moved toward the door.

"I should enjoy such comforts as your family gener-ously shared tonight." But not like this. "I am afraid it is simply not in my nature."

He grinned, and the expression was so honest and relaxed that all his finery might have fallen away to reveal a man with whom she might have found something in common over a pint of ale instead of a flute of champagne.

"Nor mine, good lady. I found my pleasure tonight in your company, and though you dutifully guarded your wilder nature from view, its memory was enough to sustain me through my exhaustive duties as host."

His hand held hers a moment longer than natural as she stepped outside, toward her waiting carriage.

Rot him. Fine. Give him something. "Perhaps we will share more quiet moments at your next premiere. I will await your invitation, my lord."

She curtsied, and he bowed. He was still a gentleman, after all.

"I shall scour flotsam itself to find a prize worthy of your continued attention."

Another curtsy freed her of his company, though he stood on the lowest step as she hurried into the curtained depths of her car. The clopping of hooves carried her down the lane and toward the main gates, and she saw through parted drapes that he watched her the entire way.

She sat back against the seat cushions with an exaggerated sigh, letting the curtains fall into place, obscuring the house from view. Fumbled for the clasp at the small of her back and flipped it to loosen the corset, which expanded with a burst of released tension. She took her first full breath of the evening and leaned her head back.

A flare of light erupted as a match was struck against the side of a shoe. Across the carriage from her, still dressed as the lady Culpepper, *Wind Sabre*'s mechanic, Sophie, lit a cigarette and waved the flame out before tossing it between the curtains. The smoke circled in the small cabin, tobacco and clove and sweet leaf. Talis wasn't a fan of the things but breathing anything at all was a blessing.

"*Hours!*" exclaimed Sophie. "I thought you'd never escape."

Tisker leaned against Sophie's side, stirring awake at her amused bark. "Hey, Cap. When's the wedding?"

Something poked her in the back of the head. Talis scoffed at the jest as she sat up to remove hairpins and shake her hair loose. "It'd have come to marriage proposals if I'd let it, I'm sure. Was it just me, or was last night twice as long as a normal night had any right to be?"

Dug, seated next to her on the cushion and now free of the livery costume, growled low in his throat. "You were armed. You could have run when you were within feet of our carriage."

Talis thought of Arric and wondered how long it would take him to discover the theft and know her for who she was. Or at least for who she wasn't.

He would be disappointed. Maybe learn a valuable life lesson about trusting anyone with a pretty face. Or a gold-capped tooth.

"Shoot my way out, Dug? Tsk. That's why you never get invited to parties." She fixed him with a grin until he nodded and matched it, then she collapsed back against him.

A lump bit at her leg, and she wrestled with the skirt to pull the music box from her pocket. She turned the overpriced trinket over in her hands several times before finally flipping back its keyhole and winding it. The twinkling metallic notes of a classical lullaby joined in the percussion of their wheels on the stone-paved street and the hollow clop of the horses' hooves.

Who was she? Certainly not Lady Phira. She escaped the corseted life by running away as a child, and even if she was far from a bloodline heir, her latest encounter with a landlocked lifestyle gave her no cause to regret that.

Who was she? Talis, captain of *Wind Sabre*. Smuggler, salvager, and occasional thief. About to get paid, after having more than earned it.

And, with the morning star crossing the skies and glow pumpkins turning from lavender to gold, she was fast asleep against her first mate's shoulder.

Want more? Don't miss Flotsam, the first book of the Peridot Shift series.

Captain Talis just wants to keep her airship crew from starving, and maybe scrape up enough cash for some badly needed repairs. When an anonymous client offers a small fortune to root through a pile of atmospheric wreckage, it seems like an easy payday. The job yields an ancient ring, a forbidden secret, and a host of deadly enemies.

Get it at rjtheodore.com.

PICK YOUR POISON

1. *I'm not done! Let's hunt renegade androids.* Head to "Sparrow" by G.J. Ogden

2. *Wait, wait. Let's find out what happened to our partner.* Head to "The Silent Passage" by Patrick Swenson

3. *I read them all!* Congratulations! Turn the page to learn more about the fabulous contributors to this anthology—and don't forget to check out CROOKED V.1 for even more sci-fi crime stories.

CONTRIBUTOR BIOS

FRASIER ARMITAGE

Frasier Armitage writes science fiction. Which is another way of saying he's a self-confessed geek who sits alone in a room scribbling in notebooks about things that are currently impossible.

When he's not writing, you'll find him with his wife and son, watching Keanu Reeves movies, reviewing books for the FanFiAddict blog, or noodling on his guitar. He's a part-time robot, full-time nerd, imaginer of worlds, and resident of Earth.

Frasier has won the 'Matthew Cross Writing Contest' multiple times, received a 'Silver Honourable Mention' from the Writers of the Future Award, and is the winner of the Pen To Print Audio Drama Competition 2022. His short stories have been published in blogs, magazines, and anthologies, and his debut novel is coming soon.

Website: frasierarmitage.com
Twitter: @FrasierArmitage

C. E. CLAYTON

C. E. Clayton is an award winning author born and raised in the greater Los Angeles area. After going the tradi-tional career route and becoming restless, she went back to her first love—writing—and hasn't stopped. She is the author of the young adult fantasy series "The Monster of Selkirk", the creator of the cyberpunk Eerden Novels, and her horror short stories have appeared in anthologies across the country. When she's not writing you can find her treating her fur-babies like humans, constantly drinking tea, and trying to convince her husband to go to more concerts. And reading. She does read quite a bit. More about C.E. Clayton, including her blog, book reviews, social media presence, and newsletter can be found on her website.

Website: ceclayton.com

MADDI DAVIDSON

Maddi Davidson is the pen name for two sisters living on opposite sides of the country: Mary Ann Davidson in Idaho and Diane Davidson in Virginia. Together they have published several novels, a non-fiction book, and numerous short stories. Their tales range from the murder of a deranged scientist resurrecting the dodo to a spurned wife hacking the pacemaker of an ex-husband who richly deserved it.

"Narrow EscApe" is the first story in a planned series of Tastee Brioche Twistletoe adventures.

Website: maddidavidson.com

CAITLIN DEMARIS MCKENNA

Caitlin Demaris McKenna is a science fiction writer and freelance editor. She currently lives, works and writes in

Vancouver, British Columbia. When not writing, she enjoys reading, watching video game Let's Plays, and entomology. She grew up in the Minnesota woods, where on clear winter nights, she would look up at the stars and wonder.

Website: expansionfront.com

AUSTIN DRAGON

Austin Dragon is the author of over 20 books in science fiction, fantasy, and classic horror. His works include the sci-fi noir, cyberpunk detective **Liquid Cool** series, the epic fantasy **Fabled Quest Chronicles**, the international epic sci-fi **After Eden** series, the classic **Sleepy Hollow Horrors**, and new military sci-fi **PLANET TAMERS** series. He is a native New Yorker but has called Los Angeles, California home for more than twenty years. Words to describe him, in no particular order: U.S. Army, English teacher, one-time resident of Paris, ex-political junkie, movie buff, Fortune 500 corporate recruiter, renaissance man, futurist, and dreamer.

He is currently working on new books and series in science fiction, fantasy, and classic horror!

Website: austindragon.com

GREG DRAGON

Greg Dragon brings a fresh perspective to fiction by telling human stories of life, love, and relationships in a science fiction setting. This unconventional author spins his celestial scenes from an imagination nurtured from being an avid reader himself. His exposure to multiple cultures, religions, martial arts, and travel lends a unique dynamic to his stories. You can enjoy excerpts from his work by visiting his website.

Twitter: @hobdragon
Facebook: facebook.com/anstractor
Website: gregdragon.com

ERIK GROVE

Erik Grove is a writer, long distance runner, and little dog wrangler living and doing things in Portland, OR. You can find his work in places like ESCAPE POD, the SPACE TOUCANS anthology series, the Zombies Need Brains NOIR anthology, and upcoming in NIGHT-MARE. Follow him on Twitter @erikgrove or check out his webpage www.erikgrove.com for dog glamour shots, marathon training nonsense, and sundry writerly shenanigans.

Twitter: @erikgrove
Website: erikgrove.com

JIM KEEN

Jim Keen writes books about the people who fascinate him in worlds that amaze him. He loves crime, thrillers, and stories about people with secrets. If there's not a big twist along the way, he'd never write the first word.

The international bestselling Alice Yu series takes

place forty years from now, in a world transformed by mechanical intelligences—AI's big brother. Yu is a loner cop atoning for past sins. Through the series she discovers what it is to be human, while becoming something much more in the process. If you like the steely future noir of William Gibson, James S. A. Corey, and Martha Wells, you'll love these sci-fi thrillers.

Website: jimkeen.com

JESSIE KWAK

Jessie Kwak has always lived in imaginary lands, from Arrakis and Ankh-Morpork to Earthsea, Tatooine, and now Portland, Oregon. As a writer, she sends readers on their own journeys to immersive worlds filled with fascinating characters, gunfights, explosions, and dinner parties. When she's not raving about her latest favorite sci-fi series to her friends, she can be found sewing, mountain biking, or out exploring new worlds both at home and abroad.

She is the author of supernatural thriller *From Earth and Bone*, the Bulari Saga series of gangster sci-fi novels, the Nanshe Chronicles series of space pirate adventures, and productivity guide *From Chaos to Creativity*.

Twitter: @jkwak
Instagram: @kwakjessie
Website: jessiekwak.com

WILLIAM BURTON MCCORMICK

William Burton McCormick is a Shamus, Thriller, Derringer, Silver Falchion and Claymore awards finalist and his Santa Ezeriņa novella "House of Tigers" was an Honorable Mention for the Black Orchid Novella Award. He is the author of the thrillers A STRANGER FROM THE STORM and KGB BANKER and the historical novel of the Baltic Republics LENIN'S HAREM. William has lived in seven countries including Latvia and Ukraine, the settings of "The Crimson Vial."

Website: williamburtonmccormick.com

MARK NIEMANN-ROSS

Mark Niemann-Ross is an author, educator, and chicken wrangler living in Portland, Oregon. He teaches "R"—a programming language, and "Raspberry Pi"—a small computer used for the Internet of Things. Both topics influence his writing, which fits solidly in the genre of "Hard Science Fiction."

Mark co-authored his first story in 2005 with Richard A. Lovett in *Analog, Science Fiction and Fact*. Since then, he has published additional stories in *Analog* and *Stupefying Stories*, has self-published two collections, and collaborated on a children's book.

Most recently, Mark published *Stupid Machine*, a science fiction murder mystery solved by a refrigerator.

Mark lives in Portland, Oregon. He does not have cats because his chickens would object.

LinkedIn: linkedin.com/in/markniemannross

Twitter: @marknr
Goodreads: goodreads.com/niemann-ross
Website: niemannross.com

G J OGDEN

G J Ogden is the author of numerous space opera and military sci-fi series that have collectively amassed over 5,200 5-star ratings on Amazon. He is a physics graduate and a former technology journalist with a lifelong love of science fiction and anything nerdy. On the rare occasions when he's not writing, he is usually getting whooped in games of Warhammer 40K by his son.

Website: ogdenmedia.net

E.L. STRIFE

Strife enjoys crafting science fiction novels in various subgenres including space opera, cyberpunk, and fantasy. Sometimes she writes about aliens and colonization, other times she sticks to genetic engineering, the supernatural, and corrupt futuristic societies. Strife's Sci-Fi is often crude and graphic, features strong women, and typically includes people who like to blow s--- up.

Strife enjoys connecting with readers and welcomes all feedback and questions. If you'd like to know when Strife's next books will be out, and to ensure you hear about her giveaways, visit her website.

Website: elstrife.com
BookBub: E L Strife
Goodreads: E L Strife

KATE SHEERAN SWED

Kate Sheeran Swed loves hot chocolate, plastic dinosaurs, and airplane tickets. She has trekked along the Inca Trail to Macchu Picchu, hiked on the Mýrdalsjökull glacier in Iceland, and climbed the ruins of Masada to watch the sunrise over the Dead Sea. She currently lives in New York's capital region with her husband and two kids.

Kate is the author of several sci fi and fantasy series, including the *Interstellar Trials*, a new YA dystopian space opera series, and the *Parse Galaxy* adult space opera series. Her short fiction has appeared in publications such as Fireside, the Young Explorers Adventure Guide, and Electric Spec.

Website: katesheeranswed.com
Instagram: @katesheeranswed
Tik Tok: @katesheeranswed

ANDREW SWEET

Andrew Sweet explores the "why" of how societies work through the "what if" of science fiction—he loves science and possibility! He maintains a personal 5-year project on cellular automata that has evolved into a CLI and an "infinitely scalable" (hardware limited of course) CA platform as he continues his obsessive search for cellular automata that can perform simple math functions. Former lead guitarist for the grunge/punk band Permanent Ascent, Andrew has been involved in music as long as he's been writing. Now proud owner of a Takamine, Andrew has traded his rapid punk chops for chaotic jazz riffs. Finally, last but definitely not least, Andrew's reasons for living are his wife and two children in their home in Portland, OR.

Website: andrewsweetbooks.com

PATRICK SWENSON

Patrick's first novel, *The Ultra Thin Man,* appeared from Tor Books. The sequel, *The Ultra Big Sleep*, debuted soon after. The third Ultra novel will be out next year. His novel *Rain Music* was published recently. He was the editor and publisher of *Talebones*, which began in 1995 and ended with its 39th issue in 2009. In 2000, he began Fairwood Press, a book line, which is still running. He has sold short fiction to the anthologies *Unbound II*, *Unfettered III*, *Seasons Between Us*, *Gunfight at Europa Station*, *Like Water for Quarks,* and also to a number of magazines. He has been a high school teacher for 37 years, and is the proud poppa of Artemis, an artist and budding designer. Patrick lives in Bonney Lake, Washington.

Website: patrickswenson.net

MARK TEPPO

Mark Teppo divides his time between Portland and Sumner, and he tends to navigate by local bookstore positioning. He writes historical fiction, fantasy, speculative fiction, and horror, and has published more than a dozen novels. If he's writing a mystery, he's pretending to be Harry Bryant.

He also runs Underland Press, an independent publishing house.

Twitter: @markteppo
Instagram: @mark.teppo
Website: markteppo.com

R J THEODORE

R J Theodore (they/she) is an author, graphic designer, and all-around collector of creative endeavors and hobbies. They enjoy writing about magic-infused technologies, first contact events, and bioluminescing landscapes.

Their love of SFF storytelling developed through grabbing for anything-and-everything "unicorn" as a child, but they were subverted by tales of distant solar systems when their brother introduced them to *Star Trek: The Next Generation* at age seven. A few years later, *Sailor Moon* taught them stories can have both.

Their short fiction has appeared in *MetaStellar*, *Lightspeed*, and *Fireside Magazines* as well as the *Glitter + Ashes* and *Unfettered Hexes* anthologies from Neon Hemlock Press.

They live in New England, haunted by their childhood cat.

Website: rjtheodore.com

Thank you so much for reading!

If you enjoyed this anthology, please let others know by leaving a review or telling a friend. As a scrappy crew of authors, we depend on word of mouth to connect with new readers.

Looking for more great sci-fi crime reads?

Don't miss the stories in CROOKED V.1.

Head to jessiekwak.com/crooked

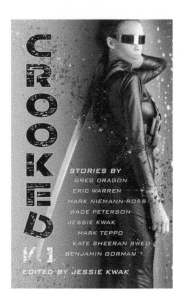